ARBORIS MYSTERIUS

ARBORIS MYSTERIUS

Stories of the Uncanny and Undescribed from the Botanical Kingdom

Chad Arment, Editor

COACHWHIP PUBLICATIONS

Greenville, Ohio

Arboris Mysterius, Chad Arment, editor.
© 2014 Coachwhip Publications
Front cover: Tree © Gigglebox Photography
No claims made on public domain material.

ISBN 1-61646-246-9
ISBN-13 978-1-61646-246-8

CoachwhipBooks.com

CONTENTS

FROM *THE TRUE HISTORY*, BOOK 1
LUCIAN OF SAMOSATA (2ND CENTURY, A.D.)

STARTING ON A CERTAIN DATE from the Pillars of Heracles, I sailed with a fair wind into the Atlantic. The motives of my voyage were a certain intellectual restlessness, a passion for novelty, a curiosity about the limits of the ocean and the peoples who might dwell beyond it. This being my design, I provisioned and watered my ship on a generous scale. My crew amounted to fifty, all men whose interests, as well as their years, corresponded with my own. I had further provided a good supply of arms, secured the best navigator to be had for money, and had the ship—a sloop—specially strengthened for a long and arduous voyage.

For a day and a night we were carried quietly along by the breeze, with land still in sight. But with the next day's dawn the wind rose to a gale, with a heavy sea and a dark sky; we found ourselves unable to take in sail. We surrendered ourselves to the elements, let her run, and were storm-driven for more than eleven weeks. On the eightieth day the sun came out quite suddenly, and we found ourselves close to a lofty wooded island, round which the waves were murmuring gently, the sea having almost fallen by this time. We brought her to land, disembarked, and after our long tossing lay a considerable time idle on shore; we at last made a start, however, and leaving thirty of our number to guard the ship I took the other twenty on a tour of inspection.

We had advanced half a mile inland through woods, when we came upon a brazen pillar, inscribed in Greek characters—which however were worn and dim—'Heracles and Dionysus reached this point.' Not far off were two footprints on rock; one might have been an acre in area, the other being smaller; and I conjecture that the latter was Dionysus's, and the other Heracles's; we did obeisance, and proceeded. Before we had gone far, we found ourselves on a river which ran wine; it was very like Chian; the stream full and copious, even navigable in parts. This evidence of Dionysus's sojourn was enough to convince us that the inscription on the pillar was authentic. Resolving to find the source, I followed the river up, and discovered, instead of a fountain, a number of huge vines covered with grapes; from the root of each there issued a trickle of perfectly clear wine, the joining of which made the river. It was well stocked with great fish, resembling wine both in colour and taste; catching and eating some, we at once found ourselves intoxicated; and indeed when opened the fish were full of wine-lees; presently it occurred to us to mix them with ordinary water fish, thus diluting the strength of our spirituous food.

We now crossed the river by a ford, and came to some vines of a most extraordinary kind. Out of the ground came a thick well-grown stem; but the upper part was a woman, complete from the loins upward. They were like our painters' representations of Daphne in the act of turning into a tree just as Apollo overtakes her. From the finger-tips sprang vine twigs, all loaded with grapes; the hair of their heads was tendrils, leaves, and grape-clusters. They greeted us and welcomed our approach, talking Lydian, Indian, and Greek, most of them the last. They went so far as to kiss us on the mouth; and whoever was kissed staggered like a drunken man. But they would not permit us to pluck their fruit, meeting the attempt with cries of pain. Some of them made further amorous advances; and two of my comrades who yielded to these solicitations found it impossible to extricate themselves again from their embraces; the man became one plant with the vine, striking root beside it; his fingers turned to vine twigs, the tendrils were all round him, and embryo grape-clusters were already visible on him.

We left them there and hurried back to the ship, where we told our tale, including our friends' experiment in viticulture. Then after taking some casks ashore and filling them with wine and water we bivouacked near the beach, and next morning set sail before a gentle breeze. . . .

THE GIANT WISTARIA
CHARLOTTE P. GILMAN

"MEDDLE NOT with my new vine, child! See! Thou hast already broken the tender shoot! Never needle or distaff for thee, and yet thou wilt not be quiet!"

The nervous fingers wavered, clutched at a small carnelian cross that hung from her neck, then fell despairingly.

"Give me my child, mother, and then I will be quiet!"

"Hush! hush! thou fool—some one might be near! See—there is thy father coming, even now! Get in quickly!"

She raised her eyes to her mother's face, weary eyes that yet had a flickering, uncertain blaze in their shaded depths.

"Art thou a mother and hast no pity on me, a mother? Give me my child!"

Her voice rose in a strange, low cry, broken by her father's hand upon her mouth.

"Shameless!" said he, with set teeth. "Get to thy chamber, and be not seen again to-night, or I will have thee bound!"

She went at that, and a hard-faced serving woman followed, and presently returned, bringing a key to her mistress.

"Is all well with her,—and the child also?"

"She is quiet, Mistress Dwining, well for the night, be sure. The child fretteth endlessly, but save for that it thriveth with me."

The parents were left alone together on the high square porch with its great pillars, and the rising moon began to make faint shadows of the young vine leaves that shot up luxuriantly around them; moving shadows, like little stretching fingers, on the broad and heavy planks of the oaken floor.

9

"It groweth well, this vine thou broughtest me in the ship, my husband."

"Aye," he broke in bitterly, "and so doth the shame I brought thee! Had I known of it I would sooner have had the ship founder beneath us, and have seen our child cleanly drowned, than live to this end!"

"Thou art very hard, Samuel, art thou not afeard for her life? She grieveth sore for the child, aye, and for the green fields to walk in!"

"Nay," said he grimly, "I fear not. She hath lost already what is more than life; and she shall have air enough soon. To-morrow the ship is ready, and we return to England. None knoweth of our stain here, not one, and if the town hath a child unaccounted for to rear in decent ways—why, it is not the first, even here. It will be well enough cared for! And truly we have matter for thankfulness, that her cousin is yet willing to marry her."

"Hast thou told him?"

"Aye! Thinkest thou I would cast shame into another man's house, unknowing it? He hath always desired her, but she would none of him, the stubborn! She hath small choice now!"

"Will he be kind, Samuel? Can he—"

"Kind? What call'st thou it to take such as she to wife? Kind! How many men would take her, an' she had double the fortune? And being of the family already, he is glad to hide the blot forever."

"An' if she would not? He is but a coarse fellow, and she ever shunned him."

"Art thou mad, woman? She weddeth him ere we sail to-morrow, or she stayeth ever in that chamber. The girl is not so sheer a fool! He maketh an honest woman of her, and saveth our house from open shame. What other hope for her than a new life to cover the old? Let her have an honest child, an' she so longeth for one!"

He strode heavily across the porch, till the loose planks creaked again, strode back and forth, with his arms folded and his brows fiercely knit above his iron mouth.

Overhead the shadows flickered mockingly across a white face among the leaves, with eyes of wasted fire.

"O, George, what a house! What a lovely house! I am sure it's haunted! Let us get that house to live in this summer! We will have Kate and Jack and Susy and Jim of course, and a splendid time of it!"

Young husbands are indulgent, but still they have to recognize facts.

"My dear, the house may not be to rent; and it may also not be habitable."

"There is surely somebody in it. I am going to inquire!"

The great central gate was rusted off its hinges, and the long drive had trees in it, but a little footpath showed signs of steady usage, and up that Mrs. Jenny went, followed by her obedient George. The front windows of the old mansion were blank, but in a wing at the back they found white curtains and open doors. Outside, in the clear May sunshine, a woman was washing. She was polite and friendly, and evidently glad of visitors in that lonely place. She "guessed it could be rented—didn't know." The heirs were in Europe, but "there was a lawyer in New York had the lettin' of it." There had been folks there years ago, but not in her time. She and her husband had the rent of their part for taking care of the place. Not that they took much care on't either, "but keepin' robbers out." It was furnished throughout, old-fashioned enough, but good; and "if they took it she could do the work for 'em herself, she guessed—if *he* was willin'!"

Never was a crazy scheme more easily arranged. George knew that lawyer in New York; the rent was not alarming; and the nearness to a rising sea-shore resort made it a still pleasanter place to spend the summer.

Kate and Jack and Susy and Jim cheerfully accepted, and the June moon found them all sitting on the high front porch.

They had explored the house from top to bottom, from the great room in the garret, with nothing in it but a rickety cradle, to the well in the cellar without a curb and with a rusty chain going down to unknown blackness below. They had explored the grounds, once beautiful with rare trees and shrubs, but now a gloomy wilderness of tangled shade.

The old lilacs and laburnums, the spirea and syringa, nodded against the second-story windows. What garden plants survived were great ragged bushes or great shapeless beds. A huge wistaria vine covered the whole front of the house. The trunk, it was too large to call a stem, rose at the corner of the porch by the high steps, and had once climbed its pillars; but now the pillars were wrenched from their places and held rigid and helpless by the tightly wound and knotted arms.

It fenced in all the upper story of the porch with a knitted wall of stem and leaf; it ran along the eaves, holding up the gutter that had once supported it; it shaded every window with heavy green; and the drooping, fragrant blossoms made a waving sheet of purple from roof to ground.

"Did you ever see such a wistaria!" cried ecstatic Mrs. Jenny. "It is worth the rent just to sit under such a vine,—a fig tree beside it would be sheer superfluity and wicked extravagance!"

"Jenny makes much of her wistaria," said George, "because she's so disappointed about the ghosts. She made up her mind at first sight to have ghosts in the house, and she can't find even a ghost story!"

"No," Jenny assented mournfully; "I pumped poor Mrs. Pepperill for three days, but could get nothing out of her. But I'm convinced there is a story, if we could only find it. You need not tell me that a house like this, with a garden like this, and a cellar like this, isn't haunted!"

"I agree with you," said Jack. Jack was a reporter on a New York daily, and engaged to Mrs. Jenny's pretty sister. "And if we don't find a real ghost, you may be very sure I shall make one. It's too good an opportunity to lose!"

The pretty sister, who sat next him, resented. "You shan't do anything of the sort, Jack! This is a *real* ghostly place, and I won't have you make fun of it! Look at that group of trees out there in the long grass—it looks for all the world like a crouching, hunted figure!"

"It looks to me like a woman picking huckleberries," said Jim, who was married to George's pretty sister.

"Be still, Jim!" said that fair young woman. "I believe in Jenny's ghost as much as she does. Such a place! Just look at this great wistaria trunk crawling up by the steps here! It looks for all the world like a writhing body—cringing—beseeching!"

"Yes," answered the subdued Jim, "it does, Susy. See its waist,—about two yards of it, and twisted at that! A waste of good material!"

"Don't be so horrid, boys! Go off and smoke somewhere if you can't be congenial!"

"We can! We will! We'll be as ghostly as you please." And forthwith they began to see bloodstains and crouching figures so plentifully that the most delightful shivers multiplied, and the fair enthusiasts started for bed, declaring they should never sleep a wink.

"We shall all surely dream," cried Mrs. Jenny, "and we must all tell our dreams in the morning!"

"There's another thing certain," said George, catching Susy as she tripped over a loose plank; "and that is that you frisky creatures must use the side door till I get this Eiffel tower of a portico fixed, or we shall have some fresh ghosts on our hands! We found a plank here that yawns like a trap-door—big enough to swallow you,—and I believe the bottom of the thing is in China!"

The next morning found them all alive, and eating a substantial New England breakfast, to the accompaniment of saws and hammers on the porch, where carpenters of quite miraculous promptness were tearing things to pieces generally.

"It's got to come down mostly," they had said. "These timbers are clean rotted through, what ain't pulled out o' line by this great creeper. That's about all that holds the thing up."

There was clear reason in what they said, and with a caution from anxious Mrs. Jenny not to hurt the wistaria, they were left to demolish and repair at leisure.

"How about ghosts?" asked Jack after a fourth griddle cake. "I had one, and it's taken away my appetite!"

Mrs. Jenny gave a little shriek and dropped her knife and fork.

"Oh, so had I! I had the most awful—well, not dream exactly, but feeling. I had forgotten all about it!"

"Must have been awful," said Jack, taking another cake. "Do tell us about the feeling. My ghost will wait."

"It makes me creep to think of it even now," she said. "I woke up, all at once, with that dreadful feeling as if something were going to happen, you know! I was wide awake, and hearing every little sound for miles around, it seemed to me. There are so many strange little noises in the country for all it is so still. Millions of crickets and things outside, and all kinds of rustles in the trees! There wasn't much wind, and the moonlight came through in my three great windows in three white squares on the black old floor, and those fingery wistaria leaves we were talking of last night just seemed to crawl all over them. And— O, girls, you know that dreadful well in the cellar?"

A most gratifying impression was made by this, and Jenny proceeded cheerfully:

"Well, while it was so horridly still, and I lay there trying not to wake George, I heard as plainly as if it were right in the room, that old chain down there rattle and creak over the stones!"

"Bravo!" cried Jack. "That's fine! I'll put it in the Sunday edition!"

"Be still!" said Kate. "What was it, Jenny? Did you really see anything?"

"No, I didn't, I'm sorry to say. But just then I didn't want to. I woke George, and made such a fuss that he gave me bromide, and said he'd go and look, and that's the last I thought of it till Jack reminded me,—the bromide worked so well."

"Now, Jack, give us yours," said Jim. "Maybe, it will dovetail in somehow. Thirsty ghost, I imagine; maybe they had prohibition here even then!"

Jack folded his napkin, and leaned back in his most impressive manner.

"It was striking twelve by the great hall clock—" he began.

"There isn't any hall clock!"

"O hush, Jim, you spoil the current! It was just one o'clock then, by my old-fashioned repeater."

"Waterbury! Never mind what time it was!"

"Well, honestly, I woke up sharp, like our beloved hostess, and tried to go to sleep again, but couldn't. I experienced all those moonlight and grasshopper sensations, just like Jenny, and was wondering what could have been the matter with the supper, when in came my ghost, and I knew it was all a dream! It was a female ghost, and I imagine she was young and handsome, but all those crouching, hunted figures of last evening ran riot in my brain, and this poor creature looked just like them. She was all wrapped up in a shawl, and had a big bundle under her arm,—dear me, I am spoiling the story! With the air and gait of one in frantic haste and terror, the muffled figure glided to a dark old bureau, and seemed taking things from the drawers. As she turned, the moonlight shone full on a little red cross that hung from her neck by a thin gold chain— I saw it glitter as she crept noiselessly from the room! That's all."

"O Jack, don't be so horrid! Did you really? Is that all? What do you think it was?"

"I am not horrid by nature, only professionally. I really did. That was all. And I am fully convinced it was the genuine, legitimate ghost of an eloping chambermaid with kleptomania!"

"You are too bad, Jack!" cried Jenny. "You take all the horror out of it. There isn't a 'creep' left among us."

"It's no time for creeps at nine-thirty A.M., with sunlight and carpenters outside! However, if you can't wait till twilight for your creeps, I think I can furnish one or two," said George. "I went down cellar after Jenny's ghost!"

There was a delighted chorus of female voices, and Jenny cast upon her lord a glance of genuine gratitude.

"It's all very well to lie in bed and see ghosts, or hear them," he went on. "But the young householder suspecteth burglars, even though as a medical man he knoweth nerves, and after Jenny dropped off I started on a voyage of discovery. I never will again, I promise you!"

"Why, what *was* it?"

"Oh, George!"

"I got a candle—"

"Good mark for the burglars," murmured Jack.

"And went all over the house, gradually working down to the cellar and the well."

"Well?" said Jack.

"Now you can laugh; but that cellar is no joke by daylight, and a candle there at night is about as inspiring as a lightning-bug in the Mammoth Cave. I went along with the light, trying not to fall into the well prematurely; got to it all at once; held the light down and *then* I saw, right under my feet—(I nearly fell over her, or walked through her, perhaps),—a woman, hunched up under a shawl! She had hold of the chain, and the candle shone on her hands—white, thin hands,—on a little red cross that hung from her neck—*vide* Jack! I'm no believer in ghosts, and I firmly object to unknown parties in the house at night; so I spoke to her rather fiercely. She didn't seem to notice that, and I reached down to take hold of her,—then I came upstairs!"

"What for?"

"What happened?"

"What was the matter?"

"Well, nothing happened. Only she wasn't there! May have been indigestion, of course, but as a physician I don't advise any one to court indigestion alone at midnight in a cellar!"

"This is the most interesting and peripatetic and evasive ghost I ever heard of!" said Jack. "It's my belief she has no end of silver tankards, and jewels galore, at the bottom of that well, and I move we go and see!"

"To the bottom of the well, Jack?"

"To the bottom of the mystery. Come on!"

There was unanimous assent, and the fresh cambrics and pretty boots were gallantly escorted below by gentlemen whose jokes were so frequent that many of them were a little forced.

The deep old cellar was so dark that they had to bring lights, and the well so gloomy in its blackness that the ladies recoiled.

"That well is enough to scare even a ghost. It's my opinion you'd better let well enough alone!" quoth Jim.

"Truth lies hid in a well, and we must get her out," said George. "Bear a hand with the chain?"

Jim pulled away on the chain, George turned the creaking wind-lass, and Jack was chorus.

"A wet sheet for this ghost, if not a flowing sea," said he. "Seems to be hard work raising spirits! I suppose he kicked the bucket when he went down!"

As the chain lightened and shortened there grew a strained silence among them; and when at length the bucket appeared, rising slowly through the dark water, there was an eager, half reluctant peering, and a natural drawing back. They poked the gloomy contents. "Only water."

"Nothing but mud."

"Something—"

They emptied the bucket up on the dark earth, and then the girls all went out into the air, into the bright warm sunshine in front of the house, where was the sound of saw and hammer, and the smell of new wood. There was nothing said until the men joined them, and then Jenny timidly asked:

"How old should you think it was, George?"

"All of a century," he answered. "That water is a preservative,—lime in it. Oh!—you mean?—Not more than a month; a very little baby!"

There was another silence at this, broken by a cry from the workmen. They had removed the floor and the side walls of the old porch, so that the sunshine poured down to the dark stones of the cellar bottom. And there, in the strangling grasp of the roots of the great wistaria, lay the bones of a woman, from whose neck still hung a tiny scarlet cross on a thin chain of gold.

KASPER CRAIG
MAUD HOWE

IT WAS AT A LONDON FLOWER-SHOW that Leonard Ebury first met the strange old man who was destined to exert so strong an influence over his life. It was in mid-May, the weather was on its best behavior, and Hurlingham was a paradise of bloom and perfume. In the great tents where the roses were displayed, on the banks of the river and in the club-house, scores of gorgeously-dressed ladies flitted about among the flowers, like so many brilliant butterflies. The band was playing an intoxicating Strauss waltz; the sun was shining brightly, its warmth tempered by a gentle breeze from the river.

Leonard was alone; in all that gay company, there was not one person whose face he had ever seen before. He had been in London but two days, and had not yet made an acquaintance. From his seat beneath a spreading oak-tree he watched the jocund scene, forgetting his own loneliness in contemplating the ever-changing crowd before him.

"May I share your seat, sir?" said a voice at his side; and as he moved to make room for the owner of the voice, his eyes fell upon a man who was an incongruous figure in the gay assemblage.

"You seem to be alone like myself," said the newcomer. "And if I am not mistaken, you are a stranger in London as well."

"You are not mistaken. I never felt so much alone in all my life as I have for the last hour among all these pleasure-seekers."

"Your interest, like mine, is in the flowers, I fancy. That is another point of resemblance between us: but we are in the minority to-day, sir. Most of the people"—here he indicated a group of ladies—"have come here to exhibit their own unfolding or unfolded charms." The stranger spoke in a smooth, courteous voice, his last words followed by an odd, chilly laugh which gave the young American a singular sensation of cold.

"To be quite frank with you, sir," Leonard replied, "I will confess that no higher motive than a desire to kill time brought me to Hurlingham this morning. The flowers are very interesting, no doubt. But I have just returned from the home of flowers, where the hybiscus and the flame-acacias flaunt their gorgeous colors through the dark forests, where the airy orchids hang from palm and fern-tree, but where the sight of a fair woman's face is as rare as snow in July."

"Of what country do you speak?"

"Of the island of Java, where I have passed the last five years. These human flowers have a greater charm for me than the finest roses. Look, now, at that lady in the sapphire dress! Is she not as beautiful, as graceful as yonder peacock, sunning himself on the balcony? See! He spreads his fan, and she turns her lovely head in the sun, and lets its light glisten on her fair curls!"

"I perceive that you are a student of nature like myself. The lady and the bird belong, indeed, to the same class of beings. She wears the colors of his plumage, and imitates his graceful posturing—and see, further, how this woman has found her kin in the other kingdoms. She wears diamonds, hard, sparkling stones, whose glitter masks their shallowness; and she carries camellias: showy, scentless, heartless as herself."

The stranger spoke with a sudden energy.

"Do you know the lady's name?" inquired the young American, who was growing interested in the conversation.

"I never saw her before, but I know her species," answered the stranger with some bitterness. Leonard, who had his full share of the national trait of curiosity, regarded his new acquaintance with a growing interest. He was a tall man, and very slender, but much bent with age. His long, grayish hair and beard floated about his thin face, which wore a greenish pallor and was characterized by an expression of eager inquiry. Whatever else he might be, the man was surely a seeker.

"I perceive that you are no common person," continued the old man, "and I believe that some of my theories may be of interest to you. They are the result of a long life devoted to the study of nature. If I have learned some of her secrets, it is in return for years of labor.

"First in importance I hold the great law of harmony, which runs through all nature and is recognized by men under the blind name of destiny. Every created thing is in harmony with some creation in every other sphere of nature; is, in fact, one note in a vast chord which echoes through the whole universe. It is the first unconscious effort of man to find his kindred elements in the other spheres. Only when this is accomplished does he attain his full development; not till he learns to commune and borrow from these kindred substances in the mineral and vegetable worlds the qualities which they possess, does he reach the zenith of his power."

"You interest me more than I can express," said the young man, falling in with the stranger's mood with the facile adaptability of his race. "This new science is allied to astrology. I believe that a man cannot fail to be influenced by the stars under whose light he was born; and if these remoter forces affect his destiny, why not the nearer ones of which you speak?"

The old man nodded assent, and Leonard begged him to unfold more of his theory.

"All in good time, young sir. I feel that I have found in you one whom I may at once profit by and befriend. If I am not mistaken, you are not in the best of circumstances. Come, now! Would you not be glad of a position which would fall in with your taste for travel, and at the same time reward you handsomely?"

Leonard blushed under the keen gray eyes fixed on him from beneath the old man's shaggy brows. He was conscious that his clothes were somewhat shabby, but the old man's dress was in a much worse condition. "He may be a lunatic, and he may be a rich eccentric," thought Leonard. "Well! I have been a soldier of fortune too long to resign my commission now."

"Sir, you have guessed my case," he said, frankly. "This morning I had but two guineas in the world."

"And you spent one of them to gain admittance to the flower-show! Come, I like your spirit. I have often spent my last ha'penny to buy a posy. I will show you something that will repay your generous outlay. Half his fortune on the mere chance of seeing a beautiful flower!"

The old man rose as he spoke, and led the way to the large tent.

"Here you will see an illustration of what I have just said"—they were now among the prize roses. "Women are more material than we are, and the coarser ones have little sympathy with flowers, preferring to find their counterparts in the grosser mineral world. Their passion for gems is, perhaps, the strongest sentiment of which they are capable. Those of the finer mould only aspire to the higher, more spiritual union with the flora; and even these are keyed to the note of the more fleshy flowers. Women and roses are forever coupled together. Women have always been the most successful rose-growers. I myself first cultivated the rose, a flower of a low order of beauty nearly allied to the sensuous side of man. It is the flower that the lover brings to the tryst, that the beloved wears as a love-signal in her breast, the votive-offering which dresses the altars of Cytherea and of Eros. See that young woman breathing the fragrance of that deep-hearted *Gloire de Dijon*. Its perfume affects her like wine, or like a lover's kiss."

"I think them a most charming pair," said Leonard, stoutly.

"Doubtless; I should have thought so at your age. The trivial passions of youth are necessary to strengthen us for the mightier passions of age. You now, who love a fair face better than all the flowers in the world, will hardly believe that your admiration of woman is a puny sentiment beside my passion for my flowers—the only one that remains to me after a lifetime of passions."

"Which of the flowers did you choose as your favorite when you discarded the rose?" inquired Leonard.

"All in good time, friend," answered the enthusiast. "At first I gave myself to the lily; a purer blossom, but still too earthly. It is the flower we lay in dead hands, the symbol of mortality."

"How can we learn to find our floral affinities?" asked Leonard, curious to hear more of his companion's wild talk.

"How lightly you ask me for a secret that I have given my life to learn! And yet it is possible that I may some day share it with you, if you can do the service I shall ask of you. Be satisfied that you have learned what few men ever dream of—that the secret exists, and may be learned. Bonaparte knew it. What mighty councils he held with the violet, who shall ever tell? Not till he became inflated, vainglorious, worshipping his power and ignoring the source from which it was drawn, did Napoleon fail. On the morning of Water- loo, why was the familiar knot of violets missing from his coat?"

"I follow you," cried Leonard. "The corn-flower of the German Kaiser, the primrose of Lord Beaconsfield—these may have been the most powerful allies of these two great men!"

"Even so," rejoined the visionary. "Did you never suspect that there lurked in the red and white roses of York and Lancaster a deeper significance than the dull historians, who treat them as the mere badges of the rival factions, have ever dreamed?"

They had left the rose-tent, and now entered a small building whose interior was arranged in imitation of a tropical forest. Palm- trees and giant ferns lifted their tall tops to the vaulted roof; the ground was carpeted with moss; a pool of water was filled with rare aquatic plants, some of which Leonard recognized as natives of the tropical countries where he had lived. Amidst the foliage were gorgeous tropical birds; and high up in the branches of the taller trees hung the wonderful orchids, to which the miniature forest merely served as a background.

"Capital!" cried Leonard. "This is the work of an artist! I could almost fancy myself in the forests of Java again. Look at that beau- tiful night-moth! I have seen it growing from the highest branches of a copal-tree, so lofty, that the flower twinkled from its leaves like a white star. And that cyprepedium—I never saw a more per- fect specimen! I almost fancy that I shall see through yonder win- dow the mighty outlines of Java's volcano, crowned with clouds and fire, and draped with its royal purple haze."

The old man was delighted with the youth's enthusiasm. He shook him warmly by the hand, saying:

"Away with hesitation! Let us at once make our compact of friendship. Never was there a fitter partnership. You are young, a poet, an enthusiast. I am old, and a little wiser than you, possessing experience which you lack, lacking the fire of youth which is still yours. You are poor and I am rich. Lend me your strong sinews, your young, active limbs, and I will give you all that you require to live like the sybarite and the adventurous spirit that you are. What say you? Are the terms fair?"

"More than fair; generous!" answered Leonard. "But what is the nature of the service you require of me? I am, as you surmise, an adventurer, and frankly declare myself to be one who has lived too late; a knight-errant of the nineteenth century, seeking for adventure wherever I may find it; stipulating only that I may keep unspotted my honest name, the only inheritance my poor parents left me."

"Come now! Is it likely I should ask you to rob a hen-roost?" said the old man, testily. "If I were in want of a villain, I should hardly give a chance acquaintance like yourself the power to denounce me. I have made my offer; it is for you to accept or decline it."

Just as Leonard was about to refuse this preposterous proposition of an unquestioning obedience, a young girl passed by and stopped to admire a beautiful nepenthe growing near him. She lifted a sweet, pale face to the flower; and as she stood thus, her slight figure reaching upward, she looked at Leonard whose eyes were fastened on her. The young man's heart stood quite still, and then gave a mighty throb. The girl's large, soft eyes returned his intense gaze frankly; then their expression changed to one of pleading; then they were hidden by the smooth, white lids. A faint wave of color spread over her transparent cheek, and she drew a sudden, long breath which loosened the modest moss-rose in her bosom so that it fell to the ground. Leonard dropped upon his knee and, kneeling at her feet, restored the flower to her. She thanked him with a gentle inclination of the head and another tremulous glance. No word had been spoken. A careless observer would only have seen that a pretty young girl had let fall a rose, which a good-looking young man had picked up and returned to her with a rather extravagant politeness. But in that brief moment this youth and this girl, strangers till then, looked into each other's eyes and knew that they were lovers for all time.

"So, Mary Heather, you have come to see your friends in their new surroundings. That is well; but do not linger too long amid this rank vegetation. I shall not return until late to-night."

It was the old man who thus addressed the newcomer.

"All will be ready, sir," she answered, in a voice that sounded to Leonard like that of his dead mother. She turned to go, but at the entrance started back. A scorpion lay on the threshold.

"Do not be afraid! I took care to draw his sting; and that green snake you saw gliding up the palm is as harmless as those pretty lizards. I wished to make the imitation as true to nature as possible," continued the old man turning to Leonard, "and I have been at great pains to be exact in these minor details. But you have not given me your answer. Are we to be friends, or do our paths separate here?"

Leonard's resolve was already taken. Mary Heather had disappeared. His best chance of ever seeing her again was through this strange old man, who seemed on such intimate terms with her.

"As my Mistress Chance has led me to you, sir, I will not break faith with her, nor with you. I accept your offer," he exclaimed, holding out his hand.

"Good!" cried the stranger, laying his cold hand in Leonard's warm grasp. "I am rarely deceived in a face. My name is Kasper Craig. How are you called?"

Leonard handed him his card; and after giving the young American an appointment for the next evening, Kasper Craig left him and melted, like a gray shadow, into the gay crowd that was beginning to pour into the orchid-grove.

"Who was that old man I was just talking with?" asked Leonard, of one of the attendants.

"I don't wonder you ask," replied the man. "I never saw him outside his own garden before. That was Kasper Craig, the greatest orchid collector in the world. This is his exhibit. Folks say that he is a little touched here," tapping his forehead significantly.

Ebury soon after left the festival of flowers, and made his way home to his poor lodgings. He could remember Mary Heather's sweet face better in his bare attic-chamber than in that gay crowd, out of which she had dawned for a moment on his sight, like a modest country daisy astray in a garden of splendid court-flowers.

The next evening he knocked at the door of a poor cottage in Hammersmith a little before the hour named by Kasper Craig. The house was a crazy, old affair, but behind it there was a large, well-kept garden and some glass-houses, the whole inclosed by high, brick walls.

He rapped several times without receiving any attention from those within. After a delay of some minutes, the door was cautiously opened and a small, withered hand was put out toward him. Leonard seized it in his own and held it firmly.

"Let me go," cried a shrill voice. "Give me what you have brought for Kasper Craig, and let me go."

"I have brought nothing but my muscles," said Leonard, pushing the door open, "and those are the only things I possess that Kasper Craig has asked me to use in his service."

The young man had forced himself into the dimly-lighted passage. He still held the little hand in his; but when he saw the crippled child to whom it belonged, his grasp grew more tender.

"Come, my boy," he said gently; "play no pranks with me. I have come by appointment to see Kasper Craig. Lead me to him."

"What is your name?" said the cripple, suspiciously.

"Leonard Ebury. What is your's?"

"Edward Heather," answered the child. "You are to wait till Kasper Craig returns. You can either sit here, or go out into the garden." Outside, the weather was damp and it was beginning to drizzle; inside, the prospect of the bare passage, which contained nothing but a dusty hat-rack and a few botanical prints hanging on the walls, was hardly more inviting.

Leonard laughed and patted the child's thin hand.

"You are not very hospitable, Edward; but if you will stay and talk with me, we will sit on the stairs till Kasper Craig comes home. Is Mary Heather your sister?"

"Yes," said the boy, fixing his large, hollow eyes on Ebury with an intent, questioning gaze. "What do you want with my Mary?"

"Only to see her, to speak with her. If that cannot be, to know if she is in this house."

The boy's eyes seemed to read Leonard's very soul.

"No," he said, shaking his head with an air of elfin sagacity. "No, Leonard Ebury, you cannot see her. If you are a friend of Kasper Craig's, you shall not see my Mary."

"I am no friend of Kasper Craig's. I have come to do some work for him, for which he pays me. Do you understand? If I could see your sister—if only once—I care not if I never see that strange old man again."

"Why?" said the child. "Why do you want to see Mary? Do you love her, too?"

Leonard trembled under those sad, questioning eyes. He could not have lied to the child to save his life.

"Yes, Edward, I love Mary Heather."

"Are you her sweetheart?" whispered the child, angrily. "She never told me of you."

"I never spoke, to her—but I have seen her. I love her, and I believe that she loves me."

"And will you take us away from here, away from Kasper Craig—now—to-night—if I let you see Mary?"

They are all mad in this house, thought Ebury; but he answered the child soothingly.

"If Mary wishes it, yes. But take me to her. He may return at any moment."

"Come then," said the child resolutely, leading the way up the dark stairway. Leonard groped his way behind him as best he might. Edward tapped lightly at a door at the end of the passage, which was immediately opened by Mary Heather.

"There she is," said the child, pointing to his sister. "Say what you have to say quickly."

"I am afraid that I have intruded upon you, Miss Heather," Ebury began. "I came by appointment to seek Kasper Craig, and I find that I am before the hour."

"Come in," said the young girl. "You are welcome to sit here till Kasper Craig returns. He will not be long."

Leonard still hesitated on the threshold, hat in hand. He felt all unworthy to enter that white, maiden room, so rich in purity, so poor in all else.

"Come in. Mary says you are to come in," said the child, petulantly, pushing Ebury into the room and shutting the door. "How cold it is! I will stir the fire while you talk."

"He is very nervous to-day. Do not notice him," said Mary in an undertone, as she placed a chair for the visitor near the fire and took her place at a work-table. She was soon stitching at some coarse work, and the home-like air of the large, pleasant chamber, together with Mary's quiet grace and dignity, soon made Leonard forget the child's wild talk. Ebury learned that the brother and sister were orphans and dependent upon Kasper Craig, to whom they were distantly related. Mary told him their simple history in answer to his adroit questions.

She barely remembered her parents, both of whom died when Edward was a baby. The children assisted Kasper Craig in caring for his orchids; and in addition to this, Mary made drawings from certain of the rarer specimens. Her easel, with an unfinished sketch of a white orchid, stood near the window. The flower from which the drawing was made, bloomed from the branch of a tree hanging against the wall near the little white bed. The great, tropical flower hung languidly from the fragment of dead wood. It was unlike any orchid Leonard had ever seen. As he was admiring the weird blossom, the door opened and Kasper Craig entered.

"You were prompt indeed, friend," said the famous collector with his chilly laugh. "But I shall not apologize for keeping you waiting, for my tardiness has given you a glimpse of my greatest treasure, my last discovery. Tell me, frankly. Have you ever seen anything as beautiful as this in Java, or anywhere else?"

"I have certainly never seen anything like this orchid," said Leonard, "but I am not sure that I think it beautiful. It is such a savage-looking flower! Look at that open mouth and throat—they have almost a human look. Those coarse, white spikes are like teeth. They would hold fast and devour any unfortunate bee that came in search of honey."

"It is allied to the *dionæa muscipula*, which, as you know, feeds upon insects. But this flower has a much more highly-developed organism. In evolution, it is as far from the Venus's fly-trap as you are from the river-drift man. Linnaeus, and Gray, and all the famous botanists between them, have failed to establish the line between animal and vegetable life. There is a good and sufficient cause for this: the line does not exist. There is no break in the chain of creation. The orchid stands midway between the plant and the animal. It is capable of movement and it is carnivorous, but it has not yet attained to its full development. It is the highest and latest expression of nature, the crowning triumph of creation. This hybrid is the result of the experiments of thirty years of my life. Step by step, I have raised the standard of its race's organism. This wonderful creature already sleeps, breathes, moves, feeds itself like many of its predecessors. It will do more. Hitherto it has been nourished only by the grosser forms of animal life: flies and other insects. Deprived of this sustenance, it will grasp the strong, subtle life-essence which belongs only to some few of the higher animal species."

Leonard's attention had wandered from the subject of the old man's discourse. His eyes were fixed on Mary Heather, who was sitting at the other end of the room, stitching steadily at her work. Her soft hair, her dewy, violet eyes, her pure, flower-like face were already more familiar to him than his own features; and yet, every time that his eyes fell upon her loveliness, it seemed that a rich, new treasure had been given to him.

"You are looking at Mary Heather," said the collector. "You may well look at that girl. What a rare, orchid-like growth she is! Her father was a drunkard. Her mother, an overworked seamstress. From their union sprang this perfect flower. Can you fancy that her delicate tints, her perfect form, her airy grace, were inherited from a sot and a drudge? No, no; nature does not perform miracles; there are causes for all her so-called phenomena. The scientists have not yet learned the A, B, C, of her wonderful methods. From her babyhood Mary Heather has lived among my plants. Her mother would bring the child in her cradle in the morning, and leave her with me all day. She has breathed the breath of the rarest flowers that the world has ever seen. She has drawn her life from them. Her flesh is more like their flesh than like yours or mine. Frail growths, that have never before lived out of their native soil, have flourished under her hands; plants that have ever been considered sterile in a state of cultivation have grown fruitful under her care; for she is of their kind, and knows the secrets of their mystic marriage-rites. How closely the two forms of life approach each other! This girl is the flower of the human family. If we could produce an animal-flower, with more animal attributes even than the *dionæa*, should we not have found the link in the chain that binds the two kingdoms together? Would not the man who should produce that flower, who should publish that great secret to the world, be remembered with Galileo, with Newton, with Darwin?"

Kasper Craig had whispered this flood of wild talk into the ear of the young American, who was now thoroughly convinced of the old man's insanity. Leonard looked at Mary and Edward Heather. The boy was crouching in his invalid-chair, his fearful eyes fixed upon Kasper Craig, his whole figure expressive of a terrified anticipation. Mary had laid down her sewing, and sat leaning back in her arm-chair, pale and weary, but showing no sign of the brother's nervous agitation. The sweet, faint color had faded from her cheeks. She was drooping like the lilies in his mother's garden at home, on a hot, summer afternoon. He thought of Kasper Craig's comparison. She was, indeed, a human flower.

"What you say is very ingenious, at least," said Leonard, "and I am pleased to have seen this rare flower, of which Miss Heather is making so faithful a drawing. But how is this?" He had stepped close to the little bed, and in passing touched the white pillow, leaving a benediction on the fair linen. "The artist is painting the flower white, while the orchid surely has a faint rose tint on the lower petals."

"I had not noticed that," said Mary. "Is there not some reflection that gives it that color? I am quite sure the flower was as white as snow when I began the drawing yesterday."

"It was white, Mary!" said Kasper Craig. "But see for yourself. The young man is not mistaken."

There was a ring of joyous exultation in his chilly voice, at the sound of which the cripple cowered in his chair. Mary Heather came slowly to the old man's side, and moved the flower into a better light. The rose tint was now unmistakable. Leonard noticed how white and worn the girl looked, and determined for her sake to break up the interview.

"It grows late, sir," he said. "Let us not longer intrude upon Miss Heather, who seems in need of repose. We have not yet spoken of the matter that brought me here to-night."

At this reminder Kasper Craig led the way down-stairs; at the doorway Leonard was detained by the child, who had darted from his chair the moment the old man left the room.

"Remember that you are to take us away, soon," he murmured, "very soon, or it will be too late. Mary will die."

Leonard lifted the misshapen little creature in his arms and soothed him tenderly, whispering in his ear:

"I will come again, soon. Tell her—tell your sister—that I am her friend, and would give my life to help her if she were in trouble."

"Are you coming, young man?" called Kasper Craig from the stairs; and with a last, lingering look at Mary, her lover left the room.

The two men sat together until midnight; and when they parted, it had been agreed between them that Leonard Ebury should start for Bogota, in search of a rare specimen of the South American orchid, as soon as his outfit could be arranged. He received the most careful instructions from his employer, who was familiar with the ground he was to go over, and who proved himself a practical business-man in everything that concerned the proposed journey.

Leonard came to the house the next day in the vain hope of seeing Mary Heather or her brother; but he was admitted by Kasper Craig, who accompanied him to the door at the end of his visit. He found some pretence each day to make a pilgrimage to Hammersmith, but the fair girl and the little cripple were never to be seen. Leonard sometimes asked himself if the two children had any existence outside of his dreams. That wonderful morning among the flowers, when the maiden for whom he had waited all his life suddenly appeared before him, to be lost a moment after in the crowd—was she real, or a vision betwixt sleeping and waking? There remained, however, the reality of Kasper Craig, who seemed to have forgotten his odd theories, and talked of his flowers as any other enthusiastic collector of rare and choice plants might have done.

One day Leonard plucked up courage to ask to see the young girl, but he was told shortly that she was too busy to receive visits from young men. Leonard resorted to every device to postpone his departure; but the morning of his last day came and he had not caught another glimpse of Mary Heather.

"I will not leave London without seeing her," he said to himself. "I will tell the old man so, plainly; and if he will not give me the opportunity, he may send someone else in my berth, to-morrow."

He arrived at the cottage earlier than was his wont, and ere he had time to knock, the door was noiselessly opened by Edward Heather, who beckoned him to enter quietly. The child carefully closed the door, and then seizing Leonard by the hand, dragged him up the stairs with an incredible force. The door of Mary's room stood slightly ajar, and without giving any warning, the child drew the visitor in and closed the door. Mary was seated at her easel, her back towards them. She did not look up from her work, and Leonard saw that she was unconscious of his presence.

"Look at her!" whispered the child. "She is dying, dying! The flower is killing her!"

Leonard followed the direction of the child's eyes. They were fixed upon the orchid. The flower was strangely altered. Instead of drooping gracefully against the branch, it was now a robust and vigorous plant, standing boldly forth from the bark on which it had bloomed. The faint, rosy tinge had deepened and spread over the whole flower. The mouth was scarlet, and the throat with its cruel spikes was spotted here and there with flecks of dark red.

It was a sinister-looking plant, indeed, and one that might easily terrify a nervous, imaginative invalid like Edward Heather.

"What made it grow like that?" murmured the child. "Does it get all that blood from that dead branch?"

Here Mary Heather looked up from her work, and for the first time Leonard saw her face. It was white as marble. As she rose to greet him, the young man saw that she was wasted to a shadow of her former self.

"What ails you, Mary Heather? Are you ill?" he asked, taking her thin hand in his.

"Ill? No! Only a little tired." Her voice was like an echo of herself, her wan smile a piteous thing to see.

It seemed to Leonard Ebury that his reason deserted him at that moment, and for the life of him he could not have told why he did the thing—but before Mary Heather's pale lips breathed another breath of the heavy air of that chamber, he had torn the flower from the wall and trampled it into a bleeding mass beneath his feet.

"Are you mad?" cried a voice beside him. Kasper Craig had gripped him by the arm, and stood glaring down upon him with a look of rage upon his face which Leonard Ebury never forgot.

"I don't know; we are all mad here, I think," he said, shaking the old man from him. Kasper Craig dropped on his knees and gathered up the mangled flower; the oozing juice stained his hands a dull red; a peculiar, sickly odor pervaded the room. Leonard Ebury threw open the window and let the light summer breeze blow through the chamber. This action seemed to remind the old man of his presence, which in his despair over his shattered treasure he had ignored.

"Ruined!" he cried, staggering to his feet. "Ruined—and by the man I have befriended. Ingrate, fool! Is it thus you requite my confidence, my generosity? You shall pay dearly for this!"

Leonard was speechless and confused. Now that all was over, he was half-ashamed of having yielded to that strange impulse of destruction. He stood with crossed arms leaning against the wall, his eyes fixed upon the floor, trying to regain his self-possession. Kasper Craig came slowly toward him, his hands hidden under his long cloak.

"Have a care, Leonard," cried Mary Heather. The girl's warning came none too soon, for at that moment the old man sprang at Leonard's throat, the long, sharp pruning-knife which he always wore at his belt clutched in his hand.

"A life for a life!" he cried furiously. But before he had time to deal the blow which he had aimed, the younger man closed with him and, after a short struggle, wrested the knife from him and tossed it out of the open window into the garden below. Disarmed and exhausted, the old man sank panting and trembling into a seat. There was a long silence, broken at length by Ebury:

"I don't know what this all means. You have bewitched us all, it seems. You must find another to do your bidding in South America, Kasper Craig. I have other work to do. Mary Heather, I do not know what power this dark old man has over you and your brother, but it is one from which I would fain free you both. Will you come with me out into the world? I have nothing to offer you but my love, my honest name, and the service of my life. Will you come with me?"

Mary had revived a little in the last few moments, and the voice in which she answered the young man's appeal was like her own again.

"Yes, Leonard Ebury, we will go with you."

The child was running about the room, collecting their few possessions.

"Leave all behind, Edward. There is nothing that is ours, here," she said.

Kasper Craig had listened, speechless and ireful, to what was said.

"What nonsense is this, girl?" he at length exclaimed. "You to leave your home and the only friend you have in the world, at the bidding of this penniless adventurer!"

"He gives us love, which suffices for all things. You have never loved us, Kasper Craig, and we owe you nothing. We have worked for you all the years that we have eaten your bread, and we leave you as poor as we came to you."

"Come, Mary, come," said the child, impatiently pulling his sister's skirts. "Come out into the sunshine."

"Remember that you can never come back, Mary; the door will be closed against you forever. My fortune, which would have been yours"—he stopped and hesitated.

"Your fortune!" laughed Edward. "When you were killing her, what good would that do her? Come away, Mary. We must go now, or stay forever."

"Farewell, Kasper Craig," said the girl. "I am going out of the gray world in which you have kept me, out into the warm sunlight. Farewell!"

Leonard Ebury drew her white hand through his arm, and with the child upon his shoulder, they left the house. When they were out in the street the girl drew a long breath.

"How good it is to be away from that sombre house," she said. "You were sent by Heaven to deliver us from our joyless life with that strange old man."

"Murderer, murderer!" cried the child, shaking his tiny fist at the dingy house.

"Do not mind him," murmured Mary Heather. "He is often strange, like this. Kasper Craig meant no harm to us, I am sure. I never saw him in anger until this afternoon." She touched her lover's arm with a shudder at the danger in which he had been from the old man's knife. "But let us forget him," she continued. "Edward, Leonard, let us agree never to mention his name again."

"With all my heart," cried Leonard; "for I cannot even think of him without doubting my own sanity."

"She does not know," whispered the child in Leonard's ear, "she never did know; but you and I know that the flower was a"—

"Hush, boy," interrupted Leonard Ebury, sternly. "Let Kasper Craig be forgotten, as Mary wills."

"Yes," laughed the child. "We will never see him, we will never think of him again. He cannot hurt us now, for the flower is dead!"

THE GOLD PLANT
GEORGE GRIFFITH

THIS IS THE STORY of the Gold Plant—not exactly, I admit, as I had it from the old skipper, for the voluminous manuscript which he left me by will, among two or three other legacies, mostly in the curious line, to "knock into shape," as he expressed it in his somewhat original statement, needed a good dose of the blue pencil, for he had added to it, interlined it, and partially rewritten it, until it was a very maze of literary involution.

I don't say either that it is strictly true, or that it is even mainly true, though, personally, I believe it, for the skipper, at any rate, towards the latter end of his life, was a sober, steady-going man, a regular church-goer, and a highly respected citizen of the little East Coast fishing town in which I made his acquaintance. I don't think he would lie wantonly, even in a posthumous form, and I certainly owe it to him to record that with the manuscript he left me two or three leaves of a plant, utterly unlike any plant known to botany until quite recently, which certainly afforded strong collateral evidence as to the truth of the story.

The leaves are something like oak leaves in shape, but larger. They are very thin, but as stiff as sheet steel, and they shine in the light with a golden metallic lustre so like that of the real thing that, but for their hardness, you might almost imagine them to be stamped out of gold. After I had read the story I took them to a botanist friend of mine, who worried about them for a long time, and then sent them to Kew, whence they came back with the information that they were certainly true leaves, but of an unknown plant, and, further, that metal of some sort, and probably an alloy of gold, had in some strange manner entered largely into their composition.

This was corroboration enough for me, and so I set to work upon the skipper's manuscript, and the result was the following narrative, which may be taken as a fairly faithful unravelling of the tangled skein that he had got knotted up with the point of his pen in the course of the only literary labour he undertook.

"IT WAS AWAY BACK in the early forties, and I was first officer of about the smartest schooner that ever ran the middle passage between the Slave Coast and Cuba. Her name was the *Spindrift*, and as I shall be beyond the reach of all laws but one when this is made public, I need make no bones about saying that she was not only a slaver by trade, but a bit of a pirate, too, when the game was handy, and not too many people looking. She was commanded by as smart a man as ever made his living out of his own wickedness and other people's suffering. His name was Peter Johnson when he was within earshot and Sandy Pete when he wasn't.

"I don't say it was the sort of name you'd give a pirate slaver in a novel, but you see it was his name, and there's an end of it. It seemed to fit him, too, for he didn't look a bit the sort of man that you'd expect to find at a trade like that. He was neither short nor tall, but a bit slim in build, so that he looked taller than he was. His hair was between red and yellow, as you will have guessed, and rather thin, though he took the greatest possible trouble to dress it so that you wouldn't think so.

"His face wouldn't have been bad if it hadn't been for the eyes, and they were green. Not grey or light blue, mind you, but green, as green as deep sea-water, and when he got angry they used to light up and burn just like a cat's in the dark. He never showed he was angry any other way. Never a drop of blood came into his smooth, sallow face. You scarcely ever heard him blaspheme, except when he was pleased, and then only for amusement like; but when you saw those eyes of his begin to glitter, and heard him speak even more politely than usual, it was time to stand by and let everything go with a run.

"None of us liked him, least of all myself, but business was business in that line, same as in any other, and Captain Pete was the smartest and luckiest man on the Coast, so shares ran high accordingly.

"Captain Pete had just one weakness, and that a pretty common one. He didn't care about drink, or women, or glory, not a bit, but he was greedy right up to the roots of his sandy hair, and if he once got it into his head that there was money in the game, he'd go through with it at any cost and any risk. Still, I ought to say that he never took any risks that he didn't get through all right with but once, and that was the last risk but one that he ever took.

"He had made a very respectable pile at the time I speak of, and although he was only about thirty-five, he was thinking seriously of selling the *Spindrift* and settling down somewhere quiet and respectable like to enjoy, as he used to put it, the hard-earned fruits of his toils and perils. He had got all his money in a bank at Port Royal, and on the particular trip I am going to tell about he had taken over with him as a passenger from Cuba to the Coast a man who had been skipper and part-owner of a Yankee clipper running between Baltimore and Liverpool, and who had found the game rather slow, and was thinking of going into the black ivory line.

"He was looking out for a ship, and so Captain Pete took him across to show him what the *Spindrift* could do with her heels, and, if he persuaded him to buy, to introduce him to the chiefs and dealers on the coast as his successor in the business, because, of course, the goodwill would go with the ship.

"There was a fine lot of slaves waiting for us in the calabooses, and the Yankee skipper was very much pleased with the prospect, and told Captain Pete that he didn't think there would be any difficulty about buying the *Spindrift* with the people who were finding him the money—solid, respectable Yankee merchants, every one of them—when he took his report back. But Captain Pete had sailed his last trip in the *Spindrift*, and this is how it came about that the Yankee took her home instead of him.

"Among the slaves that were waiting for us there was a lad and a girl—brother and sister they were—quite different from any of the others. Their skins were almost white, whiter, in fact, than some of ours, and their features were thin and regular, and like anything but a negro's. Indeed, the girl was a regular beauty, and her brother, when he got washed and had some cotton clothes on him, was as pretty a lad as you would wish to see. The girl seemed about seventeen, and her brother might be a year or so younger.

"Now Captain Pete was, as I have said, a very smart man, and a lot more intelligent about things in general than most men in his line, and when he spotted those two he had them fetched out from among the others, got them washed and dressed a bit decent like, took them into a hut that he used as a sort of office, and started talking to them to find out where they came from. He knew most of the dialects that were used along the Coast, and he found they could understand one of them pretty well, so they had quite a long jaw, and when it was over he left them in the hut, got a nigger woman to take them some food and look after them just as if they had been visitors or customers, instead of slaves, and then came to me to go for a walk with him outside the village.

"I saw there was something in the wind, so I said 'Yes,' and when we had got clear away from the huts and out of earshot he took hold of me by the arm, and said:

"'Martin, have you ever heard that story about a race of white people up in the mountains yonder to the eastward?'

"'Yes,' I said, 'I've heard it, and I believe I once read a book about them, but never took much account of it except as a traveller's yarn. Why?'

"'Well,' he said, lowering his voice a bit, 'it's a fact, and that boy and girl that came down with the last batch belonged to then, and I've been getting all the particulars out of them.'

"'And do you believe them, Captain?' I asked, with just a bit of a laugh.

"'Believe! Yes, I do,' he said. 'Do you believe that?'

"He opened his other hand, and showed me a nugget of virgin gold that might have weighed about an ounce and a half. 'And do you know what that means?' he went on. 'It means that they know of gold mines different to any that the Arabs or niggers about here know of, for all their gold is dust, washed out of river beds—see?'

"'That's so,' I said, 'There is no doubt about that. Did you get that from them?'

"'Yes,' he said, 'The girl gave it to me as a sort of earnest penny, on a bargain that I've been making with them. How she managed to hide it all the way down I don't know, but there it is, and they've promised to get me as much of that as I can take away with me as a ransom if I'll release then, and let them guide me back to their own country. Now, Martin, they might be valuable as slaves if we got them safely over, but they wouldn't be worth a gold mine, would they?'

"'No,' I said, 'they wouldn't, always supposing you got that gold mine for them.' For, to tell you the truth, I thought it was a bit of a wild-cat scheme, and little better than foolishness to take such a big story on trust from a boy and girl like that, even making all allowance for the nugget. But Captain Pete's heart was set on it already, and I saw that he meant going.

"'Don't you see,' he said, when I'd told him what I thought of the plan, 'that there isn't any more risk in it than there is in our own trade? We've been lucky so far, but it's always the hundredth time that you come to grief, and it's just as likely as not that one of those infernal cruisers might drop on us on our very last passage, and then how should I look with all my hard-earned little pile in the bank and myself in irons going to Port Royal to be tried for slavery, and, perhaps, something worse?

"'Now this game, you see, has no harm in it, and if it turns out right it means a fortune, not only for me, but for you, too, if you'll come along with me as I want you to do. We'll get half-a-dozen men out of the schooner, arm them well, and fit out a regular expedition. Wilkins shall give me an order on his people for the value of the ship and cargo, and I'll send it by a respectable trader from Lagos to my bank in Port Royal, and tell them to draw the money. Then every-thing will be safe until we come back. Now, what do you say?'

"I thought about it for a bit and then decided to go. I hadn't any pile to trouble about, for I spent my shares as fast as I had

drawn them—a bit faster, sometimes, and, besides that I was a bit
sick of slaving, and, like most young chaps of my age—for I was
only twenty-five when this happened—I wasn't at all averse to a
bit of an adventure, so I said:

"'Well, Captain, I don't say that I have the same hopes of the
job as you have, but if you'll give me the money that should be
coming to me this voyage, and pay for the fitting-out of the trip,
and give me a fair share of the plunder—if you get it—I'm your
man, and I'll start when you like.'

"'Good!' he said; 'then that's all fixed. I needn't tell you to keep
your mouth close shut on it, and now I'll go straight and settle
things up as well as I can with Wilkins, and get Wilson to take your
place and see about the men, and then tomorrow I'll drop down to
Lagos in the coasting schooner and get what's wanted, while you
stop here with the men and look after the boy and girl. I'll be back
in under the week, and then we can make a fair start.'

"I agreed, and, not to make too long a story of it, Captain Pete
managed to get everything arranged as he wanted it. Wilkins loaded
up the *Spindrift* with as pretty a cargo as ever you saw, and took
her out of the river, and that's the last that ever was seen or heard
of her. Whether she would have got on better with Captain Pete I
don't pretend to say. Maybe not; maybe it was just his luck that
got him out of her in time, though no one can say that his luck
turned out very rosily after all.

"We made our start about eight days later, well found and fitted in every way, ten of us all told, including the boy and the girl,
and took with us a train of six mules and twenty negro drivers and
bearers, for Captain Pete had fairly set his heart on the job now,
and was determined to do the thing properly.

"At first the men knew nothing except that they were to have
double pay until they got back to the Coast. But when we had been
travelling up-country for a week the Captain told them—the white
men, of course, not the niggers—that he was going gold-seeking
on information that he had picked up and thought trustworthy.
Then he showed them the nugget, and told them the story of the
boy and the girl, and let it simmer in their minds for a bit. A day or

two later he said something else to them that I didn't hear at the time, but it came out later, as you'll see, and the result was that the men pushed on contented and eager to get there, and as the road wasn't bad, considering the country, we got over the ground pretty fast.

"It would take me too long to tell all about the journey, for we travelled eastward across the Kwara river and through the Adamawa country, and then into the unknown wilds beyond, trending a bit more southward, for four months, during which we must have covered something like fifteen hundred miles of all sorts of country, from swamps and forests to meadow lands and mountains, that only wanted getting to and cultivating to make a paradise of them.

"The further we went the more I got to believe in the story, for that boy and girl just took us straight along, road or no road, by some sort of instinct, until at last they brought us to the foot of a high, steep mountain range, running nearly due north and south, that looked too steep for anything but a bird to get over. We hadn't seen a trace of human beings for two or three weeks, but the morning after we camped at the foot of those mountains we had it proved to us that the story of the white people was no traveller's yarn, but a real fact.

"We had let Koomru, that's the boy, go out of the camp the night before, keeping the girl back as hostage, and he came back just after sunrise with about a dozen others of the same colour and features as himself, only, of course, older and much more finely dressed. They were the gentlest and most peaceable folk I ever came across, and I can tell you their delight at getting the boy and girl back was a sight that did even a stony-hearted lot of slavers like us good.

"Of course, they looked on Captain Pete and us almost like angels sent from Heaven to save the boy and girl from slavery, and we guessed, too, that this boy and girl must have been something very considerable in the country from the respectful way they were treated. They were ready to deal fairly by us, too, for they promised not only to give us, as the girl had said, as much gold as each of us could carry, but to load the four mules and the twelve bearers that we had left with it as well. But there was one thing they wouldn't do at any price—they wouldn't show us the way through the mountains or tell us anything at all about the country beyond.

"Now, this was just what Captain Pete and most of us wanted, and, as you know by this time, he wasn't the man to stick at much to get his way. He let the boy go to and fro as he pleased, but he kept the girl and a couple of women attendants that they had sent out to her in the camp till the last ounce of the ransom had been paid—and paid it was honestly, in good bars and nuggets and dust, that footed up around two hundred pounds weight, and as gold was fetching about £4 10s an ounce in those days this was worth over £5000 sterling.

"This was pretty good, but it wasn't enough for Captain Pete. He wanted nothing less than the mines that the gold came out of, and he meant to have them, and the country beyond the mountains as well, if he could get it. So when all the gold had been handed over and packed up, he gave a feast, and got about two score of the people, including the boy and girl, into the camp, and then he got up and told the head-man that unless they showed him the mines and let him take as much as he wanted out of them, not one of them should leave the camp alive, except the boy and the girl, and he'd take them back with him and make slaves of them, and force them to guide him back again with a force of men strong enough to conquer the country.

"They listened to him in a dazed sort of way as if they could not understand it. They had never seen any treachery like that before, but when they came to see that we really meant business they showed plenty of courage. The head-man told him that every citizen in the country was bound by an oath and under pain of death never to show anyone outside the mountains the way in or to reveal the location of the gold mines, and that they were all ready to die sooner than give up the secret, for if they did give it up they would be killed by their own people, and so should we, too, for the matter of that.

"Then Captain Pete got angry, and his eyes began to burn green. We had firearms and they hadn't, so, of course, they were entirely at our mercy. One of them tried to slip off and run to the mountains to give the alarm, but he hadn't gone forty yards before the Captain dropped him with a bullet through the head. Then there was a stampede, and when it was over there were only six of them left, including the head-man and the boy and girl.

"It was a horrible thing to do, but if you have ever seen men with the gold fever on them as we had it then, you'd understand. There is no other madness like that to make wild beasts of men, and that's just what it made us. Those that were left still held out as obstinately as ever, and told the Captain to do his worst—and he did, for he tied the head-man and the three others up to trees and burnt them to death one after the other; but they died like heroes to the last man, and not a word would they say.

"Nobody else came out of the mountains. Everything remained still and as lonely as death, so we had to conclude either that the people knew nothing about what was going on, or else that they had made up their minds that only those who had been dealing with us should come out in case someone betrayed the secret. When the last man was dead, Captain Pete threatened the boy and girl with all sorts of horrors and tortures if they didn't show us the way through the mountains; but it was no good, they told him to do as he liked, and then held their tongues.

"He tied them up and flogged them both, one after the other, but not a word did he get out of them; so at last he gave it up, and we started to search for the opening ourselves. We spent over a week at it, and lost a man every day, for, so sure as a man went prospecting alone, he never came back. At last, when there were only four white men and six niggers left, we were forced to give in; so we loaded up the gold, leaving everything else that we could spare behind us, and started off back.

"The first night the boy and girl stabbed themselves to death, and there we were in a strange country, all those hundreds of miles from the Coast, without guides. A week later the niggers bolted to a man, each of them taking as much of the treasure as he could lay his hands on, and if we hadn't kept the arms strictly to ourselves I suppose they'd have shot us down and taken the lot. So we four white men pushed on with the mules as fast as we could, for it wasn't a bit of good trying to chase the niggers, and for a fortnight everything went on all right.

"Then we lost one of the mules in a swamp, and two or three days after that one of the men sickened, and as we had to choose between taking him or a load of gold, we left him mad with fever to die in the bush. It was just as though there was a curse on the whole thing, as I daresay now there was. Last of all, when we were coming down the western slope of the steep mountain that we had to cross, our last man fell over a precipice with one of the mules—and that was the end of the expedition for the present.

'The Captain and I discussed things, and decided that there was nothing for it but to bury the treasure—we still had about £4000 worth of it left—in a spot in the mountains that we could readily find, and push on with the two mules we had left and the lightest possible loads down to the Coast, and then organize a regular expedition to cone back, find the treasure, and go on to the Gold Country, as we called it, force our way into it and conquer it, like Cortez had conquered Mexico.

"After a bit of seeking we found a place at the head of a deep valley running into the side of the mountain. This valley had a natural pyramid of rock at the mouth of it, so there would be no mistaking it when we came back; so we buried the treasure there, took the exact latitude of the mountain and worked out the longitude by dead reckoning as well as we could. Then we started hone, pretty well down-hearted, as you may guess, but none the less determined on that account to come back and find the mines of the Gold Country at any cost.

"We got back to the Coast all right, and went down to Lagos, and the first thing Captain Pete heard there, was that the bank in which he left all his money had gone to smash, and that every dollar of it was lost; and so there we found ourselves with only a few ounces of gold in our pockets and no money to fit out the expedition with. Still, Captain Pete wasn't beaten, and neither was I, for the matter of that, though, of course, I hadn't been anything like as hard hit as he was.

"We managed to raise about £50 between us, and with this we bought four mules and trading stuff, got six niggers on credit from a dealer we had done business with for a long time, and off we started back again for the mountain. Ten weeks afterwards I and the Captain found ourselves with two mules in the valley once more; the other two mules and three of the niggers had died and the others had run away, for the bad luck had come back worse and worse as we got nearer to that treasure which had the curse of blood upon it.

"But there was more bad luck in store for us yet, for when we reached the place where we had buried the treasure we found the ground covered with the most extraordinary looking plant that anybody had ever seen. It was a sort of shrub about two feet high; but it wasn't vegetable—it was metal. The stems and branches were as tough and hard as wire, and the leaves—well, you have got some of those, so you can see them for yourself.

"Of course, we thought it very wonderful, but we didn't know the real meaning of it until we had worked like slaves for two good days clearing it away, and then we dug down—and what do you think we found? Just nothing but a few little scraps of the bar gold, eaten away as if they had been in some acid, and a sprinkling of the gold dust. Every other scrap of the treasure had been eaten up by this wonderful infernal plant; and, more than that, it had changed it, for anyone with half an eye could see that, though they had a golden sort of look, the stems and leaves of the plant were no more gold than they were iron.

"That night Captain Pete shot himself. He did it quite quietly, and never said a word to me about what he was going to do, but he seemed to be altogether broken up by this last cut of fate, and after all, perhaps, he had done the best thing he could, for he was a bad man, and if ever gold was bought with blood and treachery that treasure of his was. As for me, I picked up what was left, got a few of the leaves of the Gold Plant, as I called it, buried Captain Pete in the hole where the treasure had been, and started off, just about as miserable a man as there was in Africa, to get back to the Coast.

"It took me nearly six months, but I got there and went back into the old line and did very well, but I had learned a lesson. I saved two out of every three dollars that I made, and when the trade got altogether too risky, about ten years later, I left it and bought a little trading schooner, and she made me enough money to retire on for good."

THAT WAS THE END of the skipper's story. For the sake of possible explorers and treasure-seekers, I regret to say that he seems to have thought better about leaving the latitude and longitude of the mountain behind him, for it was not in his manuscript, and the most careful search among his papers failed to reveal the slightest indication, other than what was given in his story, either of the mysterious country of the White People, or of the unknown valley in which the Gold Plant had flourished in such costly soil.

THE STORY OF THE GREY HOUSE
KATE AND HESKETH PRICHARD

Mr. Flaxman Low declares that only on one occasion has he undertaken, unasked, the solving of a psychical mystery. To that case he always refers as the "affair of the Grey House." The house bears a different name in the annals of more than one scientific society, and much controversy has raged over the strange details of a story that seems to open up a new province of fantastic horror. Papers and treatises have been written about it in almost every European language, and many dismaying facts of a somewhat analogous nature have thus been brought to light. There was some hesitation at first about laying this matter—backed as it is by an explanation, which, though terrible, is not altogether unsupported—before the public, but it has finally been decided to incorporate it in the present series.

During the dry summer of 1893 Mr. Low happened to be staying in a lonely village on the coast of Devon. He was deeply immersed in some antiquarian work connected with the old Norse calendars, and therefore limited his acquaintance in the neighbourhood to one individual, a Dr. Fremantle, who, beside being a medical man, was a botanist of some note.

One afternoon, when driving together, Mr. Low and Dr. Fremantle passed through a valley which nestled cup-like in the higher ground a few miles inland. As they passed along a deep, steep lane with overhanging hedges they caught a glimpse, through a break in the leaves, of a grey gable peeping out between the horizontal branches of a cedar.

Flaxman Low pointed it out to his companion.

"That's young Montesson's house," answered Fremantle, "and it bears a very sinister reputation. Nothing in your line, though," with a smile. "Indeed, no ghost would lend the same hideous associations to the place it now possesses as the result of a succession of mysterious murders that have occurred there."

"The grounds seem neglected. I don't remember to have seen such rank growth anywhere."

"Certainly not inside the British Isles," returned Fremantle. "The estate is left to take care of itself, partly because Montesson won't live there, partly because it is impossible to find labourers to work near the house. Our warm, damp climate and this sheltered position give rise to extraordinary luxuriance of growth. A stream runs along the bottom, and I expect all the low-lying land, where you see that belt of yellow African grass, is little better than a morass now."

Fremantle drew up as they gained the top of the slope. From there they could overlook the tangle of vegetation, dimmed by a rising mist, which surrounded and almost hid the roof of the Grey House.

"Yes," said Fremantle, in answer to an observation of Mr. Low, "Montesson's guardian, who lived here and looked after the property for him, turned the place into a subtropical garden. It used to be one of my chief pleasures to wander about here, but since my marriage my wife objects to my doing so, on account of the tales she has heard."

"What is the danger?"

"Death!" replied Fremantle shortly.

"What form of death? Malaria?"

"No disease at all, my dear fellow. The persons who die at the Grey House are hanged by the neck until they are dead!"

"Hanged?" repeated Flaxman Low in surprise.

"Yes, hanged. Not only strangled but suspended, as the marks on the necks show. If there were any hint of a ghost in it you might investigate—Montesson would be only too grateful if you could fathom the mystery."

"Tell me something more definite."

"I'll tell you what has happened in my own knowledge. Montesson's father died some fifteen years ago and left him to the guardianship of a cousin named Lampurt, who, as I told you, was a horticulturist, and planted the place with a wonderful variety of foreign shrubs and flowers. Lampurt had a bad name in the county, and his appearance was certainly against him—a squint-eyed, pig-faced fellow, who sidled along like a crab, and could not look you in the face. He died first."

"Was he hanged? Or did he hang himself?"

"Neither, in this case. He dropped in a kind of fit, right up in front of the house, while he was engaged in planting some new acquisition. Had it not been for the evidence of the persons who were present at the time, I should have said his death resulted from some tremendous mental shock. But the gardener and his relation, Mrs. Montesson, agreed in saying that he was not exerting himself unduly, and that he had had no disturbing news. He was a healthy man and I could see no sufficient reason for his death. He was simply gardening, and had apparently pricked himself with a nail for he had a spot of blood upon his forefinger.

"After that all went well for a couple of years, when, during the summer holidays, the trouble began. Montesson must have been about sixteen at the time, and had a tutor with him. His mother and sister—a pretty girl rather older than himself—were also here. One morning the girl was found lying on the gravel under her window, quite dead. I was sent for, and, upon examination, discovered the extraordinary fact that she had been hanged!"

"Murder?"

"Of course, though we could find no trace of the murderer. The girl had been taken from her bedroom and hanged. Then the rope was removed and she was thrown in a heap under her window. The crime caused a tremendous sensation in the neighbourhood, and the police were busy for a long time, but nothing came of their inquiries.

"About a fortnight later, Platt, the tutor, sat up smoking at the open study window. In the morning he was found lying out over the sill. There could be no mistake as to how he met his death, for in addition to the deep line round his throat, his neck was broken as neatly as they could have done it at Newgate! As in the other case, there was nothing to show how he came by his death, no rope, no trace of footsteps or any struggle to lead one to suspect the presence of another person or persons. Yet from the facts it could not have been suicide."

"I see you had some suspicion of your own," said Flaxman Low.

"Well, yes, I had. But time has passed, and I now think I must have been mistaken. I must explain that the branches of the cedar you saw jut to within a few feet of the windows of the rooms occupied by Miss Montesson and Platt respectively at the time of death. I told you there were no traces of anyone having approached the house. It therefore struck me that some active person might have leaped from the cedar into the open windows and escaped in the same way, for the windows open vertically, and when both leaves are thrown back, there is a large aperture. But the murders were so purposeless and disconnected that they suggested irresponsible agency. I recollected Poe's story of the Rue Morgue, where, you remember, the crimes were committed by an ourang-outang. It seemed to me possible that Lampurt, who was of a morose and strange temper, might, among other things, have secretly imported an ape and turned it loose in the woods. I had a thorough search made in the park and grounds, but we found nothing, and I have long ago abandoned the theory."

Low thought silently over the story for some time, then he asked for the dates of the three deaths. Fremantle answered categorically, and it appeared that all had taken place about the same season of the year—during summer, in fact. Upon this Mr. Low made an offer to investigate the affair on psychical lines, if Montesson made no objection. In answer to this message Montesson took the next train down to Devon, and begged to be allowed to accompany Mr. Low in his inquiries.

Flaxman Low quickly saw that Montesson might prove a very useful companion. He was a blond, heavily built man, and plainly possessed of a strong will and temper. Low put aside his books

and went off at once with Montesson to have a closer look at the
Grey House while the daylight lasted.

It is difficult to give any adequate impression of the teeming
exuberance of wild and tangled growth through which they had to
cut their way. Young, lush, sappy leafage overlay and half disguised
the dank rottenness of the older vegetation beneath. After wading
more than breast-high through the matted reeds, below which the
spreading stream was fast reducing the land to a swamp, they
emerged into a fairly open space that had once been the lawn round
the house.

Here brambles and lusty weeds now grew abundantly under
the untended trees. Curious shrubs and plants flourished here and
there. As they came up a stoat sneaked away by a narrow footpath,
nettle-grown and caked with damp, which led past blackened
bushes round the house. Otherwise the place was deserted, not a
leaf seemed to move in the windless heat of the afternoon. The
squat, grey face of the house was scarred across by a dark-leaved
creeper, hung with orchid-like blossoms, a little to the left of which
Low noticed the cedar mentioned by Dr. Fremantle.

Low drew up at the weed-twisted, sunken little gate that gave
upon the lawns and spoke for the first time.

"Tell me about it," and he nodded towards the house.

Montesson repeated the story already told, but added further
details. "From here," went on Montesson, "you can see the exact
spot where all these things took place. The upper of these two windows surrounded by the creeper and under the shadow of the cedar, belonged to my sister's room; the lower is that of the study
where Platt died. The gravel path below ran the whole length of
the house, but it is now over-grown— Has Fremantle told you of
Lawrence?"

Low shook his head.

"I hate the very sight of the place!" said Montesson hoarsely;
"the mystery and the horror of it all seem in my blood. I can't forget! My mother left on the day of Platt's death, and has never been
here since. But when I came of age I resolved to make another attempt to live here, meaning to sift the past if I got the chance of

doing so. I had the grounds cleared about the house, and after leaving Oxford, came down with a man of my own year, called Lawrence. We spent the Easter vacation here reading, and all went right enough. Meanwhile I had the house examined, thinking there might be a secret entrance or room, but nothing of the kind exists. This house is not haunted. Nothing has ever been seen or heard of a supernatural character—nothing but the same awful repetition of blind murder!"

After a few seconds he resumed.

"During the following summer Lawrence came down with me again. One hot evening we were smoking as we walked up and down the gravel under the windows. It was bright moonlight, and I remember the heavy scent of those red flowers—" Montesson glanced round him strangely.

"I went in to fetch a cigar. It took me some minutes to find the box I wanted, and to light the cigar. When I came out, Lawrence lay crumpled up as if he had fallen from a height, and he was dead. Round his neck was the same bluish line I had seen in the two other cases. You can understand what it was to leave the man not five minutes before, in health and strength, and to come back to find him dead—hanged—to judge from appearances! But as usual, no trace of rope or struggle or murderer!"

After some further talk, Mr. Low proposed to go into the house. It had evidently been deserted in haste. In the room once occupied by Miss Montesson, her girlish treasures still lay about, dusty, moth-eaten, and discoloured. Montesson paused on the threshold.

"Poor little Fan! It's just as she left it!" he said hurriedly.

The cedar outside threw a gloomy shade into the room, and the fantastic red blossoms drooped motionless in the stagnant air.

"Was the window open when your sister was found?" inquired Low after he had examined the room.

"Yes, it was hot weather—early in August. This room has not been occupied since. After Platt's affair, I have always avoided this side of the house, so that it was only by chance Lawrence and I came round to this part of the lawn to smoke."

"Then we may suppose that the danger, whatever it is, exists on this side of the house only?"

"So it seems," replied Montesson.

"Your sister was last seen alive in this room? Platt in the room directly below? and your friend—what of him?"

"Lawrence was lying on the gravel path just under the study window. All of them have died under the shadow of the cedar. Did Fremantle give you his idea? Poor Lawrence's death disposed of that theory. No big ape could live in England all those five years in the open, and in any case it must have been seen sometime in the interval."

"I think so," replied Low abstractedly. "Now as to what we must do to try and get at the meaning of all this. Do you feel equal, considering all you have gone through in this house, do you feel equal to remaining here with me for a night or two?"

Montesson again glanced over his shoulder nervously.

"Yes," he said. "I know my nerves are not as stiff and steady as they should be, but I'll stand by you—especially as you would not find another man about here willing to run the risk. You see it is not a ghost or any fanciful trouble, it means a real danger. Think over it, Mr. Low, before you undertake so hazardous an attempt."

Low looked into the blue eyes Montesson had fixed upon him. They were weary, anxious eyes, and, taken in combination with his compressed lips and square chin, told Low of the struggle this man constantly endured between his shaken nervous system and the strong will that mastered it.

"If you'll stand by me, I'll try to get to the bottom of it," said Low.

"I wonder if I should allow you to risk your life in this way?" returned Montesson, passing his hand over his prematurely lined forehead.

"Why not? Besides it is my own wish. As for risking our lives—it is for the good of mankind."

"I can't say I see it in that light," said Montesson in surprise.

"If we lose our lives it will be in the effort to make another spot of earth clean and wholesome and safe for men to live on. Our duty to the public requires us to run a murderer to earth. Here we have a murderous power of some subtle kind; is it not quite as much our duty to destroy it if we can, even at risk to ourselves?"

The result of this conversation was an arrangement to pass the night at the Grey House. About ten o'clock they set out, intending to follow the path they had more or less successfully cleared for themselves in the afternoon. By Flaxman Low's advice, Montesson carried a long knife. The night was unusually hot and still, and lit only by a thin moon as they made their way along, stumbling over matted weeds and roots and literally feeling for the path, until they came to the little gate by the lawn. There they stopped a moment to look at the house, standing out among its strange sea of overgrowth, the dim moon low on the horizon, glinting palely upon the windows and over the deserted countryside. As they waited a nightbird hooted and flapped its way across the open.

At any moment they might be at handgrips with the mysterious power of death which haunted the place. The warm lush-scented air and the sinister shadows seemed charged with some ominous influence. As they drew near the house Low perceived a sweet, heavy odour.

"What is it?" he asked.

"It comes from those scarlet flowers. It's unbearable! Lampurt imported the thing," replied Montesson irritably.

"Which room will you spend the night in?" asked Low as they gained the hall.

Montesson hesitated. "Have you ever heard the expression 'grey with fear'?" he said, laughing in the dark; "I'm that!"

Low did not like the laugh, it was only one remove, and that a very little one, from hysteria.

"We won't find out much unless we each remain alone, and with open windows as they did," said Low.

Montesson shook himself.

"No, I suppose not. *They* were each alone when—good night, I'll call if anything happens, and you must do the same for me. For Heaven's sake, don't go to sleep!"

"And remember," added Low, "with your knife to cut at anything that touches you." Then he stood at the study door and listened to Montesson's heavy steps as they passed up the stairs, for he had elected to pass the night in his sister's room. Low heard him walk across the floor above and throw wide the window.

When Mr. Low turned into the study and tried to open the window there, he found it impossible to do so: the creeper outside had fastened upon the woodwork, binding the sashes together. There was but one thing left for him to do, he must go outside and stand where Lawrence had stood on the fatal night. He let himself out softly and went round to the south side of the house.

There he paced up and down in the shadow for perhaps an hour.

In the deceptive, iridescent moonlight a pallid head seemed to wag at him from the gloom below the cedar, but, moving towards it, he grasped only the yellow bunched blossom of a giant ragwort. Then he stood still and looked up into the branches above; the gnarled black branches with their fringes of black sticky leaves. Fremantle's theory of the ape passing stealthily among them to spring upon his victims found a sudden horror of possibility in Low's mind. He imagined the girl awaking in the brute's cruel hands—

Out upon the quiet brooding of the night broke a scream—or rather a roar, a harsh, jagged, pulsating roar, that ceased as abruptly as it had begun.

Without a moment's consideration, Mr. Low seized the branch nearest to him and, swinging himself up into the tree, he climbed with a frantic effort towards the window of Montesson's room, from which he was almost sure the sound had come. Being an unusually active and athletic man he leaped from the branch towards the open window, and fell headlong in upon the floor. As he did so, something seemed to pass him, something swift and sinuous that might have been a snake, and disappear out of the window!

Remembering a candle on the toilet table, he lit it when he regained his feet and looked about him.

Montesson lay on the floor "crumpled up" as he had himself described Lawrence's position. Low recalled this with misgiving as he hurried to his side. A dark smear like blood was on Montesson's cheek, but though unconscious, he was still alive. Low lifted him on to the bed and did what he could to rouse him, but without success. He lay rigid, breathing the slow almost imperceptible respiration of deep stupor.

Low was about to go to the window, when the candle suddenly went out, and he was left in the increasing darkness, to all intents alone, to face an unknown though tangible assailant.

Silence had again fallen upon the house—that is, the silence of night, and woodlands, and many-folded leafage, and the things that go by night. He stood by the window and listened. His senses were acute and throbbing; he felt as if he could hear for miles. The scent of the scarlet blossoms rose like deadening fumes into his brain, and he drew away from the window, and, feeling strangely spent, threw himself upon a couch. Then he drew out the knife at his belt, and strung himself up to watchfulness with an effort.

He knew that the attack he had to expect would be likely to come from the direction of the window. He saw the faint, swimming moonlight that fell through the leaves and tendrils of the creeper fade slowly away. Probably clouds were coming up over the sky, for the steamy heat was even more oppressive.

The low window-sill was scarcely more than a foot above the floor, and presently he fancied something was moving along the carpet among the entangling shadows of the leaves, but the darkness was now intensified, and he could not be sure. Montesson's breathing had become quieter. It was the dead hour of the night; hardly a sound was to be heard.

Suddenly Low felt a soft touch upon his knee. His whole consciousness had been so absorbed in the act of listening that this unexpected appeal to another sense startled him. Here and there, rapid, soft, and light, the touches passed over his body. It might have been some animal nosing about him in the dark. Then a smooth, cold touch fell upon his cheek.

Low sprang up, and slashed about him in the darkness with his knife.

In that instant the thing closed with him—a flexuous, snaky thing that flung its coils about his limbs and body in one swift spring like a curling whiplash!

Flaxman Low was all but helpless in the winding grasp of what?—the tentacles of some strange creature? or was it some great snake, this sentient thing that was feeling for his throat? There was not an instant to lose. The knife was pressed against his body; with a violent effort he drew it sharply, edge outwards, against the tightening coils. A spurt of clammy fluid fell upon his hand, and the thing loosed and fell away from him into the stifling gloom.

IN THE MORNING Montesson came to himself in one of the lower rooms at the other side of the house. Fremantle was beside him.

"What's the matter?" he asked. "Ah, I remember now. There's Low. It has beaten us again, Fremantle! It is hopeless. I don't know what happened—I was not asleep, when I found myself seized, lifted up, drawn towards the window, and strangled by living ropes. Look at Low!" he went on harshly, raising himself. "Why, man, you're all over blood!"

Flaxman Low glanced down at his hands.

"Looks like it," he said.

"It has beaten even you, Low!" went on Montesson. "There is something much more terrible and tangible than a ghost in this cursed house! See here!"

He pulled down his collar. A faint bluish circle with suffused dots was drawn round his throat.

"It is some deadly species of snake," exclaimed Fremantle.

Low sat down astride a chair thoughtfully.

"I'm sorry to disagree with both of you. But I am inclined to think it is not a snake, and on the other hand I fancy it has a great deal to do with what we may roughly call a ghost. The whole evidence points in only one direction."

"You mustn't let your prejudice in favour of psychical problems run away with your reason," said Fremantle drily. "Has a ghost actual, palpable power?—to go further, has it blood?"

Montesson, who had been looking at his neck in the glass, turned quickly. "It's some horrible thing in nature! Something between a snake and an octopus! What do you say to it, Low?"

Low looked up gravely.

"In spite of Fremantle's objections the steps from beginning to end are very clear."

Fremantle and Montesson exchanged a glance of incredulity.

"My dear fellow, much learning has warped your mind," said Fremantle with an embarrassed laugh.

"First of all," continued Low, "we know where all the deaths have occurred."

"To speak precisely, they have all occurred in different places," interposed Fremantle.

"True; but within a strictly limited area. The slight differences have been of material help to me. In all cases they have occurred in the vicinity of one thing."

"The cedar!" cried Montesson, with some excitement.

"That was my first idea—now I refer to the wall. Will you tell me the probable weight of Lawrence and Platt at the date of death?"

"Platt was a small man—perhaps under nine stone. Lawrence, though much taller, was thin, and could not have weighed more than eleven. As for poor little Fan, she was only a slip of a girl."

"Three people have been killed—one has escaped. In what way do you differ from the others, Montesson?" asked Low.

"If you mean I'm heavier, I certainly am. I scale something like fifteen. But what has that to do with it?"

"Everything. The coils have evidently not sufficient compressive power to destroy life by strangulation simply—there must be suspension as well. You were simply too heavy for them to tackle."

"Coils of what?"

"Of this." Low held up a tapering, reddish-brown tendon or line, which had red curved triangular teeth set on it at intervals.

The two other men stared at this object, and then Montesson burst out: "The creeper on the wall!" he said, in a tone of disappointment. "It couldn't be! Besides, has a plant blood?"

"Let us go and look at it," said Low. "This creeper has never been cut because it withers away every winter to the ground and grows again in the spring. Look here!" He took out his knife and cut a leathery shoot. A crimson stain spurted out on his cuff. "The only person, as far as I can gather, who cut this plant was Mr. Lampurt in nailing it to the wall. He died of shock when he saw the red stain on his finger, as he knew something of its deadly properties. But though stupefying—as your condition last night proved, Montesson—they are not fatal. Even to stupefy they must get into the blood. Now the deaths have all occurred within reach of the tendrils of this plant. And all have happened at the same season of the year, that is to say, at the time when it attains its full annual strength and growth. Another point in favour of Montesson's escape was the dryness of the season. The growth is not quite so good as usual this summer, is it?"

"No, the tendrils are thinner—a good deal thinner and smaller."

"Just so. Therefore your weight saved you, though you were stupefied by the punctures of the thorns. I feared that, and warned you to use your knife."

"But the brain of the thing?" cried Fremantle. "Why, man, has a plant will and knowledge and malevolence?"

"Not of itself, as I believe," answered Low. "Perhaps you will prefer to attribute much to the long arm of coincidence, but the explanation I can offer is one that has long been held by occultists in other countries. Pythagoras and others have taught that the forms of incarnation change as the soul raises or debases itself during each spell of Life. Connect with this the belief of the Brahmins, and I may add of various African tribes, that an earth-bound spirit, at the moment of a premature or sudden death, may pass into plants or trees of certain species, by virtue of an inherent attraction possessed by these plants for such entities. To go further, it is said that these degraded souls have intervals during which they have power of voluntary action to do good or evil, and such action has influence on their future incarnations."

"What do you mean? What do you intend us to believe?" Montesson said, and stopped.

"It is hard to put it into words in these latter days of unbelief," said Low, "but the evidence goes to show that a man—presumably not a good man—dies a sudden death near this plant, even innoculated with its sap. Fremantle knows this plant to be a Malayan creeper, belonging to a family that possesses strange powers and properties. I may recall the old story of the upas tree, and more lately still the murder tree discovered near Kolwe, in East Africa, by Herr Boltze. There are also other instances."

"It is incredible!" said Fremantle almost angrily.

"I don't ask you to believe it," said Flaxman Low quietly, "I only tell you such beliefs exist. Montesson can do something towards proving my theory. Let him have the plant destroyed, and judge by results."

The tendril of the creeper severed by Mr. Low in his struggle was presented by him to the authorities at Kew.

Mr. Montesson has acted upon Mr. Flaxman Low's suggestions. The Grey House is now occupied and safe, and it is a strange fact that no plant, not even the hardy ivy, will live where the red-blossomed creeper once grew.

THE FLOWER OF DEATH

A. V. PANKEY

I LOVED ELIZABETH and she loved me until Morrison came. Henry Morrison (may his bones lie in an unhallowed burying place) was my nemesis; I knew it from the first. Young, laughing, handsome, his dashing manners would have carried him past the portals of any woman's heart. But Elizabeth! I had merely taught her love! Not love of me, but love, just love. So when Morrison came I was doomed. Oh, how plainly I see it all now! Too late, alas, forever too late!

I though she loved me. Fool that I was! I mistook passion for love—the senses for the soul. In time she might, but there was no time; no time at all when Henry Morrison was around.

Shall I tell you the story of our love, (for such I call it even now). I believe I shall; confession is good; it frees a man's soul from the thraldom of himself.

Elizabeth was a child when I first met her. It was I who watched over her as she entered woman's estate. My tongue it was that taught her passion, my caresses that brought her sensual nature into being.

Did I love her then? Yes, and no—I loved to play on her as a musician plays on his instrument. You see, I was older than she, and she trusted me. To her, for a time, I was a god. I told her great things about my life and my achievements—lies, all of them, lies of the basest sort. But she never suspected! I pleased myself by thinking all I did was for her good. I inculcated high ideals—in words. What my tongue professed my looks, and actions, nullified.

Thus we lived in a fool's paradise of falseness. Our life breathed sentiments which our bodies controverted. We knew the glory of the platonic kiss! and of the fraternal hug! and the brotherly-sisterly caress! Yes, we talked, and thought, and lived a lie.

Mind you, now, I am not saying that we violated the written code—Elizabeth remained a virgin—I a man of honor. Deep in my soul I still believe all would have come out right in the end. My protestations of undying love were not all false, affection was present, love might have appeared. We really liked one another. We were temperamentally suited, of that there can be no doubt.

When two people, a male and a female, see each other constantly day by day, evening by evening, for years; when all the changing fancies of young womanhood are cloaked under a genuine regard; love may some day come. Fool that I was, I began to dream of love.

Love, the holiest of all passions, acquires a certain sanctity all its own. Where love comes all sham goes out. The hollow mockery of pretense can never take the place of true love. When I began to really love Elizabeth my whole course of action towards her changed. I discouraged all intimacy as a thing tending to make love less than real. I wanted a genuine transition into a new estate. The love for which I was yearning was a vital thing, one far removed from the sensuousness of the past. And I had almost succeeded. Elizabeth and I were estranged; beings apart. New barriers had been erected, barriers essential to full enjoyment of the matrimonial alliance—when Morrison came!

He came like a thief in the night; like a thunderbolt from a clear sky. Just when I had Elizabeth in the condition I wanted her; just when she was dangling, a soulful peach on a ripened limb only awaiting the harvester to complete the gathering—Henry Morrison came and spoiled it all.

In his big automobile they skimmed like larks over roads that Elizabeth and I had trodden on foot. With his power launch they tossed hours behind them in pleasant circling over the secluded bosom of the lake. I had none of these, riches had never been mine, so I could only sit by and watch Morrison win away the girl I loved.

He won her! Fully prepared, as I had made her, she was a temptation both to herself and to him. On her part inhibition was gone; in its place was substituted aboveboard feminine charm. He fell, she fell.

Naturally I did not sit idly by. In every conceivable way I worked to break the spell I had consciously woven. In vain! I protested my love; she remembered my apparent neglect! I tried force, she carried the story to my new rival, Morrison. We fought, he and I. We fought long and hard. In the end he won. He was the better man. After that I hated—him?—Her?—No! I hated them both. But, hating as I did I left them alone.

They were married, as I knew they would be. She followed him and lived in his beautiful home. Just as she followed him so I followed them both. Disguised as a Malay servant, I, too, took up residence in that beautiful mansion.

Henry Morrison was a liberal provider. He was particular, but he was generous even beyond his means. The place resembled a palace, large building, enormous estate, green lawns for a solid emerald mile. My descriptive ability is insufficient when I try to picture the inside of Henry Morrison's palatial residence. There were private baths of heroic dimensions, a library stocked with rare and valuable books, and a conservatory unparalled in the whole world.

I am something of a scientist myself. I specialize on flowers. But in all my experience I have never seen flowers of so rare a sort as those Henry Morrison had. There were red, white, blue, yellow, green, purple and black flowers; large, small, long, short, light and heavy flowers. There were roses and plants and orchids and shrubs. Some of the flowers were beautiful, so beautiful as to lead the senses astray; while some were so ugly and so ill-smelling as to be positively nauseating.

Amid all this oriental splendor Elizabeth, my Elizabeth, wandered. She was happy. To all intents and purposes I might as well have been forever gone from the surface of the globe. Under cover of my disguise I moved at will over the house. Many and many a time I stood within arm's reach of her without giving a sign to signify who I was. Once! So it seemed to me, I was about to embrace her. But the death of the passion was as sudden as its birth. I wanted revenge, not satisfaction. I wanted Henry Morrison to feel the power of my hatred. Elizabeth I would spare, but for Morrison there could be no escape. Night after night I repeated my prayer,

"O, God, deliver mine enemy into mine hands."

The opportunity came in a way I had not anticipated. One evening a Malay, a genuine man from the East, came to the door. I met him. Certain signs learned while I was on my travels made us as brothers. I questioned him. He had a rare plant which he would sell to my master, Henry Morrison. At my request he showed me what the flower was like.

Can I describe it? The mind cannot comprehend all things. This was a most unusual flower. Encased in oil silk it seemed more an animal than a flower. It was potted in a magnificent pot of early Egyptian workmanship. The plant resembled a snake in that a long fine body was coiled about a central stem, upraised on which was the bulb or bud. This bud or bulb, or head was tinged with a living, vital red.

"Oh!" I said, mistaking it, "this is the flower of passion!"

"No, master," the man from the East made reply. "This is called the Flower of Death, the vampire plant."

"And why so?" I asked, interested at once.

"Because, master, it lives by sucking human blood."

I begged to see. In a flash it came over me that here was just the thing I had been looking for. I drew Brahma Mahomet after me into my little office and there we talked of many things.

The next day, as if it had come from a great distance, I presented my master with the Flower of Death. I told him it was a good luck plant. I explained the oiled silk as being necessary to protect the bloom. Henry Morrison was pleased. He needed a new toy to entertain Elizabeth. He commanded me to present it to her forthwith. This I did.

It was growing dark in Elizabeth's chamber when I entered. The last light from the fading sun shone only feebly through the gorgeously colored glass in her windows. She was asleep. Worn out with the petty activities of the day, her head had fallen forward on her arms as she sat composing a letter by the marble table, and she slept. Did I awaken her? Not I! Instead, I tore away the silken cover from the vampire plant. Waiting only long enough to see the slender hose-like tentacle uncoil, reach out, and gently touch the sleeping woman's neck, I retreated to my room and thought—

Hours later a great confusion broke out. Servants ran hither and yon. Bustle temporarily took the place of effective service. Calm in the midst of it all, I entered the room of my mistress—Elizabeth.

Here, more than anywhere else, was disorder rampant. Servants were doing ten thousand useless things. What good, I ask, is any service rendered the dead? Elizabeth was lying as I had left her, snow white—dead. Ivory itself was not as alabaster as her complexion as she lay there half sprawled out over the table. Henry, for once confronted by a situation where his money was valueless, swayed helplessly in the center of the room. It was my hour.

"Master," I said, tapping his arm, "This plant, see? The vase in which it rests is foul."

I led him over to the great Egyptian vase in which was the Vampire Plant. Its bloom glowed and sparkled in the light of the many tapers like a woman's unspotted soul.

"How beautiful the flower is!" he, Henry, my master, exclaimed.

"Yes," I said, "but see! This stuff in the vase here—'tis red! What can it be?"

He got a whiff of it and his face paled. Tentatively he dipped in his finger. Obeying some inner impulse I grabbed his arm and shoved it to the elbow in the warm red fluid.

"My God!" he cried, "It's blood!"

"Yes, yes, yes!" I shrieked, "It's blood, blood, blood! It's Elizabeth's blood, and it's on your hands. Man, can't you see? I'm revenged on you for stealing the woman I loved!"

THE LURE OF THE LAVENDER TREES
MARYLAND ALLEN

"Go on," said the bartender.

The man leaned farther across the polished surface of the bar. "It's true. Let me tell you—"

"Go on," said the bartender with the same weary contempt.

"It's true," cried the man again.

"What's true?" broke in Abbott. It was night in San Francisco, and we were looking for the Great Adventure.

"What's true?"

"Oh, he was mate of the *Idalee*," said the barkeeper, jerking his thumb and speaking as if the stranger was dead or deaf. "She was wrecked somewhere, and he gets picked up and comes back here with his hair white and a screw loose and wants to tell me some rip-snortin' lie or other. But no, he don't, and so I tell him. He don't work off his nightmares on me for free drinks."

The man turned his back on the bar. It was plain that he followed the sea, and that he was educated. He took off his soft hat and ran his thin, brown fingers through hair that was thick and white as cloth.

"Chaps," he said appealing—he kept his face curiously averted as he spoke, but his black eyes looked up at us dilated and a little wild— "Chaps, if you would have a drink with me and let me tell you—"

The barkeeper helped us carry our drinks to the table farthest across the room. "He's nutty, I tell you," he growled, and put down the handful of cigars that Abbott had ordered. "You don't even remember where the blamed old ship went down, Jim Moylhan."

He glared the stranger accusingly in the face.

"It was south of the line," burst out the man with a kind of dreadful eagerness as if he must be telling, and yet was afraid. "It was south of the line, I can tell you that much. And we saw them a long distance away. They were streaming purple against the sky like a banner from the sea; bending and beckoning even at that distance. They were lavender in the lingering, gorgeous hues of sunset and lavender in the quick flash of day. A strange sight for shipwrecked men, chaps, but it seemed a welcome one to the bride. She saw them first.

"'Oh,' she cried, and pointed. 'Oh, God be praised!'

"We rested on our oars, the captain, her man, and I. We looked, and I think we did praise God. And that shows, chaps, what poor, dense, helpless creatures human beings are.

"'Land!' said the captain, and he looked grave. 'Land there!'

"The bride's man laughed. 'You're all turned around without your compass, cap'n,' he says, 'and your broken-backed Findlay's at the bottom of the sea. Sure enough it's land. Let's go.'

"But the captain looked dubious. 'I've sailed these seas for thirty years,' says he, 'and I've never missed so much as a pipeful of land, chart or no chart. It don't seem familiar to me.'

"Then the bride laughed." His somber, brown face lightened. "Well, chaps, that closed the argument.

"All day we pulled toward that swinging purple signal in the sky. Then the trades died; the sun set and we moved over a sea of molten gold. The white clouds burned crimson, the soft blue of the sky seemed to reflect the glow, and against the red furnace of the western horizon the lavender banner hung motionless.

"Very slowly the glory faded and the moon rose. It seemed to swing far out of the sky and dimmed the brightness of the stars. The water moved in gentle swells and peaceful, shining ripples. The whole great silence of the sea was filled with restful calm. And we, struggling with the oars, tortured by hunger and thirst, still shaking with the horror of a great ship's death—we seemed intruding out of place, and chaps, somehow I felt ashamed. The purple banner moved very gently then. It beckoned slowly all through that night, and the captain said something about the land breeze.

"The bride slept close against the shoulder of her man, and the rest of us were intended to sleep. But I know we did, and I now the boat still moved forward. Maybe it was the current—I don't know. South of the line, chaps, currents are not only things that are queer. I do know that when the day came in that single lightning stroke the bride set us all leaping with a cry.

"'They're trees,' she screamed; 'they're trees!'

"The tide was out. As far as we could see on either hand the top of the reef hunched up, deep yellow and sea-stained. Directly opposite us gaped the opening like a missing front tooth. The water in the lagoon was bright green; the beach shone dazzling white. Beyond that came a wide strip of soft, velvety turf, a shade darker green that the lagoon. Then, like a solid wall, from where the beach curved to where the beach ended, arose the lavender trees.

"They stood up tall and straight, and yet seemed to droop. Chaps, even the stems were lavender. It was very still and blazing hot, and they stood so motionless you could hardly tell the leaves from the branches. They were strangely beautiful with the blue sky behind them and the dark green turf, the white beach, and the pale green lagoon in front. But they were terrible. You could not see through nor beneath them. There was not a crack nor a cranny for the eye to pierce. They seemed placed together with a devilish contrivance of color to protect or to conceal, and there were no other trees in sight.

"We sat in that boat, chaps, like foolish, gasping images, and stared. Then the bride began to whimper and crouched beside her man.

"'Let's go away,' she whined. 'I am afraid. Let's go away.'

"Her man pulled back, too, and the flesh of his face seemed to fall away and leave his eyes sticking out. But the captain picked up his oar and put it over the side of the moving boat.

"'There's a hell of a current here,' said he; 'steady aft, there, Moylhan.'

"So we two worked our oars in the water, and the boat flew through the opening, skimmed the lagoon, and darted half-way up the beach. I ask you to remember, chaps, that we were weak and exhausted and the tide was running out.

"Where the boat grounded in the sand a bright, clear stream of water ran out of the trees. It made a crystal streak across the soft grass and down the white beach to the lagoon. The captain was in the bow, and he fell down before it first. He did not seem at all surprised to find a running stream on an atoll. He had been rather startled at the mere thought of land in those seas, but he fell on his hands and knees beside that water, and drank like a pig, grunted and sucking it into his throat. As for me, honestly, chaps, I didn't think. A mate's not paid to kick. If the captain's suited, that settles the business. I did feel a little surprised, but I was mostly angry because he didn't wait for the bride. And then the water sickened me.

"It was sweet and fresh enough, all right, and, God knows, I had dreamed of nothing else since that night the ship went down. But I couldn't drink to amount to anything; I couldn't—there was something wrong. It ran down my naked throat, cool and wet, and stopped there. Somehow my mind wouldn't let it go any farther, and I ejected it upon the sand. Then the bride jerked upright and began the same thing. But her man and the captain kept on drinking. Only the bride's man did not drink so much.

"I felt so weak that I sat right down where I was, and then I saw that the lavender-trees were watching. I saw something come out of them, chaps. It was something that I could only sense with my nerves, but it felt and felt about, up and down, and came closer with every breath I drew.

"The captain was still drinking, and the bride's man knelt as if dazed with his hand up to his head. The bride came and sat down beside her man. Out of the blue sky the sun poured down. The sea drummed against the reef and washed its yellow back with foam. The beach glared white, the strip of turf shone like a dark emerald, the bright water flowed through it without a murmur and made a little ripple against the life-boat's gray side, and, reaching out from that misty, mysterious wall of lavender foliage and wood, the something that I could only sense swayed this way and that, feeling, feeling, feeling.

"The same thing that spoke in my mind about the water told me to take hold of the boat, and when I did so the thing drew back into the trees. Perhaps I looked white; I know I felt like death. The bride stared up at me from where she knelt beside her man, and I saw that she knew.

"Then the captain got to his feet with a satisfied grunt. 'We'll have to forage for some food,' says he, 'but we'll sleep first. When the trades begin to blow I'll put up a signal.'

"He looked aloft and seemed to notice the trees for the first time. 'Are they purple?' says he. 'Are they purple?'

"But the bride's man was already asleep. I hung onto the boat and looked at the bride, and neither of us answered. We thought, and each knew the other was thinking—fear. I felt hysterical, all wild and confused. But I could see her growing calmer, calling on her courage and getting a prompt reply. Somehow the captain did not seem to expect an answer. He slumped down where he stood and I watched him begin to snore. I wanted to tell the bride that she was brave, but my tongue was stuck behind my teeth, my eyes closed, and I slept in the shadow of the boat.

"It was the bride's scream awoke me. 'Drop him!' she screeched."

The stranger paused and looked from Abbott to me with those wild, terror-dilated eyes. The sweat burst out across his lined, sunburnt forehead.

"Gods, chaps," he whispered, "I never heard a woman cry like that before—I couldn't—I couldn't stand it again."

A tense silence fell about the table. Abbott and I exchanged glances. He looked horrified at the sequel to his friendly offer, but very eager.

As for me, I longed to cry fake, if only to show that I still retained my sanity, but the words would not come. I looked across at the burly barkeeper serving out drinks so stolidly, and I wanted to hear him say again that the stranger was "nutty."

I was wild to speak to the man, too, and get him started again, but I did not dare. At last:

"'Drop him, drop him!' She said it over four times. 'Drop him, drop him!'

"I dragged myself up beside the boat, chaps, while the bride clung to her man and he fought her with his hands, and there lay the captain upon the soft turf half-way to the lavender-trees. The bride looked at me.

"'Go and get him,' she croaked.

"I tried to walk and my bare feet felt like they were suckered to the sand. I got the captain about his middle and he bellowed like a bull. The trades had come up while we slept. The purple branches swept and swayed and the leaves stood up in the wind without a sound. As I lifted the captain a drooling lavender branch streamed across the green turf and swept about my waist. Oh, God! chaps, I—I—but the bride screamed again, the branch blew away, and I dragged the captain to the beach.

"The captain lay where I threw him and soon he slept and breathed hard. About his neck there was a thin, purple mark like a string tied close. I saw the bride look at it and catch her breath. Then she glanced at me. But she did not speak and we both turned away. Chaps, we saw the fear in each other's eyes.

"The bride's man still sat with his knees hugged in his arms and his black eyes moved swiftly here and there, up and down. Sometimes he shivered and the sweat dripped from him like water and his legs jerked convulsively.

"Then with a deep sigh the stiffness would go out of him and his chin flop limply on his knees. I knew he felt the thing—the thing that moved in and out between those purple tree stems seeking, seeking, seeking, like fingers among sand.

"When the sun went over behind the grove the captain groaned and sat up. No light came through the lovely cloud of silent moving leaves, and there were no shadows on the green turf.

"The captain stared at the reef, the peaceful evening sky, and then at the lavender trees. He looked awfully worried.

"'This ain't the place for an island,' he muttered. He said it over again. 'This ain't the place for an island.' Then he said very loud, 'The hell I'm thirsty!'

"He tried to drag himself to his feet, but he couldn't; so he went for the water on his hands and knees. The bride looked at me and ran her dry tongue along her black lips.

"'Stop him!' she croaked like a frog in the marsh. 'Stop him!'

"But the captain made it before I did, and glued his mouth to the water that had no more business to be there than the land. I couldn't pull him away. I did get my arms about him, but he would not budge an inch. So I started to creep for the boat. But the bride looked at me, and I turned back. Chaps, I felt ashamed.

"Somehow the captain got to his feet. He turned and stared us over very slowly. He looked at me creeping toward him on my hands and knees, at the bride squatting in the shadow of the boat, holding tightly to her man's arm, and the bride's man shivering and sweating, watching that thing which was feeling closer and closer and closer.

"'I'm goin' to find us something to eat,' says the captain. His voice sounded thick and guttural, and the thin, purple mark about his neck seemed to tighten like a pulled string. He went up the beach to the green sod.

"The bride looked at me again. 'Stop him,' she rasped. But I, chaps, what could I do?

"The purple branches tossed high toward the blue sky, swept out across the soft turf, and all without a sound. The captain grasped the air close in front of his neck as if the string pulled too hard.

"Then he began to run in queer, skipping strides, and all the while his hands fought to loosen up that choking grip. The bride's man scuffled and kicked up the sand trying to follow, and the bride struggled to hold him down.

"But I crouched beside the water and watched the captain run under the purple trees. The color closed about him like a quick-shut door. The branches dipped and beckoned as before and the leaves stood out straight without a whisper. Then he began to scream and the bride's man answered."

Again there was a tense, strained silence. My cigar was out. I looked from Abbott to the stranger and back to Abbott again. I saw they both were panting.

"The bride looked at me," said the stranger, "and I crawled back to help. She was fighting like a cat to keep him down beside the boat. My God, chaps, I didn't know any man, even a half dead one would treat a woman the way he did. I bumped his head against an oarlock and that didn't help. He was weak, but not so weak as we two, and he scrambled to his feet at last. Then the bride caught him about the knees, his head cracked against the boat and he lay between us. And all the while, behind those silent purple branches, the captain screamed and screamed.

"I started to go after him, chaps, but the bride caught me back. She took her man by the feet and made me lift his shoulders. We pulled and twisted and got him into the boat. Then I started again, but she took my head between her hands and turned it so that I looked out to sea.

"'Don't turn back,' she whispered.

"'Moylhan, Moylhan!' the captain shrieked. 'Jim, oh, Jim!'

"'Our Father,' says the bride—and she begins to push the boat—'who art in heaven, hallowed be Thy name—'

"She pressed her tender bosom against the bow. Chaps, I helped. But it seemed to me that the boat had grown there to that white beach and the captain's screams rose higher. They went through my head like white-hot knives.

"'Jim, Jim! Help me, oh Jim!'

"I stopped pushing on the boat and started to turn around—'Thy kingdom come, Thy will be done,' croaked the bride.

"Chaps, we got that boat into the lagoon. The water was waist deep in a second. I heard the captain still screaming, but the bride was close beside me.

"'—on earth as it is in heaven. Give us this day our daily bread—'

"Perhaps it was her praying that made me push harder. It was that or her eyes. The next I remember she was in the boat and I felt her fingers pulling at mine.

"I scrambled, she pulled. Then I fell flat in the bottom beside the bride's man and we passed through the opening and out to sea. The bride took an oar. I did the same, and we worked with the bride's man in the bilge water at our feet.

"It was the *Tropic Queen* picked us up. We were not rowing then. Three days after I asked if the bride was living and the bride's man. The doctor told me that they were and likely to live a long time.

"In another week I heard the passengers running up and down the deck; I heard a tug whistle and smelled the green freshness of the land. The doctor slapped me on the back.

"'Look up,' he said. 'Look up, man. This is God's country and San Francisco.'

"Then, chaps, I raised my eyes for the first time since the bride turned them from the lavender trees."

In the tense silence which followed Abbott drew a deep breath.

"Well?" he demanded.

The stranger started and passed his hand through his damp, white hair.

"Well!" he repeated blankly.

"Yes, well?" burst out Abbott. "What's the answer, what's it all about, what's the explanation?"

"Answer, explanation?" groped the stranger. "I—I don't understand," he finished slowly.

Then a deep red burned in Abbott's smooth cheek, and he pushed back his chair quickly.

"And I have wasted my time and money on a mystery without an explanation!" he cried angrily. "An hour spent on stuff that is absolutely worthless. No magazine will buy a mystery story that is not explained in detail."

"Explained in detail," repeated the stranger dazedly. "It's true, I tell you."

But Abbott was on his way across the room, muttering disgustedly.

"Abbott!" I cried. I caught him as he stepped into the street. "May I try it?" I asked.

"Yes, you can try it," he snorted contemptuously, "but it won't go. I tell you no editor will take a mystery story that is not fully explained. You can try it."

Well—I have.

THE WARLOCK OF GLORORUM
HOWARD PEASE

"BUT ARE YOU SURE your father wouldn't object?" I asked of my companion—a most bright and amusing Eton boy—to whom I was playing bear leader. "Not a bit," replied he; "my father is a naturalist and Darwinian; not a sceptic, but *Agnosticus suavis* or *Verecundus, ordo compositae*, you know. 'Hunt the ghost by all means,' said he, when I suggested a ghost 'worry,' and then as he does sometimes over coffee and a cigarette after dinner he talked with a real keen interest on the whole subject. He talked so long that old Mac (the butler) got quite shirty, and finally—after putting his head round the door two or three times—came in like the Lord Mayor and bore off the whisky decanter to the smoking-room. Now, the pater said that the love of the marvellous was native to mankind, and Tertullian had acquired a false credit for his motto, *Credo quia impossible*, since that was the natural failing of the untrained intellect, and, scientifically speaking, he ought to have been shot sitting.

"Then he went on to tell a jolly story which some great educationalist had told him of the little girl playing in the garden, who saw Fifine, the poodle, unexpectedly appear, and at once rushed in crying to her mother, 'Mummy, mummy, there's a bear in the garden!' Her mother, being a wholly unimaginative creature, promptly put Maggie into the corner, and told her to beg God's pardon for having told a lie. Presently Maggie comes out of her corner radiant, 'It's all right, mummy,' she cried, 'God tells me He has often mistaken Fifine for a bear Himself.' No doubt, as he said,

Maggie had had a momentary fright, and for half a second had thought of a bear, but she knew, too, that if she stayed to investigate she would find out it was Fifine, so preferring the luxury of the marvellous, she fled crying in to her mother. Sometimes, of course, he added, the ghost is the resultant of some horrible cruelty or murder, mankind, from various motives, refusing to let the memory of the crime die out, but more usually the ghost is born of the early mythopoeic imagination of man that cherishes the marvellous. One never hears of a new ghost nowadays. Science, no doubt, is an iconoclast in the matter."

"Well," said I, "how do you propose to proceed? I have gathered that there was once a warlock or wizard here in the sixteenth century—one of your forebears—who bore a most unhallowed reputation. Is he your ghost, or is the ghost the result of his 'goings on'?"

"Both," replied Dick, smiling. "At least there are a number of tales about him and his misdeeds; one version has it that he built himself a secret chamber wherein he conferred with the 'Auld Enemy' in person, and no one has yet discovered his 'dug-out.' Here's a quaint woodcut of the old warlock," he continued, taking down as he spoke a foxed print from the wall and holding it out for my inspection.

"Ain't he a fearsome figure? Looks as if his liver were cayenne pepper. Astrologer, botanist, poisoner, he is said to have been, and I don't wonder."

The ancient warlock possessed indeed a most mischancy visage: hard, curious, inhuman eyes he had, thin, sunken cheeks, and a black straggling moustache, the whole surmounted by a great bald dome of brow. "By Alchemist out of Misanthropos," I suggested, after a lengthy scrutiny, "and perhaps Misogynist as well." My companion laughed appreciatively. "That's about it," he said; "yet there is a tale of a fisherman's daughter, the belle of the village below.

"Well," he continued with animation, "our job is now to discover his secret chamber. 'Tis as good as a treasure hunt with the supernatural thrown in. By the way," he went on, "it's the first time I've ever been in Glororum Castle, as it is called, for the old place has only just come back to us, that is, to my father as representative of the senior branch of the Macellars, by the death of a cousin who died S.P. What nerves they had, these old chieftains! Fancy, like the Maclean, setting out your wife—even if a trifle *passée*—on the Skerry to drown before your dining-room window, or, like the Macleod, lowering her into the dungeon beneath the drawing-room that you might the better enjoy the charms of Amaryllis—your gardener's daughter—above. Well, it's too late this afternoon to begin our 'worry,' but to-morrow morning we must start by flagging all the windows with towels, as the inquisitive lady is said to have done at Glamis Castle."

I willingly agreed to his proposal, which jumped well enough with my own humour, and then as Dick went off to unpack I determined to go without and view the castle from every side.

Dusk was now closing in on the dark and frowning tower that was perched like an osprey upon the basalt cliffs that overlooked the sea. The building was really rather a peel tower than a castle, for it was of no great extent, consisting merely of the tall, gaunt tower with a wing added on to its western side. Situated on the edge of the bare sea, like a lighthouse abandoned, scarred by the fierce nor'-easters, with the mutter of the waves about it below and the scream of sea-fowl above, one could scarce imagine a more desolate or forbidding human abode than fitly-named "Glower-o'er-'em" Tower.

The neck of land by which it was approached from the west had been protected by a wall, within which a garden had sheltered, wherein the warlock had grown his herbs and poisons, but all was now ruinous and weed-grown, and gave only an added touch to the general forlornness. The place had been let as a shooting-box in recent years, but neither landlord nor tenant had thought it worth while to spend any money on reparation or embellishment. 'Twas indeed a fitting retreat for a warlock or wizard, I thought, as with a final regard I turned to go within doors.

Just at that moment I caught a glimpse of a fisher lass with a pannier rounding the corner. She looked back, and I saw a roguish Romney eye lighting a charming profile. "Too pretty," I thought, remembering Dick, as she tripped onward into the shadow of the Tower.

The sea was moaning under a heavy cloud-wrack; away to the west above the Lammermoors the sunset flared like a bale-fire, scattering sparks on the windows of the Tower. 'Twas cheerier within than without, for the walls were thick and kept the wind at bay, the wood fires were lively with hissing logs, and scarce heeded a chance buffet from the down draught lying in ambush within the open chimney-stack. We slept in the wing without any dread of the warlock, for it had been added on to the tower long after his time, and save for the sound of the sea far below, resembling the dim "mutter of the Mass," or the spell of a necromancer, I heard nothing throughout the night.

Next morning after breakfast was over Dick produced a pile of towels, which we divided up between us for our voyage of discovery. "After all," I said, "we shan't want many, for bows and arrows in the far past, and later, the window tax, kept the number of openings down."

We ascended by the ancient stone newel stair that circled up from the old iron "yett" of the entry to the battlements above, and laid a towel below the sash of every window. In the topmost storey in some servants' rooms that had been long disused we discovered certain windows with broken cords that entirely refused to open.

Dick's way here was of the "Jethart" kind. He simply knocked a pane out with the poker, and thrust the towel through.

When we had finished we descended in haste and perambulated the tower without, counting up our tale of towels in some excitement.

"As many windows, so many towels," I said with disappointment, as I checked them off carefully.

"Damn!" said Dick meditatively. Then after a moment or two's thought, "The old boy's cell must have been on the roof; he was sure to have been an astrologer. Let's go up again and start afresh." So saying he led the way up to the parapet of the battlements, and there we surveyed the roof. The main part of the roof consisted of a gable covered with heavy stone tiles, but the further part that lay between the north-east and north-west bartizans was flat and covered with lead, and at the verge of this were iron steps that led down to the roof of the new wing below. This latter we did not concern ourselves with, as we knew it dated since the wizard's day, but carefully examined the stone tiles and the further leads without, however, any discovery resulting.

We were just about to give up our quest when Dick's quick eyes noticed a chink in the lead that formed the channel or gutter for the rain water leading either way to the gargoyles beneath the bartizans outside.

"Look here!" he cried. "See the dim light showing! I swear it's a glimmer of glass. Evidently this particular lead was meant to be drawn aside and admit the light." I hastened to the side and peered with him into the dirt-laden crack.

Opening my pen-knife I scraped away the dirt and soon verified his conjecture that there was glass below. "You're right!" I cried in my excitement. "It is glass. Now let's search and see if we can find anything like a hinge, or at least some indication that the lead could be withdrawn at will." We sought all along by the containing wall and found that the lead did not end in a flat sheet, as is usual, against the wall, but was turned over, and evidently continued below.

"It looks very much as if it was meant to roll up and be turned over like a blind on a roller below," I said to my companion.

"I'm sure of it," Dick replied with conviction. "I'll tell you what we must do. We'll pull up the lead, make sure of the extent of the glass, then go below and search for the wizard's cell from the exact indication we shall then have of its whereabouts."

"Right!" said I, "that's the method."

We set to work, and soon had doubled back a strip of lead a foot broad from the centre till the glass ended by the bartizan on either side. We could not pull the lead right back because of the iron steps, which had evidently been inserted when the new wing was built, and now interfered with our further action.

The glass was set in heavy leaded panes, which were so engrained with the grime of centuries that we could discern nothing through them.

"We must search for the wizard's cell from below," I said. "If we cannot discover it there we must return and break in from above."

"Yes," agreed Dick, "it would be a pity to smash the roof in if we can find an entry below without causing damage."

The orientation was now easy, and as we studied the position from the parapet we could select the towelled window below which fitted best with the position of the glass roof.

The curious thing was that the window was not situated in the centre, but at the side of the torn up lead.

"We'll find out the reason below," I said, as we descended in great excitement, hastening on our quest.

The room we made for was one of the disused chambers on the top storey, which we had remarked for its narrowness when we broke the window and thrust a towel through.

"There must be a secret passage," cried Dick, as he flashed his torch upon the walls; "we're not below the glass; we're to the right hand of it. Wherefore search the left wall."

Dick's inference seemed excellent, and full of eagerness I tapped with my knife, he with his poker, all along the western wall.

"There's a hollow here," cried Dick, overjoyed, as his poker rang with a strange lightness. "Let's hunt for an opening or crack, or some betraying sign."

"Here! Look here!" he shouted. "I believe this stone pulls out."

Hastening to his side and applying my knife to the thin ragged crevice he had discovered, I found the stone was loose. I worked feverishly while Dick held the torch. "Now it's coming!" I cried, and even as I spoke it fell forward and crashed on to the floor. To us scrutinising the aperture, there seemed evidently a spring or catch concealed behind it.

Thrusting in my arm I pressed it home. A creak sounded; there was a rusty wheeze, and a portion of the wall seemed to shake and move slowly inwards.

"We've got it!" yelled Dick, as he pressed his shoulder against the receding portion, "it's a wooden door covered over with thin slabs of stone."

"Forrard!" cried Dick. "Forrard on!" and as he shouted he pressed forward down a narrow, dusty aperture towards a chamber beyond where a dim light showed through the begrimed roof above.

I pressed on hotly at his heels through the six feet of passage. We were now within the threshold of the secret cell. But what was that horrible thing beneath the dim sky-light? Dick's electric torch was failing, and we could not see distinctly, and a very oppression of fear seized upon us both. What was the gruesome object in front that resembled a dead octopus with decayed black arms?

There was a sickly taint in the air, and as I stood there fascinated by fear Dick took a step forward and threw the faint light of his torch upon the atrocious figure.

Surely it was a gorilla grasping its victim, and bending it in to itself as in some horrid act of rape!

Dick advanced yet another foot. Then I perceived that it was worse even than I suspected, for I now distinguished a giant species of *Nepenthes* (*Nepenthes Ferocissimus*) most monstrously developed, clutching in its long arms and horrid ascidiums the remains of a human victim—apparently a woman—for a gleam of yellow satin showed beneath the black embrace. Good God! I thought of the "fisherman's daughter" with a shudder.

I heard the torch drop. Then came a rustling shiver. The monstrous growth had sunk to the floor under pressure of the fresh air!

I thought I had fainted, but the next moment I felt Dick's hand shaking upon my sleeve, and heard a voice quaver in my ear:

"Let's get out of this! It's altogether too damned beastly."

AN ORCHID OF ASIA: A TALE OF THE SOUTH SEAS
EDNA WORTHLEY UNDERWOOD

JACQUES D'ENTRECOLLES and Dr. Ribot were riding together where the sand-wastes sweep back from Calais and begin to flatten out into level land. It was November, and the first dim edge of evening. The road stretched ahead, a coffee-colored, twisting thread, toward the farmhouse of d'Entrecolles, which they could see, and which was the color of the road. About it stood pale green poplars, which the wind was whipping wildly. The world was coffee-color and pale green. Over beyond the sand ripples, in a distance they could not see, a cold ocean, the color of the bending poplars, was beating against cliffs of yellow earth.

"It's no use, d'Entrecolles!" said the gray-haired doctor. "No use at all!" turning toward him a kindly, red, weather-beaten face. "My coming over to see you, and giving you first one medicine and then another is foolishness. You've got to get out of the country! You must breathe richer air than this. For three generations your ancestors have lived in the tropics. The thing for you to do is to go back there. There's something in the surroundings there that you need to keep life in you."

His companion turned upon him a face that was startling in its emaciation and began to cough as he spoke.

"Don't try to talk out here, Jacques! I should think you'd know better! Wait until we get to the house."

Later in the evening, when they were sitting in chairs drawn up in front of the fire, to which from time to time Jacques d'Entrecolles stretched out his thin hands eagerly, the old doctor took up the subject.

"You've got to go away! Your brother can take care of the estate—well enough, *now*—"

"But—where shall I go? And when I get there what shall I do? Must I be an exile?"

"Yes—very likely," answered the doctor, replying to the last question first. "Do? What shall you do? That's easy enough when money-making is not a necessity. You are interested in lots of things. Indulge some of your hobbies, preferably one that will keep you out of doors, in a country where the sun is hot."

Jacques d'Entrecolles's bright, dark eyes looked meditatively into the fire.

"I believe you are right. It is heat I need. This climate takes the vitality out of me."

The two men sat without speaking for a time, while d'Entrecolles turned over in his mind and then rejected vague plans for the new life that he was forced to begin.

The doctor was the first to break the silence. "I'll tell you what to do! It will combine business, health and pleasure. You are crazy over orchids. Be an orchidologist! Start an orchid farm."

"Yes, I'd like that—perhaps—"

"Now, I have the idea exactly," interrupted the other. "An old acquaintance of mine—Jean Labat—is here in Calais for a visit. He has been to Paris to put his ten-year-old daughter, Clarice, and his eight-year-old daughter, Marie, into a convent school. He was in government employ for a number of years in South America. He got into some kind of trouble there. Nothing disgraceful at all! Some political mix-up in which he got the worst of it—which is probably to his credit. He's an orchid fancier, too! He is living now—a sort of voluntary exile because he likes the tropics—on one of the Powell Islands, southwest of India, not far from the equator, either just above or just below it. He's the only white man on the island. Now, that's the place for you to go and establish an orchid farm. I'll run across him in a day or two in Calais, and have him come over."

"That's not bad. There is nothing in the world that has fascinated me so peculiarly as orchids."

A week later, Labat drove over from Calais and, at d'Entrecolles's invitation, stayed a few days at the farm.

"The island where I am," he replied in answer to one of
d'Entrecolles's requests for information, "is the most southerly and
least known of the Powell groups. I do not think it is found on small
maps. It is not very long and a few miles wide. In the Indian tongue it
is called Vpra-na, which means 'the land where the dead come back.'"

"That must be just the place I need," said d'Entrecolles, smiling. "They say I look more like a dead man than a live one."

Jean thought so, too, but he did not say it. Had it not been for
Dr. Ribot's assurance that all the man needed was change of air,
he would have considered it folly for a man who looked like this to
plan upon going anywhere.

At the end of the visit the arrangements were made and the
plans for the new home drawn. Jean Labat and his wife, who came,
on one side, of a South American Indian race, were to start for the
island at once. Near the opposite end from which they lived—at a
comfortable walking distance—Labat was to build a bungalow and
furnish it. D'Entrecolles selected gardeners from his French farm
to accompany him. He stipulated, in drawing plans for the grounds,
that the front of the bungalow should form a half circle, and that
the house to be set there should be bordered by a wide veranda.
From this veranda he wished to look down avenues of trees that
started from the building as a center and radiated like the spokes
of a wheel. The other half of this circling veranda was to face the
sea. The trees, which should be selected for height and size, must
be cleared of vines and trimmed high to give space and air, and
orchids set growing upon them. Some groups of trees—forming
a square—he wished cut level on top and orchids placed here, in
order to form, at some future time, an even, outspread flower-car-
pet. No other flower should be permitted to grow in this garden.

"This is my plan, Labat: to send plant-hunters to the cold countries, where it is inexpedient for me to go, and have them send on
to you the result of their work. Now in Siberia there is a variety

colored like smoked crystal. It is small and not fragrant, and looks more like a night-moth than anything else. It thrives on the cold steppe where dry winds blow. In the bogs of New England there are delicately tinted 'maiden tresses.'

"Have you been planning for this all your life?" laughed Labat, interrupting him.

"No, but I find I have read more than I thought and I am slowly recalling it—and what I've heard. The moccasin flower, too, is in New England. In the high valleys of the Alps, near the snow-line, there is a small, sweet-scented variety of a marvelous blue—almost a Wedgwood blue. There are a good many small ones in the north."

"When do you plan to reach Vpra-na, Monsieur d'Entrecolles?"

"Not for a long time! Not until the plants are blooming. I've got to get well, for one thing! It will take time to go to the flower-haunts; and it will take four years at least to adapt the plants to new surroundings. I do not wish to see the estate until everything is as I have planned it—bungalow built, plants in flower. I intend to make it the greatest orchid farm in the world, something worth a trip around the globe to see. I will arrange with my banker in Calais to look after the money end for you."'

The next day he wrote to Veitch and Son of London, celebrated specialists and pioneers in cross-fertilization, to ship to Labat specimens of everything they had, and to give him advice on hybrid-izing.

In February, he set out upon his own long wanderings. He took ship for the Cape of Good Hope—and with grief at leaving the brother whom he loved. The precarious state of his health, the waterways to be traversed, made it possible they might not meet again. Winter rain fell like tears over the eager, boyish face that looked after him from the pier as the steamer moved away.

He went to the Cape of Good Hope in search of the waxen blossoms called *Bonatea speciosa,* which he found in reasonable abundance. He packed them in dry moss, sent them away by the first steamer and started north. He traveled slowly, keeping to the center of the continent, resting frequently and spending altogether more than a year in Africa. From Africa he sent to Labat hundreds of plants. In Madagascar he made a find—a white, six-rayed, waxen orchid, huge in size, from whose center depended long, pale green, swinging whips. The islands south of Asia he knew grew orchids in abundance. From the Andaman Islands in the Bay of Bengal he procured quantities of tree orchids, whose flowers were little white stars, and fragrant; here, too, was a violet-hued natural hybrid (purple *Dendrobium*), the large, mauve-colored *Vanda teres*. In the Mergui Islands there were orchids of enchanting hues. In Penang he came upon a plant that at a distance the unaided eye could not distinguish from the spotted tropical spider. From the South China Sea he shipped six long boxes of white orchids that have down-hanging roots and resemble a bird of paradise; and pale blue, waxen specimens that form a trailing vine. In the Botanical Gardens of Buitenzorg, Java, they make a specialty of orchids, and he shipped to Labat seven cases. At the request of Mr. Niemen-huysen—curator of the gardens and a famous orchid specialist—he remained in Buitenzorg to learn something of methods of culture. In reply to d'Entrecolles's statement that he had written to Labat to cross the richly colored *Vandea* from Malay with the *Angræcum sesquipedale* of Madagascar, the old man replied with a heat of utterance that caused a sensation of surprise in his hearer.

"You'll learn things when you get to your estate and settle down to orchid farming! Strange things—which you wouldn't listen to in a fairy tale!"

"What do you mean?" asked d'Entrecolles.

"I can't explain! And that's the strangest thing of all. But you'll find out for yourself. Oh, I'm sure you'll be more successful than I have been! You have wealth. Your time is your own. And you are young—and good to look at." He noticed as he spoke that the face of d'Entrecolles had the golden pallor of those whose ancestors have lived in hot lands. "I shouldn't be a bit surprised—if *you* found out!"

"What has youth to do with it?" d'Entrecolles questioned, knowing that it was futile to probe the other matter, which interested him most.

"Youth? Everything! They are a queer lot—these orchids. They have likes, dislikes, nerves—passions— And, then, you like them differently from the way in which I like them. My interest has been purely scientific. You are nearer to them, d'Entrecolles! The other day you were standing under that purple hybrid down there—the one with the mouth the color of fresh blood and little white ripples along the edge like angry teeth—and I said to myself, 'D'Entrecolles does not look out of place among them!' You have changed, *physically,* too, have you not, since you have been on this quest?"

"Oh, yes!" Then he recalled how life and strength had suddenly swept back into his body like a tidal wave from an unknown deep. He had taken on flesh. His skin had grown dark. It had acquired certain coppery tints.

"And when you come to experimenting with hybrids by cross-fertilization, you'll find it's like being a god. There's no limit yet to the degree to which you can push it. You can see life, new, wonderful, which you yourself have willed, created right under your hand."

The word *life* gave him a peculiar thrill, as if he were in the presence of unguessed and invisible intelligence. The boundaries of the word expanded unpleasantly.

"Now I have made a plan for your journey. You won't be offended or think I'm officious, will you?"

"No, indeed! I'm grateful for advice from an expert."

"The best place to get orchids for experiments in cross-fertilization is South America. They have reached highest development there. The rarest, most wonderful flowers in the world are found in the South American jungles. I have not seen them, but a traveler, a friend of mine who is an artist, made sketches of them, which I am going to show you."

He went into the house, brought out a brown portfolio and opened it. "Now, what do you call that?" he questioned triumphantly.

"A white dove."

"I knew you'd say so! That's the orchid of the holy dove from Panama. The foot-hills of the Andes are full of orchids of different kinds. And so is Peru! Over the buried cities of the Incas they float like the souls of the dead. He—the artist who made these pictures—said that.

"To the hill-forests of Colombia you must go for the *Odonto-glossum*. In the jungles of Ecuador there are trees which are enveloped with orchid blossoms. These orchids—from the old Spanish Main—are gorgeous and splendid, like the lustful dreams of the *conquistadores*. Did you ever see a red like that? What are these, you ask? Bee, frog, lizard, butterfly orchids. Notice, if you will, that they do not in the least resemble a flower. These I have shown you I wish you to collect first and send to Vpra-na. Now I've kept the best for the last," he added, closing the book. "And I haven't any picture of this to show you. All I can do is to tell you about it. Did you ever hear of the 'death-orchid' of Venezuela?" D'Entrecolles shook his head.

"I thought not! Not many white men have heard of it. And none has seen it. But the man who made these drawings says that he knows that it does exist. He traveled in Venezuela. Different Indian tribes told him about it. Its perfume causes either death or a narcotic sleep—to the Indians—from which they never awake in their right mind. No one has gathered it. It might not have the same effect upon a white man, you see. Now there's your chance. Go! Find it! Bring it back! If I were not so old, I'd go with you," the little old Dutchman exclaimed, his face burning with eagerness and excitement.

"I'll do it!" cried d'Entrecolles, with equal fervor.

"And you'll succeed, d'Entrecolles, "because—they like you—"

"*They?*"

"Yes—"

He arose, said good-night, and without a word of explanation took the portfolio and went into the house.

When d'Entrecolles left Java for South America, it did not seem to him that he was setting out on a flower quest. It was as if the object of his journey had changed. It was as if he were going in search of a lost and unknown race. The dried plants that he had not shipped to Labat, he hung by the windows and around the walls of his room. They bloomed, covering his little cabin with fantastic color and form. Then he found it was the flowers that supplied need of companionship and made the presence of his Frenchmen more and more negligible. This discovery did not please him. It made him vaguely apprehensive, like the approach of indeterminate danger. At night, particularly, did their fantastically focused shadows seem uncanny.

In the arrangement of this new journey he took the old man's advice. He went first to the West Indies, where he sought out and sent back, one by one, the flowers of which the Buitenzorg botanist had told him. As soon as this was done, he secured three trusty Spanish-speaking Indians and started for the jungles of Venezuela. He followed the Orinoco toward the Colombian border, inquiring at every settlement of natives if they had heard of the death-flower. Some admitted they had heard of it but declared they did not know anything about it. Others shook their heads and refused to reply. Others seemed frightened when the subject was mentioned and hastened away. When they reached Colombia, they turned north. They traveled until they saw foot-hills of the Andes and felt fresher air. Here they came upon a deserted pueblo. All had left with the exception of one old, wrinkled man, who was getting ready to follow.

"Do you know anything about the death-orchid?"

He did not answer at once.

"Do you mean the flowers that kill?"

"Yes. Can you tell us where they grow?"

"That's why we are moving," he answered vaguely. "At night their perfume is blown over here. It has made some of our people mad."

"But where is the place?"

"North—straight north; but higher in the mountains. In the first valley on the other side of that range there," pointing toward ripples of ash-colored summits beyond.

"Will you go with us?"

His face at once expressed such terror that it was useless to wait for an answer.

They camped that night on the site of the deserted pueblo. Just as the twilight was thickening into blackness, whiffs of peculiar, compelling fragrance came to them. It affected the senses like two high, long notes when a violinist slowly draws his bow across the strings.

With the first light, they set out for the foothills and the range of mountains to the north. Two days later, they crossed the foot-hills and entered a pleasant, fresh valley in which there was a little river where gray herons waded, and whose bordering hills on the other side were thick with trees. They made camp under a clump of *guabos churimos,* the thick leaves of which they plucked to make beds. Red and blue macaws flew over them. Within the thickets, hidden from sight, they heard the *chilacoas* calling.

When the camp, which was near the second range of foot-hills, was nearly completed, one of the Frenchmen exclaimed: "That can't be snow shining there, on the crest of that hill! The hills are not high enough."

D'Entrecolles brought his field-glass. "No; it isn't snow. As you say, the hill is not high enough. It's flowers. Huge, white, shining flowers!"

"But we smell no perfume; so it cannot be the ones we are after," objected one of the Frenchmen.

"It might be! You can't tell. There are orchids that give off per-fume only at certain hours, and different perfume on different days," exclaimed d'Entrecolles. "And sometimes they imitate scents of other flowers, just as mocking-birds imitate bird voices."

Later in the day, with the first lengthening of the shadows of the Andes, faint breaths of fragrance were discernible. To Jacques d'Entrecolles the fragrance was like music—the first, faintly out-lined notes of a prelude. The Indians felt it quickly. It made them dizzy. They declared they would not stay, and grabbing up hand-fuls of grass to hold to their faces, they started back toward the deserted pueblo. The two Frenchmen found the odor irritating, but it did not make them ill. Its severity of effect was evidently not for the white race. The perfume increased with the night, growing stronger and stronger, like some orchestral composition rising to a climax of tone. When day had gone from the valley, leaving two far, high Andean summits rosy, the flowers began to glow with a baleful phosphorescence. An occasional flower shone out for a moment more brightly than others, and then darkened, and another took up the glow, like an orchestra whose keys were color and light instead of tone. At midnight, the perfume lessened. At daybreak, it was gone.

For a number of days d'Entrecolles observed this hill of flowers from the distance of the camp, and felt for the first time the effect of the fateful perfume. To his French companions it was merely unpleasant. To him it was perilously pleasant. When it swept over him as he was dropping off to sleep, it bore him to a hasheesh world of visioned splendor. And the vision in its significance was always the same: He floated above a cataract more terrible and tremendous than Niagara; a cataract made, not of water, but of fantastic, angry flowers, which were being lashed by some power he could neither see nor comprehend, from one form of life to another—on and on. And the upflung foam was a writhing agony of beauty. When day came, this vision of night remained in his mind as a definite symbol of material change. For several days he was content to watch the flowers from his vantage across the valley. They repelled and attracted him. He hesitated to invade their presence.

"It will not be difficult to procure the flowers," he declared reassuringly to his companions. "They are harmless by day. They have no light. They have no power."

The French gardeners did not feel inclined to accompany him. But at length he persuaded them. He was right. The flowers were harmless as other flowers by day. They had neither scent nor light. To the touch they were not poisonous.

For shipment they selected plants upon which the buds were starting. They packed them in dried grass. Thus sheltered from dust and moisture, they reached the Orinoco, where a steamer of the Iquitos Company bore them to the coast. Here the grass packages were crated and shipped to Labat. A letter went on the same steamer, directing Labat to cross one of the Venezuelan death-flowers—as soon as the blossom should be developed—with the flower he had obtained by crossing the great Malay *Vandea* with the *Angræcum sesquipedale* of Madagascar.

"Push this intercrossing to the highest limit! Choose the largest, strongest specimens. I am not sailing for Vpra-na, now. I plan to visit the Castleton Gardens in Jamaica, take a look at the collection of exotics the Jesuit fathers started on Martinique, visit for a week or two the botanical gardens of Rio, and go on to Bogota to study in earnest. Bogota, you know—since you yourself told me— is the head of the orchid industry of the world."

TEN YEARS AFTER THE DEPARTURE from France, d'Entrecolles stood in the wonder-garden Labat had created. Indeed, he stood beside the botanical marvel that had resulted from the blending of the three great flowers. Labat had called it *Vita Nuova,* a name which d'Entrecolles changed, to the older man's displeasure, to *La Revenante.*

"*La Revenante,* d'Entrecolles, means dead life come back again. Can't you see that this is new life—*Vita Nuova*—which we ourselves have created?"

"I wish you wouldn't use that word *life,* Labat," replied d'Entrecolles in a new tone of vexation.

The orchid that caused this discussion, and that was, in truth, something new in the world, surpassed the others in size. It was of a nameless pale pink-violet color, which the night bleached to white. Its center was of a deep, unusual crimson upon which shone two round, white velvet dots. From this center depended four white, satiny substances which, in the African mother-orchid, had been called whips, but which recalled to the mind of d'Entrecolles a picture by an Italian of the Renaissance. It was a picture of an angel— or was it a demon?—anyway, something beautiful, and it wore the guise of a woman; and in order to impress the idea of swift motion, that it was winging its way *toward something,* the artist had painted four arms.

While Labat had been experimenting with the heights of flower life, he himself had been doing the opposite. He had been making one of the species grow backward. He had made it lose color, form, beauty, fragrance, texture, and become a pulpy, poisonous, disgustingly dotted monster. In doing this, he experienced savage joy.

As he moved about his fantastic estate, engaged in one duty

and another, he became conscious that the white orchid-eyes of *La Revenante* followed him, focusing upon him everywhere their expressionless immobility. The flower bent and flecked him as he passed. And the touch was as the touch of flesh: a cold, startlingly colored, stinging flesh that left the trailing sensation of flame. The petals were white, floating, voluptuous arms. The flower clung to his fingers. It moved toward him when he approached. And it poured over him waves of sensual delight which crippled his will.

When he came up each morning from his dip in the sea to begin the work of the day, he saw the swaying curtains of bloom with fresh surety of vision. The cumulative impression made upon him was that of floating, detached symbols of human life. It was as if from some perfect distance, some vantage-point of vision, they would be focused in the eye into a complete form of living beauty, of which now each petal was a disintegrated part. They became tantalizing symbols, flower caricatures, which were beginning to cause more and more confused emotions.

"Are they life," he questioned himself eagerly, "climbing up to some glittering culmination? Or are they life dissolving in fluttering particles of charm?"

He began to talk aloud, as if arguing with himself. "The sensation that a beautiful orchid causes is not wholly pleasure. Mingled with pleasure, although in a lesser degree, there is something that resembles fear, then surprise, and to those who are sensitive, a vague, unsatisfied questioning. It is as if some monster, sensed but not seen, were trying to wing its way toward me across aeons of time." He paused in dismay at his own words.

"The rose, the lily, are beautiful—royally beautiful—but within the safe realm of little flowers. But *La Revenante*"—he started nervously at the consciousness that he had not only spoken but thought of the orchid, at the moment, as a living woman—"*La Revenante* is beautiful with a different beauty; the perplexing, almost grievous beauty of something transcending known and definite boundaries of the flower world."

At mid-day, when he settled himself comfortably upon the bamboo couch on the veranda for his daily siesta, there fell across his face the wan, green shadows of the jungle day. He lay where he could look down the avenues from which the swaying curtains depended. As he watched them idly, the shadows of the orchids, which the semi-perpendicular sun flung upon the smooth ground, showed forms that at first were startling, at length terrifying, as they moved, combined, or parted, at direction of the wind. He could not sleep. He left the couch, defied the tropic sun and moved about his garden. Mid-day lays command of silence upon tropic life. The sun is god; the world is hushed before him. Color alone lives. In this silence, he felt eyes looking at him that he could not see nor escape.

He was glad when Vlei-la, the native girl whom Labat had educated, trained for a house-servant, and taught to speak French, joined him. Accidentally her hand touched him. The flesh of natives of the tropics, he found, is sweet and cool like the petals of the flower. Looking down upon the almost bare brown body that walked beside him, he reflected how perfectly in place she was here, and how out of place she would be in a house in France. Reversely, he knew that not the most delicately intuitioned French woman could keep from being inharmonious here. Vlei-la, indeed, did not vibrate with a personality more dominant than the flowers. And he was not sure that he himself did. Nature dominated them both. Under this sun that melted everything in its blinding flame, differences and distinctions lessened.

Vlei-la caught the drift of his thinking. "We are just little dark bugs beside that, aren't we?" she questioned, pointing to the volcanic summit down whose slopes poured riotously the green life of the forest.

He laughed and agreed with her.

As they turned from one to another of the spoke-like avenues of the garden, it became evident that they were both trying to avoid a certain place, the rear corner of the bungalow, where grew the hybridized Venezuelan death-orchid. The instant this fact became clear to d'Entrecolles, there swept before his brain a vision—the mournful, mephitic loveliness of *La Revenante*. Taking Vlei-la playfully by the arm he pulled her along. "Come—why not this path?"

"No—no. Not—there!" she returned decidedly.

"Why not?"

She did not explain. She seemed afraid. She escaped from him and attempted to draw his mind away by changing the subject. "Look there—those gray-yellow flowers! Aren't they ugly little faces? They have long, hairy ears, silly eyes and hanging mouths—looking like this!" She tried to imitate them.

D'Entrecolles saw, as he followed her pointing finger, a band of imps exhibiting a spirit grotesque, ironic, mocking.

Vlei-la was not larger than a twelve-year-old child in France. He could hear the satiny sound of her bare feet as she walked beside him. He felt toward her the tenderness one cherishes for a pet. She marked a distance about half way between himself and the pallid flower.

When they had finished their tour of the garden, she curled up on one end of the veranda and looked with bright, tireless eyes at the blazing blue levels of the sea. She did not speak. The sea has stolen the voice of island dwellers and speaks itself with multiple power and personality. He wondered what it could be that held her attention as she sat so motionless, so silent.

Night came and lit a sudden splendor in the stars. The tropic night is not silent like the day. It is filled with noises. There is a shrieking, calling, trilling. Underneath there is a faint network of phantom sounds. He knew it was for this he had been waiting throughout the day. This had been the suppressed motive of thought and action—the longing for the hour to come when he could smell again the perilous perfume.

The consciousness that the hour had come brought its reaction: that it was duty to resist the impulse; that the hours of intoxication spent under the perfume were just as injurious as hours of intoxication obtained in a more usual way. He thought bravely that he could resist. But as he sat toying with the anticipated pleasure, a charming presence over him. It inspirited like sunlight or clean swept wind. Something within the soul of him laughed back and joined it. As swiftly as without use of feet he was beside *La Revenante* in his perfidious paradise.

The great flower glowed sadly with a grayish lustre tinged with violet. But when he reached its side and touched it, it burst into a primrose-yellow phosphorescence. The perfume called like a voice. He pressed *La Revenante* lovingly against his cheek. He felt the cold tentacles, the satin pendants, a soft-skinned, fragrant face, in which shone two round, white, magnetic eyes, whose expressionlessness held a terrible power. The perfume poured madness into his brain. Caressing words rose to his lips: "Exquisite waxen grotesque! Beautiful terror swaying beside me in the night! Where were you born? Under what moon of time?"

The impetuosity of his words aroused him. He turned just in time to see a white skirt disappearing around the corner of the bungalow. Vlei-la had been watching him.

Never had he felt an emotion that equaled this in intensity. It was a woman who stood beside him. With his hands of flesh he could not touch her. With the words of his mouth he could not speak to her. With his physical body he could not see her. And yet he caressed her, spoke to her, saw her. And the developing faculties which enabled him to do so were sweeping him away from ordinary life. They were dehumanizing him. These hours of overwhelming passional reverie induced by the drug-perfume were shutting off from him—or veiling—certain perspectives of memory, which were dear, and which kept alive his contact with the past.

A thin wind came crisping the tops of the tall canary trees. There was a haunting sense of cosmic change. The wind moved the flower nearer and nearer to him. It seemed to dance for joy. And the voice of the sea borne on the morning was its voice. Night had gone.

Throughout the day he slept. And the sleep had neither dreams nor remembrance. Occasionally, where its tissue was worn thin, he felt a face looking down at him. He knew vaguely that it was Vlei-la. At night, when he awoke, he was weary. He was exhausted. He felt a peculiar prostration of will. After he dressed, he took down from the wall a round mirror and looked at himself intently. He did not know what it was that impelled him to do so. It was as if he were looking for something that had not yet appeared, some change in himself. When he stepped out upon the veranda, day had already dropped in a yellow fury behind the waves.

"Don't go there tonight, Monsieur Jacques!" pleaded Vlei-la, stepping in front of him as if to bar the way.

He sat down wearily, waiting for what she would say next.

"If you could have seen your face when the great flower shed its light over you, you would not want to go. It was frightful! I should not have known you! And when you left to go to bed—just before day—the face of the flower was a white, grinning skeleton."

He looked at her helplessly. He heard terror in her tone.

"Let us go out in the boat tonight. I will row you myself. And I will sing you a song of my people."

Limply he let himself be led away.

For the space of a week he did not revisit *La Revenante*. It was not because he did not feel an impulse to go, so strong that he had to fight against it continually. It was the will of Vlei-la added to his own.

He began to feel happy, light-hearted, just as of old. He began to plan for the visit of the brother whom he had loved so dearly. He could not understand why he had not seen him or made an effort to have him come to Vpra-na in all these years. It was as if he had lived them through in a swift intoxication that had dazed his brain. He and Labat were on more friendly terms. The latter told him that his daughter, Clarice, who had finished her studies in the *Sacré Cœur* in Paris, would soon be with them. He spent two happy days with the family on their end of the island. He saw clearly that he had been at fault in the various disagreements with Labat. Life and its facts fell into their old reasonable adjustments. Almost every evening, he and Vlei-la rowed out upon the ocean.

Vlei-la saw the change in d'Entrecolles, and she determined to make it permanent. She chose early morning to destroy the great flower and the plant upon which it grew. When she came near enough to reach it, it poured a flood of perfume upon her like a sword thrust, and she staggered back toward the house, dizzy and faint. The next morning, she made another attempt, and lifted her hand, after covering her face. The arm fell limp, with a stinging sensation. Later in the day, she saw outlined fluctuatingly beneath the skin, near the shoulder, miniature red death-flowers. She showed her arm to d'Entrecolles and told him the cause.

"I am going back to Madame Labat. I am afraid of it! It will kill me if I stay. After I am gone, do not ever go near it again, Monsieur Jacques," she pleaded.

As he saw her disappear down the road that led to the other end of the island, terror assailed him. For three days, he did not perform his duties in the garden. He was careful to keep away from it. He idled by the sea. He explored the volcanic peak. He pretended he had interest in scientific investigation of the extinct crater. Each day he felt more strongly the impulse that called him back. Now the impalpable presence sometimes stood beside him in the day. Its loveliness was a sensation instead of a visual perception. The instant it came there arose a barrier between himself and all that he had loved before. With ears that were not the ears of his physical body he heard a step, a moving garment, a determined and planned approach, and *La Revenante* stood beside him. The fourth night, because he tried to think that the emotion induced by *La Revenante* reached certain heights of recompensing vision, he deliberately went to the corner of the bungalow. The great flower shone with an icy whiteness. The whiteness changed to dusky malevolence, which made him think of the dulled, day-stung eyes of the great owl. This was followed by wave after wave of perfume of varying intensity, like an angry voice that reproached. With a sense of the old, resistless charm, fear was joined.

The white eyes had the hypnotic power of evil attraction possessed by two shining, swift-turning wheels of steel. He could not look away from them. Color darkened, deepened, paled, changed, like the blushing and paling of emotion. He went nearer. Standing close beside this monstrous flower, he felt distinctly the vibrations of a seething, cruel life. Shut up within it there was a voiceless something that writhed for deliverance, for change, for power— something eager to press on to an attainment he could not foresee. *La Revenante* possessed a life as highly developed as his own, but upon a different plane. Through the ordinary medium, words, they could not converse. But *La Revenante* had found other ways.

Within his dazed brain this fact arose to confront him and to sober him. He had cultivated a flower beyond the limits of flower life. He had made an orchid-woman. The beautiful, pallid, silent flower was mocking his misery with her velvet-white, expressionless eyes. *La Revenante* was a vampire that sat upon his soul.

Swinging over the sea, the day came with a swift surprise. When d'Entrecolles went to bed, he gave directions to be called in three hours. He could not waste the day in sleep. There was something he must think about. He admitted to himself now what he had so long denied. Now, instead of resorting to vague evasions, he determined to seek reasons. As he sat in the sunlight, a face flashed upon him. He saw it with his mind, not with his eyes. Perhaps, indeed, it was the nerves of his body that saw. New senses were being developed in him, extensions perhaps of embryonic senses that all possess. He could see that they were being developed to meet this new requirement of life.

Ten years in the tropics had brought physical and mental changes, in both of which was discernible a drawing nearer to the speechless life about him. He thought less. He felt more. He relied upon instinct instead of reason. His body was more sensitively alert. His mind was duller. The crisp boundary between reality and vision was melting. The motive power of life was beginning to be, not his own mind and will, but a magnetic, irresistible power of the tropic earth. By some alchemy he was being transformed. Added to this there was an excitation of the senses caused by color and light. This was so great that beside it self-directed thinking seemed dull. One did not feel like expressing one's own thoughts so decidedly in the presence of this tremendous nature. It was easy to sink into a torpor in which body and nerves communicated in their own way with the silent life about them. In addition, the atmosphere was like a presence, a personality, embracing ranges of mood. Spicy, nameless scents were borne to him continually upon the tropic wind. The dim, steaming fragrance of the jungle was the fragrance of exuberant life. This was being inhaled into his body, mingled with his blood. An interchange of conscious and unconscious life was going on; a silent weaving together of two separate kingdoms—animal and vegetable. It was as if in Vpra-na his blood changed gradually to a sap. On this tropical island where the flaming sun made life a crucible of decomposition and reconstruction, he had noticed that the flesh of the natives was more like flower-tissue than elsewhere. Repeatedly he had thought of this when with Vlei-la. Here the growing things of the volcanic mountain suggested to him continually that there might be abnormal and sporadic extensions, both of substance and sense, toward a more powerfully sentient plane. The application of the word *Vpra-na* showed the sure instinct of unscientific jungle people. He had noticed in himself since he had been in Vpra-na, that dormant senses had been quickened without effort. It was as if a part of him had been pulled off, leaving an undersurface that was sensitive.

He had begun to be conscious of a sentient force in the growing things of the mountain above his head and his garden that overhung the sea. Here there was a converging of the planes of life. It was that point in nature's perfected plan, where parallel lines, seen from a certain height and distance, become one. And he was caught in their riotous inter-lapping. There was, however, no good reason to believe, he saw, that for him this experience was an advance in life. It was just as likely to be a going down on the other side of the circle, toward the old, primeval life, in some unnamed geological period, when changing environment was developing special faculties, and the green, waving arms of the vine, with their uncertain motions at the mercy of the winds, was becoming, by infinite gradations of slow time, *determined* motion. In this experience he felt that he was describing a descending curve. For him it was a deterioration. But for the orchid, it was an upward curve, a betterment, a drawing near to some culmination of desire. In the orchid, the accumulated yearning of a voiceless flower-race was reaching out to touch him. A flower-soul as ancient as the sea itself was drawing toward him. And its approach aroused not wonder, nor intellectual curiosity, but a vague terror, which he could neither express nor overcome. He saw clearly what had happened.

He and the flower were caught in the rhythmic swing of cosmic waves, and now they were being swept together at that point of visible time that we call today, but that is really tomorrow. He saw now a new meaning in the term *La Revenante*. It meant when the dead come back to live again a life of joy in the sun.

Now that he had admitted that he was confronting a peculiar condition based upon some fact he did not understand, that it was not the result of fancy or imagination, he made less effort to resist the drug-perfume. Every night found him under the great flower, eagerly inhaling the intoxication. There, all alone, he paced the deserted garden paths and gave himself over unrestrainedly to his perilous, polychrome festival.

The orchid does not keep to the color simplicity of garden flowers. The orchid owns only tints, shades. These color variations are so subtle, so unusual that they may not be named. They are like fractions of musical notes that may not be stated in exact mathematical terms. With the pleasure, there is mingled a feverish, tantalizing suggestiveness. They are peculiarly evocative of emotion. They stimulate the senses to perplexing pursuits. They are color spiritualized with grief. They are color intellectualized with experience. And the line of the orchid is as over-freighted with meaning as its color. These line-rhythms signify agony and revolt, with certain satin interspaces of cold triumph. As d'Entrecolles walked toward the bungalow the faces that followed him were beautiful caricatures of humanity, just as the ape and the monkey are disgusting caricatures.

He began to consider afresh this protoplasmic adventure. Was it improbable, impossible, that *La Revenante* was a person, living upon a different plane? He knew that wherever we think we see a fixedly drawn line, we see, not the limit of fact, but the limit of our minds. Does anyone know the exact difference between animal and vegetable protoplasm? In both are life. Life means impulse. Impulse means change—progress. Perhaps the fragile lines marking a flower carry sensation. A nerve is nothing but protoplasm.

He had made scientific experiments himself with the great flower. He had tried the effect upon it of loud and harsh noises, of chloroform, gases, music. In each case it had responded. And the response showed an organized attempt toward self-preservation. There was in it, too, a husbanding of energy which this complication of life was squandering so recklessly in him. Sex was defined in it. A structural change toward greater strength than its Madagascan ancestor possessed had taken place. The flower had the power to perpetuate itself beyond the limits of flower-life. He had measured the temperature of the blossom. It was higher than that of other flowers. Heat means greater molecular activity. A more intense life was going on within it. It was changing more than the others. Then he recalled that the power of change "*marks things which live little from things which live much.*" This "*lives much*" echoed for days in his memory.

He saw that *La Revenante* possessed an occult intelligence swifter of action and more delicate of comprehension than his own. She was the supreme expression of a race. In her persistent growth above plant life, she had sought and found places of oscillating resistance. Now she was poised and ready for flight higher.

Then his mind slipped beyond control and performed mad feats of imaginative thinking. While he sat there, meditating, the cell-eyes of *La Revenante* might be looking across space at stars—and at worlds beyond the stars—and registering impressions that were impossible for him. Just as a person climbs perilous mountains in order to look upon an enlarged world-vista, so had *La Revenante* climbed patiently to a dizzy peak of cosmic vision, and now she was reaping her reward. Who could formulate a guess as to what she was looking upon? And beyond what she saw, what was it that she dreamed? He was learning that it is the brain, not the eye unaided, that sees farthest. What was it that dwelt within him and thought? Did he know? Could he tell? Might there not be a like nameless presence dwelling within the flowers? Had he any right to say that this presence was of greater or less importance?

By daylight the face of the flower was fresh, unwearied, disconcerting, while the nights of furious brain-visions left him worn and exhausted. Beside this coldly shining, splendid youth, his body was of no more account than a withered leaf. It was a rag of flesh. He felt peculiarly ashamed, too, just now, that he must die and

grow old. Then he thought of *La Revenante's* infinite prolonga-
tion of soul, whose memories had not been destroyed as his own
had been. Where had been its beginning? When would it end? And
in this cosmic adventure of hers, what had been the scenes by the
way? In comparison with *La Revenante's* life, his own had been
brief and its experiences shabby. She must have scorn of him. He
was insignificant beside her of the infinite past who had cast off
life after life. He began to suffer from jealousy and envy. Was there
some mighty, semi-immortal lover whom this intensified life did
not burn up, as these futile visions of the brain were burning up in
him the previous substance of life. Where had she been with him?
Upon all the stars? What had he said to her of love?

All moods induced by *La Revenante* had this too great blending of pain. In her cold, sleepless soul a cruel ambition was hidden. There was something within him which the flower must cling
to in order to gain a desire. He was rounding a cape of experience
that jutted out into an uncharted sea. Was the flower's love of him
an end in itself? Or was it merely a means of progression toward
something dearer and of more ancient desire? Was it love of a plant
for a man as we understand love? Or was it something more irresistible for the will, more destructive for the body—chemical attraction? Were they "antagonistic affinities"? If this were true, the
unified power of earth was behind it.

But it was not good for him—this experience. Indeed, it was
quite the reverse. The effect of the perfume was becoming more
and more injurious. He did not think his own thoughts now. He
did not think or wish or will anything of his own accord. His mind
was becoming by slow degrees a mirror that reflected the perverted
passions of a flower. Less and less did memory frame for him pictures of the life he had lived with his brother before he came to
Vpra-na. Less and less did he go over the pleasant years of wandering. Most dangerous of all, this life with *La Revenante* was beginning to seem the only real life. Any other was merely fictional.
There was a something always beside him. The soul of him was
never alone. Fastened to him by invisible tentacles of emotion and
desire was a soul-parasite. He was beginning to speak haltingly

and with a too frequent searching for the word. This was because, with *La Revenante,* he had conversed so long without the need of words.

What would happen if he could not save himself? Physicians know the ultimate effect of morphine, cocaine, opium. Those drugs give ruinous pleasure. They make those addicted to them grow old, bent, misshapen. But who knew what the effects of this perfume would be? It was greatly more dangerous because its powers were unknown. When he looked at himself in the morning, now, in the little round mirror that hung upon his wall, he saw a change. But he was not growing old or bent. Quite the contrary. He was beginning to look like a flower. A new and unwholesomely colored youth was enveloping him. He was drawing nearer to the monster that controlled him. Not only his mind was changing, but his body.

The orchids moved restlessly under the prodigious splendor of the tropic moon. One could hear faint metallic sounds like crinkling of crisp silks. Was it suffering or pleasure, or a combination of both, that motived their restlessness? The perfume called to him like a voice. Like a voice it varied in emotional intensity. Again he suffered from jealousy. What did the radiant, satin-surfaced orchids say to each other under the moon, on these incredible tropic nights by the sea? What did they say to each other which he could not comprehend, because he was only a fragment of life broken off from the past, while they were life in its entirety? As the perfume passed over him it began to weaken self-directed thinking. The first touch made him vaguely fancy that, in the dreams of the orchid sleep, his mind was going backward just as he had made one of the plants grow backward and revert to an earlier state.

He had visions of vanished and unrecorded races. He saw faces that had been formed by a set of thoughts and emotions totally dissimilar to his own—faces such as the wildest dreams of poet or painter could not express drifted past. With the beauty and the strangeness were mingled horror and visioned cruelty. Against his will he became the recipient of tragic histories that had followed the birth of time. Out of the void blackness of the past, there rounded into visibility forms such as had not been seen within the modern world, and faces mirroring a race-soul that held the unexpanded power of ages.

He floated above a world to which life had not come. Bare, black, jagged, mountains rose above tawny plains as limitless as oceans. Lonely waters became sullen ebony under the night, or surfaces of steel by day.

Upon the yellow slime at length fell the disintegrated dust of dead planets dropping through space. Threadlike lines shot across the wastes. Their motions were swift as if impelled by an electric flash. They invaded the earth like an army. The green lines crawled, clung, conquered. Dots sprouted upon them. The dots expanded. They took on form: round, oblong, smooth-edged, saw-toothed. Like joined like. They formed villages. The villages fought each other. They strangled, they smothered, they murdered each other. In their cold rage they leaped at the cliffs and the mountains. They circled their heights with green cords of steel. They corroded them. They crumbled their rocks to dust. They choked and checked the rivers. They leaped from place to place with a murderous fury. They were impelled only by two passions: greed and destruction. He saw pass before his eyes the battles of pre-glacial periods when plants invaded the earth.

Then a white curse fell with the lightning. Baffled rage of defeat vibrated through the air. There was a smoking fury of hate. Motion was taken away from them. They were bound to the earth that they had tried to destroy. They must remain motionless. They must remain at the mercy of whatever approached.

Ages and ages passed away, touching his highly keyed brain like dust circles flung from passing carriage wheels.

The green, growing things upon which the prohibition had fallen, had found their rage helpless. It turned in upon them. Its concentrated power found expression in a burst of color-fury, which wrapped the earth. Flowers were born! Millions and millions of invisible, bright burning cell-eyes, freighted with cruel memories, with cruel experiences, looked out upon the earth. When he saw them—even in his dream—he shuddered at the fact that "*in organic memory there can be no shifting of truths.*"

The thin, cold, unsympathetic moon shone upon him as he stumbled heavily away to bed. He awoke in the late afternoon suffering from an exhaustion that was equal to illness. Whenever he slept now, the plant's influence over him was greatest. It was as if it were entwined within the recesses of consciousness, and there it drew him nearer to an unexplored life he feared.

As the day advanced he was unable to shake off the exhaustion. It was so pronounced it was like the annihilation of self. *La Revenante* set up a vibration too high for the human organism. This thought-transference poured ideas into his mind too quickly and in quantities too great for safe assimilation. *La Revenante* communicated by entire thoughts, not tiny, broken, ill-fitting word-particles. Too high a pressure had been placed upon brain and nerves.

Three months later Jacques d'Entrecolles awoke from what seemed to him a prolonged dream in the bungalow of Labat, on the other end of the island. After one of the numerous quarrels with d'Entrecolles, Labat had been impelled to go to the garden again by Vlei-la, who kept before his mind the idea of a danger which she either would not or could not explain. D'Entrecolles had shown a pitiful pleasure at sight of the older man and begged Labat to take him away. "I haven't the will to go alone, now. I want you to take me."

Labat saw that a peculiar change had come over the body of d'Entrecolles. Evidently, too, some change had touched his mind. But Labat did not know what it was. The French gardeners were dead. And there was no use trying to get information from the sullen Indians. He believed the trouble had been caused by the dangerous Venezuelan death-flower. But there was no way to prove this.

After d'Entrecolles had been with Labat for a month he began to improve. His old self returned. But the peculiarities still marked his body. Labat now went over in d'Entrecolles's place to superintend the garden. One night after his return, when the family were at supper together, he remarked to d'Entrecolles: "The monstrous Venezuelan hybrid is dead and another is coming in its place. This bids fair to surpass the former. It bids fair to be such a flower as the world never saw."

D'Entrecolles was surprised to find that the fading of one flower and the appearing of another had no effect upon the passion that dominated him and that gave rise each day to the longing to go back.

Visitors were frequent. But he did not go over to meet them nor to tell them with pride of what he had done. He did not wish to read in the curious eyes of strangers the impressions made by the physical changes that had come upon him. He left the explaining of his wonder-garden to Labat, greatly to that gentleman's surprise. He seemed, too, to have given up his old, domineering ways.

The fame of this marvelous garden had circled the world. As a point of attraction worthy of visit it was mentioned in travelers' guides and in steamboat advertisements. The Royal Mail Steam Packet Co., of India, had just published the following statement in one of their circulars:

THE BOTANICAL WONDER OF THE WORLD

. . . the splendors of tropical orchids have up to the time of the daring and enterprising voyages of Monsieur Jacques d'Entrecolles, been only for those who could not appreciate them—for animals and serpents in the depths of impenetrable jungles. Now they are accessible to the world. A visit to this wonder-garden easily repays . . .

"We had a steamer full today, Jacques!" Labat remarked one night. "They were crazy over the *Renanthera Lowii* from Borneo. It has leaves three feet long. And each blossom spike is twelve feet in length. There are fifteen of these plants upon one canary tree. Right beside it, the blue *Vanda Roxburghii* has swinging draperies yards in length, which sweep the ground. Upon the side of the mountain I've built seats and a path. There visitors can sit and look down upon a block of trees whose leveled tops are covered with a carpet of rose-tinted *Aerides*. One of the women said they reminded her of curled, greedy flame-souls. And that same woman was afraid of *La Revenante!* She declared it was a beautiful terror. I tried to get the party to stay over night. I wanted them to see the flower give off light and change color."

When Clarice came from Paris, d'Entrecolles had recovered his former mental traits. He was glad to see Clarice. He had been cling-ing to the thought of her coming, and he gave himself over with determination to her company. She was slender, almost short. Her skin was pale and clear. She had heavy yellow hair and blue eyes so dark they were nearly black. She wore the latest fashions of France. She knew the gossip of the great city. She knew about the plays, the operas. She had a trunk full of books and magazines. All this brought freshly to his senses the other life he had once known. Her presence made him see the level fields of France he had loved; the crowded city streets filled with a life to which he belonged. He saw its gay, glittering boulevards by night. He heard the street cries. He felt the bitter, frost-gleaming winter upon the farm near Calais. He smelled the cold, invigorating breath of the pale sea that sent its spray in winter across the dunes. He went hunting with the brother he loved, whose face he could recall plainly now, and to-gether they felt upon their cheeks the tingling wind. All this meant life, strength and calm reason.

The fragile, figured-muslin frocks of Clarice pleased d'Entre-colles particularly; the little girlish ornaments she wore, her high-heeled slippers and her gracefully fashioned hats. In conversation he tried continually to get her point of view, to look at things with her eyes, not because the point of view was superior, but because he felt it took him further away from something he feared. He felt he must cling to her, keep close to her, in order to save himself from something that impended. He was conscious now that there is nothing so necessary to keep close to as commonplaceness. It rules wherever men laugh and are happy. The way to live safely is to live entangled in the intricate mesh of petty daily interests. How much better would a life be with Clarice—with its pleasant and stupid frivolities, which he could contemplate with conde-scending good nature—than a lonely life in the midst of this tragic beauty. *La Revenante* had kept him on the threshold of things—of love, of life. He had never intended to live in Vpra-na. He was vexed that he had wasted years there. He had planned to get well, gratify a caprice—perhaps do a unique thing in the world—and make money. He did not intend to be chained like a prisoner.

He would marry Clarice and go away. This determination brought him such relief and peace of mind as he did not think possible. He would go away forever from this glowing vegetation that drooped its disconcerting splendor over him. He would go away from the steaming jungle, whose green shadows floated always about him. He would go away from this riot of color, which disturbed the senses, and from the unresting rhythm of this blue, blazing ocean, whose sound beat within his body like a pulse.

One of the things that had hastened the proposal to Clarice and the arrangement with Monsieur and Madame Labat for the wedding, was a marked passage in a scientific book belonging to Labat, which he had picked up from the table, and which opened to the following sentence: "Continued pressure upon living tissue, by modifying the processes going on in it . . . gradually diminishes and finally destroys its power of resuming the outline it had at first. Thus the matter of which organisms are built up is modifiable by arrested momentum or by continual strain . . ."

With Clarice he planned the buying and furnishing of a home in Paris. She should have her carriage, her box at the opera; in short, she should be a great lady. He described to her the farm near Calais, and his brother. In a short time, he would be with his brother again. Then he would make up richly for these years of neglect. Then he would explain how it had come about. The future seemed clear.

Together they spent happy days in which d'Entrecolles was conscious of a striving, an insincerity on his part. He was trying to wish for the things he planned with Clarice. The less he really wished for them, the harder he tried. He clung to her as a child clings to its mother when it fears something. He taught her to manage a little sail-boat. He taught her to swim. One early morning as he saw Clarice floating down through the bright, aquamarine water, which had a dizzy, magnifying quality, he thought that in just this way *La Revenante* had floated down through cycles of glittering ages, from the visioned contour of some former life. And he had happened to come upon her in one of the myriad moments of progression. The vividness of the impression was uncanny. It displeased him. He tried to put it away upon the instant. He did not wish even to remember. Later in the day, another picture came to him to make him realize how powerful was that past he was avoiding so carefully. He recalled how sometimes he used to feel he had pleased the strange flower, and its petulant soul was happy, and it had laughed. This laughter was communicated to him in sensations that were neither pain nor pleasure, but a gentle shock to the intelligence. The longing to go back still possessed him. Daily he fought against it.

"But why do we not marry and go to France?" questioned Clarice for the hundredth time. "What are we waiting for?"

"Nothing," he replied. "Nothing at all."

How could he tell her when he did not know? It was his wish, too, to marry and to return to France forever. No one was more eager than he to get away. What it was that prevented him, he could not tell.

The only person who saw and knew the reason was Vlei-la. She said to Clarice when they were alone, "If you will do as I tell you, things will come out right—and in a short time."

"What do you mean?"

"This! Tomorrow morning, before daylight, while Monsieur, your father, is still sleeping, you and I will go to the orchid garden together. There is a great strange flower there, at the corner of the bungalow. At night it gives off light and changes color. Take the hatchet from the shed-room with you, and destroy it, and the plant upon which it grows. Then you will see a difference in Monsieur d'Entrecolles! Then things will be arranged at once as you wish."

Clarice tried to probe this amazing statement of Vlei-la's. But the sullen nature of the Indian reasserted itself under questioning, and she remained silent.

The next morning, while the household were asleep, they went to the garden. Vlei-la waited in the road below the slight elevation upon which the bungalow was situated, explaining to Clarice that the perfume made her ill and she did not dare go nearer. Clarice went alone to where *La Revenante* shone dimly in the dusk. Vlei-la waited what seemed a long time. Clarice did not return. The house was beginning to be astir. Soon Monsieur would come to make his daily round. She herself did not have the courage to go after Clarice. When day came she turned back by the road along which they had come. She met Labat. She told him the circumstances in detail. He ran to the garden. Clarice lay unconscious on the ground. *La Revenante* had bent down until the baleful flower hung only a few feet above the girl's face, and shadowed it with widespread petals.

The little steamer was dispatched to the nearest island for a doctor. When the doctor reached Vpra-na, Clarice was dead. And a most peculiar change had taken place in her. Her eyes were blinded and the iris was perfectly white, as if it had been burned with an acid. The pale cheeks showed crimson color like the high red of fever. The doctor said Clarice had died of a violent attack of meningitis, which often caused blindness, and left spots upon the body. Vlei-la told the doctor and the family that Clarice had been killed by the perfume and the touch of the great flower, and, by way of proof, she showed upon her own arm, near the shoulder, red spots exactly like the spots upon the face of Clarice. The doctor merely laughed at the idea and shook his head.

"Look at Monsieur d'Entrecolles, if you do not believe the influence of the flower!" retorted Vlei-la, angrily. The doctor turned and looked at him. His eyes became bright-pointed and quizzical. His face showed that some quick, startling thought had touched the brain, but he said nothing. He would make no admission. When he was climbing into the steamer to go back, he turned to give one last, searching look at d'Entrecolles.

Monsieur Labat and his wife made up their minds to return to France to join Marie, their other daughter. And they determined to take Vlei-la with them. They asked d'Entrecolles to go, too. He shook his head sadly and said he was going back to the bungalow. Vlei-la attempted to dissuade him, but she was unsuccessful. He grieved over the death of Clarice. He was gloomy and silent. He seemed to feel self-accused, as if, in some way, he were accountable. He stayed on with the family for a few days and spent his time in turning idly the pages of piles of old books and pamphlets.

When he gave himself over again to the influence of *La Revenante,* the work of destruction was swift. Once there had been something in his eyes that made men love him. That was fading now. The human light was dying. The first morning he looked at himself in his little round mirror he saw it flickering; a fleeting wisp-light, as if far within and below a surface. The perfume of *La Revenante* was establishing in him a different life-rhythm. It was impressing upon his brain the pattern of a different thought-and-action life. Under the deepening brown of his skin the coppery tints looked of reddish hue and took on contours of changing charm. They floated over his body as a thought floats across the brain. When he first realized what was happening, he succumbed to such terror that in the sickening nerve contraction that followed, he felt that the soul of him had escaped and floated away.

A change equally great had taken place in *La Revenante.* It floated more sovereignly upon the air. It recalled the sensation made by a bugle's ringing note of victory. It exceeded other flowers in size. It was more than a foot and a half in diameter. The leaf petals were thicker. They more closely resembled flesh. The round, white, velvet dots seemed now to have outlined upon them deepening circles of darker shades, focusing slowly into twin expressions of consciousness. The red velvet center was more mouth-like. Tiny white teeth edged it. It possessed power of independent motion. Its fragrance was a reasoned organ-scale of perfume-tone marvelously adapted to expression. Over it hovered vaguely the semblance of a human face. The firm presenting of its leaf-surface to the wind indicated peremptory will. It was as if it were being dilated by another soul. It was as if some unheard-of and unbelievable transfer had taken place.

AFTER THE SHOCK of fear in which d'Entrecolles felt that his soul had escaped, there was nothing to hold longer the body of him together. There was nothing to keep it from describing more and more a hideous and unhuman expansion. Gradually his mind faded. Nothing remained in the old way of organized intelligence. Motive power became perfunctory, muscular memory, the repetition of certain fixed habits established in the flesh. His mind had dissolved in the unexplored vastness of an ancient life.

Just before Labat sailed for France he came over, inspired by the insistence of Vlei-la, to make one last effort to induce d'Entrecolles to return on the steamer, with them, to his old home. D'Entrecolles was lying on the bamboo couch as Labat rounded the corner of the road that brought the bungalow in view. He came near enough to see him plainly. The first glance made him know that it was useless to speak to him. Upon the couch, facing him, he saw a crumpled, radiant-hued horror of flesh. The eyes had become the eyes of the great ape. A puzzled, defeated inquiry shone brightly within them. D'Entrecolles had taken on flesh. The cheeks, exactly in the center, were pendulous as petals. A tilting forward and curving over of the ears was traceable. The muscles that control the mouth had relaxed. It hung open and showed white tooth-edges. The increased flesh was not distributed evenly over the body in the ordinary way. There were astonishing irregularities, which echoed human standards basely. There was an increasing attempt to simulate something else—*some other form of life.*

What had been beautiful in petal texture was revolting when translated into flesh. The human eyes whence intelligence had fled were inferior to the white velvet dots upon the flower. The body suggested to Labat the result that had been obtained when d'Entrecolles had made one of the flowers grow backward. As he stood there watching, he thought the flower curtains reached out and out, and tried to swing their blossoms nearer, as if they knew that the shape upon the veranda had become one of them.

But d'Entrecolles felt nothing now. He saw nothing. He feared nothing. The splendid visions were no more. No more did the nerves respond to emotion. The helpless flesh was a riot of changing colors. The helpless flesh alone lived. Occasionally, as a shiver passes over water, the expression of his lost self passed over his face for a moment. But the mind had had nothing to do with it. It was the transient thrilling of molecular memory.

His body had become something for a monster to batten on. Each day it took on fresh repulsiveness. The colors—which now contained disgusting suggestions of decay—blazed out, changed tint, faded, in the manner in which d'Entrecolles first saw the death-flower give out light so long before on the slopes of the Andes in Colombia. Labat realized that there were probably no bounds to this disorderly growth. He knew that in the vegetal kingdom there is no limit to growth until death stops change. The body was cari-caturing the monster d'Entrecolles had hated so long—and feared.

Labat returned to his family. He knew that d'Entrecolles was past help now. And he wished to spare himself the unpleasantness of a closer view.

As DAYS WENT ON, the hideous changes in the body progressed. The ears curled over more and more. But they still kept something of their old power of sound reproduction; and they bore to him the ancient voices of unnumbered seas, unsleeping, which shook what little nerve-resistance still remained within him, with the rhythm of destruction. And before the eyes that neither saw nor knew color any longer, blazed the tragic, lazulite splendor of the tropic ocean.

"GLUED"

H. DE VERE STACPOOLE

I

BRANDT IS A HUNTER. I met him at Seattle before the war, and, a few days ago, I met him again on the boat from Calais to Dover. Hunters are getting fewer and fewer these days. I mean men like Selous and Brandt. The wild parts of the earth are getting more settled, the big herds are thinned or destroyed. Look at elephants—I mean, look for them. Places where twenty years ago they were a natural feature of the scenery, now deserted. Listen for the organ-trombone voice of the hippopotamus by the old rivers where once the hippo sang and bathed. If you hear it, it will be from some upper reach. Tomorrow or next day, you will not hear it at all.

Then again, the markets and museums are against the hunter these days; rare beasts are not so rare, and the price of furs and skins, barring sable and fox, has not increased in proportion to the higher price of living and the fitting out of expeditions. I gathered this from Brandt. He is a bit of a pessimist, and may be wrong; but, anyhow, when I met him the other day, he had "chucked hunting for good," taken up with rubber, and was able to travel Pullman.

On the train up from Dover we fell to talking of the war. Although over forty when the fighting broke out, he had served with the Canadians. That he was a German by extraction did not matter a button to him. He was more than a good shot. He was inevitable with the rifle. You can fancy the execution done by this deadly man as a sniper, till a German got him and smashed up his elbow, and turned his attention to rubber.

"How many did you kill?" I asked.

"It may have been a hundred," said Brandt; "it may have been more. I had good luck. Well, it is over now, and I will never hunt again, except for dollars."

"Are you sorry?" I asked.

"Well, I don't know," said he. "Sometimes I am sorry, and sometimes not. When I was out there in the bush or jungle I was free. I had no money to speak of. Now I have suddenly got money and I am no longer free. Money makes a man a slave. Money is business, don't you forget that.

"Lazy people say to themselves, 'Oh, how I wish I were rich.' forgetting that if they were rich they would have to guard their wealth. You buy a stock, and it goes down. Your brother says, 'Oh, that doesn't matter, it is a good investment.' Just so, but, meanwhile, your capital has shrunk, and that is not very pleasant. You buy a stock and it goes up, and you say to yourself, 'Now, I ought to get out and take my profits.' You have seen the rubber boom and the oil boom. I was in them both. I tell you, there were times when I felt afraid."

"Were you ever frightened in the old days?"

"Once."

"How was that?"

"Well, I am not a man given to talk big, as you know, or to brag. Of course, all old hunters are apt to brag a bit as to the size of beasts or the price of pelts and so on; but they don't brag of courage, because they are not proud of it. The thing comes as a necessity, just like breathing. Without courage, as people call it, a hunter would not live a month, in some places, and would not hunt long in any place—except, maybe, where there were only rabbits. He has it always with him, like his rifle.

"All the same, I lost my courage once, and I will give you a hundred guesses as to what sort of a beast or thing it was that made my heart go down into my boots. Elephant, no—lion, no—tiger, no. Something more terrible than that. What could be more terrible than a tiger? Well, to my mind, a snake is more terrible, but it was not a snake. No, it was something worse than a snake. Give it up?

Well, I will tell you, and if you doubt my word when I've done, ask Tangze. You will find him at the South Kensington Museum. He has given up collecting this fifteen years, and he has got a fixed post now—a sort of professorship, and has got married and fattened up wonderfully since I knew him out in South America.

"He was a bit of a stick of a chap in those days—looked more like one of those dried orchids he was always packing off to Europe than anything else; but there wasn't a man in the two hemispheres that knew more about tropical flora. Beasts were nothing to him; he was a vegetable hunter and nothing else—he didn't even bother about butterflies, I doubt if he would have taken the trouble to catch one, not if it was labeled as being the newest specimen.

"I met him by pure chance. I was in Para, just come back from a trip upcountry with a chap, Lord Wearmouth, who was prospecting for gold with a little hunting thrown in. I don't know who sold him the gold prospectus, but whoever did, sold him a pup. There's no gold south of the Javary. I told him so, and he wouldn't listen to me; but he was a nice chap, and the pay was big, and, as I said, there was hunting of sorts to be done, so I had gone. I was paid off in Para, and that same night I went into a gambling shop kept by a Peruvian and lost everything I had but ten dollars and my equipment.

"I suppose I'm a gambler born, and, anyhow, I've got it back in rubber and oil. But that night I felt pretty bad. It was *trente et quarante*, played in quite a decent shop with women in evening clothes eating ices, and fellows from the upper Amazon dashing down their money by the fistful. But the place seemed like hell to me when the croupier raked in my last off the red. I'd backed red right through.

"I had enough for a drink and something to clink in my pocket, and I stood there for a few minutes when all was done watching the play. Then I went back to the hotel.

II

"I WENT UP TO MY ROOM, turned on the electrics, and sat down in an armchair to have a smoke. I hadn't intended to risk more than twenty dollars when I went into that shop, but card gambling is like quicksands; you get up to your knees, and trying to recover yourself you get up to your waist—and then you're done.

"Well, as I sat there smoking, I had lots to think about. I couldn't pay my hotel bill without selling my equipment, and how to get away I didn't know. But I did know that the worst will do its worst, and that a man, to tackle his luck, isn't much good unless he's had a night's sleep behind him. So I finished my cigar and turned in, and woke next morning with the waiter bringing in my early coffee and a letter.

"It was from a chap in the same hotel. His name was Tangze; he was out on a commission from one of the Rothschilds, if I remember rightly, and his chief man had failed him. Lord Wearmouth had spoken of me to him. He was in room No. 14, and would I call and see him any time that morning? Then there was a postscript, half apologizing for saying that terms would be easily arranged, as money was not the main object of his principal.

"Well, I lay back on the pillows and laughed to think of how I'd given bad luck the slip, leaving only a few dirty dollars in his hands; for there's many a man would have left his sleep behind him, finding himself in the same fix, or maybe put a bullet through his head.

"Soon as I was dressed, I popped in on Tangze. He was a little dried-up chap, as I have said, and he was in his pajamas, writing letters. He jumped up when he heard my name, and under five minutes, from start to finish, we'd fixed terms. They were big terms for a big job. Rothschild, or whoever it was, had fixed his avaricious eye on the flora of the upper Amazon. He wanted to ransack that place, chiefly for orchids; expense was no matter—within limits, of course, and a gunman, being necessary to deal with big game, could ask his own figure.

"It was a week later that we started, taking a Royal Mail boat up the river. I only knew the lower Amazon, not far from Para, and that's as much as to say I didn't know the Amazon at all. The thing isn't rightly a river. It's a world. A world always slipping away to the sea. Day after day and day after day and day after day, pulling against the stream, it was always the same; the great forests and the birds, tracts of swamp where the 'crocs' lay like logs.

"But the one same thing that got on our nerves was the width. It never got narrower. Always the same old sea when one came on deck of a morning. It was in flood, or, more truly speaking, near the end of flood, and the Ithecraly and Javary and half a hundred streams that would have been big rivers in Europe were sending down assortments—tree trunks and dead cattle and suchlike. The water came brown as porter by the banks, and swirling as if the river was alive and in trouble.

"'It will be all right when we reach Remat des Males,' said Tangze. 'The river is sinking now.'

"'I'm thinking that we'll find the going rather stiff after these floods,' I said. 'It will take a lot of sun to dry the forests, to say nothing of the swamps.'

"He hadn't thought of that. There's an awful lot of clever people who don't do much thinking outside the line of their circle. The expedition had been timed wrong for the upper Amazon—and it had been timed by Tangze, who ought to have known better. I told him so, and he agreed. That is the sort of chap he was when he hadn't a touch of liver on him. When his liver woke up he was a different person.

"However, there was no use bothering. But you'll see our position when I tell you that just then whole tracts of country were under water, thousands and thousands of square miles. In fact, the Amazon was a lake as big as Europe in its upper part, a lake maybe not more than three feet deep in places, with forests sticking out of it. Well, when we got to Yaniero, that is to say fifteen hundred miles from the mouth, we found a town on stilts. Being built on piles, the houses in Yaniero have landing stages as well as steps.

"Lord, it's a cheerful place, especially just after the end of the rain, with the forests smoking and big, filthy clouds rolling away overhead. There's nothing fit to eat, and nothing fit to drink, sardines are five dollars a tin, and tobacco a dollar the two ounces—when you can get it. What do the people live on, there? Rubber!

"I don't mean to say they eat it, but, by Jove, they spend it! Big money they make tapping the trees on the estates roundabout. Then

they come into Yaniero and bust their earnings on sardines and
whisky and top boots and Henry Clays that never saw Havana, and
suchlike—and gambling. There was a hotel, and we stayed at it, for
there was nowhere else to stay. We had nothing to do but sit on
the hotel landing stage and watch the floods go down and shoot at
passing alligators. Then we met Ramon.

III

"RAMON WAS A SORT OF SERANG. He bossed the rubber lands on the
estate next above Yaniero on the same bank, and he used to come
to the hotel to get drunk. He led two lives, did Ramon. His sober
life and his drunken life. At work, Pussyfoot J. would have hugged
him; at play, he couldn't. He drank gin mostly, when he could get
it; when he couldn't, he would drink shoe varnish, if that was all
he could get. But, mind you, when I say he got drunk, you mustn't
take me as meaning he made a beast of himself. No, sometimes
he'd be fuddled and dull, and sometimes he'd be talkative, but he
was never objectionable; and when he was talkative, he was the
most interesting Spaniard I've ever come across—that is to say,
when he kept clear of politics.

"He wasn't long in finding us out and our business, and he took
a lot of interest in Tangze. It turned out that Ramon was of the
same sort of build of mind, a sort of born naturalist, with his tastes
running to vegetables. He knew all about orchids. Perira, his master, and the owner of the estate, was worth maybe a million dollars, and took an interest in orchids, and did a lot of collecting
through his rubber gatherers, including Ramon.

"You may fancy how this news flattened out Tangze. He had
come fifteen hundred miles up the Amazon orchid hunting, only
to find that a millionaire Portuguese had been combing the forests
for Lord knows how long. It was plain as a pikestaff that all round
there the place must be skinned, and that there was nothing likely
of interest to be found that had not been found by Perira and sent
off to the botanical gardens of God knows where. There's no use
finding new specimens for a Rothschild if some son of a gun of a

squatter of a Portuguese pops up and says, 'I've got that and stuck my name on it already'—see?

"Well, there we were in that fix, looking up the river and thinking of our new move, when Ramon turned up trumps and took us to his heart. He was pretty sick of Perira, and said so—giving us to understand that he had never done orchid hunting for Perira with any enthusiasm, so to speak. Perira was one of those rich men who'd be richer if they weren't so mean. Instead of giving Ramon full pay for orchid hunting and nothing else, he made him do the hunting in his off time and only gave him a few dollars for his trouble.

"Ramon got Tangze aside now and proposed to lead us into a part of the forests beyond the Javary which he said was no use for rubber but rich in everything else—sand box, euphorbias, mata-matas, and all such, to say nothing of climbers and orchids. He said he'd take a month's holiday which he was entitled to, and lead us, asking only a dollar a day and a commission on anything new we should find.

"Tangze asked him what the commission would be, and Ramon said he'd fix it at a quarter of the market value, that is to say at the market value estimated by Tangze. That was the sort of chap Ramon was. A good bit of nobleman, though as brown as a coffee berry, and with the reputation of having killed three men in quarrels over their wives.

"It was settled that the commission should be paid for anything found on the month's march, and, of course, we fixed it that the commission only held good for things above a certain fixed value. Tangze explained this to Ramon, and Ramon said, '*Sí, señor*.'"

IV

"WHEN THE FLOODS had gone down, we started. We were six altogether, Ramon, myself, Tangze, and three porters to carry tents and grub. I took a cordite rifle, a Luger pistol and a gun I've found the usefulest of any for everything bar big game; it was a double barrel, one barrel choke. I reckon that was the narrowest choke bore ever drilled; close to any big beast, I believe it would have been deadlier than a rifle. I've never measured, but I judge that at ten yards you could have covered the scattering of the shot with a penny—so to speak.

"We left Yaniero on a Tuesday morning at sunup, with the toucans yelping above the trees and the mist blowing away in the morning wind, and every prospect of another hot day. We left in a steam launch we'd hired, with a chap to run her and take her back, and in two minutes we'd turned a bend of the river and Yaniero was out of sight. It was the Javary we were navigating, and you should see that river after the rains, with the last of the dead logs drifting and the alligators sunning themselves, and the smell of river mud and rotten leaves and decaying vegetation and dead bodies of things that'd been drowned months ago.

"It's not a good river at any time. I'm not saying that any tropical river is good; but the Javary beats the band. It's lonesome, it's got a feeling of being tucked away, and it's ugly. Gets on one's spine. However, we weren't tied to it for life, and the place Ramon was seeking for was only thirty miles or so above Yaniero.

"We struck it about two hours before sunset on the second day, landed, camped, and sent the launch back with orders to come again in a month and stick till we turned up. Then we lit our fire and cooked supper, while the porters built a *tambo*. A *tambo's* a shack; they don't take more than a few hours to build, and on a march, unless you're moving on a track where they are already built, you put one up every night. It's like putting up an umbrella. Then, you see, on the return march, you have them ready built for you.

"That night, as we sat round the fire talking and smoking we heard the howling monkeys as we'd never heard them before. The brutes kept pretty shy of Yaniero, but ten miles from houses they came down most to the water's edge, and sang. And they don't really howl—they roar. If you can fancy a couple of dozen children turned into giants and roaring over some broken toy or another, you can fancy a howling monkey concert. We fired a few shots and drove them off a bit, and then when we could hear ourselves thinking, we went on with our talk.

"Ramon was letting himself loose on his pet subject, and I will say that, though I don't take much account of vegetables, his talk interested me a lot. He was a tree doctor as well as a rubber hunter. He seemed to know all about trees and their ailments. He said they suffered just as humans do, got cancer and consumption and so on, and that they had their likes and dislikes. He said also that they fought with one another, and from what I've seen of the jungle above Yaniero I believe he was right. They don't hit out and pelt each other over the heads, they fight with their roots.

"Ramon said that all over the jungle there was always a great battle going on underground between the roots of the pachyuhas and matamatas and rubbers and euphorbias and so on. He said that it wasn't so much tree fighting tree as species fighting species, and where you find great tracts of matamatas, f'rinstance, that was where the matamatas had won a victory long ago and taken up the land for their own people. I believe he was right.

"Well, this chap goes on talking of climbers, air shoots, and water shoots and so on and telling of their ways; and then he tells of an orchid he found and lost more than a year before. He came on it somewhere about that spot. It was hanging between two trees, and it beat creation as far as orchids went, for it had six or seven things like feelers out of it, and at the end of each feeler was a butterfly, a real butterfly as far as looks went, all different colors, yellow, blue, red, striped—and any movement of the air made the butterflies' wings go as if they were flying.

"'Oh, come!' said Tangze at this point. If he'd given Ramon a blow in the face, Ramon couldn't have taken it worse, without hitting him. Tangze had to apologize, which he did handsomely, and the orchid man gave us the end of the yarn. He'd been wandering a bit from camp when he found the thing, and he went back for a companion to help him to hive it. Then when he came back, he couldn't find it again. It had been so high up, hanging from a tree branch, that it wanted two men, one standing on the other's shoulders, to get at it. That's why he went for his companion.

"They hunted here and they hunted there, but still they couldn't find it. They got all the rubber gatherers in and offered a reward of ten dollars to the chap who would spot its whereabouts. Lost time. Then they gave it up as a bad job. Their main business was getting rubber, anyway.

"Ramon hadn't well finished before Tangze struck in with a yarn about the Malay jungle. I went to sleep under my mosquito net in the middle of it, and didn't wake till I was kicked.

"Dawn was up, and we'd got to start. Ramon said we had to negotiate a bad place. But that was an old rubber road which he thought was still open—but wasn't. Not a sign of it. I tell you in that jungle you can cut a road twenty feet broad today, and in a month you won't find it. It's not a matter of quick growing, but of quick flowing— the vegetation spreads like water. I'll give you an idea of what it was like just there where the old road had once been. First there were the trees. Big trees and little trees and thick ones and thin ones, tree ferns and bushes. Looking through the air at noon when a chap'd have got sunstroke in the open if he'd showed his nose without a hat, it was like the inside of a cloud getting along toward evening time. There was something solemner about that bit of jungle than I'd ever struck among trees, and I've seen a good many tracts of forest.

"Looking about you could see far and near as if the air was hung with lace high up. It was the liantasses, and across the lace shooting up like rockets you could see the shoots of the wild pine—air shoots and water shoots. To get a drink, you'd only to cut one of them. Then there were cables of creeper, thick ship's cables; and hanging sagging between the trees and on the cables, here and there, were orchids. Orchids by the hundred, hanging in that steaming heat. You've smelt a glass house when everything is growing, and the furnaces stoked—well, that's the smell that I'm smelling now when I think of those orchids.

"So much for the trees, and everything six feet above ground. If that had been all, traveling would have been a picnic. But Lord!— the undergrowth! It wasn't so much that things grew, but that nearly everything grew thorns. Thorns half a foot long, and thorns you couldn't see till you felt them. Wait-a-bit thorns that had hooks on them same as a fishhook held you back, and while you were dealing with them, good old lazaret thorns jabbed you here and there to make you hurry up.

"Under the thorns ran ground vines to trip you up, and where there weren't vines there were boggy patches to trap you. I'm telling you all this to show you that the Amazon forests—at least, the forests of the upper Amazon—aren't as much forests as strong houses, and that a hundredth part of the things they hold in the way of new species of plants and insects haven't been tapped by naturalists. Why, already on our first day's march, Tangze was finding all sorts of new mosses and suchlike, for the ax men were going before us cutting and slashing with cutlasses to make a road.

"That's how we traveled, cutting our way before us; and I've never felt sicker than I did the first few hours, with the smell of sap and cut, green things. You'd see the sap spurting, sometimes; and when it wasn't spurting, it was always oozing; you'd see the green stuff curling away like snakes cut across. Then after the first few hours, I got used to it, and didn't care. But somehow, ever since that, it's been in my mind that growing things are as much alive as walking things and crawling things, and a forest is almost, as you may say, a living body.

"I didn't get much use for my gun. Vegetables were what we were after, and it came in on me, making me burst out laughing once, that Tangze was a vegetable hunter and nothing else. He was after big game in the way of vegetables. I laughed at the time, when I thought about it; but it wasn't a laughing matter by any means.

"Vegetable big game sounds funny, but it's not funny when you come up against the thing itself. A pachyuha tree's as dangerous as a snake if you come up against it suddenly and feel its teeth before you see them; and there are worse things in the jungle than pachyuha trees. We weren't long in finding that out.

V

"I'M COMING ALONG NOW to the thing that scared me. Scared me stiff for fifteen seconds or so before I got the clutch on my nerves to deal with it.

"I've found out it's the new things that matter in this life. The old things don't count, as far as nerves go. Put a man right in front of what he's never seen nor realized, and his courage—well, it isn't there, just for the minute. You try an earthquake if you want to see—a good old South American seaboard earthquake—or come on what you think is a ghost! Well, it happened this way. Ramon hadn't said anything about fever in his talk at Yaniero. I suppose it was such a common thing in those parts that he forgot to mention it. And the upper Amazon jungle fever is a thing that's best forgotten, anyhow. It's not malaria, as far as I can make out, but a sort of twin brother, and you can catch it without being bitten by mosquitoes. Two days after we left the river, a man went down with it. And who was that man, do you think? Ramon. You'd have sworn that if one of us three went down, it would be either Tangze or me. But it was this chap who you'd have thought to be salted.

"We'd built our second *tambo* and there was nothing for it but to settle down till the chap was better. It took him three days to get his pins under him, and then they were so shaky we decided to stay for another day before pushing on. The *tambo* was built in a clearing, and the jungle round there was thinner than we'd met for some time. That day, having seen that Ramon wanted for nothing, Tangze and I settled to go off on a little prospecting trip of our own; nowhere far—just round a bit to see what we could pick up in the way of plants and animals. We blazed a trail and on top of that we kept the camp within helloing distance; and on top of that I'd got my compass. I'd also taken the double barrel. Of course, we were to stick together and not lose one another.

"Well, now, would you believe it, we hadn't been gone five minutes when I startled a bush pig and was after it, forgetting Tangze and every blamed thing but the game ahead. These bush pigs run queer. Give them clear ground, and they'll beat the band for running; but right in the thick jungle, they'll lie up as often as not, and let you go by them, if you haven't the eyes to spot them.

"This part wasn't specially thick, but there were thick clumps. I could see the beast ahead, or thought I could, till all at once it came to me that I'd gone too far. I stopped in my tracks and shouted. Tangze replied, and he wasn't so far off by the sound of his voice, so I took things easy, and didn't hurry to join up, for there were those patches to be avoided, and the ground was pretty soggy.

"I'd stopped for a moment to look at a water vine that ran double like two tubes connected together, when I heard Tangze's voice to the right of me, and more distant than I'd heard it last. I heard him cry out, 'Hello!' but not louder than if he was talking to a person he'd just come across. Then it came again, quick—'Hello! Hello!' Then I heard him cry out to me—'Brandt—help! help! help!' Just like that. Then I heard him scream. Scream like a stuck pig. I knew it was either pain or terror or both that made him scream like that, and I was into the thick stuff, like a bullet, in the direction of the sound.

"It was all thorns and tangle. If I'd had time I could have got to him quite easy by beating a way round, for, as I was saying, this part of the jungle wasn't bad compared to the rest; but I had no time. It was life or death, and I knew it.

"I hadn't reached him when the screams stopped, but I was right on to him, and the sound of his struggling gave me the last directions. I broke from the tangle into a clearing, and then I saw Tangze. He was standing and struggling there in the twilight, fighting dumbly with something I couldn't tell what, till I saw it was a spider.

The thing was hanging between the trees and the body of it wasn't more than twice as big as a coconut, but it seemed to have fifteen hundred arms, and a lot of them seemed tangled round Tangze. That was my first impression. Then, in the next flash, I saw that the arms were all curled at the ends like tendrils, and I knew for certain that the thing was no spider but a plant made in imitation of a spider—only ten hundred times bigger. I didn't notice the heap of bones of bush pigs and monkeys the thing had been feeding on, but I did notice that Tangze was being lifted off the ground by the tendrils that had got him.

"He was in a Venus flytrap, only made different, and a hundred times bigger. A trap for catching monkeys and pigs and jaguars.

"What did I do? Well, I had no time to think, but by instinct I treated that vegetable as if it had been an animal. I took aim at the body of the brute as it hung there between the trees and sent the contents of both barrels through it. Killed it. The tendrils curled down, and Tangze was dropped on the ground. But that didn't mean he was free.

"When I got up to him, he began to come round, and he shouted to me to keep off, or I'd get stuck up, too. Then it broke on me without any more explaining what was the matter, and how the thing had seized him.

"As he told me after, it was like this: He was working along through the thick stuff when he came to the clearing. He wasn't looking up, else he'd have seen the thing above him. What he did see was long, green tendrils hanging down and curled a bit at the ends. He hadn't more than noticed them, when, making a step forward, his leg touched one of the tendrils, and it stuck to his trousers as if it had been glued. He bent down and caught hold of the tendril to pull it away. It stuck to his bands. He got it away from the cloth of his trousers, but somehow, in doing so, it had glued itself to his coat sleeve—right coat sleeve. He twisted round, trying to free the sleeve, and found he had blundered into another tendril that was round his left leg just above the knee.

"You understand, the plant didn't do a thing, or make a move. All the trapping was done by the chap struggling to free himself. All the same, and it's a pretty grim fact, the plant must have been constructed so's to take advantage of the nervous terror of animals that find themselves trapped.

"A bush pig or a lynx, for instance, passing along there, would have almost sure been caught by the leg. Having no hands to free itself, it would try with its teeth, and get properly glued, for the thing sweated glue from its tendrils when food was near it, just as a man's mouth waters at sight or smell of a good dinner. A monkey caught would have carried on same as Tangze did. The more he struggled, the more he was tangled, and he said it wasn't so much the feeling of being trapped as being glued that made him shout and lose his senses and fight like a maniac. He said the feeling of being caught by stickiness was a lot worse than the feeling of being caught by a tiger.

"Well, with the help of caution and using big leaves to get a grip of the tendrils, I managed to undo him, though I nearly got stuck myself once. Then, when I'd got him free, I looked up to where the rags and remains of the body of the beastly thing was hanging in the air and, putting in two more cartridges, I shot it away.

"I've often thought of what its anatomy must have been. That body and head combined would have sure sucked Tangze's blood when the tendrils had raised him up to it. But I wonder what the mechanism was. Probably not more than the inside of a leech.

"Quite simple, and yet, as I've told you, it was the only thing I've ever shot that frightened me, and I've shot a good few things in my time in the way of beasts and men.

"Here's Victoria."

THE TREE
H. P. LOVECRAFT

"Fata viam invenient."

ON A VERDANT SLOPE of Mount Maenalus, in Arcadia, there stands an olive grove about the ruins of a villa. Close by is a tomb, once beautiful with the sublimest sculptures, but now fallen into as great decay as the house. At one end of that tomb, its curious roots displacing the time-stained blocks of Panhellic marble, grows an unnaturally large olive tree of oddly repellent shape; so like to some grotesque man, or death-distorted body of a man, that the country folk fear to pass it at night when the moon shines faintly through the crooked boughs. Mount Maenalus is a chosen haunt of dreaded Pan, whose queer companions are many, and simple swains believe that the tree must have some hideous kinship to these weird Panisci; but an old bee-keeper who lives in the neighboring cottage told me a different story.

Many years ago, when the hillside villa was new and resplendent, there dwelt within it the two sculptors Kalos and Musides. From Lydia to Neapolis the beauty of their work was praised, and none dared say that the one excelled the other in skill. The Hermes of Kalos stood in a marble shrine in Corinth, and the Pallas of Musides surmounted a pillar in Athens near the Parthenon. All men paid homage to Kalos and Musides, and marvelled that no shadow of artistic jealousy cooled the warmth of their brotherly friendship.

But though Kalos and Musides dwelt in unbroken harmony, their natures were not alike. Whilst Musides revelled by night amidst the urban gaieties of Tegea, Saios would remain at home; stealing away from the sight of his slaves into the cool recesses of the olive grove. There he would meditate upon the visions that filled his mind, and there devise the forms of beauty which later became immortal in breathing marble. Idle folk, indeed, said that Kalos conversed with the spirits of the grove, and that his statues were but images of the fauns and dryads he met there for he patterned his work after no living model.

So famous were Kalos and Musides, that none wondered when the Tyrant of Syracuse sent to them deputies to speak of the costly statue of Tyché which he had planned for his city. Of great size and cunning workmanship must the statue be, for it was to form a wonder of nations and a goal of travellers. Exalted beyond thought would be he whose work should gain acceptance, and for this honor Kalos and Musides were invited to compete. Their brotherly love was well known, and the crafty Tyrant surmised that each, instead of concealing his work from the other, would offer aid and advice; this charity producing two images of unheard of beauty, the lovelier of which would eclipse even the dreams of poets.

With joy the sculptors hailed the Tyrant's offer, so that in the days that followed their slaves heard the ceaseless blows of chisels. Not from each other did Kalos and Musides conceal their work, but the sight was for them alone. Saving theirs, no eyes beheld the two divine figures released by skillful blows from the rough blocks that had imprisoned them since the world began.

At night, as of yore, Musides sought the banquet halls of Tegea whilst Kalos wandered alone in the olive Grove. But as time passed, men observed a want of gaiety in the once sparkling Musides. It was strange, they said amongst themselves that depression should thus seize one with so great a chance to win art's loftiest reward. Many months passed yet in the sour face of Musides came nothing of the sharp expectancy which the situation should arouse.

Then one day Musides spoke of the illness of Kalos, after which none marvelled again at his sadness, since the sculptors' attachment was known to be deep and sacred. Subsequently many went to visit Kalos, and indeed noticed the pallor of his face; but there

was about him a happy serenity which made his glance more magical than the glance of Musides who was clearly distracted with
anxiety and who pushed aside all the slaves in his eagerness to
feed and wait upon his friend with his own hands. Hidden behind
heavy curtains stood the two unfinished figures of Tyché, little
touched of late by the sick man and his faithful attendant.

As Kalos grew inexplicably weaker and weaker despite the min-
istrations of puzzled physicians and of his assiduous friend, he
desired to be carried often to the grove which he so loved. There
he would ask to be left alone, as if wishing to speak with unseen
things. Musides ever granted his requests, though his eyes filled
with visible tears at the thought that Kalos should care more for
the fauns and the dryads than for him. At last the end drew near,
and Kalos discoursed of things beyond this life. Musides, weeping,
promised him a sepulchre more lovely than the tomb of Mausolus;
but Kalos bade him speak no more of marble glories. Only one wish
now haunted the mind of the dying man; that twigs from certain
olive trees in the grove be buried by his resting place-close to his
head. And one night, sitting alone in the darkness of the olive grove,
Kalos died. Beautiful beyond words was the marble sepulchre which
stricken Musides carved for his beloved friend. None but Kalos
himself could have fashioned such basreliefs, wherein were displayed all the splendours of Elysium. Nor did Musides fail to bury
close to Kalos' head the olive twigs from the grove.

As the first violence of Musides' grief gave place to resigna-
tion, he labored with diligence upon his figure of Tyché. All honour
was now his, since the Tyrant of Syracuse would have the work of
none save him or Kalos. His task proved a vent for his emotion
and he toiled more steadily each day, shunning the gaieties he once
had relished. Meanwhile his evenings were spent beside the tomb
of his friend, where a young olive tree had sprung up near the
sleeper's head. So swift was the growth of this tree, and so strange
was its form, that all who beheld it exclaimed in surprise; and
Musides seemed at once fascinated and repelled.

Three years after the death of Kalos, Musides despatched a
messenger to the Tyrant, and it was whispered in the agora at Tegea

that the mighty statue was finished. By this time the tree by the tomb had attained amazing proportions, exceeding all other trees of its kind, and sending out a singularly heavy branch above the apartment in which Musides labored. As many visitors came to view the prodigious tree, as to admire the art of the sculptor, so that Musides was seldom alone. But he did not mind his multitude of guests; indeed, he seemed to dread being alone now that his absorbing work was done. The bleak mountain wind, sighing through the olive grove and the tomb-tree, had an uncanny way of forming vaguely articulate sounds.

The sky was dark on the evening that the Tyrant's emissaries came to Tegea. It was definitely known that they had come to bear away the great image of Tyché and bring eternal honour to Musides, so their reception by the proxenoi was of great warmth. As the night wore on a violent storm of wind broke over the crest of Maenalus, and the men from far Syracuse were glad that they rested snugly in the town. They talked of their illustrious Tyrant, and of the splendour of his capital and exulted in the glory of the statue which Musides had wrought for him. And then the men of Tegea spoke of the goodness of Musides, and of his heavy grief for his friend and how not even the coming laurels of art could console him in the absence of Kalos, who might have worn those laurels instead. Of the tree which grew by the tomb, near the head of Kalos, they also spoke. The wind shrieked more horribly, and both the Syracusans and the Arcadians prayed to Aiolos.

In the sunshine of the morning the proxenoi led the Tyrant's messengers up the slope to the abode of the sculptor, but the night wind had done strange things. Slaves' cries ascended from a scene of desolation, and no more amidst the olive grove rose the gleaming colonnades of that vast hall wherein Musides had dreamed and toiled. Lone and shaken mourned the humble courts and the lower walls, for upon the sumptuous greater peri-style had fallen squarely the heavy overhanging bough of the strange new tree, reducing the stately poem in marble with odd completeness to a mound of unsightly ruins. Strangers and Tegeans stood aghast, looking from the wreckage to the great, sinister tree whose aspect was so weirdly human and whose roots reached so queerly into the sculptured sepulchre of Kalos. And their fear and dismay increased when they searched the fallen apartment, for of the gentle Musides, and of the marvellously fashioned image of Tyché, no trace could be discovered. Amidst such stupendous ruin only chaos dwelt, and the representatives of two cities left disappointed; Syracusans that they had no statue to bear home, Tegeans that they had no artist to crown. However, the Syracusans obtained after a while a very splendid statue in Athens, and the Tegeans consoled themselves by erecting in the agora a marble temple commemorating the gifts, virtues, and brotherly piety of Musides.

But the olive grove still stands, as does the tree growing out of the tomb of Kalos, and the old bee-keeper told me that sometimes the boughs whisper to one another in the night wind, saying over and over again. "*Οιδα! Οιδα!*—I know! I know!"

THROUGH THE CRATER'S RIM
A. HYATT VERRILL

I

Through the Crater's Rim

"I TELL YOU IT'S THERE," declared Lieutenant Hazen decisively. "It may not be a civilized city, but it's no Indian village or native town. It's big—at least a thousand houses—and they're built of stone or something like it and not of thatch."

"You've been dreaming, Hazen," laughed Fenton. "Or else you're just trying to jolly us."

"Do you think I'd hand in an official report of a dream?" retorted the Lieutenant testily. "And it's gospel truth I've been telling you."

"Never mind Fenton," I put in. "He's a born pessimist and skeptic anyhow. How much did you actually see?"

We were seated on the veranda of the Hotel Washington in Colon and the aviator had been relating how, while making a reconnaissance flight over the unexplored and unknown jungles of Darien, he had sighted an isolated, flat topped mountain upon whose summit was a large city—of a thousand houses or more—and without visible pass, road or stream leading to it.

"It was rotten air," Hazen explained in reply to my question. "And I couldn't get lower than 5,000 feet. So I can't say what the people were like. But I could see 'em running about the first time I went over and they were looking mightily excited. Then I flew back for a second look and not a soul was in sight—took to cover I expect. But I'll swear the buildings were stone or 'dobe and not palm or thatch."

"Why didn't you land and get acquainted?" enquired Fenton sarcastically.

"There was one spot that looked like a pretty fair landing," replied the aviator. "But the air was bad and the risk too big. How did I know the people weren't hostile? It was right in the Kuna Indian country and even if they were peaceable they might have smashed the plane or I mightn't have been able to take off. I was alone too."

"You say you made an official report of your discovery," I said. "What did the Colonel think about it?"

"Snorted and said he didn't see why in blazes I bothered reporting an Indian village."

"It's mighty interesting," I declared. "I believe you've actually seen the Lost City, Hazen. Balboa heard of it. The Dons spent years hunting for it and every Indian in Darien swears it exists."

"Well, I never heard of it before," said Hazen, "What's the yarn, anyway?"

"According to the Indian story there's a big city on a mountain top somewhere in Darien. They say no one has ever visited it, that it's guarded by evil spirits and that it was there ages before the first Indians."

"If they've never seen it how do they know it's there?" Fenton demanded. "In my opinion it's all bosh. How can there be a 'lost city' in this bally little country and why hasn't someone found it? Why, there are stories of lost cities and hidden cities and such rot in every South and Central American country. Just fairy tales-pure bunk!"

"I know there are lots of such yarns," I admitted. "And most of them I believe are founded on fact. Your South American Indian hasn't enough imagination to make a story out of whole cloth. It's easy to understand why and how such a place might exist for centuries and no one find it. This 'little country' as you call it could hide a hundred cities in its jungles and no one be the wiser. No civilized man has ever yet been through the Kuna country. But I'm going. I'll have a try for that city of Hazen's."

"Well, I wish you luck," said Fenton. "If the Kunas don't slice off the soles of your feet and turn you loose in the bush and if you *do* find Hazen's pipe dream, just bring me back a souvenir, will you?"

With this parting shot he rose and sauntered off towards the swimming pool.

"Do you really mean to have a go at that place?" asked Hazen as Fenton disappeared.

"I surely do," I declared, "Can you show me the exact spot on the map where you saw the city?"

For the next half hour we pored over the map of Panama and while—owing to the incorrectness of the only available maps—Hazen could not be sure of the exact location of his discovery, still he pointed out a small area within which the strange city was located.

"You're starting on a mighty dangerous trip," he declared as I talked over my plans. "Even if you get by the Kunas and find the place how are you going to get out? The people may kill you or make you a prisoner. If they've been isolated for so long I reckon they won't let any news of 'em leak out."

"Of course there's a risk," I laughed. "That's what makes it so attractive. I'm not worried over the Kunas though. They're not half as bad as painted. I spent three weeks among them two years ago and had no trouble. They may drive me back, but they don't kill people offhand. Getting out will be the trouble as you say. But I've first got to get in and I'm not making plans to get out until then."

"Lord, but I wish I were going too!" cried Hazen. "Say, I tell you what I'm going to do. I'll borrow that old Curtiss practice boat and fly over there once in a while. If you're there, just wave a white rag for a signal. Maybe the people'll be so darned scared if they see the plane that they'll not trouble you. Might make a good play of it—let 'em think you're responsible for it you know."

"I don't know but that's mighty good scheme, Hazen," I replied, after a moment's thought. "Let's see. If I get off day after tomorrow I should be in the Kuna country in a week. You might take your first flight ten days from now. But if things go wrong I don't see as you can help me much if you can't land,"

"We'll worry over that when the time comes," he said cheerfully. A few days later I was being paddled and poled up the Canazas

River with the last outposts of civilization many miles behind and the unknown jungles and the forbidden country of the wild Kunas ahead.

It was with the greatest difficulty that I had been able to secure men to accompany me, for the natives looked with the utmost dread upon the Kuna country and only two, out of the scores I had asked, were willing to tempt fate and risk their lives in the expedition into the unknown.

For two days now we had been within the forbidden district—the area guarded and held by the Kunas and into which no outsider is permitted to enter—and yet we had seen or heard no signs of Indians. But I was too old a hand and too familiar with the ways of South American Indians to delude myself with the idea that we had not been seen or our presence known. I well knew that, in every likelihood, we had been watched and our every movement known since the moment we entered the territory. No doubt, sharp black eyes were constantly peering at us from the jungle, while bows and blowguns were ever ready to discharge their missiles of death at any instant. As long as we were not molested or interfered with, however, I gave little heed to this. Moreover, I believed, from my brief acquaintance with the Kunas of two years previously, that they seldom killed a white man until after he had been warned out of their country and tried to return to it.

At night we camped beside the river, making our beds upon the warm dry sand and each day we poled the cayuca up the rapids and deeper into the forest. At last we reached the spot where, according to my calculations, we must strike through the jungle overland to reach the mountain seen by Hazen. Hiding our dugout in the thick brush beside the river we packed the few necessities to be carried with us and started off through the forest.

If Hazen were not mistaken in his calculations, we should reach the vicinity of the mountain in two days' march, even though the going was hard and we were compelled to hew a way with our machetes for miles at a stretch.

But it's one thing to find a mountain top when flying over the sea of jungle and quite another to find that mountain when hidden deep in the forest and surrounded on every side by enormous trees. I realized that we might wander for days, searching for the mountain without finding it. It was largely a matter of luck after all. But Hazen had described the surrounding country so minutely, that I had high hopes of success.

By the end of the first day in the bush we had reached rough and hilly country, which promised well, and it was with the expectation of reaching the base of the mountain the following day that we made camp that night. Still we had seen no Indians, no signs of their trails or camps, which did much to calm the fears of my men and which I accounted for on the theory that the Kunas avoided this part of the country through superstitious fears of the lost city and its people.

At daybreak we broke camp and had tramped for perhaps three hours when, without warning, Jose, who was last in line, uttered a terrified cry. Turning quickly I was just in time to see him throw up his hands and fall in a heap with a long arrow quivering in his back. The Kunas were upon us.

Scarcely had the realization come to me when an arrow thudded sharply into a tree by my side and Carlos, with a wild yell of deadly fear, threw down his load and dashed madly away. Not an Indian could be seen. To stand there, a target for their missiles was suicidal, and turning, I fled at my utmost speed after Carlos. How we managed to run through that tangled jungle is still a mystery to me, but we made good time, nevertheless Fear drove us and dodging between the giant trees, leaping over rocks, we sped on.

And now, from behind, we could hear the sounds of the pursuing Indians; their low guttural cries, the sounds of breaking twigs and branches; constantly they were drawing nearer. I knew that in a few minutes they would be upon us—that at any instant a poisoned blowgun dart or a barbed arrow might bury itself in my body; but still we strove to escape.

Then, just as I felt that the end must be at hand—just as I had decided to turn and sell my life dearly—the forest thinned. Before us sunlight appeared and the next moment we dashed from the jungle into a space free from underbrush but covered with enormous trees draped with gnarled and twisted lianas. The land here rose sharply and, glancing ahead between the trees, I saw the indistinct outlines of a lofty mountain against the sky.

Toiling up the slope, breathing heavily, utterly exhausted, I kept on. Then, as a loud shout sounded from the rear, I turned to see five hideously painted Kunas break from the jungle. But they did not follow. To my utter amazement they halted, gave a quick glance about, and, with a chorus of frightened yells, turned and dashed back into the shelter of the jungle.

But I had scant time to give heed to this. The Kunas' cries were still ringing in my ears when a scream from Carlos drew my attention. Thinking him attacked by savages I rushed toward him, drawing my revolver as I ran.

With bulging, rolling eyes, blanched face and ghastly, terror stricken features he was struggling, fighting madly, with a writhing, coiling gray object which I took for a gigantic snake. Already his body and legs were bound and helpless in the coils. With his machete he was raining blows upon the quivering awful thing which slowly, menacingly wavered back and forth before him, striving to throw another coil about his body.

And then as I drew near, my senses reeled, I felt that I was in some awful nightmare. The object, so surely, relentlessly, silently encircling and crushing him was no serpent but a huge liana drooping from the lofty branches of a great tree!

It seemed absolutely incredible, impossible, unbelievable. But even as I gazed, transfixed with horror, paralyzed by the sight, the vine threw its last coil about the dying man and before my eyes drew the quivering body into the trees above.

Then something touched my leg. With a wild yell of terror I leaped aside. A second vine was writhing and twisting over the ground towards me! Crazed with unspeakable fear I struck at the thing with my machete. At the blow the vine drew sharply back while from the gash a thick, yellowish, stinking juice oozed forth. Turning, I started to rush from the accursed spot but as I passed the first tree another liana writhed forward in my path.

Utterly bereft of my senses, slashing madly as I ran, yelling like a madman, I dodged from tree to tree, seeking the open spaces, evading by a hair's breadth the fearful, menacing, serpent-like vines, until half-crazy, torn, panting and utterly spent dashed forth into a clear grassy space. Before me, rising like a sheer wall against the sky was a huge precipitous cliff of red rock. Now I knew why the Kunas had not followed us beyond the jungle. They were aware of the man-killing lianas and had left us to a worse death than any they could inflict. I was safe from them I felt sure. But was I any better off? Before me was an impassable mountain side. On either hand and in the rear those awful, bloodthirsty, sinister vines and, lurking in the jungles, were the savage Kunas with their fatal poisoned darts and powerful bows. I was beset on every side by deadly peril, for I was without food, I had cast aside my gun and even my revolver in my blind, terror-crazed escape from those ghastly living vines, and to remain where I was meant death by starvation or thirst.

But anything was better than this nightmare-like forest. At the thought I glanced with a shudder at the trees and my blood seemed to freeze in my veins.

The forest was approaching me? I could not believe my eyes. Now I felt I must be mad, and fascinated, hypnotized, I gazed, striving my utmost to clear my brain, to make common sense contradict the evidence of my eyes. But it was no delusion. Ponderously, slowly, but steadily the trees were gliding noiselessly up the slope! Their great gnarled roots were creeping and undulating over the ground while the pendant vines writhed and swayed and darted forth in all directions as if feeling their way. And then I saw what had before escaped me. The things were not lianas as I thought— huge, lithe, flexible tentacles springing from a thick, fleshy livid- hued crown of branches armed with stupendous thorns and which slowly opened and closed like hungry jaws above the huge trunks.

It was monstrous, uncanny, supernatural. A hundred yards and more of open ground had stretched between me and the forest when I had flung myself down, but now a scant fifty paces remained. In a few brief moments the fearsome things would be upon me. But I was petrified, incapable of moving hand or foot, too terrified and overwhelmed even to cry out.

Nearer and nearer the ghastly things came. I could hear the pounding of my heart. A cold sweat broke out on my body. I shivered as with ague. Then a long, warty, tentacle darted towards me and as the loathsome stinking thing touched my hand the spell was broken. With a wild scream I turned and dashed blindly towards the precipice, seeking only to delay, only to avoid for a time the certain awful death to which I was doomed, for the cliff barred all escape and I could go no further.

II

Amazing Discoveries

A DOZEN LEAPS and I reached the wall of rock beyond which all retreat was cut off. Close at hand was an outjutting buttress, and thinking that back of this I might hide and thus prolong my life, I raced for it.

Panting, unseeing, I reached the projection, ducked behind it, and to my amazement and unspeakable delight, found myself in a narrow canyon or defile, like a huge cleft in the face of the precipice.

Here was safety for a time. The terrible man-eating trees could not enter, and striving only to put a greater distance between myself and the vegetable demons I never slackened my pace as I turned and sped up the canyon.

Narrower and narrower it became. Far above my head the rocky walls leaned inward, shutting out the light until soon it was so dim and shadowy that, through sheer necessity, I was forced to stop running and to pick my way carefully over the masses of rock that strewed the canyon's floor. Presently only a narrow ribbon of sky was visible between the towering walls of the pass. Then this was blotted out and I found myself in the inky blackness of a tunnel—an ancient watercourse—leading into the very bowels of the mountain.

But there was no use in hesitating. Anything was preferable to the cannibal trees, and groping my way I pressed on. Winding and twisting, turning sharply, the passageway led, ever ascending steeply and taxing my exhausted muscles and overwrought system to the utmost. Then, far ahead, I heard the faint sound of dripping, falling water and with joy at thought of burying my aching head in the cold liquid, and of easing my parched, dry throat, I hurried, stumbling, through the tunnel.

At last, I saw a glimmer of light in the distance and in it the sparkle of the water. Before me was the end of the tunnel and sunlight and with a final spurt of speed I rushed towards it. Then, just as I gained the opening, and so suddenly and unexpectedly that he seemed to materialize from thin air, a man rose before me.

Unable to check my speed, too thunderstruck at the apparition to halt. I dashed full into him and together we rolled head over heels upon the ground,

I have said he was a man. But even in that brief second that I glimpsed him, before I bowled him over, I realized that he was unlike any man I or anyone else had ever seen. Barely three feet in height, squat, with enormous head and shoulders, he stood shakily upon the tiniest of bandy legs and half supported his weight by his enormously long muscular arms. Had it not been that he was partly clothed and that his face was hairless, I should have thought him an ape. And now, as I picked myself up and stared at him, my jaws gaped in utter amazement. The fellow was running from me at top speed upon his hands, his feet waving and swaying in the air!

So utterly dumbfounded was I at the sight that I stood there silently gazing after the strange being until he vanished behind a clump of bushes. Then as it dawned upon me that as he had shown no sign of hostility, they were likely peaceable, I hurried after him.

A narrow trail led through the brush and running along this I burst from the shrubbery and came to an abrupt halt, utterly astounded at the sight which met my eyes. I was standing at the verge of a little rise beyond which stretched an almost circular, level plain several miles in diameter. Massed upon this in long rows, compact groups and huge squares, were hundreds of low, flat-roofed, stone buildings, while upon a smooth green plot at a little distance, stood a massive truncated pyramid.

Unwittingly I had reached my goal.

Before me was the lost city of Darien. Hazen had been right!

But it was not this thought not the strange city and its buildings that held my fascinated gaze, but the people. Everywhere they swarmed. Upon the streets, the housetops, even on the open land of the plain, they crowded and each and every one an exact counterpart of the one with whom I had collided at the mouth of the tunnel. And, like him too, all were walking or running upon their hands with their feet in air!

All this I saw in the space of a few seconds. Then, to add to my astonishment, I saw that many of the impossible beings actually were carrying burdens in their upraised feet! Some bore baskets, others jars or pots, others bundles, while one group that was approaching in my direction, held bows and arrows in their toes, and held them most menacingly at that!

It was evident that I had been seen. The excitement of the beings, their gestures and the manner in which they peered toward me from between their arms, left no doubt of it, while the threatening defensive attitude of the bowmen proved that they were ready to attack or defend at a moment's notice.

No doubt, to them, my appearance was as remarkable, as inexplicable and as amazing as they were to me. The greater portion were evidently filled with terror and scurried into their houses, yet many still stood their ground, while a few were so overcome with curiosity and surprise that they dropped feet to earth and rested right side up in order to stare at me more intently.

I realized that it behooved me to do something. To stand there motionless and speechless, gazing at the strange folk while they stared back, would accomplish nothing. But what to do, what move to make? That was a serious question. If I attempted to approach them a shower of arrows might well end my career and my investigations of the place then and there. It was equally useless to retrace my steps, even had I been so minded, for only certain death lay back of me. By some means I must win the confidence or friendship of these outlandish beings if only temporarily. A thousand ideas flashed through my mind.

If only Hazan would appear the creatures of the city might think I had dropped from the sky and so look upon me as a supernatural being. But it was hopeless to expect such a coincidence or to look for him. I had told him to fly over on the tenth day and this was only the seventh. If only I had retained my revolver the discharge of the weapon might frighten them into thinking me a god. But my firearms lay somewhere in the demon forest, I had heard no sounds of voices, no shouting, and I wondered if the beings were dumb. Maybe, I thought, if I should speak—should yell—I might impress them. But, on the other hand, the sound of my voice might break the spell and cause them to attack me. A single mistake, the slightest false move, might seal my doom. I was in a terrible quandary. All my former experiences with savage unknown tribes passed through my mind, and I strove to think of some incident, some little event, which had saved the day in the past and might be put to good use now.

And as I thus pondered I unconsciously reached in my pocket for my pipe, filled it with tobacco and placing it between my lips, struck a match and puffed forth a cloud of smoke. Instantly, from the weird-creatures, a low, wailing, sibilant sound arose. The archers dropped their bows and arrows and, with one accord, the people threw themselves grovelling on the ground. Unintentionally I had solved the problem. To these beings I was a fire-breathing, awful god!

Realizing this, knowing that when dealing with primitive races full of superstitions one must instantly follow up an advantage, I hesitated no longer. Puffing lustily at my pipe I strode forward and approached the nearest prostrate group. Motionless they buried their faces in "the dust, bodies pressed to earth, not daring to look up or even steal a surreptitious glance at the terrible, smoke-belching being who towered over them. Never had I seen such a demonstration of abject fear, such utter debasement. It really was pitiful to see them, to view their trembling, panting bodies quivering with nameless terror; terror so great they dared not flee, even though they knew by my footsteps that I was among them, and feared that at any moment an awful doom might descend upon them.

But their very fright defeated my purpose. I had won safety and even adoration perhaps, but there could be no amity, no intercourse, no means of mingling with them, of securing food, of learning anything if they were to remain cowering on the ground. By some means I must win a measure of their confidence, I must prove that I was a friendly beneficent deity and yet I must still be able to impress them with my powers and control through fear.

It was a delicate matter to accomplish, but it had to be done. Almost at my feet lay one of the archers—a leader or chieftain I thought from the feather ornaments he wore—and stooping, I lifted, him gently. At my touch he fairly palpitated with terror, but no frightened scream, no sound save an indrawn snake-like hiss, escaped his lips, and he offered no resistance as I lifted him to a kneeling position.

Hitherto I had had no opportunity to obtain a good view of these people, but now I saw this fellow close at hand I was amazed at his repulsive ugliness. I have seen some rather ugly races, but all of them combined and multiplied a hundredfold would be beauties compared to these dwarfed, topsy-turvy, denizens of the lost city. Almost black, low browed, with tiny, shifty eyes like those of a reptile, with enormous, thick lipped mouths, sharp, fang-like teeth and matted hair, the bowman seemed far more like an ape than like a human being. And then I noticed a most curious thing. He had no ears! Where they should have been were merely round, bare spots covered with light colored thin membrane like the ears of a frog. For an instant I thought it a malformation or an injury. But as I glanced at the others I saw that all were the same. Not one possessed a human ear! All this I took in as I lifted the fellow up. Then as he tremblingly raised his head and eyed me I spoke to him, trying to make my tones gentle and reassuring. But there was no response, no sign of intelligence or understanding in his dull, frightened eyes. There was nothing to do but to fall back on sign language and rapidly I gestured, striving to convey to him that I would do no injury or harm, that I was friendly and that I wished the people to rise. Slowly a look of comprehension dawned upon his ugly face and then, to prove my friendship, I fished in my pocket, found a tiny mirror and placed it in his hand. At the expression of utter astonishment that overspread his ugly features as he looked in the glass I roared with laughter. But the mirror won the day. Uttering sharp, strange, hissing sounds, the fellow conveyed the news to his companions and slowly, hesitatingly and with lingering fear still on their faces, the people rose and gazed upon me with strangely mingled awe and curiosity.

Mainly they were men, but scattered among them were many who evidently were women, although all were so uniformly repulsive in features that it was difficult to distinguish the sexes. All too, were clad much alike in single garments of bark-cloth resembling gunny sacks with, holes cut at the four corners for legs and arms and an opening for the head.

But while there was no variation in the form or material of the clothing yet some wore ornaments and others did not. Leg and arm bands of woven fibre were common. Many of the men had decorations of bright hued feathers attached to arms or legs or fastened about their waists and many were elaborately tattooed. That such primitive dwarfed, ugly, degenerate creatures could have built the city of stone houses, could have laid out the broad paved streets and could have developed so much of civilization, seemed incredible.

But I had little time to devote to such thoughts. The fellow I had presented with the mirror was hissing at me like a serpent and by signs was trying to indicate that I was to follow him. So, with the crowd trailing behind us, we started up the road towards the centre of the city.

III

Before the King

TRULY NO STRANGER procession had ever been seen by human eyes.

Before me, the chief archer led the way, walking upon his great calloused hands and with his bow grasped firmly in one prehensile foot and his precious mirror in the other. On either side and in the rear were scores of the weird beings hurrying along on their hands, keeping up an incessant hissing sound like escaping steam; black legs and feet waving and gesticulating in air and, at first glance, appearing like a crowd of headless dwarfs. How I wished that Fenton might have been there to see!

Apparently my actions had been closely watched from the safe retreats of the houses and word passed that I was not to be feared, for as we reached the first buildings, the edges of the roofs and the tiny window slits were lined with curious, ugly faces peering at us. It was then that I noticed that none of the buildings had doors, the walls rising blank to the roofs save for the narrow windows, while ladders, here and there in place, proved that the inhabitants, like the Pueblo Indians, entered and left their dwellings through the roofs.

Now and then as we passed along, some of the more venturesome beings would join the procession, scrambling nimbly down the ladders, sometimes upside down on their hands, often using both hands and feet, but always using hands only as soon as they reached the ground.

How or why they had developed this extraordinary mode of progression puzzled me greatly, for there seemed no scientifically good reason for it. Among tribes who habitually use boats, weak legs and enormously developed shoulders, chests and arms are common, and I could well understand how a race, depending entirely upon water for transportation, might, through generations of inbreeding and isolation, lose the use of legs.

But here was a people who apparently had no conveyances of any kind, who must of necessity travel about to cultivate their crops, who must carry heavy burdens in order to construct their buildings and to whom legs would seem a most important matter, and yet with legs and feet so atrophied and arms so tremendously developed that they walked on their hands and used their feet as auxiliaries. It was a puzzle I longed to solve and that I would have investigated thoroughly had fate permitted me to dwell longer in the strange city. But I am getting ahead of my story.

Presently we reached a large central square surrounded by closely set buildings. Approaching one of these, my guide signalled that I was to follow him as he swiftly ascended the ladder to the roof. Rather hesitatingly, for I doubted if the frail affair would support my weight, I climbed gingerly up and found myself upon the broad, flat roof. Before me were several dark openings with the ends of ladders projecting from them and down one of these my guide led the way. At the bottom of the ladder I was in a large, obscure room, lit only by the slits of windows high in the walls, and for a moment I could see nothing of my surroundings, although from all sides issued the low hissing sounds that I now knew were the language of these remarkable people. Then, as my eyes became accustomed to the dim light, I saw that a score of beings were squatted about the sides of the room, while, directly before me, on a raised dais or platform, was seated the largest and ugliest individual I had seen.

That he was a ruler, a king or high priest, was evident. In place of the sack-like garment of his people he was clad in a long rove of golden green feathers. Upon his head was a feather crown of the same hue. About his wrists and ankles were golden bands studded with huge uncut emeralds, and a string of the same stones hung upon his chest.

The throne, if such it could be called, was draped with a green and gold rug and everywhere, upon the walls of the chamber, were paintings of strange misshapen, uncouth creatures and human beings all in the same green and yellow tints. Something in the surroundings, in the drawings and the costume of the king, reminded me of the Aztecs or Mayas and while quite distinct from either I felt sure that, in some long past time, these dwellers of the lost city had been influenced by or had been in contact with, these ancient civilizations.

As I stood before the dais my guide prostrated himself before the green robed monarch and then rising, carried on what appeared to be an animated account of my arrival and the subsequent happenings.

As he spoke, silence fell upon those present and the king listened attentively, glancing now and then at me and regarding me with an expression of combined fear, respect and enmity. I could readily understand what his feelings were. No doubt he was a person of far greater intelligence than his subjects, and while more or less afraid of such a strange being as myself, and superstitious enough to think me supernatural, yet in me he saw a possible usurper of his own power and prominence and, if he had dared, he would have been only too glad to have put me out of the way.

At the end of the archer's narrative the fellow handed his mirror to the king who uttered a sharp exclamatory hiss as he saw his own ugly countenance reflected in it. Forgetting court etiquette and conventions in their curiosity, the others gathered about and as the mirror passed from hand to hand their amazement knew no bounds.

All of these men I now saw were clad in green or green and white and were evidently of high rank, priests or courtiers I took it, but otherwise were as undersized and repulsive as the common people on the streets.

Suddenly I was aroused from my contemplation of the room and its occupants by my guide who came close and by signs ordered me to perform the miracle of smoking. Very ceremoniously and deliberately I drew out my pipe, filled it and struck a match. At the bright flare of the flame king and courtiers uttered a wailing hiss of fear and threw themselves upon the floor. But they were of different stuff from their people, or else the guide had prepared them for the event, for the king soon raised his head, and glancing dubiously at me and finding I had not vanished in fire and smoke, as he no doubt expected, he resumed his sitting posture and in sharp tones ordered his fellows to do likewise.

But despite this it was very evident that he and his friends were in dread of the smoke from my mouth and nose while the tobacco fumes caused them to sputter and cough and choke. This at last was more than even the king could stand, and by signs he made it clear that he wished me to end the demonstration of my fire eating ability. Then he rose, and, to my unbounded surprise, stood erect and stepped forward like an ordinary mortal upon his feet. Here was an extraordinary thing. Was the king of a distinct race or stock or was the use of nether limbs for walking confined to the royal family or to individuals?

It was a fascinating scientific problem to solve. I had no time to give it any consideration, however, for the king was now addressing me in his snake-like dialect and was trying hard to make his meaning clear by signs. For a moment I was at a loss, but presently I grasped his meaning. He was asking whence I had come, and from the frequency with which he pointed upward I judged he thought I had dropped from the sky.

Then a brilliant idea occurred to me as I remembered Hazan's story and his suggestion regarding his return by plane. Pointing upward I made the best imitation of a motor's exhaust that I could manage. There was no doubt that the monarch grasped the meaning. He grinned, nodded and swept his arm in a wide semicircle around his head, evidently to represent the course of the plane when Hazen had flown over the city.

Seemingly, satisfied and, I judged, deeply impressed as well, he resumed his seat, gave a few orders to his fellows and summoning my guide spoke a few words to him. Thereupon the archer signalled me to follow and led the way across the room. But I noticed that the king had not returned the mirror.

Ascending the ladder to the roof the fellow hurried across to a second building, scrambled down another ladder and we entered a large room. In one corner swung a large fiber hammock; in the centre was spread cloth decorated in green and gold, and as we entered two women appeared, each carrying handsome earthenware dishes of food whose savory odors whetted my already ravenous appetite.

Marvelous as it was to see these impossible beings carrying food in their uplifted feet and walking on their hands, yet I had now become somewhat accustomed to the people and I was so famished that I hardly gave the upside down serving maids a second glance.

The food was excellent—consisting of vegetables, some sort of fricassee game and luscious fruits—and as I ate my guide squatted near and regarded me with the fixed, half adoring, half frightened look that one sees on the face of a strange puppy.

I judged that he had been appointed my own personal guard or valet—it mattered little which—and I was not sorry, for he seemed a fairly decent specimen of his race and we already had become pretty well accustomed to each other's signs and gestures. Wishing to still further establish myself in his confidence, and feeling rather sorry for him because of the loss of his treasured mirror, I searched my pockets for some other trinket. My possessions however were limited. They consisted of a stub of a lead-pencil, a note book, a few coins, my handkerchief, my watch, my pocket-knife, a few loose pistol cartridges, my pipe and tobacco and a box of matches. As I drew all these out a sudden fear gripped me. I had barely a dozen matches remaining and my supply of tobacco was perilously low. What would happen when I could no longer produce fire and smoke when called upon to do so?

But I controlled my fears and comforted myself with the thought that possibly, after having felt the effects of tobacco smoke, the king would not soon demand another miracle at my hands and that, before either matches or tobacco was exhausted, something might well happen to solve any problems that might arise. Nevertheless I heartily wished that I had arranged with Hazen to bring supplies in case they were needed and which he could have easily dropped as he flew over.

It would, I now realized, have proved an extremely impressive thing for the people to have seen me secure my magic from the giant roaring bird in the sky. But I had never of course dreamed of such adventures as I had met and could not possibly have foreseen the need of such things. Just the same I cursed myself for a stupid fool for not having provided for any contingency and especially for not having arranged a series of signals with Hazen, However, I was familiar with wigwagging and decided that, if necessity arose, it would be quite feasible for me to signal to him by means of my handkerchief tied on a stick. Also, I felt a bit easier in my mind from knowing that near the city was a splendid landing place for the plane and that Hazen, if signalled, would unquestionably attempt a descent.

Truly it was not every explorer in a predicament like mine who could count on being able to summon aid from the clouds if worst came to worst or who knew that a friend in an airplane would keep track of his whereabouts, indeed, I almost chuckled at these incredible folk and yet within two hundred miles of the Canal and civilization and with another American due to hover above—and even communicate with me—within the next three days. It was all so dreamlike, so utterly preposterous that I scarcely could force myself to believe it and, having dined well and feeling desperately tired, I flung myself into the hammock and almost instantly dropped off to sleep.

It was still daylight when I awoke and the room was empty. Ascending the ladder to the roof without meeting anyone, I climbed down the other ladder to the street. Many people were about and while a few, especially the women and children, threw themselves on their faces or scampered into their houses at my approach, yet the majority merely prostrated themselves for a moment and then stood, supporting themselves in their ape-like way, and stared curiously at me. I had gone but a short distance when my valet came hurrying to my side. But he made no objections to my going where I wished and I was glad to see that my movements were not to be hampered as I was anxious thoroughly to explore the city and its neighborhood. Curious to learn the purpose of the pyramidal structure I had noticed I proceeded in that direction and was soon in a part of the town given over to stalls, shops and markets. There were also several workshops, such as pottery makers', a woodworking shop and a weaver's shop and I spent some time watching the artisans at their work. Somehow, from seeing the people walk upon their hands, I had expected to see them perform their tasks with their feet and it came as something of a surprise to see these fellows using their hands like ordinary mortals.

Beyond this portion of the city the houses were scattered, the outlying buildings were more or less patched and out of repair and were very evidently the abode of the poorer classes, although the inhabitants I saw, and who retreated the instant they saw me, were exactly like all the others as far as I could see, both in dress and feature. Passing these huts, I crossed the smooth green field, which I now saw was a perfect landing place for the plane. Tethered to stakes and grazing on the grass were a number of animals which, as I first noticed them, I had taken for goats and cattle. But now I discovered that they were all deer and tapirs. It was a great surprise to see these animals domesticated but, after all, it was not remarkable, for I should have known, had I stopped to give the matter thought, that goats, sheep and cattle were unknown to the aboriginal Americans and that this city and its people, who had never been visited and had never communicated with other races, would of necessity be without these well known animals.

Moreover, I knew that the Mayas were supposed to have used tapirs as beasts of burden, and while I was standing there watching the creatures a man approached riding astride a big tapir and driving a second one loaded with bags of charcoal and garden produce. Here then was a partial solution of the manner by which these weak, dwarfed people built their stone houses. For with the powerful elephant-like tapirs—and I noticed all were the giant Baird's tapir which reaches a weight of seven or eight hundred pounds— they could easily haul the blocks of stone from a quarry and by means of tackle and inclined planes, could readily hoist the stones to the tops of the walls.

I had now reached the base of the pyramid and found it a massive structure of the same flinty stone as the other buildings. Running from base to summit was a spiral path or stairway and instantly I knew that it was a sacrificial pyramid exactly like those used by the Aztecs and on which unfortunate beings were killed and sacrificed. This discovery still further confirmed my suspicions that these people were either of Aztec or Maya blood or had been influenced by those races. Filled with curiosity to see the altar on the summit I started up the sloping stairs. I was at first doubtful if my companion would permit this for the structure was sacred and doubtless only priests of the highest order were permitted upon it. Evidently, however, my guide thought that such a supernatural being or god as myself had every right to invade the most sacred places, and he offered no objection, but prostrated himself at the base of the pyramid as I ascended. At the summit I found, as I had expected, the sacrificial stone, a huge block elaborately carved in hieroglyphs and with channels to permit the blood to drain off, while, close at hand, was a massive carved stone collar or yoke exactly like those which have been found in Puerto Rico and have so long puzzled scientists. From the blood stains upon this I felt sure it was used to hold down the victim's head and neck, while strong metal staples, set into the stone, indicated that the man destined for sacrifice was spread-eagled and his ankles and wrists bound fast to the rings.

It was a most interesting spot from a scientific standpoint, but decidedly gruesome, while the stench of putrefied blood and fragments of human flesh clinging to the stones was nauseating and I was glad to retrace my steps and descend to the ground.

From the top of the pyramid I had obtained a fine view of the plain and city and I had noted that the former was surrounded on all sides with steep cliffs, and I realized that the plain was not a flat topped mountain as I had thought but the crater of an extinct volcano.

I saw no path, pass or opening by which the crater-valley could be entered, but I knew there was the one by which I had arrived. As the sun, here on the mountain top, was still well above the horizon I decided to visit the entrance to the tunnel, for I was anxious to know what the people should leave this avenue open when, on every other side, they were completely cut off from the outer world. Possibly, I thought, they knew of those horrible man-eating trees and trusted to them to guard the city from intruders. Or again, they might keep the entrance guarded, for the fellow I had knocked over as I dashed in had been at the tunnel mouth and for all I knew he might have been an armed guard and was merely so thunderstruck at my precipitate appearance that he forgot his duties and his weapons.

With such thoughts running through my mind I strolled across the plain, past well-tilled gardens and fields, in several of which I saw men ploughing with well made plows drawn by tapirs. Even the farmers stopped their work and prostrated themselves as I passed, and it was evident that word of my celestial origin and supernatural character had gone forth to every inhabitant of the valley.

Following the path, I reached the little rise from which I had first viewed the city and soon came to the spot where I had entered. Imagine my utter surprise when I saw no sign whatever of the opening. I was positive that I had not missed my way. I recognized the clumps of bushes and the forms of the rocks, but there was no dark hole, no aperture in the cliff. Then, as I drew near to the precipice, I made an astounding discovery. Closely fitted into the rock and so like it that it had escaped my attention, was an enormous stone door. How it was operated, whether it was hinged or slid or whether it was pivoted, I could not determine. But that it covered and concealed the entrance to the tunnel I was convinced. Why the people had left the tunnel open as though to clear the way for me, why they should have fitted a door to it, why they should ever use the tunnel which could bring them only to the death-dealing forest, were problems which I could not solve.

At any rate there was nothing to be gained by staying there and I started back towards the city. Thinking to return by another route, I took a path that led towards the opposite mountain side and presently from ahead, I distinctly heard the sound of metal striking stone.

Oddly enough my mind had been so filled with other matters that I had hardly wondered how these people cut or worked the hard stone. But now that my attention was attracted by the sound my curiosity was aroused and I hurried forward. What metal I wondered, did these people use? For metal I knew it must be from the ringing, clinking noise. Was I about to see hardened bronze tools in actual use or had these marvelous folk discovered the use of iron or steel? So astounding had been all my experiences, so paradoxical and incredible everything I had seen, that I was prepared for almost anything. I, or rather we, soon came to the verge of a deep pit wherein, laboring at great masses of white stone, were scores of workmen. Standing like skeletons among the blocks were derricks; hitched to sledge-like drags loaded with stone were teams of tapirs and on the further side was a big outjutting. Hurrying down the steep trail I reached the bottom of the pit to find every man flat on the ground. Signalling to my companion that I wished to have the fellows go on with their work, I approached the nearest slab of rock. It was the same fine-grained whitish rock of which the city was built, and, lying upon it where they had been dropped by the stone cutters, were several small hammers, chisels and an adze-like tool. That they were not bronze or any alloy of copper I knew at the first glance. Their color was that of tempered steel and they seemed ridiculously small for the purpose of working this hard stone. If these people used steel then I had indeed made a discovery, and intent on this matter I picked up one of the tools to examine it. No sooner had I lifted it that I uttered an involuntary exclamation of surprise. The hammer, although hardly larger than an ordinary tack hammer, weighed fully ten pounds! It was heavier than if made of solid gold. There was only one known metal that could be so heavy and that was platinum. But platinum it could not be, for that metal is softer than gold and would be of no more use for cutting rock than so much lead. The tools, however, were undoubtedly hard—the polished surface of the hammer-head and the chisels, and the unscarred keen edges of the latter, showed this, and, anxious to test their hardness, I held a chisel against the rock and struck it sharply with a hammer.

Once more I cried out in wonder, for the chisel had bitten fully half an inch into the stone! It had cut it as easily as if the rock were cheese! What marvel was this? What magic lay in these tools? And then the secret dawned upon me and a moment's examination of the stone confirmed my suspicions. It was not that the tools were so very hard or keen but that the rock was soft—so soft that I could readily cut it with my pocket knife, a wax-like earthy rock which no doubt became hard upon exposure to the air exactly like the coral rock of Bermuda, which may be quarried with saws and even planed, but becomes as hard as limestone after exposure to the elements. Still, the tools were far harder than any metal except tempered steel, and for some time I puzzled over the matter as I watched the workmen, now over their fright and adoration, skillfully cutting and squaring the blocks of stone. It was one more conundrum I could not solve, and it was not until long afterwards, when a careful analysis of the metal was made, that I knew the truth. The metal was an alloy of platinum and iridium—the later one of the hardest of all known metals.

As we left the quarry and made our way toward the city I noticed an immense aqueduct stretching across the land from the apparently solid mountain side just above the quarry. I had given little thought to how the people secured water here in the crater. But it was now apparent that it was brought from some source by the stone conduit. Keenly curious to know whence it came, for I could not imagine how a river, lake or spring could exist on the crater rim, I wished to investigate, but darkness was coming on, I was tired and I deferred further exploration until another day.

Although I suppose I should have been grateful for being able to communicate with the people at all, yet I keenly felt the lack of a common medium of conversation, for the sign language was limited and I could not secure information I so much desired about many matters that puzzled me.

Nothing further of interest transpired that night. I was supplied with food, I slept soundly and did not awaken until roused by the women with my breakfast. Very soon afterwards I was summoned to the throne room by Zip, as I called my companion, and once more I had to strike a match and smoke my pipe for the king's benefit. This time a second personage of high rank was beside him, a villainous looking hunchbacked dwarf with red, vicious eyes and cruel mouth but who, like the king, walked on his feet. From his elaborately decorated white robes and the mitre-like crown of quetzal feathers on his gray head, I concluded he was a high priest, for in the designs upon his costume and the form of his crown, I saw a decided resemblance to the Aztec priests as shown in the picturegraph of that race. Moreover, the quetzal or resplendent trogon was, I knew, the sacred bird of the Aztecs and Mayas, and while I was aware that it was common in the northern portions of Panama, I had never heard of its occurrence in Darien, a fact which still further confirmed in my belief that these people were of Aztec stock. But if this were the case it was a puzzle as to why they should be so undersized, malformed and physically degenerate, for both the Aztecs and Mayas were powerful, well-formed races. The only solution I could think of was the supposition that isolation and intermarriage through centuries had brought about such results.

But to return to my audience with the king. I was not all pleased at thus having to use my precious matches and tobacco and I foresaw some very unpleasant developments in store for me if the performance was to be of daily occurrence. It was manifest that I must devise some new and startling exhibition of my powers if I were to retain my prestige and my freedom, for I well knew, from past experiences with savage races, and from the character of these potentates, that if I failed to perform miracles, and became, in their eyes, an ordinary mortal, my career would come to an abrupt end.

To be sure, there was the reassuring fact that Hazen would or should appear within the nest forty-eight hours, but it was decidedly problematical as to whether I could communicate with him or could receive any aid from the air. However, there was nothing to be done but obey and puff away at my pipe. With the idea of cutting the exhibition short I stepped closer to the throne and blew the smoke towards the faces of the king and the priest. The monarch was soon coughing and spluttering, but he was game, while the priest, to my amazement, sniffed the smoke and seemed to enjoy it. Here was trouble. Evidently he had a natural taste for tobacco and this fact caused me a deal of worry, for if the old rascal took it into his head to acquire the habit and demanded I should let him try a puff at the pipe I would be in a pretty fix indeed.

However, my fears on this score were groundless, and presently the king, who could stand it no longer, signalled for me to depart, which I did most gladly.

I still had it in mind to investigate the water supply, and with Zip— reminding me of an acrobatic clown—beside me, headed for the aqueduct. This I found was of stones, dovetailed together in water-tight joints, and built like an open trough and the speed of the water flowing though it proved the supply well above the city's level. It was an easy matter to follow the conduit, for a well-trodden path was beside it, but it was a steep upgrade climb for nearly a mile before I gained the spot where the aqueduct tapped the mountain rim. Here the water gushed from a hole in the solid rock and from its volume I knew it must come from some large reservoir. From where I stood I could look directly down into the quarry and the thought flashed through my mind that if the people continued to quarry in the place for many more years they would undermine and weaken the foundations of the aqueduct.

It was their lookout not mine, however, and still intent on tracing the water to its source I turned up a trail that appeared to lead
to the mountain top. In places this was excessively steep and here
Zip exhibited a new habit of his people. Dropping his feet first and
his prehensile toes grasping every projection and bit of rock to draw
him along while his immense, powerful hands supported his
weight; and pushed him onward. He looked more like a gigantic
spider than anything, and not in the least human. Panting and
blown I at last gained the summit and looked down upon a lake
of dismal black water filling a circular crater about half a mile in
diameter. Close by was an aperture in the rock and half-filled with
water, and it was evident that this was connected with the outlet
below by means of a shaft. Whether this was a natural formation
or had been laboriously cut by hand I could not tell, but I was prepared for almost anything by this time and was not greatly surprised to find a cleverly constructed sluice gate arranged above
the opening to regulate the flow of water. I had seen similar crater
lakes in the extinct volcanoes of the West Indies, but I was surprised that Hazen had not mentioned it. But on second thought I
realized that when flying over it, the dark water surrounded by
vegetation would hardly be visible and might easily be mistaken
for heavy shadow or an empty crater, while the aviator's surprise
at the city would fix his attention upon it to the exclusion of all
surroundings.

Standing upon the rock ridge several hundred feet above the
city I had almost the same view as Hazen had from his plane and I
could understand how, at an elevation of 5000 feet or more, he
had been unable to obtain any very accurate idea of the buildings
or people. I also realized, with a sinking of my heart, that it would
be next to impossible for him to recognize me or to see any signals
I might make.

The most prominent spot in the entire valley was the pyramid,
for this was isolated upon the green plain and the sun, striking
through a gap in the eastern rim of the crater, shone directly upon
the altar's summit, this bringing it out in sharp relief. Indeed,
it looked for all the world like a pylon on an aviation field. If I

expected to make my presence known to Hazen or to signal to him, my best point of vantage would be the summit of the pyramid and I determined to climb there and await his arrival when he should be due, two days later.

Little did I dream at the time of the conditions under which I would await him upon that gruesome altar.

IV

The Sacrifice

BY THE TIME we had descended the mountain and had reached the city it was noon, and going to my quarters I was glad to find an excellent meal. Having finished eating I threw myself into the hammock and despite my scarcity of matches and tobacco, indulged in a smoke. Then, feeling drowsy, I took off my coat, placed it on the floor beside my hammock and closed my eyes.

I awoke refreshed and reached for my coat only to leap from the hammock with a cry of alarm. The coat was gone! Quickly I searched the room, thinking Zip might have placed the garment elsewhere while I slept, but the place was bare. Zip was nowhere to be seen, and even the rug on which meals were served had been removed.

Here was a pretty state of affairs. My coat contained my matches, pipe, tobacco, pocket knife and handkerchief. Without it I was lost, helpless, incapable of maintaining my prestige of position. Death or worse hovered over me. My life depended on regaining my precious garment and its contents. Who could have taken it? What could have been their object? And instantly the truth flashed upon my mind. It was that rascally high priest. He had seen me take pipe, tobacco and matches from my coat pocket. He had watched me narrowly, perhaps had kept his eyes upon me through some hidden peep-hole or opening, and had seen me remove my coat, and white I slept had seized it. Or perhaps he had ordered Zip to secure it for him. It made little difference which, for if it were in his possession he would have me in his power. He could order by fair means or foul, and knowing that every second I delayed increased my peril, I rushed to the ladder and across the roofs to the throne room.

From beneath me, as I started to descent, came the sounds of the hissing language in excited tones, and as my head came below the level of the roof my heart sank. The dark air of the room was heavy with tobacco smoke!

The next instant my feet were jerked from beneath me, I was seized, tumbled on the floor, and before I could strike or rise I was bound hand and foot. Dazed, startled and helpless I glanced about. Surrounding me were a dozen of the repulsive dwarfs. Gathered about the sides of the room were crowds of people, and seated upon the throne, puffing great clouds of smoke from my pipe, a wicked leer upon his ugly face, and thoroughly enjoying himself, was the priest, while beside him the king coughed and sneezed and looked very miserable.

All this I took in at a glance. Then I was seized and dragged roughly before the throne. I fully realized my doom was sealed. I was no longer a supernatural being to be feared and adored—my treatment proved that—but merely a prisoner, an ordinary mortal. Oddly enough, however, I was no longer frightened. My first fears had given place to anger, and I raged and fumed and prayed that the grinning fiend before me might be stricken with all the torturing sickness, which usually follows the beginner's first smoke.

But apparently he was immune to the effects, and as soon as I was dragged before the throne he rose, and pointing at me, addressed the crowd before him. That he was denouncing me as an imposter and at the same time tremendously increasing his own importance was evident by his tones, his gestures and the expression on his dark face. Moreover, he had another card to play. Pointing upward and waving his arm and making quite creditable imitation of an airplane's exhaust, he spoke vehemently and then pointed to a man who crouched on the dais.

At first I was at a loss to grasp his meaning, and then, as the trembling creature beside the throne spoke in frightened tones and gesticulated vividly, I realized he was the chap I had bumped into upon my arrival. He had spilled the beans and had informed the old scarecrow of a priest, that I had arrived via the tunnel and not from the sky.

I felt sure now that my doom was sealed. But there was nothing I could do or say. There was one chance in a million that I might be escorted from the valley and turned loose in the tunnel; but that gave me no comfort, for I knew that hideous certain death awaited me on that slope covered with the devilish man-eating trees.

The chances, however, were all in favor of my being tortured and butchered. Strangely enough my greatest regret, the matter which troubled me the most and made me curse my carelessness in removing my coat while I slept, was not that I should be killed—I had faced death too often for that—but the fact that I would be unable to report the wonderful discoveries I had made or give my knowledge of the city and its people to the world. Indeed, my thoughts were so concentrated on this that I gave little attention to the priest, until he stepped forward, and, with a nasty grimace, struck me savagely across the face. Maddened at the blow I lunged forward like a butting ram. My head struck squarely in the pit of his stomach, and with a gasping yell he doubled up and fell sprawling on the dais while the pipe flew from his lips and scattered its contents far and near. Before I could roll to one side, my guards seized and pulled me across the room. Despite my plight and the fate in store for me I laughed loudly and heartily as I saw the priest with hands pressed to stomach, eyes rolling wildly and a sickly greenish pallor on his face. The blow plus the tobacco had done its work. I had evened the score a bit at any rate.

The next moment I was hauled through a low doorway hidden by draperies, and, bumping like a bag of meal over the rough stones, was pitched into an inky black cell. Bruised, scratched and bleeding I lay there unable to move or see while the occasional sounds of shuffling footsteps, or rather handsteps, told me a guard was close at hand. For hour after hour I lay motionless, expecting each minute that I would be dragged out to torture or death and wondering dully what form it would take, until at last—numb, exhausted and worn out, I lost consciousness.

I was brought to my senses by being seized and jerked to a sitting posture, and found the cell illuminated by a spluttering torch, while two of the men supported my shoulders and a third held a gourd of water to my lips. My throat was parched and the liquid was most welcome, and a moment later, a fourth man appeared with food. It was evident that the priest had no intention of letting me die of thirst or starvation, and I wondered why he should be so solicitous of my comfort if I were doomed to an early death.

As soon as I had eaten, the guards withdrew, taking the torch, and I was once more left in stygian blackness with my thoughts. I wondered whether it were day or night, but I had no means of judging. It had been the middle of the afternoon when I had missed my coat, and, reasoning that the food served was probably the evening meal, I decided that it was now about sundown. In that case I should probably be put out of the way the next morning. That would be a full twenty-four hours before Hazen was due and I wondered what he would think when he saw no sign of me in the valley—whether he would surmise that I had not reached the city and had been killed by the Kunas, and what he would report to my friends in Colon.

But Colon, friends and Hazen seemed very far away as I thought of them there in that black hole awaiting death at the hands of the strange black dwarfs and, as far as any aid they could give me, was concerned I might well have been in Mars.

My thoughts were interrupted by my guards reappearing with the torch. Lifting me to my feet they loosened the bonds about my legs and urged me through a small doorway, where I was compelled to bend low to pass, and along a winding, narrow, low-ceilinged stone tunnel. That I was on my way to my execution I was sure, and vague thoughts of selling my life dearly and of overpowering my puny guards crossed my mind. But I dismissed such ideas as useless, for even were I to succeed I would be no better off. There were thousands of the tiny men in the city, it was impossible to escape from the valley unseen, and I had not the least idea where the underground passage led. To attempt to escape meant certain death, and there still remained a faint chance, a dim hope that I might yet be spared and merely deported. So, ducking my head and with stooping shoulders, I picked my way along the tunnel by the fitful glare of the flaming torch.

For what seemed miles the way led on and I began to think that the entrance was outside the valley and that was being led to freedom, when a glimmer of light showed ahead, the floor sloped upward, and, an instant later, I emerged in the open air.

For a moment my eyes were blinded by the light after the darkness of the passage and I could not grasp where I was. I had thought it evening, but I knew the night had passed and another day had come. Then, as I looked about at my surroundings and it dawned upon me where I was, a shudder of horror, a chill of deadly fear swept over me. I was on the summit of the pyramid. The sacrificial altar was within three paces. Beside it stood the fiendish priest and his assistants, and gathered upon the green plain were hordes of people with faces upturned towards me. I was about to be sacrificed, to be bound fast to the bloodstained awful stone, to have my still-beating heart torn from my living body!

Anything were preferable to that and with a sudden bound I strove to gain the altar's edge and hurl myself to certain death. But to no avail. Two of the dwarfs held me fast by the cord which fastened my wrists and I was jerked back to fall heavily upon the stones. Before I could struggle up, four of the priest's assistants sprang forward and, grasping me by legs and shoulders, lifted me and tossed me upon the stinking sacrificial stone. I was helpless, and instantly my ankles were tied fast to the metal staples, the bonds of my wrists were severed, my arms were drawn apart and securely lashed to other staples, the stone collar was placed about my neck forcing my head far back and I was ready for the glowering priest to wreak his awful vengeance.

Stepping close to the altar he drew a glittering obsidian knife—and even in my terrible predicament I noted this, and realized that he was adhering strictly to Aztec customs—and, raising his arms, he began a wailing, blood-curdling chant. Up from the thousands of throats below came the chanting chorus, rising and falling like a great wave of sound. How long I wondered, would this keep on? How much longer must this agony, this torture of suspense be borne? Why did he not strike his stone dagger into my chest and have it over with?

And then, from some dormant cell in my brain, came the answer. I was to be sacrificed to the sun god, and I remembered that, according to the Aztec religion, the blow could not be struck until the rising sun cast its rays upon the victim's chest above the heart. The priest was awaiting that moment. He was delaying until the sun, still behind the crater's rim, should throw its first rays upon me.

How long would it be? How many minutes must pass before the fatal finger of light pointed to my heart? With a mighty effort I turned my head slightly towards the east. Above the rugged mountain edge was a blaze of light. Even as I looked with aching eyes a golden beam shot across the valley and flashed blindingly into my face. It was now only a matter of seconds. The priest raised his knife aloft. The chant from the multitude ceased and over city and valley fell an ominous, awful silence. Upon the sacrificial knife the sun gleamed brilliantly, transforming the glass-like stone to burnished gold. With his free hand the priest tore open my shirt and bared my bosom. I felt that the end had come. I closed my eyes. And then, at the very instant when the knife was about to sweep down, faint and far away, like the humming of a giant bee, I caught a sound. It was unmistakable unlike anything else in all the world— the exhaust of an airplane's engines!

And my straining ears were not the only ones that heard that note. Over the priest's face swept a look of deadly fear. The poised knife was slowly lowered. He turned trembling towards the west and from the waiting throng below rose a mighty sigh of terror.

A new hope sprang up in my breast. Was it Hazen? He was not due until the next day and it might be only some army plane that would pass far to one side of the valley. No, the sound was increasing, the plane was approaching. But even were it Hazen would it help me any? Would he see my plight and descend or would he fly too far above the city to note what was taking place? For a space my life was saved. The fear of that giant, roaring bird would prevent the sacrifice. The priest feared he had made a mistake, that I was a god, that, from the sky, vengeance would swoop upon him and his people for the contemplated butchery. But if the plane passed? Or would his dread of it be greater than his fear of defying the sun god by failing in the sacrifice?

Now the roar of the motor sounded directly overhead and the next moment I glimpsed the plane speeding across the blue morning sky. Then it was gone. The exhaust grew fainter and fainter. All hope was lost. Whoever it was had flown on, all unsuspecting the awful fate of a fellow man upon that sunlit pyramid.

And now the priest was again towering over me. Once more he raised his knife. I could feel the warm sun beating upon my throat and shoulders. I could feel it creeping slowly but surely downward. The knife quivered in the impatient hand of the priest, I saw his muscles tense themselves for the blow, I caught the grim smile that flitted across his face as he prepared to strike.

An instant more and my palpitating heart would be held aloft for all to see.

But the blow never fell. With a deafening roar, that drowned the mighty shout of terror from the people, the airplane swooped like an eagle from the sky and clove the air within a hundred feet of the altar. With a gurgling cry the priest flung himself face down, and his knife fell clattering with the sound of broken glass upon the stones.

Was it Hazen? Would he see me? Would he alight? Was I saved?

The answer was a thunderous, fear-maddened cry from below, a swishing whirr as of a gale of wind and a dark shadow sweeping over me.

And then my overwrought senses, my frazzled nerves could stand no more and all went black before my eyes.

Dimly consciousness came back. I heard the sounds of rushing feet, the panting labored breath of men, sharp, half uttered exclamations and terror and a deep drawn sigh of relief. Above my wondering eyes a figure suddenly loomed. A weird uncanny figure with strangely smooth and rounded head and great goggling, glassy eyes. With a jerk the stone collar was lifted from my strained neck and as full consciousness came back I gasped. It was Hazen! By some miracle he was ahead of time!

From somewhere, muffled behind that grotesque mask, came a hoarse: "My God, are you hurt?

Before I could speak the bonds were slashed from my ankles and wrists. A strong arm raised me and pulled me from the slab.

"For God's sake, hurry!" cried Hazen, as ha if supporting me he rushed toward the altar stairs. "I've got 'em buffaloed for a minute, but the Lord alone knows how long it'll hold 'em."

Rapidly as my numbed limbs would permit I rushed down the sloping, spiral way. Half carried by Hazen I raced across the few yards of grass between the base of the pyramid and the plane, and as I did so I caught a fleeting glimpse of a huddled, shapeless, bloody bundle of green and white. It was all that remained of the priest whom Hazen had hurled from the altar top!

The next moment I was in the plane and Hazen was twirling the propeller. There was a roar as the motor started. Hazen leaped like an acrobat to his seat and slowly the machine moved across the plain.

Everywhere the people were prostrate, but as the machine started forward one after another glanced up. Ere we had traveled a score of yards the creatures were rising and with frightful screams were scattering from our pathway. It was impossible to avoid them. With sickening shocks the whirring propeller struck one after another. Blood spattered our faces and becrimsoned the windshield and the wings. But uninjured the plane gathered headway; the uneven bumping over the ground ceased; we were traveling smoothly, lifting from the earth.

Then with a strange wild roar the people rushed for us. Racing on their hands they came. Rocks and missiles whizzed about us. An arrow whirred by my head and struck quivering in a strut. But now we were rising rapidly. We were looking down upon the maddened hosts, their arrows and sling-flung stones were striking the under surface of the fuselage and wings. We were safe at last. A moment more and we would be above the crater rim.

A sudden exclamation from Hazen startled me. I glanced up. Straight ahead rose the precipitous mountain side above the quarry. To clear it we must ascent far more rapidly than we were doing.

"Must have splintered the blades!" jerked out Hazen. "She's not making it. Can't swing her. Rudder's jammed. Heave out everything you can find. Hurry or we'll smash!"

Before us loomed the ragged, rocky wall. We were rushing to our doom at lightning speed. At Hazen's words I grasped whatever I could find and tossed it over the side. A box of provisions, a roll of tools, a leather jacket, a thermos bottle, canteens, an automatic pistol and a cartridge belt all went, I glanced up. We were rising, faster. A few pounds more overboard, a few feet higher and we would be clear. Was there anything else I could throw out? Frantically I searched. I saw a can-like object resting on a frame. Spare gasoline I decided, but fuel was of no value now. With an effort I dragged it out. I lifted and hurled it over.

With a sudden jerk the plane sprung upward. There was a terrific muffled roar from below and with barely a yard to spare we rose above the crater rim.

"Lord, you must have dropped that old bomb!" cried Hazen. "The concussion jarred the rudder free."

I glanced over the side. Far beneath, a cloud of smoke and dust was drifting slowly aside exposing the aqueduct, broken smashed and in ruins. From the opening in the mountain side a mighty stream of water was roaring in a rushing, tearing torrent. The bomb had landed squarely in the quarry. The aqueduct had fallen, the shock had let loose the gates of the lake and the whole vast crater reservoir was pouring in a mighty flood across the valley.

In a wide arc Hazen swung the plane about. "Poor devils!" he muttered as we soared above the doomed city.

Already the green plain was shimmering with the glint of water. We could see the frantic, frenzied people running and scrambling up their ladders. Again we wheeled and circled far above them and now only the roof tops of the houses were above the flood. Presently these too sank from sight and above the sunlit waters only the sacrificial stone remained.

"It's all over!" exclaimed Hazen, and heading northward we sped beyond the encircling mountain sides. Beneath us now was forest, and with a shudder I recognized it as that death-dealing, nightmare grove of cannibal trees. Fascinated I gazed down and suddenly from the mountain side behind us burst a frothing yellow torrent. The pressure of the flood had been too great. The overwhelming waters had forced the stone door of the tunnel by which I had entered that incredible valley. Before my wondering eyes the devastating deluge swept down the slope. I saw the monstrous trees shiver and sway and crash before the irresistible force. They gave way and like matchsticks went tossing, tumbling, bobbing down the hillside.

Higher and higher we rose. The water-filled crater was now but a silvery lake. The slope up which I had fought and raced from the ravenous, blood-sucking trees was bare, red earth scarred deep by the plunging stream that flowed over it. Far to the west gleamed the blue Pacific. Like a vast map Darien was spread below us. Northward we sped. Before us was civilization. Behind us death and destruction. The man-eating trees were a thing of the past. The lost city was lost forever.

THE BLOOD-FLOWER
SEABURY QUINN

"*ALLO,*" JULES DE GRANDIN seized the receiver from the office telephone before the echo of the tinkling bell had ceased, "who is it, please? But of course, Mademoiselle, you may speak with Dr. Trowbridge." He passed the instrument to me and busied himself with a third unsuccessful attempt to ignite the evil-smelling French cigarette with which he insisted on fumigating the room.

"Yes?" I queried, placing the receiver to my ear.

"This is Miss Ostrander, Dr. Trowbridge," a well modulated voice informed me. "Mrs. Evander's nurse, you know."

"Yes?" I repeated, a little sharply, annoyed at being called by an ordinary case after an onerous day. "What is it?"

"I—I don't quite know, sir." She laughed the short, semi-hysterical laugh of an embarrassed woman. "She's acting very queerly. She—she's—oh, my there it goes again, sir! Please come over right away; I'm afraid she's becoming delirious!" And with that she hung up, leaving me in a state of astounded impatience.

"Confound the woman!" I scolded as I prepared to slip into my overcoat. "Why couldn't she have hung on thirty seconds more and told me what the matter was?"

"Eh, what is it, my friend?" De Grandin gave up his attempt to make the cigarette burn and regarded me with one of his fixed, unwinking stares. "You are puzzled, you are in trouble; can I assist you?"

"Perhaps," I replied. "There's a patient of mine, a Mrs. Evander, who's been suffering from a threatened leukemia—I've administered Fowler's solution and arsenic trioxid and given her bed-rest treatment for the past week. It looked as if we had the situation pretty well in hand, but. . ." I repeated Miss Ostrander's message.

"Ah?" he murmured, musingly. "'There it goes again,' she did say? What, I wonder, was 'it'; a cough, a convulsion, or—who can say? Let us hasten, my friend. *Parbleu*, she does intrigue me, that Mademoiselle Ostrander with her so cryptic 'There it goes again!'"

LIGHTS WERE GLEAMING through the storm from the windows of the Evander house as we came to a stop before its wide veranda. A colored servant, half clothed and badly frightened, let us in and ushered us on tiptoe to the upper story chamber where the mistress of the establishment lay sick.

"What's wrong?" I demanded as I entered the sickroom, de Grandin at my heels.

A glance at the patient reassured me. She lay back on a little pile of infant pillows, her pretty blonde hair trickling in stray rivulets of gold from the confines of her lace sleeping cap, her hand, almost as white as the linen itself, spread restfully on the Madeira counterpane.

"Humph!" I exclaimed, turning angrily to Miss Ostrander. "Is this what you called me out in the rain to see?"

The nurse raised a forefinger quickly to her lips and motioned toward the hall with her eyes. "Doctor," she said in a whisper when we stood outside the sickroom door, "I know you'll think me silly, but—but it was positively ghastly!"

"*Tiens, Mademoiselle*," de Grandin cut in, "I pray you be more explicit: first you tell Friend Trowbridge that something—we know not what—goes again, now you do inform us that something is ghastly. *Pardieu*, you have my sheep—*non, non*, how do you say?—my goat!"

In spite of herself the girl laughed at the tragic face he turned to her, but she recovered her gravity quickly.

"Last night," she went on, still in a whisper, "and the night before, just at 12, a dog howled somewhere in the neighborhood. I couldn't place the sound, but it was one of those long, quavering howls, almost human. Positively, you might have mistaken it for the cry of a little child in pain, at first."

De Grandin tweaked first one, then the other end of his trimly waxed blond mustache. "And it was the sleepless dog's lament which went again, and which was so ghastly, *Mademoiselle?*" he inquired solicitously.

"No!" the nurse exploded with suppressed vehemence and heightened color. "It was Mrs. Evander, sir. Night before last, when the beast began baying, she stirred in her sleep—turned restlessly for a moment, then went back to sleep. When it howled the second time, a little nearer the house, she half sat up, and made a queer little growling noise in her throat. Then she slept. Last night the animal was howling louder and longer, and Mrs. Evander seemed more restless and made odd noises more distinctly. I thought the dog was annoying her, or that she might be having a nightmare, so I got her a drink of water; but when I tried to give it to her, *she snarled at me!*"

"*Eh, bien,* but this is of interest," de Grandin commented. "She did snarl at you, you say?"

"Yes, sir. She didn't wake up when I touched her on the shoulder; just turned her head toward me and showed her teeth and growled. Growled like a bad-tempered dog."

"Yes? And then?"

"Tonight the dog began howling a few minutes earlier, five or ten minutes before midnight, perhaps, and it seemed to me his voice was much stronger. Mrs. Evander had the same reaction she had the other two nights at first, but suddenly she sat bolt-upright in bed, rolled her head from side to side, and drew back her lips and growled, then she began snapping at the air, like a dog annoyed by a fly. I did my best to quiet her, but I didn't like to go too near—I was afraid, really—and all at once the dog began howling again, right in the next yard, it seemed, and Mrs. Evander threw back her bedclothes, knelt up in bed *and answered him!*"

"ANSWERED HIM?" I echoed in stupefaction.

"Yes, doctor, she threw back her head and howled—long, quavering howls, just like his. At first they were low, but they grew louder and higher till the servants heard them, and James, the butler, came to the door to see what the matter was. Poor fellow, he was nearly scared out of his wits when he saw her."

"And then . . . ?" I began.

"Then I called you. Right while I was talking to you, the dog began baying again, and Mrs. Evander answered him. That was what I meant"—she turned to de Grandin—"when I said 'There it goes again,' I had to hang up before I could explain to you, Dr. Trowbridge, for she had started to crawl out of bed toward the window, and I had to run and stop her."

"But why didn't you tell me this yesterday, or this afternoon when I was here?" I demanded.

"I didn't like to, sir. It all seemed so crazy, so utterly impossible, especially in the daytime, that I was afraid you'd think I'd been asleep on duty and dreamed it all; but now that James has seen it, too . . ."

Outside in the rain-drenched night there suddenly rose a wail, long-drawn, pulsating doleful as the cry of an abandoned soul. "O-o-o—o-o-o-o—o-o-o—o-o-o-o!" it rose and fell, quavered and almost died away, then resurged with increased force. "O-o-o—o-o-o-o—o-o-o—o-o-o-o!"

"Hear it?" the nurse cried, her voice thin-edged with excitement and fear.

Again, "O-o-o—o-o-o-o—o-o-o—o-o-o-o!" like the echo of the howls outside came an answering cry from the sickroom beyond the door.

Miss Ostrander dashed into the room, de Grandin and I close behind her.

The dainty white counterpane had been thrown back, Mrs. Evander, clad only in her Georgette nightrobe and bedcap, had crossed the floor to the window and flung up the sash. Already the wind-whipped rain was beating in upon her as she leaned across the sill, one pink sole toward us, one little white foot on the window-ledge, preparatory to jumping.

"*Mon Dieu*, seize her!" de Grandin shrieked, and matching command with performance leaped across the room, grasped her shoulders in his small, strong hands, and bore her backward as she flexed the muscles of her legs to hurl herself into the yard below.

For a moment she fought like a tigress, snarling, scratching, even snapping at us with her teeth, but Miss Ostrander and I over-bore her and thrust her into bed, drawing the covers over her and holding them down like a strait-jacket against her furious struggles.

De Grandin leaned across the window-sill, peering out into the stormy darkness. "A-roint thee, accursed of God!" I heard him shout into the wind as he drew the sash down, snapped the catch fast and turned again to the room.

"Ah?" he approached the struggling patient and bent over her, staring intently. "A grain and a half of morphine in her arm, if you please, Friend Trowbridge. The dose is heavy for a non-addict, but"—he shrugged his shoulders—"it is *necessaire* that she sleep, this poor one. So! That is better.

"*Mademoiselle*," he regarded Miss Ostrander with his wide-eyed stare, "I do not think she will be thus disturbed in the day, but I most strongly urge that hereafter you administer a dose of one-half grain of codein dissolved in eighty parts of water each night not later than half-past 10. Dr. Trowbridge will write the prescription.

"Friend Trowbridge," he interrupted himself, "where, if at all, is *Madame's* husband, Monsieur Evander?"

"He's gone to Atlanta on a business trip," Miss Ostrander supplied. "We expect him back tomorrow."

"Tomorrow? *Zut*, that is too bad!" de Grandin exclaimed. "*Eh bien*, with you Americans it is always business. Business before happiness; *cordieu*, business before the safety of those you love!

"*Mademoiselle*, you will please keep in touch with Dr. Trowbridge and me at all times, and when that Monsieur Evander does return from his business trip, please tell him that we desire to see him soon—at once, right away, immediately.

"Come, Friend Trowbridge—*bonne nuit, Mademoiselle*."

"I SAY, DR. TROWBRIDGE," Niles Evander flung angrily into my consulting room, "what's the idea of keeping my wife doped like this? Here I just got back from a trip to the South last night and rushed out to the house to see her before she went to sleep, and that dam' nurse said she'd given her a sleepin' powder and couldn't waken her. I don't like it, I tell you, and I won't have it! I told the nurse that if she gave her any dope tonight she was through, and that goes for you, too!" He glared defiantly at me.

De Grandin, sunk in the depths of a great chair with a copy of de Gobineau's melancholy *Lovers of Kandahar*, glanced up sharply, then consulted the watch strapped to his wrist. "It is a quarter of 11," he announced apropos of nothing, laying down the elegant blue-and-gold volume and rising from his seat.

Evander turned on him, eyes ablaze. "You're Dr. de Grandin," he accused. "I've heard of you from the nurse. It was you, who per-suaded Trowbridge to dope my wife—buttin' in on a case that didn't concern you. I know all about you," he went on furiously as the Frenchman gave him a cold stare. "You're some sort of charlatan from Paris, a dabbler in criminology and spiritualism and that sort of rot. Well, sir, I want to warn you to keep your hands off my wife. American doctors and American methods are good enough for me!"

"Your patriotism is most admirable, Monsieur," de Grandin murmured with a suspicious mildness. "If you . . ."

The jangle of the telephone bell cut through his words. "Yes?" he asked sharply, raising the receiver, but keeping his cold eyes fixed on Evander's face. "Yes, Mademoiselle Ostrander, this is— *grand Dieu!* What? how long? Eh, do you say so? *Dix million diab-les!* But of course, we come, we hasten—*morbleu*, but we shall fly."

"Gentlemen," he hung up the receiver, then turned to us in-clining his shoulders ceremoniously to each of us in turn, his gaze as expressionless as the eyes of a graven image, "that was Made-moiselle Ostrander on the 'phone. Madame Evander is gone—dis-appeared."

"Gone? Disappeared'?" Evander echoed stupidly, looking help-lessly from de Grandin to me and back again. He slumped down in the nearest chair, gazing straight before him unseeing. "Great God!" he murmured.

"Precisely, *Monsieur*," de Grandin agreed in an even, emotion-less voice. "That is exactly what I said. Meantime"—he gave me a significant glance—"let us go, *cher* Trowbridge. I doubt not that Mademoiselle Ostrander will have much of interest to relate.

"*Monsieur*"—his eyes and voice again became cold, hard, stonily expressionless—"if you can so far discommode yourself as to travel in the company of one whose nationality and methods you disapprove, I suggest you accompany us."

Niles Evander rose like a sleep-walker and followed us to my waiting car.

THE PREVIOUS DAY's rain had turned to snow with a shifting of the wind to the northeast, and we made slow progress through the suburban roads. It was nearly midnight when we trooped up the steps to the Evander porch and pushed vigorously at the bell-button.

"Yes, sir," Miss Ostrander replied to my question, "Mr. Evander came home last night and positively forbade my giving Mrs. Evander any more codein. I told him you wanted to see him right away, and that Dr. de Grandin had ordered the narcotic, but he said . . ."

"Forbear, if you please, *Mademoiselle*," de Grandin interrupted. "Monsieur Evander has already been at pains to say as much—and more—to us in person. Now, when did *Madame* disappear, if you please?"

"I'd already given her her medicine last night," the nurse took up her story at the point of interruption, "so there was no need of calling you to tell you of Mr. Evander's orders. I thought perhaps I could avoid any unpleasantness by pretending to obey him and giving her the codein on the sly this evening, but about 9 o'clock he came into the sickroom and snatched up the box of powders and put them in his pocket. Then he said he was going to drive over to have it out with you. I tried to telephone you about it, but the storm had put the wires out of commission, and I've been trying to get a message through ever since."

"And the dog, *Mademoiselle*, the animal who did howl outside the window, has he been active?"

"Yes! Last night he screamed and howled so I was frightened. Positively, it seemed as though he were trying to jump up from the ground to the window. Mrs. Evander slept through it all, though, thanks to the drug."

"And tonight?" de Grandin prompted.

"Tonight!" The nurse shuddered. "The howling began about half-past nine, just a few minutes after Mr. Evander left for the city. Mrs. Evander was terrible. She seemed like a woman possessed. I fought and struggled with her, but nothing I could do had the slightest effect. She was savage as a maniac. I called James to help me hold her in bed once, and then, for a while, she lay quietly, for the thing outside seemed to have left.

"Sometime later the howling began again, louder and more furious, and Mrs. Evander was twice as hard to manage. She fought and bit so that I was beginning to lose control of her, and I screamed for James again. He must have been somewhere downstairs though, for he didn't hear my call. I ran out into the hall and leaned over the balustrade to call again, and when I ran back—I wasn't out there more than a minute—the window was up and Mrs. Evander was gone."

"And didn't you do anything?—didn't you look for her?" Evander cut in passionately.

"Yes, sir. James and I ran outside and called and searched all through the grounds, but we couldn't find a trace of her. The wind was blowing so and the snow falling so rapidly, any tracks she might have made would have been wiped out almost immediately."

DE GRANDIN took his little pointed chin between the thumb and forefinger of his right hand and bowed his head in silent meditation, "Horns of the devil!" I heard him mutter to himself. "This is queer—those cries, that delirium, that attempted flight, now this disappearance. *Pardieu*, the trail seems clear. But why? *Mille cochons*, why?"

"See here," Evander broke in frantically, "can't you do something? Call the police, call the neighbors, call . . ."

"Monsieur." de Grandin interrupted in a frigid voice, "may I inquire your vocation?"

"Eh?" Evander was taken aback. "Why—er—I'm an engineer."

"Precisely, exactly. Dr. Trowbridge and I are medical men. We do not attempt to build bridges or sink tunnels. We should make sorry work of it. You, *Monsieur*, have already once tried your hand at medicine by forbidding the administration of a drug we considered necessary. Your results were most deplorable. Kindly permit us to follow our profession in our own way. The thing we most of all do not desire in this case is the police force. Later, perhaps. Now, it would be more than ruinous."

"But . . ."

"There are no buts, *Monsieur*. It is my belief that your wife, Madame Evander, is in no immediate danger. However, Dr. Trowbridge and I shall institute such search as may be practicable, and do you meantime keep in such communication with us as the storm will permit." He bowed formally. "A very good night to you, *Monsieur*."

Miss Ostrander looked at him questioningly. "Shall I go with you, doctor?" she asked.

"*Mais non*," he replied. "You will please remain here, *ma nourice*, and attend the homecoming of Madame Evander."

"Then you think she will return?"

"Most doubtlessly. Unless I am more badly mistaken than I think I am, she will be back to you before another day."

"Say," Evander, almost beside himself burst out, "what makes you so cocksure she'll be back? Good Lord, man, do you realize she's out in this howling blizzard with only her nightclothes on?"

"Perfectly. But I do declare she will return."

"But you've nothing to base your absurd . . ."

"Monsieur!" de Grandin's sharp, whiplike reply cut in. "Me, I am Jules de Grandin. When I say she will return. I do not make mistakes."

"WHERE SHALL WE begin the search?" I asked as we entered my car.

He settled himself snugly in the cushions and lighted a cigarette. "We need not search, *cher ami*," he replied. "She will return of her own free will and accord."

"But, man," I argued, "Evander was right; she's out in this storm with nothing but a Georgette nightdress on."

"I doubt it," he answered casually.

"You doubt it? Why . . . ?"

"Unless the almost unmistakable signs fail, my friend, this Madame Evander, thanks to her husband's pig-ignorance, is this moment clothed in fur."

"Fur?" I echoed.

"Perfectly. Come, my friend, tread upon the gas. Let us snatch what sleep we can tonight—*eh bien*, tomorrow is another day."

HE WAS UP AND WAITING for me as I entered the office next morning. "Tell me Friend Trowbridge," he demanded, "this Madame Evander's leukemia, upon what did you base your diagnosis?"

"Well," I replied, referring to my clinical cards, "a physical examination showed the axillary glands slightly enlarged, the red corpuscles reduced to little more than a million to the count, the white cells stood at about four hundred thousand, and the patient complained of weakness, drowsiness and a general feeling of malaise."

"U'm?" he commented noncommitally. "That could easily be so. Yes; such signs would undoubtlessly be shown. Now . . ." The telephone bell broke off his remarks half uttered.

"Ah?" his little blue eyes snapped triumphantly, as he listened to the voice on the wire. "I did think so. But yes; right away, at once, immediately.

"Trowbridge, my old one, she has returned. That was Mademoiselle Ostrander informing me of Madame Evander's reappearance. Let us hasten. There is much I would do this day."

"AFTER YOU WENT last night," Miss Ostrander told us, "I lay down on the chaise longue in the bedroom and tried to sleep. I suppose I must have napped by fits and starts, but it seemed to me I could hear the faint howling of dogs, sometimes mingled with yelps and cries, all through the night. This morning, just after 6 o'clock, I got up to prepare myself a piece of toast and a cup of tea before the servants were stirring, and as I came downstairs I found Mrs. Evander lying on the rug in the front hall."

SHE PAUSED A MOMENT and her color mounted slightly as she went on. "She was lying on that gray wolfskin rug before the fireplace, sir, and was quite nude. Her sleeping cap and nightgown were crumpled up on the floor beside her."

"Ah?" de Grandin commented. "And . . ."

"I got her to her feet and helped her upstairs, where I dressed her for bed and tucked her in. She didn't seem to show any evil effects from being out in the storm. Indeed, she seems much better this morning, and is sleeping so soundly I could hardly wake her for breakfast, and when I did, she wouldn't eat. Just went back to sleep."

"Ah?" de Grandin repeated. "And you bathed her, *Mademoiselle*, before she was put to bed?"

The girl looked slightly startled. "No sir, not entirely; but I did wash her hands. They were discolored, especially about the fingertips, with some red substance, almost as if she had been scratching something, and gotten blood under her nails."

"*Parbleu!*" the Frenchman exploded. "I did know it Friend Trowbridge. Jules de Grandin, he is never mistaken.

"*Mademoiselle*," he turned feverishly to the nurse, "did you, by any happy chance, save the water in which you laved Madame Evander's hands?"

"WHY NO, I DIDN'T, but—oh, I see—yes, I think perhaps some of the stain may be on the washcloth and the orange stick I cleaned her nails with. I really had quite a time cleaning them, too."

"*Bien, tres bien!*" he ejaculated. "Let us have these cloths, these sticks, at once, please. Trowbridge, do you withdraw some blood from *Madame's* arm for a test, then we must hasten to the laboratory. *Cordieu*, I burn with impatience!"

An hour later we faced each other in the office. "I can't understand it," I confessed. "By all the canons of the profession, Mrs. Evander ought to be dead after last night's experience, but there's no doubt she's better. Her pulse was firmer, her temperature right, and her blood count practically normal today."

"Me. I understand perfectly, up to a point," he replied. "Beyond that, all is dark as the cave of Erebus. Behold, I have tested the stains from *Madame's* fingers. They are—what do you think?"

"Blood?" I hazarded.

"*Parbleu*, yes, but not of humanity. *Mais non*, they are blood of a dog, my friend."

"Of a dog?"

"Perfectly. I, myself, did greatly fear they might prove human, but *grace a Dieu*, they are not. Now, if you will excuse, I go to make certain investigations, and will meet you at the *maison* Evander this evening. Come prepared to be surprised, my friend. *Parbleu*, I shall be surprised if I do not astonish myself!"

FOUR OF US, de Grandin, Miss Ostrander, Niles Evander and I, sat in the dimly lighted room, looking alternately toward the bed where the mistress of the house lay in a drugged sleep, into the still-burning fire of coals in the fireplace grate, and at each other's faces. Three of us were puzzled almost to the point of hysteria, and de Grandin seemed on pins and needles with excitement and expectation. Occasionally he would rise and walk to the bed with that quick soundless tread of his which always made me think of a cat. Again he would dart into the hall, nervously light a cigarette, draw a few quick puffs from it, then glide noiselessly into the sickroom once more. None of us spoke above a whisper, and our conversation was limited to inconsequential things. Throughout our group there was the tense expectancy and solemn, taut-nerved air of medical witnesses in the prison death chamber awaiting the advent of the condemned.

Subconsciously, I think, we all realized what we waited for, but my nerves nearly snapped when it came.

With the suddenness of a shot, unheralded by any preliminary, the wild, vibrating howl of a beast sounded beneath the sickroom window, its sharp, poignant wail seeming to split the frigid, moonlit air of the night.

"*O-o-o—o-o-o-o—o-o-o—o-o-o-o!*" it rose against the winter stillness, diminished to a moan of heart-rending melancholy, then suddenly crescendoed upward, from a moan to a wail, from a wail to a howl, despairing, passionate, longing as the lament of a damned spirit, wild and fierce as the rallying call of the fiends of hell.

"Oh!" Miss Ostrander exclaimed involuntarily.

"Let be!" Jules de Grandin ordered tensely, his whisper seeming to carry more because of its sharpness than from any actual sound it made.

"*O-o-o—o-o-o-o—o-o-o—o-o-o-o!*" again the cry shuddered through the air, again it rose to a pitch of intolerable shrillness and evil, then died away, and, as we sat stone-still in the shadowy chamber, a new sound, a sinister, scraping sound, intensified by the ice-hard coldness of the night, came to us. Someone, some *thing*, was swarming up the rose-trellis outside the house!

Scrape, scratch, scrape, the alternate hand- and footholds sounded on the cross-bars of the lattice. A pair of hands, long, slender, corded hands like hands of a cadaver long dead, and armed with talons, blood-stained and hooked, grasped the window-edge, and a face—God of Mercy, such a face!—was silhouetted against the background of the night.

Not human, nor yet wholly bestial it was, but partook grotesquely of both, so that it was at once a foul caricature of each. The forehead was low and narrow, and sloped back to a thatch of short, nondescript-colored hair resembling an animal's fur. The nose was elongated out of all semblance to a human feature and resembled the pointed snout of some animal of the canine tribe except that it curved sharply down at the tip like the beak of some unclean bird of prey. Thin, cruel lips were drawn sneeringly back from a double row of tusklike teeth which gleamed horridly in the dim reflection of the open fire, and a pair of round, baleful eyes, green as the luminescence from a rotting carcass in a midnight swamp, glared at us across the windowsill. On each of us in turn the basilisk glance dwelt momentarily, then fastened itself on the sleeping sick woman like a falcon's talons on a dove.

Miss Ostrander gave a single choking sob and slid forward from her chair unconscious. Evander and I sat stupefied with horror, unable to do more than gaze in terror-stricken silence at the apparition, but Jules de Grandin was out of his seat and across the room with a single bound of feline grace and ferocity.

"Arroint thee, accursed of God!" he screamed, showering a barrage of blows from a slender wand on the creature's face. "Back, spawn of Satan! To thy kennel, hound of hell! I, Jules de Grandin, command it!"

THE SUDDENNESS of his attack took the thing by surprise. For a moment it snarled and cowered under the hailstorm of blows from de Grandin's stick, then, as suddenly as it had come into view, it loosed its hold on the windowsill and dropped from sight.

"*Sang de Dieu, sang du diable; sang des tous les saints de cie!*" de Grandin roared, hurling himself out the window in the wake of the fleeing monster. "I have you, vile wretch. *Pardieu, Monsieur Loupgarou*, but I shall surely crush you!"

Rushing to the window, I saw the tall, skeleton-thin form of the enormity leaping across the moonlit snow with great, space-devouring bounds, and after it, brandishing his wand, ran Jules de Grandin, shouting triumphant invectives in mingled French and English.

By the shadow of a copse of evergreens the thing made a stand. Wheeling in its tracks, it bent nearly double, extending its cadaverous claws like a wrestler searching for a hold, and baring its glistening tusks in a snarl of fury.

De Grandin never slackened pace. Charging full tilt upon the waiting monstrosity, he reached his free hand into his jacket pocket. There was a gleam of blue metal in the moonlight. Then eight quick, pitiless spurts of flame stabbed through the shadow where the monster lurked, eight whiplike crackling reports echoed and re-echoed in the midnight stillness—and the voice of Jules de Grandin:

"Trowbridge, *non vieux, ohe*, Friend Trowbridge, bring a light quickly! I would that you see what I see!"

Weltering in a patch of blood-stained snow at de Grandin's feet we found an elderly man, ruddy-faced, gray-haired, and, doubtless, in life, of a dignified, even benign aspect. Now, however, he lay in the snow as naked as the day his mother first saw him, and eight gaping gunshot wounds told where de Grandin's missiles had found their mark. The winter cold was already stiffening his limbs and setting his face in a mask of death.

"Good heavens," Evander ejaculated as he bent over the lifeless form, "it's Uncle Friedrich—my wife's uncle! He disappeared just before I went south."

"*Eh bien*," de Grandin regarded the body with no more emotion than if it had been an effigy molded in snow, "we shall know where to find your uncle henceforth, *Monsieur*. Will some of you pick him up? Me—*pardieu* I would no more touch him than I would handle a hyena!"

"Now, *Monsieur*," de Grandin faced Evander across the living room table, "your statement that the gentleman at whose happy dispatch I so fortunately officiated was your wife's uncle, and that he disappeared before your southern trip, does interest me. Say on, tell me all concerning this Uncle Friedrich of your wife's. When did he disappear, and what led up to his disappearance? Omit nothing, I pray you, for trifles which you may consider of no account may be of the greatest importance. Proceed, *Monsieur*. I listen."

Evander squirmed uncomfortably in his chair like a small boy undergoing catechism. "He wasn't really her uncle," he responded. "Her father and he were schoolmates in Germany—Heidelberg—years ago. Mr. Hoffmeister—Uncle Friedrich—immigrated to this country shortly after my father-in-law came back, and they were in business together for years. Mr. Hoffmeister lived with my wife's people—all the children called him Uncle Friedrich—and was just like one of the family.

"My mother-in-law died a few years ago, and her husband died shortly after, and Mr. Hoffmeister disposed of his share of the business and went to Germany on a long visit. He was caught there in the war and didn't return to America until '21. Since that time he lived with us."

Evander paused a moment, as though debating mentally whether he should proceed, then smiled in a half shamefaced manner. "To tell you the truth," he continued, "I wasn't very keen on having him here. There were times when I didn't like the way he looked at my wife a dam' bit."

"Eh," de Grandin asked, "how was that, *Monsieur?*"

"Well, I can't quite put a handle to it in words, but more than once I'd glance up and see him with his eyes fastened on Edith in a most peculiar way. It would have angered me in a young man, but in an old man, it both angered and disgusted me. I was on the point of asking him to leave when he disappeared and saved me the trouble."

"Yes?" de Grandin encouraged. "And his disappearance, what of that?"

"The old fellow was always an enthusiastic amateur botanist," Evander replied, "and he brought a great many specimens for his herbarium back from Europe with him. Off and on he's been messing around with plants since his return, and about a month ago he received a tin of dried flowers from Kerovitch, Rumania, and they seemed to set him almost wild."

"Kerovitch? *Mordieu!*" de Grandin exclaimed. "Say on, Monsieur; I burn with curiosity. Describe these flowers in detail, if you please."

"H'm," Evander took his chin in his hand and studied in silence a moment. "There wasn't anything especially remarkable about them that I could see. There were a dozen of them, all told, perhaps, and they resembled our ox-eyed daisies a good deal, except that their petals were red instead of yellow. Had a queer sort of odor, too. Even though they were dried, they exuded a sort of sickly-sweet smell, yet not quite sweet either. It was a sort of mixture of perfume and stench, if that means anything to you."

"*Pardieu*, it means much!" de Grandin assured him. "And their sap, where it had dried, did it not resemble that of the milkweed plant?"

"Yes! How did you know?"

"No matter. Proceed, if you please. Your Uncle Friedrich did take these so accursed flowers out and . . ."

"And tried an experiment with them," Evander supplied. "He put them in a bowl of water, and they freshened up as though they had not been plucked an hour."

"Yes—and his disappearance—name of a little green man!—his disappearance?"

"That happened just before I went south. All three of us went to the theater one evening, and Uncle Friedrich wore one of the red flowers in his buttonhole. My wife wore a spray of them in her corsage. He tried to get me to put one of the things in my coat, too, but I hated their smell so much I wouldn't do it."

"Lucky you!" de Grandin murmured so low the narrator failed to hear him.

"UNCLE FRIEDRICH was very restless and queer all evening," Evander proceeded, "but the old fellow had been getting rather childish lately, so we didn't pay any particular attention to his actions. Next morning, he was gone."

"And did you make inquiry?"

"No, he often went away on little trips without warning us beforehand, and, besides, I was glad enough to see him get out. I didn't try to find him. It was just after this that my wife's health became bad, but I had to make this trip for our firm, so I called in Dr. Trowbridge, and there you are."

"Yes, *parbleu*, here we are, indeed!" de Grandin nodded emphatically. "Listen carefully, my friends; what I am about to say is the truth:

"When first I came to visit Madame Evander with Friend Trowbridge, and heard the strange story Mademoiselle Ostrander told, I was amazed. 'Why,' I ask me, 'does this lady answer the howling of a dog beneath her window?' *Parbleu*, it was most curious!

"Then while we three—Friend Trowbridge, Mademoiselle Ostrander and I—did talk of *Madame's* so strange malady, I did hear the call of that dog beneath the window with my own two ears, and did observe Madame Evander's reaction to it.

"Out the window I did put my head, and in the storm I saw no dog at all, but what I thought might be a human man—a tall, thin man. Yet a dog had howled beneath that window and had been answered by *Madame* but a moment before. Me, I do not like that.

"I call upon that man, if such he be, to begone. Also I do request Mademoiselle Ostrander to place her patient under an opiate each night, that the howls beneath her window may not awaken Madame Evander.

"*Eh bien*, thus far, thus good. But you do come along, *Monsieur*, and countermand my order. While *Madame* is not under the drug that unholy thing beneath her window does howl once more, and *Madame* disappears. Yes.

"Now, there was no ordinary medical diagnosis for such a case as this, so I search my memory and my knowledge for an extraordinary one. What do I find in that storehouse of my mind?

"In parts of Europe, my friends—believe me, I know whereof I speak!—there are known such things as werewolves, or wolf-men. In France we know them as *les loups-garoux*; in Wales they call them the bug-wolves, or bogie wolves; in the days of old the Greeks did know them under the style of *lukanthropos*. Yes.

"What he is no one knows well. Sometimes he is said to be a wolf—a magical wolf—who can become a man. Sometimes, more often, he is said to be a man who can, or must, become a wolf. No one knows accurately. But this we know: The man who is also a wolf is ten times more terrible than the wolf who is only a wolf. At night he quests and kills his prey, which is most often his fellow man, but sometimes his ancient enemy, the dog. By day he hides his villainy under the guise of a man's form. Sometimes he changes entirely to a wolf's shape, sometimes he becomes a fearful mixture of man and beast, but always he is a devil incarnate. If he be killed while in the wolf shape, he at once reverts to human form, so by that sign we know we have slain a were-wolf and not a true wolf. Certainly.

"NOW SOME WEREWOLVES become such by the aid of Satan; some become so as the result of a curse; a few are so through accident. In Transylvania, that devil-ridden land, the very soil does seem to favor the transformation of man into beast. There are springs from which the water, once drunk, will make its drinker into a savage beast, and there are flowers—*cordieu*, have I not seen them?—which, if worn by a man at night during the full of the moon, will do the same. Among the most potent of these blooms of hell is *la fleur de sang*, or blood-flower, which is exactly the accursed weed you have described to us, Monsieur Evander—the flower your Uncle Friedrich and your lady did wear to the theater that night of the full moon. When you mentioned the village of Kerovitch, I did see it all at once, immediately, for that place is on the Rumanian side of the Transylvanian Alps, and there the blood-flowers are found in greater numbers than anywhere else in the world. The very mountain soil does seem cursed with lycanthropy.

"Very well. I did not know of the flower when first I came into this case, but I did suspect something evil had cast a spell on *Madame*. She did exhibit all the symptoms of a lycanthrope about to be transformed, and beneath her window there did howl what was undoubtedly a wolf-thing.

"'He has put his cursed sign upon her and does even now seek her for his mate,' I tell me after I order him away in the flame of the good God.

"When *Madame* disappeared I was not surprised. When she returned after a night in the snow, I was less surprised. But the blood on her hands did perturb me. Was it human? Was she an all-unconscious murderess, or was it, happily, the blood of animals? I did not know. I analyzed it and discovered it were dog's blood. 'Very well,' I tell me. 'Let us see where a dog has been mauled in that vicinity.'

"This afternoon I made guarded inquiries. I find many dogs have been strangely killed in this neighborhood of late. No dog, no matter how big, was safe out of doors after nightfall.

"Also I meet a man, an *ivrogne*—what you call a drunkard—one who patronizes the leggers-of-the-boot not with wisdom, but with too great frequency. He is no more so. He have made the oath to remain sober. *Pourquoi?* Because three nights ago, as he passed through the park he were set upon by a horror so terrible that he thought he was in alcoholic delirium. It were like a man, yet not like a man. It had a long nose, and terrible eyes, and great, flashing teeth, and it did seek to kill and devour him. My friends, in his way, that former drunkard did describe the thing which tried to enter this house tonight. It were the same.

"Fortunately for the poor drunken man, he were carrying a walking cane of ash wood, and when he raised it to defend himself, the terror did shrink from him. 'Ah ha,' I tell me when I hear that, 'now we know it were truly le *loupgarou*,' for it is notorious that the wood of the ash tree is as intolerable to the werewolf as the bloom of the garlic is unpleasant to the vampire.

"WHAT DO I DO? I go to the woods and cut a bundle of ash switches. Then I come here. Tonight the wolf-thing come crying for the mate who ranged the snows with him last night. He is lonely, he is mad for another of his kind. Tonight, perhaps, they will attack nobler game than dogs. Very well, I am ready.

"When Madame Evander, being drugged, did not answer his call, he was emboldened to enter the house. *Pardieu*, he did not know Jules de Grandin awaited him! Had I not been here it might well have gone hard with Mademoiselle Ostrander. As it was"—he spread his slender hands—"there is one less man-monster in the world this night."

Evander stared at him in round-eyed wonder. "I can't believe it," he muttered, "but you've proved your case. Poor Uncle Friedrich! The curse of the blood-flower . . ." He broke off, an expression of mingled horror and despair on his face. "My wife!" he gasped. "Will she become a thing like that? Will . . . ?"

"*Monsieur*," de Grandin interrupted gently, "she *has* become one. Only the drug holds her bound in human form at this minute."

"Oh," Evander cried, tears of grief streaming down his face, "save her! For the love of heaven, save her! Can't you do anything to bring her back to me?"

"You do not approve my methods," de Grandin reminded him.

Evander was like a pleading child. "I apologize," he whimpered. "I'll give you anything you ask if you'll only save her. I'm not rich, but I think I can raise fifty thousand dollars. I'll give it to you if you'll cure her!"

The Frenchman twisted his little blond mustache furiously. "The fee you name is attractive, *Monsieur*," he remarked.

"I'll pay it; I'll pay it!" Evander burst out hysterically. Then, unable to control himself, he put his folded arms on the table, sank his head upon them, and shook with sobs.

"Very well," de Grandin agreed, casting me the flicker of a wink. "Tomorrow night I shall undertake your lady's case. Tomorrow night we attempt the cure. *Au revoir, Monsieur*. Come away, Friend Trowbridge, we must rest well before tomorrow night."

DE GRANDIN WAS SILENT to the point of moodiness all next morning. Toward noon he put on his outdoor clothing and left without luncheon, saying he would meet me at Evander's that night.

He was there when I arrived and greeted me, saying that the main business would start soon.

"Meantime, Trowbridge, *mon vieux*, I beg you will assist me in the kitchen. There is much to do and little time in which to do it."

Opening a large valise he produced a bundle of slender sticks which he began splitting into strips like basket-withes, explaining that they were from a mountain ash tree. When some twenty-five of these had been prepared, he selected a number of bottles from the bottom of the satchel, and, taking a large aluminum kettle, began scouring it with a clean cloth.

"Attend me carefully, Friend Trowbridge," he commanded; "do you keep close tally as I compound the draft, for much depends on the formula being correct. To begin."

Arranging a pair of apothecary's scales and a graduate glass before him on the table, he handed me this memorandum.

R
3 pints pure spring water
2 drachms sulfer
1/2 oz. castorium

6 drachms opium

3 drachms asafoetida

1/2 oz. hypericum

3/4 oz. aromatic ammonia

1/2 oz. gum camphor

As he busied himself with scales and graduate I checked the amounts he poured into the kettle. "Voila," he announced, "we are prepared!"

Quickly he thrust the ash withes into a pailful of boiling water and proceeded to bind together a three-stranded hyssop of ash, poplar and birch twigs.

"And now, my friend, if you will assist me, we shall proceed," he asserted, thrusting a large washpan into my hands and preparing to follow me into the dining room with the kettle of liquor he had prepared, his little brush-broom thrust under his arm.

We moved the dining room furniture against the walls, and de Grandin put the kettle of liquid in the dishpan I had brought in, piling a number of light wood chips about it, and starting a small fire. As the liquid in the kettle began bubbling and seething over the flame, he knelt and began tracing a circle about seven feet in diameter with a bit of white chalk. Inside the first circle he drew a second ring some three feet in diameter, and within this traced a star composed of two interlaced triangles. At the very center he marked down an odd-looking figure composed of a circle surmounted by a crescent and supported by a cross. "This is the Druid's foot, or pentagram," he explained, indicating the star. "The powers of evil are powerless to pass it, either from without or within. This," he pointed to the central figure, "is the sign of Mercury. It is also the sign of the Holy Angels, my friend, and the *bon Dieu* knows we shall need their kind offices this night. Compare, Friend Trowbridge, if you please, the chart I have drawn with the exemplar which I did most carefully prepare from the occult books today. I would have the testimony of both of us that I have left nothing undone."

Into my hand he thrust the following chart:

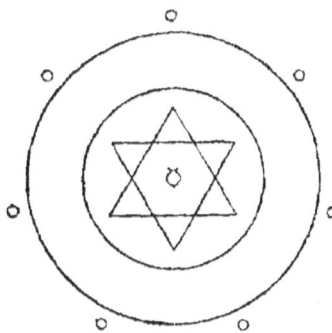

Quickly, working like one possessed, he arranged seven small silver lamps about the outer circle where the seven little rings on the chart indicated, ignited their wicks, snapped off the electric light and, rushing into the kitchen, returned with the boiled ash withes dangling from his hand.

Fast as he had worked, there was not a moment to spare, for Miss Ostrander's hysterical call, "Dr. de Grandin, oh, Dr. de Grandin!" came down the stairs as he returned from the kitchen.

ON THE BED, Mrs. Evander lay writhing like a person in convulsions. As we approached, she turned her face toward us, and I stopped in my tracks, speechless with the spectacle before me.

It was as if the young woman's pretty face were twisted into a grimace, only the muscles, instead of resuming their wonted positions again, seemed to stretch steadily out of place. Her mouth widened gradually till it was nearly twice its normal size, her nose seemed lengthening, becoming more pointed, and crooking sharply at the end. Her eyes, of sweet cornflower blue, were widening, becoming at once round and prominent, and changing to a wicked, phosphorescent green. I stared and stared, unable to believe the evidence of my eyes, and as I looked she raised her hands from beneath the covers, and I went sick with the horror of it. The dainty, flowerlike pink-and-white hands with their well-manicured nails were transformed into a pair of withered, corded talons armed with long, hornlike, curved claws, saber-sharp and hooked like the nails of some predatory bird. Before my eyes a sweet, gently bred woman was being transfigured into a foul hell-hag, a loathsome, hideous parody of herself.

"Quickly, Friend Trowbridge, seize her, bind her!" de Grandin called, thrusting a handful of the limber withes into my grasp and hurling himself upon the monstrous thing which lay in Edith Evander's place.

The hag fought like a true member of the wolf pack. Howling, clawing, growling and snarling, she opposed tooth and nail to our efforts, but at last we lashed her wrists and ankles firmly with the wooden cords and bore her, struggling frantically, down the stairs and placed her within the mystic circle de Grandin had drawn on the dining room floor.

"Inside, Friend Trowbridge, quickly!" the Frenchman ordered as he dipped the hyssop into the boiling liquid in the kettle and leaped over the chalk marks. "Mademoiselle Ostrander, Monsieur Evander, for your lives, leave the house!"

Reluctantly the husband and nurse left us and de Grandin began showering the contorting, howling thing on the floor with liquid from the boiling kettle.

SWINGING HIS HYSSOP in the form of a cross above the hideous change-ling's head, he uttered some invocation so rapidly that I failed to catch the words, then, striking the wolf-woman's feet, hands, heart and head in turn with his bundle of twigs, he drew forth a small black book and began reading in a firm, clear voice: "*Out of the deep have I called unto Thee, O Lord; Lord hear my voice . . .*"

And at the end he finished with a great shout: "*I know that my redeemer liveth . . . I am the resurrection and the life, saith the Lord; he that believeth in me, though he were dead, yet shall he live!*"

As the words sounded through the room it seemed to me that a great cloud of shadow, like a billow of black vapor, rose from the dark corners of the apartment, eddied toward the circle of lamps, swaying their flames lambently, then suddenly gave back, evaporated and disappeared with a noise like steam escaping from a boiling kettle.

"Behold, Trowbridge, my friend," de Grandin ordered, pointing to the still figure which lay over the sign of Mercury at his feet.

I bent forward, stifling my repugnance, then sighed with mingled relief and surprise. Calm as a sleeping child, Edith Evander, freed from all the hideous stigmata of the wolf-people, lay before us, her slender hands, still bound in the wooden ropes, crossed on her breasts, her sweet, delicate features as though they had never been disfigured by the curse of the blood-flower.

Loosing the bonds from her wrists and feet the Frenchman picked the sleeping woman up in his arms and bore her to her bedroom above stairs.

"Do you summon her husband and the nurse, my friend," he called from the turn in the stairway. "She will have need of both anon."

WH—WHY, SHE'S HERSELF AGAIN!" Evander exclaimed joyfully as he leaned solicitously above his wife's bed.

"But of course!" de Grandin agreed. "The spell of evil was strong upon her, *Monsieur*, but the charm of good was mightier. She is released from her bondage for all time."

"I'll have your fee ready tomorrow," Evander promised diffidently. "I could not arrange the mortgages today—it was rather short notice, you know."

Laughter twinkled in de Grandin's little blue eyes like the reflection of moonlight on flowing water. "My friend," he replied, "I did make the good joke on you last night. *Parbleu*, to hear you agree to anything, and to announce that you did trust to my methods, as well, was payment enough for me. I want not your money. If you would repay Jules de Grandin for his services, continue to love and cherish your wife as you did last night when you feared you were about to lose her. Me, *morbleu!* but I shall make the eyes of my *confreres* pop with jealousy when I tell them what I have accomplished this night. *Sang d'un poisson*, I am one very clever man, *Monsieur!*"

"IT'S ALL A MYSTERY TO ME, de Grandin," I confessed as we drove home, "but I'm hanged if I can understand how it was that the man was transformed into a monster almost as soon as he wore those flowers, and the woman resisted the influence of the things for a week or more."

"Yes," he agreed, "that is strange. Myself, I think it was because werewolfism is an outward and visible sign of the power of evil, and the man was already steeped in sin, while the woman was pure in heart. She had what we might call a higher immunity from the virus of the blood-flower."

"And wasn't there some old legend to the effect that a werewolf could only be killed with a silver bullet?"

"Ah bah," he replied with a laugh. "What did those old legend-mongers know of the power of modern firearms? *Parbleu*, had the good St. George possessed a military rifle of today, he might have slain the dragon without approaching nearer than a mile! When I did shoot that wolfman, my friend, I had something more power-ful than superstition in my hand. *Morbleu*, but I did shoot a hole in him large enough for him to have walked through!"

"That reminds me," I added, "how are we going to explain his body to the police?"

"Explain?" he echoed with a chuckle. "*Nom d'un bouc*, we shall not explain: I, myself, did dispose of him this very afternoon. He lies buried beneath the roots of an ash tree, with a stake of ash through his heart to hold him to the earth. His sinful body will rise again no more to plague us, I do assure you. He was known to have a habit of disappearing. Very good. This time there will be no re-appearance. We are through, finished, done with him for good."

We drove another mile or so in silence, then my companion nudged me sharply in the ribs. "This curing of werewolf ladies, my friend," he confided, "it is dry work. Are you sure there is a full bottle of brandy in the cellar?"

THE DEVILS OF PO SUNG
BASSETT MORGAN

OF ALL WEALTH ABOUNDING in Papua for the man who risks its myriad perils and keeps faith with the under-dogs of trade channels by which pearls and Paradise skins flow forth, Captain McTeague preferred pearls. He was a connoisseur and could state at sight and with remarkable accuracy the natal place of a nest of pearls. On the somewhat sketchy charts of tortuous outlines of the evilly lovely black sphinx of the South Seas he had painstakingly marked the location of more prolific sources of those translucent drops of tinted glory, and the finest came from a lagoon on the north coast guarded by an unspoiled, therefore indomitable tribe under the rule of Tukmoo.

In ports which splash the transient whitewash of civilization on the Papuan sea rims, it was said that Tukmoo's warriors had never met defeat; that as sorcerer, Tukmoo devised ingenious tortures that were the envy of his rivals; that he it was who punished infidelity of women by having them devour facial features of their lovers uncooked and sliced from the living victim, who was staked to the ground, and both were sentenced to the dreadful palm death which takes days of frightful agony, within sight and sound of each other.

Captain McTeague did not doubt the tales told of Tukmoo until he enquired for pearls from old Quong Yick, the Chinese who got them in exchange for alarm clocks, beads, printed silks and tin dippers, and the old trader cast the first shadow of suspicion on the hitherto gleaming hellishness of Tukmoo's intrepidity.

"Tukmoo no got. Long time he no got. He ver' sick in his liver for why he no got. He say heap debbil-debbil have got lagoon. He make plenty magic but no can do drive out debbil. Me no savvy. Maybe go look-see."

When he went north to Sarong for gum-dammar, it would not be much out of his course for Captain McTeague to investigate for himself the reason of the dearth of Tukmoo's fine pearls. McTeague headed his schooner toward that red mark on his chart which designated the best pearl lagoon known from the Curlews to the Solomons.

Starting with a sulfur-yellow sky and dead calm from which the wind moaned as it arose and lashed the Banda Sea to fury, a storm drove him from his course and delayed his arrival. With the gray seas still pursuing in hump-backed fury, McTeague saw another craft storm-harried as his own but making remarkable speed in the tail of a typhoon which had kept him on deck for forty-eight hours. She was slender and rakish, black as the hells she came from, with lurid storm-red flashes of light on her pugnacious brass guns. She seemed to be headed for some harbor until McTeague hove in sight, then she veered about as if on patrol. When he drove in closer there was a burst of white smoke, a low "boom" and the scream of a shot ricochetting too close for risking a second aim of her gunner. Captain McTeague promptly turned tail, cursing his own carelessness in not learning more about the debbil-debbils which put fear into the heart of the dauntless and devilish Tukmoo. That grim streak of a craft fast swallowed by coast shadow was manned by oily Mascats, head-hunting Dyaks and God alone knew what mixture of human wolves; but any and all of them merely spineless innocents compared with their master, who had made his own name the terror of the Banda.

McTeague knew as much as any other man about Po Sung. He was a Mongolian tainted by the worst of other strains of heritage. He spoke excellent English, was suave in company of Europeans and had so huge a grasp of trade that he was a valued confidant of port merchants and diplomats for some years while he perfected his own sovereignty in hidden realms of wealth. Po Sung was like a giant octopus with tentacles reaching to every compass point. Now that he was growing old he had brazenly disdained the guise of decency and took his true colors, secure from vengeance in some backwater shelter where he devised and executed his schemes unmolested. Captain McTeague wished he had not run across Po Sung.

He would have headed out and away only the storm had strained his schooner and snapped off a few spars and he needed to seek shelter and make repairs especially as the barometer which rose promisingly had suffered a relapse, presaging a flashback of storm.

At sunset, luridly furious behind the crouching black spine of Papuan hills, he headed the schooner into a lagoon and dropped anchor and was not surprised to be wakened shortly after he turned in by drums of the jungle talking in purring spurt and long tattoo rolls. His arrival was being broadcast by black men in the same manner in which their forebears had communicated news of the epochal upheavals of world inundation, the sunken Lemuria and Atlantis. The night was pregnant with menacing growl of drums, and a grimmer dawn poured opalescent light over a lagoon alert with darting canoes, slender as arrows, heralding the arrival of the sorcerer Tukmoo.

As THE SORCERER'S CANOE shot alongside the schooner, McTeague saw that Tukmoo wore a necklace of pearls large as his finger ends, strung between human incisor teeth. He was plumed and painted, covered from forehead to heel with blue lace of tattooing beaded with cicatrices. A scarlet loin-cloth supported a club knobbed with human knuckle-bones. The forty paddles stabbed the water as one, and McTeague was wondering (since there are but two in a set) how many incisor teeth went into that necklace, when Tukmoo reached the deck, and planting his prehensile-toed feet firmly demanded in fairly fluent pidgin-English, strong drink.

McTeague obliged with watered brandy further weakened by grenadine sirup with a chaser of coffee. He had blundered into a lagoon usurped by Tukmoo when he was driven from his heritage by Po Sung. He regretted the cruise and again wished himself far away.

"O Chief, I must make repairs to my boat," he stated. "How come you no longer guard the pearl lagoon to the south?"

Tukmoo spoke wily words of wisdom. He had the advantage of acquaintance during youth and young manhood with a zealous missionary and at the good man's death from old age had absorbed (according to his belief) wisdom of his heart, which Tukmoo ate roasted. He related a cause for deserting his pearl lagoon which was difficult to translate into pidgin. Captain McTeague shortened the tale for his Swede mate, Okey, when he announced that he would go ashore with Tukmoo.

"Okey, Po Sung has got the pearl lagoon. He's loosed a few extra fine devils and scared the giblets out of Tukmoo. I don't understand the details, but Po Sung has a flock of red devils on the river. They sound like man-eaters, whether bird or beast I can't make out. The muggers speak words. The apes chin-chin in native lingo. The land is bewitched. I suspected a phonograph, but Tukmoo has one he got from Quong Yick and knows better. His son sailed in to lick hell out of Po Sung and turned up missing just when he was ready to marry a girl all nicely ripened in the bleaching-huts. Tukmoo is ready to make bigger magic by torturing this girl, only we happened along in time to fall into the mess, and I wish to God that typhoon had piled us on the Curlews before we ran in here. Tukmoo demands that I go and make magic that will drive out Po Sung, since his own monkey-tricks have failed. There's no choice about it, Okey. I've got to go or they'll make potpourri and Irish stew of you and me and the crew. Get me my box of parlor tricks and Bengal lights and pack in a dozen sticks of dynamite with fuses and caps. If you hear me fire two shots twice in succession be ready to grab me and run for deep water. If I don't come back the schooner is yours, Okey."

"You ban damn fool to go," commented Okey. But already Captain McTeague felt the thrill of high adventure beating his blood to foam as the drums in canoes spoke to drums on shore of events going forward.

THE STILT-LEGGED HUTS of a comparatively new village were fresh-thatched and clean. Women stirred cooking-pots over beach fires. Beside Captain McTeague swaggered a black boy, Tao, carrying the box of parlor magic over which he was appointed guard. It was the first time Captain McTeague had been in league with black men or broken his wisdom of neutrality in thirty years of trading. He assumed an arrogance he did not feel as he sat at the feast of roast sea-turtle, scraped coconut cream and stewed fish washed down with fermented palm-juice. Strolling about the village afterward he saw the bereaved mother of Tukmoo's lost son Tawa, her body painted in white stripes, her hair matted with filth in token of mourning grief. He also saw old women guarding the bleaching-hut, and caught a glimpse of the bride, who stuck out her head and gazed for a long minute at this white man who came to fight Po Sung's debbil-debbils and avenge her lost lover. She was pretty as a doll, with hair like a curly feather duster, and skin bleached to creamy copper. To McTeague she called a greeting, "Halloo, *Tuan!*"

Tukmoo's rage was sudden. He yelped a command and the girl's shrieks shrilled through the village with the sound of a whip.

"Are you having that child beaten?" he demanded of Tukmoo.

"Not enough to injure her comeliness, because if she is not killed for a debbil feast, I will sell her to a big-bellied Chinese trader," explained Tukmoo.

McTeague knew the folly of interference, yet he hated the sound of the whipping, and played a bold game for a man in the power of savages whose aspect could change from friendliness to yelps of blood-lust in the twinkling of an eye.

"You are wrong to punish the woman just now," he said. "She will prove a help to our magic if she is told she will be taken with us so that her liver, hot with love for your son Tawa, will smell out the place where he is kept prisoner."

Tukmoo was impressed by this reasoning and yelped a rescinding command. The shrieks of the girl changed to quiet sobbing. The whip-wielder leaped from the hut and the girl was flung, sobbing hysterically, to the doorway, where she looked down on

McTeague with tear-streaked face and eyes like brimming golden pools. He wondered if her evident adoration of him as her deliverer might be turned to account in getting himself out of a perilous predicament.

TUKMOO COMMANDED a day of feasting. By night the *lagi-lagi* house held sodden harvest of drunken and overstuffed warriors, and Tukmoo slept with his head on the stomach of his oldest wife. McTeague, who dined and drank sparingly, prowled through the deserted village and halted beside the bleaching-hut, where a rift of moonlight splintered by palm sabers twinkled on the face of the girl at the door. Near by drowsed the young Tao with McTeague's box between his legs.

In a long day of scheming and planning escape by the river McTeague saw his first chance of success. Laying a finger on his lips for silence, he beckoned the girl down the notched log from the hut and touched the sleepy Tao, who started, snatched up the box and stood ready to accompany the white sorcerer.

McTeague pointed to the river and a canoe hauled on shore. It was slipped soundlessly to the water and the three took their places with the girl in the prow. McTeague understood the awe of his magic box which made them obey unquestioningly. Tukmoo ruled by fear of his cruelties, and the white sorcerer was greater than Tukmoo. In the face of that appraisal of his powers, McTeague did not dare command Tao to head for the lagoon and schooner. He was compelled to make some sort of farce of laying Po Sung's devils, for a cry from Tao would arouse the village and turn the moon-silvered peace to red slaughter. He saw regretfully that Tao headed the canoe inland on the black waterway.

They had not gone a half-mile when in the din of droning, humming, clacking insects came a sound which made the girl gasp with fear and held Tao's paddle dripping as he paused to listen. It was like a voice speaking through a muffled, rasping megaphone. McTeague's skin was prickling as he distinguished words, disconnected and maudlin, as if a drunken sailor mouthed a booming sea-chantey.

"Blo-ow . . . ma-an do-o-own, o-oh blo-ow tha ma-an do-own."
It was repeated and followed by obscene curses.

"Walk-about land, *Tuan!*" whispered the girl who crouched at
McTeague's feet.

"A white man in the jungle," he stated with conviction.

"Debbil-debbil!" came a low mutter from Tao.

McTeague watched the river for a canoe. Moon-silver, frail as
a spider's spinning, crinkled on the black flow which upheaved.
The long head of a crocodile lifted and it seemed to McTeague that
from its wicked jaws came a water-smothered repetition of "Blo-
ow the man do-own." Then it sank and bubbles broke. The canoe
shot forward under frenzied paddling, and in its wake the mugger
again lifted his snout and gaping jaws.

"Da-amn Po Su-ung," came a hollow growl answered by a cackle
of raucous laughter from the jungle which made McTeague snatch
the revolver at his hip.

"Orang-outang," he said as a tree branch released from the
clutch of the mighty "gray man of the woods" crashed. Again came
that outcry of terrible mirth and he saw the gray shape, a lighter
shadow in the gloom where the moonlight quivered through shaken
palms.

"The joke is on you, Red Moorphy," came a deep-chested growl.
"Ye hated wather. It took Po Sung to make ye loike ut. Why don't
ye find pearls yerself? Pearls! Hell, they got us in this mess. Made
a mugger o' you an' a monkey o' me."

Red Murphy! McTeague knew that name. It belonged to a
drunken loafer and thief who had served time for killing a Chink
trader in pearls. But he could not credit his senses as he heard a
jungle voice attribute the personality of a river mugger to Red
Murphy.

The canoe leaped like an arrow down the stream, but the gray
man of the woods kept pace and the crocodile followed. A patch of
shelving shore denuded of vegetation gave off a sickening stench.
McTeague was thankful the walk-about ground was temporarily
deserted of saurians. At his feet the girl quivered and her teeth
chattered. His hair rose in contagion of fear as the moonlight

entered a less dense patch of jungle vines where the big ape swung by one foot peering at the river. Again arose that soul-shattering human laughter ringing through the night.

"Wan more white fool," came the guttural cry. "Go on, you bloody idiot! Po Sung'll take yer brain an' sell yer dried head, an' feed yer carcass to his orchids. Like he did to Red Moorphy an' me. God . . . God . . . like he did to us fer wantin' a few pearls."

A scream from the girl contracted McTeague's nerve skeins. From behind the leathery throat of the saurian moaned a booming "Meat—whi-ite me-eat. Ee-at. Dr-rink an' be-ee merry."

"Lave 'em alo-one," growled the ape. "I'll have company when Po Sung gits 'em. Don't fill yer leather belly wid white ma-an. Here, have a nut." There was a thud as the hairy gray arm swung and a coconut hit the mugger's jaws, which snapped shut. Then it lunged on shore, the crooked-fanged jaws snapping in vain at the ape which swung just out of reach and shrilled curses as it pelted the armor-clad mugger with coconuts.

McTeague stared. He pinched his own flesh to make sure he was awake. Glancing at Tao he saw sweat pouring down the oiled black chest of the native and the gleam of his eye-whites as he strained every muscle to outdistance the river horror.

Through the overhung river channel resounded the crash of water beaten by the powerful tail of the crocodile, its booming curses of port dive origin, the thuds of coconuts on its scaly length, the horrid shrieks of the ape's mirth as it denuded palms of their nuts. The river bobbed with them. The roar and scream of the combat was like thunder, silencing the rasp of insect clatter and hard breathing of Tao. McTeague thought he should soon awake from this incredible nightmare. He assured himself it was the ravings of delirium, but the finger-nails of the girl cut his flesh as she clutched his legs in her terror.

"Catchum white-man chin-chin," she quivered. "Make magic, *Tuan*."

The river turned. The walls of matted lianas shut the sound of combat farther away; then only did Tao slacken speed.

"Debbil-debbils," he groaned. McTeague thought of the feeble frauds of parlor magic in the box shoved toward him by the girl, simple tricks he had brought to fight such magic as he never dreamed—dread, incomprehensible black magic. Had Po Sung trained an ape to speak, a crocodile to talk? He could think of no other explanation, yet that mockery was dissipated when he recalled the words of the ape and its reasoning. This was no parrotlike repetition of words, nor would Po Sung be likely to teach jungle beasts English curses. The terrible Mongolian had invented a new hell into which McTeague plunged, and in that hour his only resolve was to sell life dearly but to die rather than fall into the power of that arch-fiend.

The swish of branches nearby roused him. In the waning moonlight of the hour before dawn, he saw a second gray shape swinging along and slowly whimpering inarticulate sounds resembling native lingo. The girl stiffened as she knelt, her hands clutched her round breasts and her cry aroused McTeague's pity.

"Tawa," she moaned, "Tawa chin-chin . . . talk-talkee."

McTeague felt his hair prickling his scalp. The canoe drifted as Tao was frozen by fear. There was the drip-drip of the paddle held in air.

"Tawa, Tawa," called the girl. The ape ceased muttering, then clutched a mat of lianas and swung closer, peering down at the face of the girl now gray-yellow in the frame of bushy curls. There came a scream that curdled McTeague's blood. The hairy arm shot out and caught the girl's hair, and she was lifted from the canoe to twist slowly and struggle feebly until McTeague's gun cracked. Came a howl of pain as the hold was released, the girl slumped in the canoe and the ape streaked into the jungle. The canoe leaped forward.

McTeague let the girl lie in merciful oblivion. His own blood congealed at the horror of this demon-haunted domain of Po Sung. Behind them came the fighting mugger and first ape, and they dared not attempt to turn back.

GRAY DAWN SIFTED over moon and stars. Through densely matted lianas McTeague saw patches of pearl-tinted sky and caught lurid gleams of scarlet flowers which breathed a fetid scent as repulsive as the walkabout grounds of crocodiles. The shore was a mass of orchids, with black throats and quivering stamens of yellow, which climbed the branches of gray trees and dead ropes of vines. A bend in the river hid them from the ape and mugger. The canoe navigated a stretch of stream walled by the furious scarlet of orchids that seemed to announce the master-hand of a gardener planting them like ruddy cliffs along the black flow of river shadow.

When the sun spread gold on the upper reaches of the flower wall, McTeague observed the orchid petals quivering and folding in elongated bulb-shapes of dull yellow. The river widened into a pool, smooth as a mirror bordered with fern and feathery nipa palm. There was lurid and ominous beauty in the place, a menacing and maddening tumult of scarlet orchids of gigantic size, with petals five feet or more in length, their dusky black throats shading to maroon purple. The stamens stood out like knobbed wands thick as a man's thumb. The stench was breath-taking, overpowering, disgusting, yet when he commanded Tao to land he met vigorous protest.

"Catchum die," chattered Tao. He dropped the paddle to scoop water in his palms and suck at it noisily. McTeague snatched the paddle and sent the canoe shoreward. Its prow shoved aside the ferns and he thrust a foot to test the pool rim for a landing foothold, balancing his body with arms outthrust. Instantly the nearest giant flowers lunged forward and he was shocked to helplessness as the great petals wrapped about his bare arm with the cold sensation of serpent scales, yet repulsively flexible and soft.

Paralyzed from amazement he felt himself pulled from the canoe to flounder breast-high in the pool, the petal grip on his arm tenaciously supporting his weight. His arm pained as if constricted by a tourniquet. Tao's screech roused the girl, who first recovered her wits and snatched a knife from Tao's belt. McTeague was trying in vain to tear off the orchid petal. His senses reeled from the anesthetic stench of the orchid throat and he was only vaguely aware that the girl slashed loose gray sections of petals, the veins of which took strength to sever. He slumped into the pool over his head and came up, to clutch at the canoe stern over which he was hauled.

Tearing the petal fragments from his arm he felt the stab of pain, and blood spurted from the pores of a swelling red band. McTeague was horrified with fear of virulent poison. He jabbed his knife into the flesh and sucked vigorously, spitting into the pool as Tao sent the craft from shore.

As the canoe drifted near shore, McTeague saw the orchids move forward on their stems like gorgeous beast-heads craning toward a glut of meat. The whole wall was alert and in motion, lunging out, waving giant flowers to and fro until he could see the supporting jungle trees dead and bleached to the tops. He knew the vampire orchids of the jungle, but never before had he seen such huge ones, or animal greed so voraciously displayed. Adding to horror, the pool narrowed again to river width, arched overhead by the terrible scarlet flowers. It was like the red throat of a medieval dragon yawning for victims.

McTeague turned from the sight and observed a singular phenomenon at the pool. As the sun rose and its hot light gilded the topmost flowers, their petals jerked reluctantly shut, folded into bulb-shaped buds. At his command the paddle halted. They waited until sunlight flooded the pool and the shore was hung with leathery yellow bulbs. The shaded river yielded more slowly to the all-powerful sun. The canoe went on, and as if sentient, aware of meat near by, the tips of petals unfolded like tigers' tongues. There was the sound of creaking and rubber stems writhing like serpents. The sun had worked one of its myriad miracles, but it did not penetrate into the scarlet funnel more than a hundred yards, where McTeague faced low-hanging scarlet horrors that swayed forward, greedy for prey.

Again the craft was halted and McTeague reached for his box, then busied himself biting caps and fuses on sticks of dynamite. His right arm was swollen to twice its natural size and almost useless. His lips were hot and dry as in fever. The flower stench was terrific and making them all drowsy.

Yelling to Tao to back the canoe he tossed a stick of dynamite at each river shore, and they were drifting on the pool when a deafening roar crashed. There were tearing and slithering sounds. The river roof seemed to lift and a backwash of water rocked their craft.

For some moments debris rained down, brilliant bunches of feathers that had been Paradise birds and lories, ragged tatters of orchid petals, nooses of lianas, then the scarlet wall seemed to subside and float on the water surface, a bridge of vegetation over which McTeague assisted Tao to shove the canoe into sun-drenched water beyond.

To his incredible relief, McTeague breathed cleaner air than the stinking fetidity of the orchid pool. There was clean salt breeze from the sea and tang of ebb-tide which cleared his brain of the poison that stultified his senses. But they faced peril ahead, for as the river turned he saw the tip-tilted cornices of a dwelling built like an old temple of Cathay and knew they approached the house of Po Sung.

Much as he dreaded a meeting with that terrific personage, there was no choice. He hoped his wits and obvious blundering into the place would prove his innocence of intent to thieve pearls. He was too well-known to drop out of sight without enquiry and trouble for any man who held him prisoner. All in all, even Po Sung was a more endurable alternative than a return by the river. Yet his nerves tautened as he saw cultivated gardens, and a long pergolalike bridge spanning the river, completely covered at the far end with the scarlet orchids folded now in yellow buds.

Small channels had been cut from the river, and one of these they followed to a small pool. Red lacquer bridges arched the little streams. The sea-tang was stronger. There were hedges of fragrant ylang-ylang and frangipani, glimpses of orchards and growing plants in prim array, white crushed-coral paths, coolies in wide hats moving about stone steps of a landing-place which caught McTeague's breath and gaze.

A TALL FORM IN A ROBE of saffron yellow awaited them, its hands folded in green-banded sleeves. Captain McTeague looked into the grim black eyes of Po Sung.

"Welcome." He spoke in suspiciously bland tones. "I do not often have visitors, Captain McTeague."

His eyes darted like black quicksilver from McTeague's head down his bleeding arm to his river-wet trousers and boots.

"I heard your salute. My servants came running to report a breach in my orchid wall. I did not expect you to dynamite a way to my poor house, Captain McTeague. Why not have come by the sea?"

"No doubt you know the reason, Po Sung. Your boat took a pot-shot at my schooner yesterday. I had no idea of visiting you, but when I put in to make repairs, Tukmoo decided to detain me. I've had a bad night trying to get away and got a caress from your loving orchids. Could I trouble you for some permanganate?"

"My poor house is at your disposal, Captain McTeague."

He followed Po Sung up the path, with the girl close at his heels. Tao was sent to white-washed huts of coolie workers. On the porch of the house, copper-screened and shaded, McTeague fell into a sea-grass chair and snatched at the tall glass of cool liquid brought by a Dyak servant. He was exhausted and his eyes closed.

When he wakened he was lying on a soft mattress, clad in silk pajamas, and his wounded arm was wrapped with gauze. Light from a horn-sided ceiling lantern showed him a sleeping-room with no other furnishings than his bed and a blue jar of scentless hibiscus along one wall. He was troubled by far-away moanings and yowls from the jungle, as if the great gray men of the woods howled their hate of Po Sung.

Then again he slept and awoke greatly refreshed. The Dyak boy brought a tray of food, highly spiced chicken curry, fruit and rice wine. Evidently Po Sung lived in luxury in his hidden haven. McTeague decided that the tales told of the Mongolian were too luridly flavored by superstition. A devil he might be, but he had extended gentlemanly hospitality to Captain McTeague.

The Dyak boy shaved McTeague and trimmed his bronze beard. He was shown a coral-lined swimming-pool, where he bathed and donned pajamas of heavier silk and thick-soled sandals, returning to the porch where Po Sung sat waving a womanish fan of carved ivory and kingfisher feathers.

"You slept well, Captain McTeague?" he enquired.

"Splendidly, thanks to you, Po Sung."

"I am honored. I feared your rest would be disturbed. The big apes were noisy and my servants worked with torches in the garden. However I am free today to entertain you. No doubt you came for pearls."

He clapped his hands, and the Dyak boy appeared with a lacquer box and placed it on McTeague's lap, then opened the lid. McTeague gazed on such magnificence of pearls as he had never seen, ran his fingers in their glory, poured them from palm to palm, then realizing that his eyes too much reflected the greed he felt of such wealth he resolutely snapped down the lid and motioned the boy to take them away.

"The sight of them makes me want them, of course, but I only *trade* in pearls, and so far only through Quong Yick, who told me that Tukmoo no longer held this lagoon. I came to learn why he let it go, and I fell into his clutches. He took me prisoner and demanded powerful magic to fight your debbil-debbils. I brought my parlor tricks and dynamite. What else could I do? Tukmoo had me where he could force me to do his bidding. Then he had a big feast, and while he was drunk and asleep I came away with Tao the black boy and the girl who was to have been the wife of Tawa, son of Tukmoo. We were pretty badly scared at the apes and muggers on the way here and drifted into the orchid lagoon. I blasted my way through."

Po Sung caressed the silky black mustache which dripped like tar-streams from his upper lip.

"Tukmoo's son is braver than the sorcerer. I admire such courage in youth and have made him independent of the blacks, who are stupid pigs. But it is a pity to separate two lovers, so I was pleased when you brought the girl. They shall be united."

"That's mighty decent of you, Po Sung," said McTeague impulsively. Then, as he saw the basilisk gaze of those black eyes and the sneering smile of the cruel lips, his heart missed a beat. "You mean what you have just said?" he faltered.

"I speak the truth, Captain McTeague. In a few days you shall see for yourself. Meanwhile I should like to show you some of the

magic I have worked here, and the growth of an orchid bulb planted
only last night. Come!"

McTeague followed him toward the pergola arching the river.
It was still in shadow and the scarlet orchids wide open at the jungle
end. At the near approach, thick green stems thrust rosy tips from
soft, loose earth. Po Sung's yellow hand pointed, and McTeague
saw the stems stretch higher, growing inches as he watched, putting forth buds, and twisting through the bars of the trellis.

"Marvelous, Po Sung. You are another Burbank."

"Again I am honored by your praise. The wild orchid devoured
only insects and birds, but under my gardening it is perfected to a
man-eating flower fed by blood. It is a hungry thing, Captain
McTeague, and only for the foolish assaults of Tukmoo's warriors,
the river walls would not have flourished as they do. I planted those
bulbs in human carcasses, as this one was planted last night."

McTeague's body jerked. His head came up slowly until he
gazed into the terrible eyes of Po Sung.

"You planted a bulb in a human body last night?"

Po Sung nodded.

"Did I not say that I have decided to unite Tawa and his bride?
Tawa is now in the jungle. I heard him chattering to you as you
came up the river. I hope your shot did not maim him. Tawa's body
feeds this full-grown orchid across the bridge. His brain is in the
head of a gray man of the woods!"

"God in heaven!" breathed McTeague. "You mock me with lies."

Po Sung smiled. His black eyebrows arched.

"You shall see and believe. You are not the first man to doubt
the power of Po Sung. One year ago two thieves stole in from the
sea. One of them supplied brains to a river crocodile, the other is a
gray ape. They were companions in crime, but always fighting. They
still fight along the river shore, a most amusing sight, as you must
have found it last night."

McTeague felt the tropic heat choking him, yet cold sweat
rained down his face. He stumbled over the coral paths as he followed Po Sung to the house and through doorways he scarcely saw,
with the smell of chloroform growing stronger, until he stood in a

room with white cement walls, a skylight overhead, fitted like a hospital operating-room. Under the open skylight was a huge iron-legged cot, to which the body of a she-ape was strapped, its head swathed in bandages. Two Chinese were clearing away the evidences of surgery, and one of them spoke to Po Sung in accentless English:

"She is doing splendidly."

"The bride of Tawa," announced Po Sung, pointing to the ape. "My assistant, Dr. Feng Chu."

McTeague heard no more. The floor seemed to heave and bludgeon him. He had fainted.

FOR TIME OF WHICH he had no means of keeping track, McTeague lay on a porch couch, waited on hand and foot by the Dyak boy. Po Sung and Dr. Feng Chu, he learned from the assistant surgeon, were away in the yacht. Po Sung left orders to show Captain McTeague every respect and tell him the casket of pearls was a gift. It was advisable not to attempt to return to his schooner until Po Sung's arrival. The gray apes were troublesome lately.

They troubled McTeague. At night he heard the raucous mirth and mournful calling of Tawa, and saw the ghoulish man-shapes in the starlight. The she-ape in the surgery was also noisy, moaning piteously, and mouthing queer sounds quite different from ape-chatter.

It seemed to McTeague he was still in feverish delirium. He did not want to escape, had no power to attempt it. There were books, but he would not exert himself to read. Wandering about the grounds, he noticed the new orchid had attained a prodigious size and was already beginning to bloom. Mingled with his waking dreams were thoughts of two vampire orchids rooted in the moldering flesh of Tawa and the girl, and their brains in the heads of jungle simians.

There came a day when the assistant surgeon led the she-ape to the grounds and chained her to a tree, where she squatted as inert as McTeague on the porch. He wondered at her limpness until the Chinese told him she was under opiates to keep her quiet while her head healed. Then it flashed to the mind of McTeague that, like the ape, he was being doped. No other explanation accounted for his spineless indifference to his fate. A healthy fear intruded on his half dreams. He was being held for some sinister purpose of Po Sung, and like a fool he had supinely endured.

"Where is Po Sung?" he asked the Chinese.

"You have heard of a remarkable trained ape belonging to a scientist in Java, perhaps? Po Sung hopes to bring it back and turn it into this jungle as a companion for Tawa and the other experiment on the pearl thief, McMahon."

"I have seen pet monkeys freed among their own kind," said McTeague slowly. "The wild monkeys kill them instantly."

The Chinese did not answer, for the she-ape had roused and was leaping to the length of her chains. The tree shook with her vigorous attempts to free herself.

"Now she shall have her lesson to avoid the house when she is at liberty," said the Chinese. He went into the house and appeared again with a whip of long thin lashes barbed with metal. Watching his chance, he swung it at the she-ape. McTeague hated the cruelty of that performance, the furious suffering beast with her blood-red eyes, the streaks of blood spurting from her flanks and the cold-blooded Chinese lashing with all his strength. His own blood boiled, raced, lashed him to fury that combated the dope he was now certain had been fed him in the spicy curries at mealtimes.

When the ape sank down quivering and exhausted, the coolies rushed forward and unshackled her, and again the lash sang through the air and lifted tufts of skin. With a bound she was up and staggering uncertainly away, to disappear over the bridge into the jungle. The Chinese coiled his whip and returned to the house.

That day McTeague scraped his food into a towel and hid it under his mattress, then wandered to the gardens and ate fruit. Already he felt lighter, freer, but his nerves ached for the sedative. He realized a new peril, a craving for opium fed him, that would be worse than slavery unless he escaped at once. But he did not know how closely his movements were guarded.

He returned to the porch. The assistant surgeon was talking to a coolie, whom he dismissed. He asked McTeague to come with him to the surgery, where he filled a hypodermic needle, then laid yellow fingers on the white man's arm.

"No you don't," exploded McTeague. "You've doped me long enough. Po Sung won't use my carcass for his devil-orchids unless he kills my brain first." His fist shot out, caught the point of the yellow jaw, and with a screech the Chinese doubled up on the floor. McTeague heard running feet and slammed shut the metal door of the surgery just as yellow men lunged into view. The bolt rang home. He had barricaded himself in the cement-walled room with the unconscious yellow man.

FOR A FEW MOMENTS he felt a huge satisfaction, but it passed as the Chinese stirred. He hauled him to the cot and strapped him with bonds that had held the she-ape. Then he mopped his sweaty face and considered. From the open skylight he heard sounds of some alarm. The yellow men had thundered on the door, then departed. Using a small ladder, he climbed to the roof opening and looked from the tiers of roofs down on the domain of Po Sung, the sunset colors on the gleaming lagoon and sea, and he saw there the rakish black yacht whose guns had fired on his schooner. Po Sung had returned.

News of his return agitated the servants, who darted to and fro with flaring torches. Then McTeague saw the cause of their excitement. On the orchid-twined bridge two gray shapes swung, and the closed flower bulbs bobbed like elongated balloons on strings. The river water was stirred by a lashing black tail, and in the rapidly gathering night gloom sounded the booming curses of devils which Po Sung had created, roused now to fury against the arch-fiend.

A fierce, unholy joy filled the breast of Captain McTeague. Below him the yellow surgeon heaved against the binding thongs of the cot. A dancing light low down on the lagoon told of Po Sung's small boat leaving the yacht. He would enter the waterway and meet the rage of his victims, and from his high perch McTeague could defy them all, Po Sung, the mugger and the apes.

No, not all, for a third wavering gray ape came over the bridge, fangs bared in a horrid grin, frightening the torch-bearers back to the house as she advanced. In the smoky light McTeague could see the raw-edged scar about her head which bandages had hidden that day. Her screams were piercing and pitiful, her scrambling weak and uncertain, but she was fearless, for behind her stalked the man-apes, tremendously powerful, long arms swinging to their feet, and before that terrible sight the coolies retreated with wild screeches, slamming doors, moving furniture against all openings.

Up the river bank crawled a glistening black length of scaled ugliness, with jaws snapping.

McTeague heard the sound of ripping and tearing, the furious scream of the simians, then blood-curdling cries. He saw a glare below where the she-ape tossed torches in a heap to blaze and burn, lighting the scene of carnage. He saw human forms, broken and twisted, hurled from the porch, and strips of bamboo walls tossed on the fire. Then he knew his own peril. Sooner or later the apes would slaughter every living thing, tear the house to shreds and break into this surgery. He looked down at the bound yellow man on the cot. This was no time for petty differences.

"The jungle apes are killing the servants," he cried, "and burning the house. We are trapped up here, and Po Sung is on his way by the river to meet a doom he deserves. I'll confess I'm a coward right at this minute. I prefer a shot to that death. Is there a gun within reach?"

He dropped down and unfastened the bonds, then pointed to the ladder, which the Chinese mounted, even climbing out on the roof to look over its edge.

McTeague heard him cry out, a despairing shriek of terror. He leaped up the ladder in time to see a gray shape squatted on the roof dangling the miserable surgeon by one arm and swinging him back and forth. Suddenly her hold broke. The Chinese twisted in the air and fell to the ground, quivered, and then lay still.

McTeague looked into the gleaming red eyes of the she-ape. He had no weapon, but below were cases of surgical knives, his only defense now, his only chance of suicide to escape worse. He dropped from the skylight and his fist crashed into the glass of a case, his fingers fumbled in the darkness among queer contrivances, but none of them knives. He dashed to another case, guided

by the faint luminosity of glass, and crashed through it. Then the
faint starlight and fire reflection were blotted out. The skylight held
the she-ape, and she had dropped inside and sat on the ladder peering at him. He could see her gleaming eyes, hear his own breath
sobbing in his throat as his hands fumbled for knives and found
only small probes, useless to fight that huge gray death.

He was flattened against the wall beside the case, a fistful of
sharp probes ready for the lunge, when he heard her muttering in
piteous efforts to control the vocal mechanism of the thick throat.

"*Tuan*," she muttered, "*Tuan*," and swung down from the ladder with an arm outstretched. He felt the claws touch his arm gently, and stroke his flesh.

THEN FOR MCTEAGUE BLACKNESS FELL. He was vaguely aware of being
swung in giant arms and feeling a cool wind in his face. His eyes
opened. He lay on the upper roof, with the arm of the she-ape holding him firmly. Below, the fire leaped and the sounds of savage
destruction went on, but there were no cries of fear now, only the
guttural curses of the ape McMahon and war-cries of Papuan jungle
uttered by Tawa. Turning his head, McTeague saw the light on the
yacht's dingey coming down the river.

"Look," he muttered, and his arm pointed. The she-ape turned.

She saw and understood. In another moment McTeague was
seized bodily and swung in air as the she-ape swiftly descended by
the tiers of pointed roofs until he was dropped unhurt on the earth.
Seizing him by one wrist she ran with him toward the river, where
black gloom of trees hid them effectively. There McTeague, still
held by his captor, saw the dark swirl of water where the mugger
dived. He saw the boat sweep on under the dip of oars, to its doom.

There was an unheaved bow lantern, cries in the night, and the
lashing of the mugger's tail, the snapping of its terrible jaws and
sea-oaths from its dread throat. Later, a limp, dripping figure
crawled to the bank. McTeague could hear its gasping breathing,
and the she-ape leaped forward. He was free.

He waited until the she-ape seized that creeping victim escaped
from the mugger, and her cry summoned the man-apes, one of

whom carried a brand of flaming wood. Its light shone on the yellow face of Po Sung, distorted now by terror he had so often chiseled on faces of other men. McTeague saw the she-ape clutch the long ends of his mustache, curl them about her claws and drag Po Sung by his mouth toward the pergola.

Then he turned away at the dreadful cry that broke. The three apes were tearing Po Sung to bits and stuffing them into the orchid bulbs.

On the river the dingey floated. McTeague darted toward it, plunged in, dragged it to the shallows and secured a floating oar. He glanced back at the river bend and saw the apes flinging bits to the gaping jaws of the mugger. Then he sculled for life toward the lagoon.

A cry from Po Sung's yacht hailed him, but he paid no heed. One man could not catch McTeague on that night of fear, and the others of the crew were staining the black river water with their life-blood. A gleaming stretch of lagoon entrance beckoned to the sea, which was quiet, star-silvered. It was the time of ebb-tide, an evil hour in Papua, but Captain McTeague was beyond feeling, beyond thinking, horror-drugged, fear-driven, possessing the strength of a maniac as he sculled the boat north.

He did not remember coming to the lagoon where his schooner lay, but the mate told him later that they saw him standing in the boat, swaying from side to side like a drunken man, and through the glass they recognized Captain McTeague,

There was a tremendous feast the day after his return. Tukmoo and his warriors wakened the jungle echoes by their drums. Captain McTeague lay oblivious, and Okey the mate did the honors of the occasion, standing guard over the deck cot where McTeague lay prone, exhausted, weary to death and fighting nightmares.

"You ban wan great man, Captain," Okey explained later. "Tukmoo ban brang pearls off Po Sung. Debbil-debbils ban gone now. How come?"

Tukmoo had raked over the wreckage of Po Sung's house and found the casket of fine pearls. It seemed a trifling reward for laying the debbil-debbils of Po Sung, but Captain McTeague only shuddered and closed his eyes.

"Haul up the mud-hooks and crowd on canvas," he said to Okey. "When Red Murphy and McMahon and Tawa and the she-ape get a grouch on, there'll be hell popping in that jungle. I've seen it for the last time. Not for a ship's hold of pearls will I put in at any lagoon on the Banda shore. They nearly made a monkey of me, Okey. Honored me by fetching a trained orang-outang from Java to hold my witless brains. Maybe they had my measure at that. I was fool enough to go in and idiot enough to escape. A wise man. would never have come out alive."

WHITE ORCHIDS
GORDON PHILIP ENGLAND

MEN CALL ME MAD. They have labeled me a maniac and shut me away in this grim asylum. The more I try to convince them of the truth, the more they laugh. Bad I am; a criminal I am; but insane I am not. Now, incarcerated within madhouse walls, I will write my story; and perhaps, after I have gone, they will believe.

It all began last September; now it is June. In a tall maple outside my iron-barred window, robins are singing. To the birds it is summer; nine months ago it was summer in my heart, too. Nine months ago! How long it seems!

Nine months ago, I visited the Western Hospital of that old French-Canadian city, Montreal. And there, on a cot near the door in the fifth public ward, I saw Old Matthewson, the orchid-gatherer. Fever was devouring him, and part of the time he was delirious. But, during lucid moments, he told me his strange story; told me of the marvelous flowers for which I have sold my soul!

I laughed at him at first, I remember; laughed incredulously. Had not I myself for many years collected orchids; searched them out from the farthest corners of the globe? Certainly I had; and critics had pronounced my collection the most excellent of any—better even than that of Jasper Carrington, my most bitter rival.

Old Matthewson saw me laugh; saw my sneer of unbelief. Then with shaking fingers he drew from beneath his pillow the map, and pointed out to me the place, far in the interior of Brazil, where the flowers grew. And as his finger touched the rude sketch, his forehead contracted; a look of fear came into his pale blue eyes; and from his burning lips trembled the word, "Danger!" Suddenly he raised himself upon his elbow and stared in horror past me into nothingness. Then, uttering a sharp cry of "White Orchids!" he fell back dead.

As a nurse came hurrying from the other end of the ward, I thrust the paper into my coat pocket. After all, the man was dead, dead as a smelt. Why, then, as he could not use his map, should not I appropriate it? I calmly listened to the anger of the nurse, who accused me of exciting the patient. Then, as she turned again to the body, I walked quickly from the building.

Next morning I returned to my home in New York, taking the map with me. That evening, I spread it before me on a table in my den, and gloated over it. I studied it intently; studied it till every point upon it was firmly fixed within my mind. Finally, putting the chart aside, I sketched it from memory upon another paper; then compared the two. In delight, I found my new map was a counterpart of the original. True, I had left out a few minor details, but all important features were identical.

Placing my own sketch within a book, I folded Matthewson's, and put it in my pocketbook. Then I went down to the Collectors' Club.

Many of the members were there that night, among others, Carrington.

I behaved foolishly that evening. Excited by my discovery, I drank deeply, and became badly intoxicated. During a discussion with Carrington regarding the merits of our collections, I boasted of my new find.

Carrington laughed contemptuously: "You're dreaming, man! Or rather—you're drunk!"

Taking out the map, I waved it dramatically.

"Drunk, am I?" I exclaimed. "There's the map to prove what I've told you! Oh no, you don't!"—as he reached for it—"the secret's mine, mine alone! I'm the only white man who knows where those orchids are!"

Carrington's eyes sparkled with desire, and for a moment he appeared almost ready to assault me. Then, with a muttered oath, he turned away.

Flushed with my triumph, I called loudly for another drink. Then for another, and another.

At an early hour next morning, I staggered to a couch in an inner room, and falling upon it, lost consciousness.

WHEN I OPENED MY EYES, I remembered what a fool I had made of myself the night before. I could not recall all the idiotic things I had done, but I could remember enough. Then I thought of my map. I felt for my pocketbook. What a relief when my fingers touched it!

Reassured, I went back to my house, and entering my den, locked the door. I opened the pocketbook. The map was gone!

For several minutes I paced the room, wildly cursing. Though I had no proof, I was certain that Carrington had stolen my chart.

Then I laughed. After all, I still had a reliable map. I crossed to the table and opened the book. Yes, there lay my new map, just as I had left it.

I went to the 'phone, intending to enter a complaint at the club. Then I paused. Such a proceeding would be useless. Most of the members were good friends of Carrington's, and many were my personal enemies. If I spread the news of my loss, I should gain nothing, and besides, I should make a laughing-stock of myself.

I wished, however, to learn what Carrington was doing. So I rang him up. A servant answered, a new servant who did not recognize my voice. I asked to speak to her master. She told me that Mr. Carrington had left that morning for his house at Jacksonville. No—she didn't know how long he'd be away.

But I had found out enough. I knew why Carrington had gone to Jacksonville. It was there that his powerful biplane was housed.

I made a rapid calculation. Carrington's airplane had been used in a long non-stop flight a few weeks before, and would need a thorough overhauling before it would be fit for service. He could scarcely have it ready before a fortnight.

Then, too, an accident might delay him, nor could he depend upon finding a good landing-place in those South American jungles.

I consulted shipping lists. The fast steamer *Bolivia* was to clear for Para, Brazil, that very afternoon.

I acted immediately. When the Bolivia sailed, I was aboard.

LEAVING THE STEAMER at Para, I procured an Indian guide and a swift motor-boat, and started up the Amazon.

From the outset, disaster attended me. When near the place where I intended leaving the boat, we ran against a submerged rock. Being very near land, we managed to save both our lives and part of our supplies, including my rifle and several boxes of cartridges; but the boat sank before we could get out everything. Nearly all of my collecting paraphernalia went to the bottom; all I had left were a few large manila envelopes, such as I used for pressing flowers.

This was bad enough, but worse was to come. On the third day after we had left the river and struck inland, came tragedy. We were pushing our way through dense jungle, when suddenly my young native, who was some distance ahead of me, uttered a despairing shriek. Running forward with rifle in hand, I was horrified to see the poor lad in the embrace of a huge anaconda, anchored by its tail to a small tree. At close range, I discharged the contents of my heavy rifle into the boa's head. It sank to the ground, its coils spasmodically tightened; then it unrolled and, releasing its victim, thrashed about in its death agony.

Knowing I had nothing more to fear from the big snake, I turned my attention to the native. The poor fellow was already nearly dead. That awful hug had crushed his ribs, and driving them against his lungs, had forced the breath from his body. Even as I bent over him, the last spark of life flickered out.

Never shall I forget the despairing scream of my unlucky guide when the sinuous coils caught him, nor the sight of his broken, squeezed body. No! Nor the look of anguish pictured upon his dead face.

I buried my guide where he lay. Then, after consulting my map, I continued my journey.

Ten days later, I knew that if map and compass had not misled me, I must surely be near the place of the orchids. My heart tingling with excitement, I hastened on.

Above me on the tree branches, small green monkeys chattered indignation at my intrusion, while gaudily-feathered parrots shrilled insults.

I scarcely noticed these, so intent were my thoughts upon the flowers.

"Where is Carrington?" I wondered. Perhaps already he had reached his objective. Perhaps already he had won the rich prize!

Spurred by the unwelcome thought, I quickened my pace.

As I advanced, I saw the forest becoming more open, and felt certain that I was nearing the end of my quest.

Then, suddenly emerging from the shade of the forest into clear sunlight, I gasped in amazement.

No! The map had not lied. There, not more than a hundred yards in front of me, were the orchids—hundreds of them—in full bloom!

And such orchids! In my most fantastic dreams I had never imagined anything so beautiful. They were white, of a spotless tint of whiteness that shamed all other colorings. Petals were white, even the leaves and bodies of the plants were of the same shade. White orchids!

At first, feasting my eyes upon the orchids, I saw nothing more. Then, as my gaze dropped upon something lying on the ground a few yards from the flowers, I sprang involuntarily back. The white, sun-bleached *something* had once been a living man!

Glancing about, my terrified eyes saw other things of a similar nature. In all, scattered about near the orchids, I counted a full score of skeletons—every one a human's.

I now recalled the dark warning that Old Matthewson had uttered just as life was leaving him.

What meant these flesh-bared bones in this lovely flower garden? Look where I might, I could see nothing which appeared dangerous. Yet the skeletons showed that danger threatened.

Then again I looked at the white orchids, and desire gripped me. Momentarily or getting the grim spectacle of the dead men, I ran with outstretched hands toward the flowers.

As I drew nearer them, I became aware of a sweet, powerful scent. The aroma of it filled my nostrils; the whole atmosphere seemed clouded with the subtle perfume. I was running no longer. Instead, I was drunkenly staggering from side to side. The force of the perfume was overcoming me; my senses were reeling.

Now I realized the meaning of the danger, yet despite this, my desire for the orchids drove me on. Thunder rolled within my brain; my eyes were darkening; breath was leaving me; yet still I stumbled onward.

I had been about three hundred feet from the orchids when I had started; now I was a scant hundred. But my powers of endurance were rapidly diminishing; my very life seemed ebbing from me. And finally I fell headlong.

For some minutes I lay dazed; then with dogged effort again went forward, creeping upon hands and knees.

After covering a few feet in this manner, my limbs refused to function, and I fell again, stretched at full length on the ground, my fast-blinding eyes fixed covetously upon the orchids.

I knew now that I could not reach them. I had crossed little more than two-thirds of the distance, and already was almost lifeless. What then would be the result if I attempted to advance farther?

I hated to go back, but to remain meant death. Yet the perfume so dangerously sweet was luring me on. Every impulse in my body, mind and soul, clamored to me to go onward. But common sense told me to retreat while there was time.

So I commenced my backward journey. Too exhausted to rise, I crawled weakly toward security.

For minutes at a time strength deserted me, and I lay motionless, unable to move a single muscle.

Then my powers would return for a brief period, and again I would resume the fight. My granite-formed will urged me on. Had it not been for that, I must have lain down and let the poisonous breath of the orchids destroy me.

But that strong will saved me, and at length I again reached the edge of the forest. Rolling beneath the cooling shade of a tree, I lay still.

How long I lay there I do not know, but it was doubtless several hours.

Suddenly I heard a sound that I recognized, a sound apart from the jungle noises—the drone of a motor.

I turned my gaze upward. Was I dreaming, I wondered, or was that big, humming thing high above me in the sky really an airplane? Then I remembered Carrington.

Eagerly I watched. The machine was dropping lower; evidently its pilot had seen the flowers. He volplaned down to a perfect landing on the other side of the orchid garden.

The pilot stepped out, and at sight of him my heart thrilled. There could be no mistaking that stalwart figure.

While I looked, Carrington started toward the flowers.

Watching my rival, I could see how I, myself, must have behaved. I smiled grimly as Carrington's stride slackened and his steps became uncertain. And laughed aloud when he began to sway from side to side.

At last, Carrington fell, even as I had done. And again as I had done, he crept forward on all fours.

I now expected to see Carrington overpowered by the heady perfume, and believed he would soon abandon his attempt.

But, after some moments, I saw in mortification that he was evidently stronger than I, and that where I had failed, he might succeed.

Still he held to his course, gradually, inch by inch, cutting down the distance between him and the orchids.

Now, only ten feet separated him from the flowers.

With one last, desperate effort, Carrington flung himself forward. Seizing the nearest orchid-plant, he tore it from the ground. Then he sank unconscious beside the flowers.

I watched, expecting each instant to see him begin his return trip. But he remained motionless, and finally I realized that the scent had completely overpowered him, and if he should lie there many minutes longer, he would surely die. And then I made a decision.

Frantically I looked about, but could see nothing to aid me in my purpose. Then I thought of the airplane, and hurried over to it. In the machine I found what I had hoped for—a coil of rope.

Unrolling it, I saw I had about one hundred and twenty feet of cord.

I set quickly at work, and a few moments later held a service-able-looking lasso.

Then, drawing a long breath, I stepped into the poison-charged area.

Several times the dreadful perfume almost overcame me, but finally I arrived within about a hundred feet of Carrington.

Whirling the lariat above my head, I cast. Straight and true sped the noose, encircling my rival just below his shoulders. Carefully I drew the rope tighter. With a sigh of relief I felt the slack grow less. I began to walk backward, pulling Carrington after me. Soon both of us were beyond reach of the deadly perfume.

Still Carrington held the white orchid clutched fiercely in his hand. I took hold of the plant and tried to pull it from him. His clenched fingers were like a vise. Then I used both hands, and putting forth all my strength, bent back the rigid fingers. A moment more, and the wonderful orchid was in my possession. I cried aloud with joy; I gazed upon it in rapture.

At last, carefully laying the flower aside, I again turned to Carrington. My noose was still drawn tight about his body. His eyes were closed; I began to fear that he was already dead. I caught him by the shoulders and shook him roughly. He wriggled weakly in my grasp; his eyes slowly opened. I saw that he recognized me. He opened his mouth; tried to speak; but could not.

I smiled cruelly. I picked up the white orchid and held it above him. At sight of it, passionate desire filled his eyes; he reached for it painfully. I laughed and drew it away; his almost powerless arm dropped back; he groaned.

I laughed again. Bending over him, I said mockingly:

"You want white orchids, Carrington; then you shall have them. I will give them to you—*I will give you to them!*"

Catching hold of the rope, I savagely dragged him toward the flowers. I drew him far within the poison belt; drew him till I felt myself weakening; till my tortured lungs, crying for air, hammered at my ribs. Then I left him.

All this time, Carrington had said nothing, though he fully realized what was happening. That is: his lips had not spoken; but what a curse his cold gray eyes had uttered! They had bored me through and through.

But when I returned to the orchid, any faint qualms of conscience left me. I would have killed another man if need were—aye, a score; a hundred—to obtain the flower. From infancy I had loved flowers; almost worshiped them. But this white orchid—words cannot describe it!

I held the flower a long time, in spellbound admiration. I would have liked to take the plant intact to North America, but I knew this would be impossible. Could I have used the airplane, I might have preserved the orchid alive, but unfortunately I had never learned to operate such a machine.

But the flower, even if pressed, would excite the envy of other collectors. In my pocket were the manila envelopes. Taking one out, I carefully broke off a big blossom and placed it inside. I sealed the envelope, then returned it to my pocket. And then, going toward the orchids, I tossed the blossom-raped plant in the direction of my victim.

Going back to the edge of the woods, I picked up my rifle, which I had laid down when attempting to secure the orchids, and after casting one last look at flowers, skeletons, and Carrington, I entered the jungle.

I was now faint with hunger, but the forest teemed with game. An hour later, I killed a peccary, built a fire, and roasted it. Then I heaped on wood and made a big blaze to keep off wild beasts. Completely worn out by the day's excitement, I lay down by the fire and fell asleep.

EARLY IN THE MORNING I awoke, and continued my way back toward the river.

The fourth afternoon of my journey back, I felt sharp pains shooting through my head. I staggered on, but rapidly my strength forsook me. Fever had gripped me.

At last, my senses left me. I became delirious; what I did, I know not.

When I came to myself, I found myself in a boat on the Amazon, in the company of a party of American hunters. These told me that they had found me burning with fever, helpless in the jungle. That they had done everything within their power to aid my recovery, and were now taking me back to civilization.

My first thought was of my orchid. I searched my pocket for the envelope; found it gone. I demanded it; they told me they had seen nothing of it; that when they had found me I had not so much as a rifle or compass with me.

I refused to believe my rescuers; I became violent; I cursed them for a lot of robbers. My excitement raised my temperature; brought on a relapse; again I lost my mind.

Of course, I do not remember what happened then, but have been told that the hunters brought me to Para, where they placed me in the care of an American doctor. He recognized me, and did everything possible for me. Gradually I recovered from the fever, but for a long time my mind was a blank. The doctor took me back to New York, and some weeks later, I regained my memory.

With remembrance there came a strange feeling. I was sorry I had killed Carrington. More than sorry; I hated myself for having done so. Had I still possessed the orchid, perhaps I might not have felt remorseful, but its loss had in a measure softened me, and I realized what an awful thing I had done.

At last the strain became too great to bear. I felt that even death would be preferable to my soul-anguish. So I went to the chief of police and told my story. He only laughed at me; declared that before leaving America, Carrington had told the press he was attempting a non-stop flight across the Atlantic; that his flight had been unsuccessful, and the accepted belief was that he had fallen into the sea.

As for my own tale, the chief considered it utterly absurd. He hinted that I was suffering from hallucinations. I grew angry; a red film danced before my eyes; I struck him in the face.

It was then that they called me mad; then that they gave me a maniac's number, and dragged me to this horrible asylum. Death I would not have minded, but this—!

Since coming here, I have been tormented with awful visions. In my dreams, and often when awake, I have again seen those flowers of hell—and Carrington. I have seen his cursing gray eyes malignantly fixed upon me.

I know that if I remain longer in this lonely, dismal madhouse, I shall indeed become insane. But I will not remain!

This morning, I discovered something. One of the iron bars on my window is loose. Not very loose, but enough so I can pull it out. The maple tree where the birds are singing is quite near the window, and one of the branches is within easy reach. Tonight, when all is still, and the guards are asleep, I will escape. I have friends in the outer world who will hide me. They will give me money and help me to get away to some other country. And perhaps, when I am out in the busy world again, I shall not mind those cursing eyes; shall not behold such visions so often. Tonight, I will escape!

EXTRACT FROM THE REPORT of Charles Warren, superintendent of the asylum:

"Yesterday afternoon, Inmate No. 17 asked for pencil and paper. All the afternoon he wrote, and till nearly dark. This morning, when I entered his room, I found it empty. The pile of paper and pencil lay on the table, but Inmate No. 17 had gone. A brief examination showed that he had wrenched a bar from his window, and crawled through the opening. Going to the window, I looked out. Inmate No. 17 was lying on the ground twenty feet below. A broken branch lying beside him explained what had happened. Going downstairs, I went out and examined the body. Inmate No. 17 was dead. His neck was broken."

VINE TERROR (1934)
HOWARD WANDREI

ROMAN SHOLLA STOOD PERFECTLY STILL on his front sidewalk, bewildered. He blinked a few times, and opened and closed his mouth like a fish out of water. Then he thrust his still unlighted pipe into his pocket and ran.

There was reason enough for his fright. Sholla, proprietor of South's Cut-Rate Supplies, lived on the outskirts of the community below the hill on which stood the glass, stone, and metal faced South Experimental Laboratories.

It was about twenty minutes past seven when Sholla issued from his front door, in his hand a pipe, which he loaded methodically with a poking forefinger. He proceeded down his front walk, at which point he produced a match from his side pocket and struck it on the mailbox nailed to the oak tree. But the tree wasn't there. It had moved, moved out of reach. The earth was shouldered aside. At the base of the huge, broken-barked bole was what seemed to be a wake of turf.

"Fo' fo'teen years," he explained excitedly to Eric Shane, who lived across the street, "I strike m' match on the tree. You see me do it. What is happen?" He looked around belligerently at the little group that had collected, and which had drifted back to the scene of the novelty.

"*I* tell you what. I come down the walk and put out my hand to the postbox to strike the match. Every morning just the same. Eric will tell you so. But now I can't reach it," he said, his voice trembling. "Look for yourself. The tree has move' away from the sidewalk!" He pointed passionately at the base of the tree with his unlighted pipe. Before it, between the little huddle of men and the tree, was a plowed furrow, like a short, fresh grave.

Wiry, dark little Fred Yanotsky, who had once inspected ore at the Ashton mills, was looking up at the laboratories on the hill above Sholla's house.

"You vill find vhy up d'ere, I t'ink," he said malignantly. "No good come of machines. I know. I work wit' machines for ten, twelve year. Many funny t'ings happen. Funny t'ings." His voice trailed off ominously.

"Ah!" exclaimed Sholla contemptuously. "You talk like crazy. Because you catch yourself in the wheels one time, whose fault was it? You want to hang the big stamp, maybe, or the digger? P'r'aps you like to burn those generator' up there, like witches in the old country?"

"I do' know," said Yanotsky slowly, shaking his head. "I see some awful funny t'ings." He looked up balefully at the power plant, and fingered the mutilations of the arm that had been caught in the mill machinery many years ago.

"Ay," spoke up an old bearded fellow, Papa Freng. "What has happened to the game? Tell me, Roman Sholla."

"The game?" said Sholla. "How do you mean?"

"The game, the small game. What has happened to all the rabbits? Where are the squirrels that used to come to my window for nuts, all summer and all winter? I tell you, there has been no small game seen here these three months, nor the small green snakes, even. Roman Sholla, what of the birds?"

"Birds? What are you talking about, papa? Up there is a bird, now." He pointed off at a slow-winged turkey buzzard of remarkable size, a really gigantic specimen, that was pursuing a low, undulating flight toward the wood that surrounded the hill and the laboratories. The five men at the oak tree turned and eyed the bird warily as though they were watching Judgment approach. The buzzard passed nearly overhead, somewhat to the right of Sholla's house, and side-winged into a wide spiral as it prepared to alight in the trees half-way between the house and the laboratories on

the hill. Its trailing legs dropped a trifle, the wings spread um-
brella-wise, and momentarily it disappeared from view among the
foliage. Sholla turned to Papa Freng triumphantly, saying,

"Well, papa, there was one—or didn't I see it?"

"Look!" said the old man, seizing his arm and shaking it.

The buzzard had suddenly reappeared, beating its wings so violently that to the five astonished men it sounded like a waterfall.
The frantic bird uttered hoarse, terrified cries, thrashing the air
heavily. It was apparently working to lift some tremendous weight.
The cries ceased abruptly, as the bird seemed to erupt above the
foliage. It was heavily laden with what could only be a vine, which
was entangled in its claws and dangled with many lively twists,
dropping earth from the curling, whipping roots as the bird circled
wearily higher and higher above the woods—higher and higher, till
the silent, gaping circle of watchers strained their eyes to see. And
then, when the great black buzzard, like a living kite with its grotesque tail, was almost beyond vision above them, the vine dropped
away. It fell as though weighted, roots first. Behind its downward
plunge trailed a little flurry of leaves that had been torn away. The
vine plummeted into the trees with a distant, leafy uproar in almost precisely the same spot from which it had issued. And when
the five gaping watchers looked again into the sky the great buzzard was nowhere to be seen.

FROM THE CENTRAL CHAMBER of the laboratories a watcher commanded
at least a fifteen-mile view across the plains. This morning a tall,
gray man was standing at the windows, looking out thoughtfully
with keen blue eyes. From where he stood he could just make out
the group of men now straggling away from the front of Sholla's
house. He was smiling tolerantly.

"What cheer, fellow citizen?" said a voice behind him.

"Oh, hello, Schommer," said Haverland, turning around. "Why,
it's those confounded birds again. They don't seem to like these
woods at all. I can't imagine what the devil has got into 'em. We'll
have to beat them up one of these days and see whether there's a
hungry critter or two down there. Set traps."

"Yes," said Schommer, blinking away the dregs of sleep. "Why, I haven't seen even a squirrel around here since—well, since poor Keene got his."

That was three months ago. Haverland remembered it with regret and a great deal of embarrassment. To his complete shame, whatever it was that Keene, the senior engineer, had been working on—and those projects of his were remote enough—Haverland had destroyed. When Keene had been electrocuted, Haverland and the newcomer, Harriss, had been assisting in his experiment. Schommer stood just back of Keene. There was one peculiar aspect of the affair that Haverland thought of afterward as a remarkable, if peculiar, conception of his own. At any rate, it seemed to have been a phenomenon witnessed only by himself.

Keene had stretched forth a lean hand, and the bare wire had crossed his wrist. And then there was light, like a halo.

From where Haverland stood, watching through the poles of two huge electrodes, between which was fixed a bulb of one of the inert gases, Keene's body seemed to be aflame. He stood there like a waxwork, moments after Haverland had disconnected the current. Phosphorescent fires chased up and down his arms, and the exposed flesh of his breast and face seemed to be burning. The soft radiance brightened gradually. Harriss and Schommer, apparently blind to this aurora of light, gaped at their chief fearfully. The radiation of light was now sharply brilliant, and as Haverland gasped at its brightness there was a violent explosion of radiant energy from Keene's head that shocked him into temporary blindness.

It was a stupid, an unforgivable thing to do; it irritated Haverland to think he could be capable of such carelessness. That bulb of gas, in which had appeared a deposit of transparent, flowing crystals, might have had some important bearing on the nature of Keene's mystical and complex experiments. One almost dared suppose that the impossible was sometimes possible, and that perhaps in this one case the inert gas, or combination of inert gases, that Keene had been working on was active after all.

Still, who would know the subtle ways of Agnes, the laboratory cat? It was all chance: that it was high noon when Keene died, that

the hungry cat was mewing on the central table, and that when
Haverland set the mysterious bulb with its more mysterious contents on the table the affectionate Agnes pawed it, caused it to roll
into the sink compartment and shatter. All chance, and yet
Haverland could only blame himself for a fool's negligence.

But that radiation of light from Keene's dying body was something to be considered. In Haverland's own idiom, it was "one for
the books." Halo. The legendary gods of Greece and Rome, robed
in light. The death light. The ancient gods of India, the primitive
deities of all countries, even unto Christ and the Christian saints,
all enhaloed. Tradition somewhere originates in truth, and in the
time-forgotten genesis of that shining legend, the legend of the
halo, was the simple function of a physical law, a mystery once
visible. Haverland shook his head. There were more fools with their
follies. . . .

As he entered his own private laboratory, leaving Schommer
to luxurious yawns, he thought again of that curious, inexplicable
deposit of crystals in the bulb of stable gas—crystals that seemed
to be composed of microcosmic glass beads by the billion, and that
surely had an involved, slow, endless motion of their own. Haverland felt that he was peering into the unknown, and again and again
the sensation of his personal connection with the death of Keene
filled him with uneasiness and with shame, as though he had committed some vast error.

He noted something unusual in the condition of his room, and
stopped short. At the end of the laboratory table the window had
been broken, possibly by a vine which passed through the opening. The vine twisted along the tabletop, and was entangled in
Haverland's microscope. A pile of glass slides was knocked down.
Several had fallen to the floor and shattered.

Haverland toed the fragments irritably. A great deal of damage had been done. He started to untangle the vine from the
microscope and crowd it back through the window, swearing mildly
to himself, then dropped it and pulled absently at his lower lip,
perplexed. It struck him suddenly as being very, very odd that a

clumsy, meandering growth like this tortuous creeper should have worked so much of itself into the room.

Some four or five days later Haverland experienced a moment of pure fright. The window had been repaired, but was now open. Haverland sat on the sill, looking over rolling country that was farmed by the hunkies of South. He could see a fan of men spreading through a distant plowed field, for what, he didn't know. As he watched, he was aware of something crawling along his bare forearm. A small beetle, a fly. He brushed it off, then froze in position, panic-stricken. The beetle was not a beetle at all, but a tendril of the vine that grew outside the window. In one eternal minute he took account of many things: of the fact that the vine, which had never been any more remarkable than any of its kind, was now unimaginably luxuriant, hanging from the side of the building in a vast cloud of leaves; of the fact that a pungent, unpleasant odor moved about and among this cloud; and that a small tendril of this inexplicable new growth was visibly insinuating its way along his forearm.

Haverland had watched the slow unfolding of the cereus, but this thing crept along like a wooden worm vested in leaves. It was encircling his arm deliberately. The delicate shoots seemed to be freckled with infinitesimal suckers, and wherever they touched they clung. Haverland plucked at the thing and it resisted. Suddenly it seemed to grow into his flesh. With the shock of pain the engineer snatched it violently from his arm and flung it out. The thing had been sucking his blood.

Vegetable vampires!

All along his arm were tiny red beads, like a perspiration of blood, as though he had been pricked with a thousand needles all at once. At this moment there was an impatient rapping at the door. It was Schommer.

"Grave-robbers," he said shortly, and with an expression on his face that Haverland was not to forget.

"What?" he said, astonished.

Schommer's blue eyes glared.

"They've dug him up," he said furiously. To which he added, meeting Haverland's blank look, "Keene."

Keene had been buried at the bottom of the hill according to his own often-expressed wish. Schommer and Haverland, hastening toward the small cleared plot that contained his grave, could see nothing until they reached the place because of the foliage-banked iron grillework around it. Then Haverland stopped dead, dismayed, while Schommer watched him grimly, almost accusingly, thought Haverland. The grave was torn up. Plowed up. A few bars of the grille were bent, and impaled on the spears of these bars was Keene's body. It had apparently been so displaced for some time, vines having partially enwrapped it and broken into the flesh.

"When did you discover it?" asked Haverland, appalled.

"Only this morning. My wife reminds me to put flowers on the grave once a week." Schommer pointed to a scattered bunch of flowers on the ground—fresh flowers, and the dried stalks of the past. "Now, who would do this thing?" he said bitterly, looking at Haverland. Then he was silent.

Afterward, though, the whole horror of it seemed to be crystallized in something almost irrelevant. When the body was removed to the cemetery in town, it had first to be disengaged from those horrible vines. The trained eyes of Haverland and Schommer were alone in seeing that the flesh in nearest conjunction with the vines presented a most remarkable appearance. It looked raw. Haverland thought of the word "digested." Schommer was staring at him. And Haverland looked at Schommer, while the disgusted deputies of South's coroner quickly practiced their trade.

The potentialities of the vine. Vines that climb, and vines that hang. Creepers that find their ways upward to the sun. Tough vines that bind, vines that clutch and choke, that gripe the best life out of the vegetation that gives them foothold. The gleaming, wholly denuded skeleton of a squirrel, still intact, entangled in the vine that girdled the body of Keene.

Keene's death seemed in some way to have laid a curse over the woods and the small game that inhabited them. The three months afterward were a chronicle of desertion, the small cries of birds and the chuckling calls of wild things decreasing in number day by day till there were only long silences, broken by sounds that could not be identified. The quick, flying skip of a rabbit was as rare now as the cadenced flight of the jay and the gull. The pleasant, frightened movement of wild things disturbed and the splash of leaves had given place to queer, long, meaningless rustles; rustles that marked the insinuating course of large snakes, or perhaps the rustles of heavy vines, that, overweighted, were dropping by degrees from their places among the oaks, the birches, and the cottonwoods. Continuous movements unseen. The threat of invisibles.

EXCEPT WHEN SOME PROBLEM kept him in the building overnight, Haverland habitually rode into the city with Schommer. And both men were thankful for Schommer's car. It was a good three-quarters of a mile from the laboratories into South, and the dense woods, denser now with this monstrous new growth of underbrush, overhung the road all the way. A lonely walk, at night.

"Not even an owl," said Schommer. "Used to be a lot of them."

He was driving slowly, and now stopped the car to listen. Not a sound of bird or beast. He looked at Haverland, who had his lean gray head cocked forward listening intently.

"This place is like a cellar," Schommer continued, in his peculiar clipped style of speech. "Nothing moving; not a sound. Even a beastly smell."

His broad lips curled with displeasure as he released the brake and the car began to move.

"Wait!" said Haverland, gripping his arm.

Schommer looked at him inquiringly, then thrust his head farther out of the window to listen also. There was never a sound; the woods were deathly still.

"Hear something?" he asked skeptically. "Only living thing I've seen around here in three months was our friend the buzzard this morning. *C. a. septentrionalis*, and for such a big one even he didn't stay long."

"Listen!" said the sharp-eared Haverland, and with so commanding a voice that Schommer obeyed, opening the door and stepping outside the car. At once there was an explosion of sound in the woods near by. The air was filled with outburst after outburst of agonized cries, cries that seemed to be neither brute nor human.

Schommer snatched a flashlight from the pocket of the car and plunged through the brush at the side of the road, Haverland following. They had scarcely entered the woods, the beam of light playing through the leaves ahead of them, when the uproar terminated in a cutting scream. They advanced through the woods hastily, still hearing an unaccountable, wild thrashing sound close at hand.

When they found the origin of the disturbance not fifty feet within the woods, they stopped, gasping with horror. All about them were trees hung with vines. Directly in front of them was a large specimen at the foot of a huge cottonwood, in movement. It was thrashing about like a whip. The end of it was wound tightly about some object, which, as they watched it thrown bloodily against the trunks of the cottonwood and the surrounding trees, they saw was a dog.

Schommer ran forward for a closer view.

"Stop, you fool!" shouted Haverland instinctively, and at that moment a creeper on the ground entangled itself in Schommer's leg and tripped him headlong. He tried to get up and found himself tied hand and foot. Tender young vines enwound his wrists and ankles like steel wires; he wrestled with them, grunting with pain.

Cannibalism. Kind eating kind. Haverland stood there nerveless, and felt, sickeningly, that he was looking again into the unknown. When Schommer fell, the light had been thrown from his hand, and now shone directly on the base of the cottonwood. The vine moved slightly, like a tentacle, as though the dog somewhere off in the darkness were still struggling to free itself, slowly. Schommer was still trying to raise himself from the ground, the great veins of his neck and forehead standing out darkly in the oblique light of the flash.

"I'm caught!" he said helplessly, and then cried out with terror as a creeper cut into one fleshy wrist and made a bracelet of spouting blood.

"Help! Help me!" he screamed. At which Haverland, nervously aware of black, black shadows banked on shadows blacker still among the depths of the tall trees, stumbled blindly forward, produced a knife from his pocket and flicked it open. The vine holding the dog was perfectly still then, and Schommer suddenly managed to free himself; upon which, having brushed off his clothes, he proceeded to bind up his wrist with a handkerchief. Then, feeling highly resentful, and perhaps a little foolish because of the wholly deserted character of the still woods, he picked up the flashlight and directed it toward the ground at his feet.

"Well, that's funny," he said, taking up the vine that had tripped him and dropping it again. "Did you ever see any wood like that?"

The vine was limp, flabby, and draped along the ground like a leafy rope. Schommer stepped on it, and grimaced as it gave under his heel like flesh.

"Ugh!" he exclaimed. "What the devil do you suppose it is? Never saw anything like it!"

Haverland examined the root of the vine, and was about to draw his knife through it. But there was a windless rustle in the trees, and the vine, which had been lying as loose as a newly dead snake, and as cold, was now rigid and hard in his hand. He caught the fleeting impression that he was the object of eery, unearthly attention. He felt that he was threatened. The woods were now completely still, watching, waiting; the silence was a tangible menace, suffocating him, moving against him.

"Shall we take it along?" asked Schommer. "Might have to get a spade, unless—"

He stooped over and gripped the vine at its base, now quite limp, and tried to pull it out by the roots. Haverland held the light. Schommer was generously built, and his contorted face showed tremendous exertion, but the vine wouldn't give an inch. As he straightened up, nursing his wrist and swearing softly, Haverland saw the root of the creeper withdraw fractionally into the ground, for all the world like an earthworm.

"Hm-m," said Schommer, clearing his throat. "Queer vine, that. How about the other one?"

"Let's go see," said Haverland, and walked carefully through the dark litter of brush toward the big cottonwood, holding the light before him.

The vine that had trapped the dog was a large climber. Closely involved in its foliage was the dead, mangled animal, which he stooped to examine. Schommer grasped the main stem of the plant and shook it experimentally; it seemed to have the character of any other vine, but when he turned aside to toe the battered, bloody ruin of the dog, the vine wobbled drunkenly.

Compact, gnarled arms of fiber that thought. Intricately contrived, sap-carrying tubes, sap that pulsed, sap that beat through wooden arms. Arms that looked about for supporting trees and moved deliberately like the tentacles of a land octopus. Haverland shivered with the thought. He received the uncomfortable impression that he had entered a stranger's house by some freak, or had the dubious privilege of wandering through the devil's own garden, of being tolerated in that journey.

"Let's get out of this, Schommer," said Haverland. "We can look this thing over in the daytime." He tried to make his voice sound casual, but the words came out harsh and knotty.

Schommer joined him, and as the two picked their way back to the car he said,

"What the devil do you suppose happened to that dog?"

"Looked like some cat's work," Haverland lied; "probably the beast that's been accounting for all the game that's disappeared. Got away before either of us saw him."

Schommer shook his massive, leonine head. No cat in the country was big enough to kill a dog so horribly. Why, the thing he had touched with his foot was no more than shreds, a red puddle of flesh and splintered bones. No, it was a stronger, more savage beast than a cat. A beast so thorough and so subtle in its destruction that it absorbed living things into itself without its existence being suspected.

A LIGHT BREEZE MOVED through the woods as the two engineers approached the car, a moist, muggy breeze, and the grove of cottonwoods below the laboratory was filled with sound. The majestic trees were scarcely distinguishable against the black sky, but fireflies illuminated the foliage here and there, and briefly showed vast and looming walls of leaves and branches, in whose enclosure the two men at the car seemed to be at the bottom of a well of shadows. The effect was that of a great beast lying prone and still which had suddenly commenced to breathe. There was no freshness in the air, rather the effluvia pouring out of a boundless swamp. The sensitive Haverland harkened to the sound of the night breeze through the leaves, and noted the peculiar leatheriness of their motion and collision with each other. The familiar, fresh sound of the wind playing through poplars and cottonwoods had taken on the character of a confident, jubilant, multitudinous handclapping.

He remembered that sound. Later, among the realities of his home in the city, those engulfing shadows flocked about him and marched endlessly through his dreams, through dreams of leafy cordings and living ropes, dreams of phosphorescent foliage and vines enhaloed, all sounding before the violence of cyclonic winds that blew the radiance into flame.

Hurried, harried by dreads and he knew not what, next day he busied himself with an apparatus which he had set up in his rooms a day or two before. This consisted chiefly of a microscope and a common broad beaker. In the beaker, and filling it to the brim, was a pulpy mass in which could be discerned indisputable chlorophyll; leaves ground into a kind of rough paste; macerated vines with their foliage, which he had clipped from the creeper outside the window (the writhing, the leaping, and the voiceless fury). Near the microscope was a delicate, graduated instrument used for some kind of measurement. Alongside the microscope stood a small glass-stoppered bottle nearly full of a transparent umber fluid which had been expressed from the pulp.

Still doubtful, hesitating, never convinced, Haverland delayed his investigation one moment more. He approached a locker and removed from it a soggy paper package. With as much deliberation as he could muster, he opened it and produced a large piece of raw meat. He walked to the window with it, opened the window, and then, lingering still, stepped back. Wind outside plucked at the tower of vines, and its whole length undulated with a confusion of whispers.

Haverland wiped his brow, sagging with perspiration, and flung the meat outside. The vine thrashed out across the window. In a moment the meat had been torn into minute shreds, and the whole disappeared among the foliage. Haverland slammed the window and leaned against it. When the leaves patted the glass against his back he sobbed. Pound after pound of fresh, raw meat, vanishing thus in midair. Below the window, if he desired to look, was a sprinkling of clean-picked bones, even to the skeleton of a bird or two. There remained one certain test which the engineer felt was final.

As he stood before the odd collection of objects on the laboratory table, silent and thoughtful, he was aware of remarkable hootings and whisperings outside the building. It was as though the wind, finding small apertures and irregularities in the construction of the place, were deriding him and his work, making sport of his loneliness.

The day had been overcast. The light breeze that had begun the day before had blown up banks of clouds all day long, till by late afternoon the sky was obscured with a thick, uninterrupted blanket the color of dusty metal, that seemed to serve as a sounding-board for dull thunders in the distance.

SCHOMMER, SINCE HE LIVED near by and wanted to finish up the business of the night before, had called for his chief in the morning. Early as they were, when they had passed through South and entered the road leading through the woods below the South laboratories they found their way blocked by a man at work.

Eric Shane, who lived at the far end of South, was one of the more capable laborers among the community of foreigners. Because of his war record, when such things were of importance in employment, he held the position of road patrolman along the network leading out of South. His grader, built after the fashion of the wartime tanks with which he was familiar, was stalled in the middle of the road. He was proceeding on foot along the ditch at one side, industriously wielding a scythe. At the sound of Schommer's brakes he turned about.

After observing the two in the car silently for a moment, he said deliberately,

"Wery juicy."

"What's that, Eric?" asked Schommer.

"The wines. Wery juicy," Shane repeated. He held out his scythe, from which yellow sap was dripping.

"Vines? Well," said Schommer, puzzled, "what're you cutting 'em for?"

"Big fellahs," said Shane, shaking his head. "Across the road, blowing around from the wind. Lots easier to cut."

"I don't see any," said Schommer, craning his neck to look beyond the grader. "Cut the rest of them already?"

Shane looked steadily up the road, then stared owlishly at the two engineers as though he had seen them for the first time.

"Maybe, maybe not," he said. "I ain't been vorking wery long. I t'ink maybe vind blow him back."

He picked up the creeper he had just slashed and threw it hastily into the woods, delivering a kick at one heavy, dragging end of it. Then he wiped his sap-stained hands on his coveralls and looked at Schommer shyly.

"Should I move him?" he asked, pointing to the grader.

"Later," said Schommer. "We've got a little job for you in the woods. Bring along your spade."

Eric unhooked the spade from the grader and looked at it perplexed as he followed Schommer and Haverland through the brush. In a moment the three men arrived at a spot where the ground was broadly disturbed.

"This is it," said Schommer.

"Minus the dog," said Haverland, staring at his companion. He was suddenly filled with a great wrath, and a hatred enough to drive out any fear of the unknown. The great creeper that had been lying on the ground at the base of the cottonwood now mounted upward and was lost among the foliage of the tree. There was no trace of the dog.

Both Schommer and Haverland advanced to the base of the vine and looked about.

"X marks the spot," said Schommer grimly. He scraped a cross into the ground with one foot, where lay a loose scattering of splintered bones. "Marrow and all," he continued. "Nothing left but splinters."

It was uncommonly dark in the woods, for today there was no sun. Eric looked all around carefully, then planted his shovel firmly in the soft earth. He eyed the two engineers earnestly and rather uneasily as they examined the creeper wound all about the cottonwood.

"The devil! That's a big fellow, Charlie," said Schommer. "That surely can't be the one we saw lying on the ground last night."

Haverland shrugged. The vine was thick as a small tree, but it was as gnarled and twisted as though it had been through torture.

"You know," he said, "this is all kind of backward. I've seen wind tear a vine free, but blowing it back up is a horse of another color."

"I don' like it," said Eric. The air was charged with a musty, pungent animal smell, at which he wrinkled his nose with dislike. "I t'ink maybe I better go now."

"O. K., Eric," said Schommer. "We don't need you after all."

As he turned around, and Haverland stooped to examine the bark of the vine, there was a rustle in the foliage overhead that was not caused by any wind. It was the sound of innumerable bats in flight, the sound of leather in motion. Eric jumped up and down with excitement, his jaws moving soundlessly as he pointed. Schommer stared at him, marveling.

"Watch himself! Watch himself!" shouted the Finn, finding his voice. "*Wine come!*"

Schommer glanced up, then snatched at Haverland and hurled himself forward. The two men sprawled headlong as the "wine" slipped from the tree and fell behind them. The leaves of the vine were massed like, a great green mushroom, and the whole growth fell limply and heavily, all at once, smothering the base of the cottonwood with a thud, in a solid mound of foliage.

"Well, I *will* be damned!" said Schommer, finding his feet and brushing himself off. "Now, what do you suppose made that happen?"

"It fell," said Haverland slowly, as if to himself. "Simply came loose and fell in a heap. And we were directly beneath it."

"Looks as though someone were wishing us a lot of bad luck," said Schommer, laughing nervously. "Now, if I were superstitious—"

HAVERLAND SAID NOTHING, but he was subdued as he tramped back to the car with Schommer. He had seen what Schommer had not seen, just before the vine had fallen. That vine had a most unnatural surface of flexible, wrinkled wood, all covered with a kind of unholy sweat. The crevices of the bark were thickly packed with parasites, countless numbers of small insects which conceivably could only be battening on the vine itself. These insects were lice, uncommonly large, well-fed lice in great numbers. He considered this phenomenon judiciously and humorously as the car left the grader behind (with the panting, exhausted Eric) and mounted the drive to the garage behind the laboratories. Half-way up the drive his restless eyes saw something new.

"We're late," he said, breaking the silence. "That's sloppy work, too."

"Eh?" Schommer was surprised out of a mood of his own. When he had locked the car and issued from the garage with Haverland he looked at his watch.

"As a matter of fact, Charlie," he said, "we're early. Only ten minutes to."

Haverland verified the time with a glance at his own timepiece. Then he looked mystified down the hill and said,

"Plumbers are early, then. They've dug in."

"Where?" asked Schommer, puzzled, as he loaded his pipe. Haverland pointed toward an oak near the bottom of the hill, where the ground was spaded up.

"Something clogged up the drain," he said. "Probably the roots of that tree. Looks as though they've used a plow, doesn't it?"

Schommer squinted at the tree without recognition. The turf was broken all the way down the lawn, so that clods formed a rough ditch running from the walls of the laboratory directly into the tree.

"Sloppy work," repeated Haverland, shaking his head.

Schommer removed the pipe from his teeth and followed the course of the ditch with troubled eyes. Something beyond the tree attracted him; he walked a few paces down the lawn. The ditch continued on the other side of the tree, to the extreme bottom of the hill. Curious technique—as though the plumbers were hunting for the tree and couldn't find it. Haverland, slowly taking his place beside Schommer, saw the loose flesh of Schommer's face harden, tighten, till he seemed ten years younger.

Schommer raised his arm and pointed at the tree with his pipe as though it were a target and the pipe a gun. Then he looked at Haverland with eyes whose perplexity had something also of terror.

"Wonderful!" he ejaculated. "Charlie, that tree wasn't there before!"

"What?"

"No! The hill has always been clear. That tree is a good twenty paces up!"

"Schommer—" said Haverland through his teeth. Then he checked himself; no need yet for the wild statements he could make. After all, no one could be really sure, really certain that the fantastic things he suspected had any basis in fact. He was silent. Schommer only regarded him curiously, placing the pipe again between his teeth. Then he drew hurriedly against the almost dead fire in the bowl as Haverland proceeded farther down the hill. An oak tree, that looked all of a hundred years old. Immovable as rock. A fresh leaf sailed out of the foliage and reached the ground about ten feet in front of him. He picked it up absently, and as he stood there for a moment, genuinely troubled, he twisted the leaf idly in his fingers and noted that it was as limp and as tough as leather. He turned slowly and retraced his steps up the hill.

More of those leaves, and the leaves of other trees in the woods, flapped against the windows of the building during the day. The wind was steadily rising. Leaves like patterns cut in the skins of animals.

Some time ago, there was that item in the local paper concerning the tree that had moved. The Laboratories people told jokes about the ignorance and superstitions of the people who lived in

South: how the hunkies hated the whine of the generators, the complicated glass and metal apparatus, and the living blue sparks that jumped all over the laboratories like fireflies. But finally the tree had left the yard entirely to stand at the edge of the woods. Now there was an investigation; sliding substrata were discovered, in which the roots were involved. Odd that the layer of earth should have moved uphill! And now a tree on the very hill on which the laboratories were built, playing the same tricks, tearing up the sod.

During the day Haverland several times discovered Schommer standing at the window area looking down speculatively at the woods. Young Harriss had the phenomenon pointed out to him, and twice left his work to make an examination. Cowl shrugged; he would not have been surprised if a hen had crowed after laying an egg.

The plumbers did come in the afternoon. Having taken a sounding from the building they dug in at a point midway between the tree and the laboratories. Advantage was taken of the ditch in the turf, since it was discovered that below it, down to the sewer, was a cleavage line of broken, friable earth. It was as though a giant plow had followed the sewer-pipe from end to end, breaking the ground. Actually, one of the extraordinarily long .roots of the oak tree had entered a joint in the pipes. All manner of refuse had caught on the obstruction and damned the sewer effectively. The difficulties of repair, however, were negligible.

By this time the wind outside had become rather heavy, in the midst of which the laboratories were an isolated calm. The wind occasionally gusted with still increasing violence, and now and then small objects struck the walls and windows with faint rappings. Haverland could fancy he heard shoutings from down the hill; there was a waterfall of sound among the cottonwoods. At this moment the night-bell rang.

With some degree of surprise and curiosity he left his chambers to see what was wanted. He was alone in the building, it was late, and this was a place where few visitors came. He had locked the door, of course, after Schommer had gone at last; and now, to his further surprise, there was no one on the steps when he opened it. He stood there in the doorway wondering. It was those queer little dark people in South, and their total lack of comprehension of the purpose in these researches, their distrust of everything mechanical, and their absolute fear of electricity; but it was rather a quaint expression of hatred, to ring the bell because the machinery whined. Annoying, too.

It was an unlucky night for ignorant, fearful people, though. The sky was heavy with storm, and the wind was speaking angrily through the cottonwoods. A handful of glossy leaves swept up the hill, and a creeper which had been torn from the side of the building blew across the walk and was shaken against the steps. Haverland locked the door and walked slowly back to his table.

Mysterious. Something grimly facetious about the whole business. All the earmarks of a practical joke on a grand scale. Trees that move. Vines that plummet down fatly from trees that hold them like great green spiders. Game gradually and wantonly slaughtered; skeletons and splintered bones scattered all through the woods. Something in the woods concealed, foul-smelling enough to attract a ranging turkey buzzard. Vines, spongy with sap, blowing around in the road with the slightest breeze. A laborer's fear of still, disinhabited woods, and his flight from them. A vine had tripped Schommer, and so held him that he became frightened. Vines clustering along the road that provided the only means of approach or retreat to the laboratories. Blowing across it. The way Haverland came to work and went home. Vines tough enough to stop a road grader. The voice of Eric Shane, saying, "Wery juicy."

Vines.

Anger filled him again, and he exclaimed aloud, "It's a lie!"

But the walls of the building flung the shout into a trail of echoes; from some remote corner of his brain he plucked out the impression of a bulb of sliding crystals, that Agnes, the laboratory cat, had broken into the sink. Down the sewer, down the hill, into the woods. A thirsty oak, mounting the hill along the sewer, using its roots like the tentacles of an enfoliaged devil-fish, a wooden mole. In this whirl of half-thoughts he found the skeleton of the cat outside his own window, the bones completely disarticulated, but still recognizable. He heard the voice of Eric Shane say,

"I hear' a cat scream—one time, two times, up those hill'."

There was something deadly in the woods. A killer that worked ceaselessly, stealthily, that was not caught in any trap set for it.

In the meantime the first few drops of rain were being flung against the windows with smart rappings like thrown sand. The vine that had been torn from the walls thrashed against the building and occasionally struck the windows in the central chamber with that brittle, short sound peculiar to glass.

Haverland hesitated only a moment as pale violet lightning flickered among the clouds, then turned to the microscope on the table. He prepared a slide cleverly, like a magician's trick, and slipped it under his lenses. One certain test. He adjusted his focus, found something, and rigged up the delicate, graduated instrument that was apparently intended for some occult measurement. There he sat, hands on hips, peering, his face as grim as death. His thin lips recited some ritual without sound.

"Yes, Schommer," he heard himself saying, "those are mighty queer vines; you can tell me nothing. Do you know there's salt in their sweat, eh? Did you know their sap clots? That it takes a blood count, like your blood and mine? *Ever hear 'em talking to each other at night in those cursed woods with their damned clicks, and rubbings, and whispers?* What do you suppose they talk about? *Death!*"

But Schommer was far away in the city, asleep by now. Haverland leaped to his feet and knocked the microscope crashing to the floor. He had a grim purpose in mind, but even now was arrested by the second ringing of the bell, which broke the comparative silence in the building in the most startling manner.

IT WAS A LATE HOUR for anyone to return, and the hunkies of South had all rather sleep in coffins than come anywhere near this place. The bell continued to ring as he made his way to the door. Someone out there was passionately, or mischievously, ringing the bell again and again. Longs and shorts. Staccato rings in series, rings that set the nerves on edge; a whole wild, weird variety of ringings by some impatient lunatic. The bell still sounded alarmingly when he reached the door, which he snatched open at once. The steps were devoid of any presence but his own.

Nearly hysterical with exasperation, Haverland looked into the black, wrathful night, but not for long. A blockade of vines crowded up the steps with a rush, and advancing tendrils whipped through the doorway. Haverland flung the door to with a re-echoing crash. A few short lengths of the vine were caught in the crack, and there they writhed, like the sprouting tails of snakes. One he gripped, which instantaneously snapped about his wrist and entered the flesh. He cried out with pain; taking a shorter grip on the vine with his other hand, at the same time bracing his feet against the door, he tugged with all his might, gasping with panic. It was like trying to break a wet leather thong, but the gods gave him the advantage of weight and terror. The vine parted abruptly; he caught himself as he staggered crazily past the first of the series of generators that ran back from the door.

It was the thing that had nearly got Schommer. Vines gone soft; vines turned animal. Vines as flexible as rubber. Vines whose wooden hearts had been turned into some kind of unholy flesh, vile with rich, putrid yellow sap. Those tendrils remaining in the door writhed spasmodically; there was a heavy scraping sound, and they were withdrawn through the crack with a powerful jerk, leaving a leaf or two in the room. Haverland still held the piece that had broken off. It was quite limp, like a rounded, dirty strip of flesh, and was bleeding that sticky, pale yellow sap into his hand. He flung the thing away across the floor and walked unsteadily back to his rooms, drawing the palms of his hands heavily down his cheeks. He could hear vines beating against the door and grinding along the walls, unimaginable vines, foul things that were hosts to billions of lice. There was something definite and malicious in their movement as they worked along the window-ledges, tapping at the panes that were now streaming with moisture.

In the downpour outside, the trees in the woods arched and lashed the air with foliage. Haverland listened bewildered to the stunning impact of barrage after barrage of thunder, and fancied that the living voices that issued from the grove of cottonwoods were many times multiplied. Then the lights throughout the laboratories brightened unbearably. As the engineer approached the end of his table the lights went out. The wires had gone down in the storm.

He stumbled over some rope-like thing on the floor, and noticed wildly as he fell that the window was open. Something had come in. He reached out in the darkness, however splintered with lightnings, and found it, pulled at it. Clutching it was like squeezing the compact, corded flesh of a squid. A long, eel-shaped thing that passed through the window into the outside.

At that moment ragged lightning seemed to tear the southern sky in two, answered by an eruption of light in the north. As the following thunder battered the place with sound, Haverland stood up thrilling. He had a brilliant vision of the dying Keene; for indeed, this again was the legendary halo. The two colossal charges of electricity in the sky seemed to serve as electrodes, each bolt a pole, the laboratory between; and in this room the halo appeared once more, just as Haverland had seen it over the tube of gas three months past. There was a full, mysterious effulgence throughout the room. A pale, thin radiance flowed out from the thing on the floor and filled the room with a glory of soft light. By this illumination the engineer saw that it was really a denuded length of vine, now more like a hideous, tapering worm; saw, too, that there was scarcely a leaf remaining on the tangle of vines at the window. In the glory of the halo these boneless arms serpentined in a terrible dance; every tentacle glittered with sweat in small beads, that winked at the lightning like innumerable eyes. The vine in the room began to raise itself from the floor.

And now, having formed a towering, closed palisade about it, and accompanied by the sound of shouting leaves and colliding trunks, the vine-hung grove of cottonwoods was advancing on the house. It was the sound of earthquake; the hill shook, and metal clanged in the central chamber of the laboratories. Followed a stupendous crash. Haverland hurried to the door, half stunned.

Through the broad windows of this central chamber one commanded a view of the entire countryside. The hill itself was just high enough to permit sight over the foliaged heads of the oaks and cottonwoods. Haverland, looking down at the trees, saw the entire woods bathed in cold flame. The grove was one vast phosphorescence. The tree-trunks glowed, and the masses of leaves shone like soft, burnished metal. All the great vines were alive with light, and hung from the trees in waterfalls of flame. It was a thing seen in a nightmare or read in a fairy-tale. Another Birnam Wood, that was coming by degrees, but surely, toward the central point that was the laboratories. The laboratory hill seemed to rise from a chasm whose walls were solid light. Trees and vines in motion. Before their advancing trunks and stems the earth was rolling away in waves. Then, dark off in one end of the chamber, the engineer saw that the oak on the hill had already entered the building. The end generator had been shouldered aside and crashed through the floor into the basement. Commotion was in the air. The storm entered the chamber with the oak, and rain beat on Haverland's face.

And still it was not too late. The engineer whirled and retreated through his own laboratories, leaping the handful of twining creepers in his way. In the back of the building he picked up a sledgehammer, then raced back through the smother of rain to the garage, in which stood three full drums of gasoline. He ran up the incline on which the drums rested, and worked rapidly with a wrench. He stepped back a little, swung the sledge in one heavy blow. The drums, released, tumbled booming down the runway, spilling their contents as they went, and bounded out the doorway to go careering down the hill.

Haverland waited, dripping with rain and perspiration, then produced a box of matches. As he was about to strike a light the heavens gaped and a volcano of flame plunged cracking and thundering into the woods like the finger of God.

Haverland flung himself out of the garage in time to escape the arm of fire that leaped up the hill. From the back of the laboratories he watched a tower of flame boom up in the declining storm. Above low thunders he heard three successive explosions as the gasoline drums went. There was enough of it, he felt, to suffocate, if not to consume. A shift of wind carried the sound of crackling and hissing vegetation, and carried into the engineer's nostrils the charnel stench of all the pyres of history. Sickened, he stumbled back into the laboratories.

THE FOLLOWING DAY dawned calm and clear. Roman Sholla came out early and stood on his front lawn, smoking his pipe deliberately and looking up at the hill. A crew had appeared several hours before, and were making much noise as they repaired the damage done to the laboratories by a falling oak. There had been a strong, unpleasant odor in the air all morning, which likely enough came with the shift of the wind from the packing-plant in the city. The members of the crew, as one occasionally came down into South, found the work distasteful, the stench seemingly worse the higher one got up the hill.

One man alone in the building, the chief engineer, Haverland, had escaped serious injury when lightning had touched off three drums of gasoline in the garage and burned it. The South woods had suffered heavily, with a number of the trees and the extraordinarily large vines that grew here either totally burned or badly charred. The famous oak that had taken a journey away from Sholla's own yard, though not burned, was now dead, its leaves already withered.

Eric Shane came out presently, scratching his head and blinking cautiously. He and Sholla were joined shortly by little Fred Yanotsky and Papa Freng. Sholla, situated as he was nearest the laboratory, took on some importance. He told how the storm had wakened him. The woods had caught on fire somehow, and three explosions ("when those gasoline go off") illuminated the room he slept in.

"It was one big bonfire," he said, holding out his arms.

He told of seeing the lightning strike. "Big," he said helplessly, shaking his head. The bolt was indescribably huge. He could tell of the sharp burned-leather and ozone smell in the air afterward, though, and did. But the thunder, ah! They all remembered that sound of cataclysm when the big bolt struck, but that could not be described either.

Sholla's three friends were silent. They had said nothing yet, and seemed very much satisfied about something as they looked up at the crew busy at the shattered masonry and twisted metal above them.

"Well, Fred," said Sholla, "what you think of it, eh?"

"I t'ink," said dark little Yanotsky, "maybe it vas a good t'ing if all the plant fall in. Never, no good come of machines."

"Ah!" said Sholla contemptuously. "Always the same. Crazy stubborn like your father. You should go to school, Fred Yanotsky!"

"This morning," said white-haired Papa Freng, "a squirrel came to my window for nuts. He was very tame, and the first I have seen in a long time." His eyes were fixed on the dreaming distance. As he spoke, something moving near by brought him to sharp attention. With something of eagerness in his voice he exclaimed, "Look!"

He pointed up the road. A small cottontail, pursuing a rather aimless course of exploration or foraging, was proceeding along the ditch, nibbling at green shoots. Its way was blocked presently by a creeper that lay along the road and sagged under its own weight. It was remarkable in being almost totally leafless.

The rabbit, in skipping over it, suddenly froze, as beast does in the presence of beast. But if the grotesque old Keene had been responsible for the mockery of sentience in these singular growths of South, his ghost must have rested at last. The watchers saw the rabbit pass carelessly, unmolested, over the stiff tangle of vines and disappear among the ruins of the South woods. Roman Sholla walked the few paces up to the vine, and, toeing its snarled trunks and leafless tendrils, said,

"Dead."

THE DEVIL FLOWER (1939)
HARL VINCENT

"WHAT A JOB I PICKED OUT!" Dr. Frank Robeson was talking to himself grumpily.

A crudely stenciled sign on the main highway had said "Gregory Pines Sanitarium . . . two miles." Frank had followed the tortuous windings of the steep and narrow side road for more than twice that distance.

Abruptly his roadster nosed out into a clearing. "For crying out loud!" Frank whispered to himself, "where am I?"

Across this clearing he was in, there was the entrance to a rocky gorge that cut into the sharply rising slope ahead.

Frank shifted gear and clung to the wheel as his protesting car bumped into the shadows.

Here the going was even worse. The dry floor of the canyon was strewn with boulders and loose rock. The ravine twisted as had the road through the woods. Suddenly from around one of its contours came a roaring, clattering Juggernaut. A hoarse shout, the screech of brakes. Frank wrenched his wheel, swerving the roadster to the wall of the canyon. Too late. A careening flivver struck his car with a sickening grind of fenders, caromed off and rolled over. At once it burst into flames.

In swift fear for the driver of the other car, Frank stumbled toward the blazing wreck. His assistance was not needed—or wanted. A cadaverous, thick-spectacled individual in soiled dungarees crawled from the heap and made off down the ravine without a backward glance.

"Hi, there!" Frank sang out. "Are you hurt?"

The stranger wheeled jerkily, his narrow chalky features contorted with an emotion which might have been either fear or rage. "Lemme be!" he snarled. "If I was you I'd be gettin' along outa here before this gas tank blows up."

He turned and shambled away until lost to view around a bend. Amazed and angered, Frank stared after him. But he heeded the advice of the churlish yokel and returned speedily to his own car.

Ruefully he surveyed its damaged side. But the motor purred softly when he depressed the starter pedal, and his roadster lurched forward with its usual vigor. The running gear, fortunately, was undamaged.

Soon there echoed through the canyon the rumbling detonation which told him that fire had reached the gasoline tank of the wrecked car.

"And that," grinned Frank Robeson, "is that."

Then his grin froze to a grimace of horror. On the hood of his own car was a blob of bloody, fleshy substance. But it was not meat, either animal or human. It was something infinitely more ghastly, tentacle-like, translucent—evidently blown away from the explosion. Shuddering, Frank jumped to the ground and wiped it from the metal with a greasy rag, then slid back under the wheel and drove crazily toward his destination.

His broad face again relaxed and a puzzled light was in his steel-blue eyes when he came out of the gorge and looked up at the rambling frame structure that nestled amid the pines on the mountainside before him. It was the institution he had come so far to visit. An indefinable gloom lay over it—like a pall.

Pulling off at the side of the road, he regarded the place thoughtfully. Nothing marked it as greatly different from the many health resorts in the mountains. The broad porch, the green shutters, the spacious grounds with the inevitable croquet court, the arched signboard—all were conventional. And yet . . .

FRANK WAS PROBABLY the only staff member of New York's Park Medical Center who had entertained any doubts at all regarding Dr.

Gregory's hospital. And only recently at that. He had voiced his suspicions to his old friend, Dr. Dudley Cowan, chief of the surgical staff.

"Nonsense," Cowan had said. "Frank, we've been sending private patients to Gregory for years. You've sent many of your own. You know as well as I do that all who return are enthusiastic."

"*Some* haven't come back," was Frank's rejoinder.

Cowan's wrinkled brow had furrowed more deeply at this. "True," he admitted grudgingly, "and both were your patients. I know how you must feel, but I still think you're barking up the wrong tree. We can't question Gregory's trustworthiness."

"All the same, I'm going to run up there to look the place over," Frank told him stubbornly. "Tomorrow."

Frank had set out on the tiresome motor trip with grim determination. Two of his patients had died at Gregory Pines within six months. Of pernicious anaemia, the death certificate read. Peculiar. But Gregory's reputation was spotless; it would be folly to question his diagnoses. And unethical.

At first Frank had been only puzzled. Later he had sent Lemuel Curtis to the institution to recuperate from a severe operative case of double mastoiditis. Vague misgivings assailed him when Curtis left, but he was utterly unprepared for the telephone message that came from Curtis a few days later. Curtis was a wealthy broker.

"The whisper of *death* is in the air here," Curtis told him over the wire. "I'm *panicky*, Doctor. I've lost hope."

"Keep a stiff upper lip. I'll be up to see you."

Frank Robeson was a man of his word. But now that he was here he was not at all sure of himself. If Lem Curtis died . . .

He shivered. An uncanny silence was upon the place of the wind in the pines. He remembered the fear-husky voice of Curtis over the telephone. And he even thought of that gory blob in the gorge.

Shaking off his feelings, he started his car. There was but one thing to do. He'd make himself known to Gregory and ask to see Curtis professionally. He'd stay a few days and watch things.

The breeze whipped his shock of sandy hair into a tangle as the roadster labored up the steep drive. Grim lines were around his lips and his shoulders squared aggressively. Seeing him thus, observers might have thought him a determined sportsman rather than one of the cleverest surgeons of the metropolis. Which Frank was.

MARTIN GREGORY WAS A GENIAL if somewhat pompous man in his early fifties. A Vandyke beard and owlish eyes gave him a professorial air. His was the assured manner of one long used to deference. He was a man satisfied with his own success. But his hand was flabby and moist in the hearty grip of his caller.

Frank came to the point at once. "Any objection to my visiting Lemuel Curtis, Doctor?" he asked.

"None at all." Gregory was hesitant and his pudgy fingers were tapping the desk top. "Curtis, I might warn you, is not improving as we had expected."

"No?" Frank raised his left eyebrow in the disconcerting way he had. "There has been no change in treatment, I presume?"

"None. You are at liberty to examine the patient's chart."

Still those thick fingers tapped the desk. Frank thought that he saw an uneasy flicker in the other's eyes.

"Gregory," he blurted, "you're holding something back."

The older man flushed, then paled. "I resent that, Doctor," he spluttered. "What do you mean?"

"I'll reply with another question. Does Curtis have symptoms resembling those of Galloway and Ingalls before their deaths?"

"A-ah!" Gregory rose angrily, then dropped into his chair. "You've asked for it and I'll tell you. Yes, the symptoms are the same—and you should know them well." He stared accusingly.

"I!" Amazed, Frank returned the stare blankly.

"Who else?" Gregory's voice dropped suggestively and his eyes were shifty. "It had struck me that your last three patients arrived in quite different condition from that reported by you. Why did you send them, Doctor Robeson?"

Frank had caught a Tartar. The older man had turned the tables adroitly and was regarding him from beneath lowered lids. What had been implied was plain enough.

"You surprise me," Frank replied slowly, checking his rising ire, "I've sent my patients to you in good faith and usually with excellent results. But Galloway and Ingalls died here. Curtis, you say, is in a condition similar to theirs. You infer that I know something about it, that I knowingly sent you hopeless cases. This I deny, and I want your explanation."

Gregory smiled oilily. "Perhaps we're talking at cross purpose," he offered, again placatingly. "I admit these three cases puzzled me. Possibly I was wrong in mistrusting you."

"You *were* wrong,"—curtly. "Do I take it from you that the Galloway and Ingalls death certificates were falsified?"

"That's damned impertinence!" bellowed Gregory, purpling. "I did not understand—do not—" He subsided glumly.

"In other words you don't know what *is* wrong with Curtis?"

"Do *you?*" His bovine placidity returning, Gregory leered.

"I only know his condition when he left New York,"—stiffly. "It was satisfactory outside of the usual post-operative weakness."

"Come, come, Doctor!" Gregory arose, genial once more. "You and I are beating about the bush. We must admit that conditions seem to be odd. We'll see Curtis immediately; then I'll leave it to you to say who is at fault."

Though unsatisfied, Frank assented. On the way he mused darkly.

More than ever he was suspicious. Certainly no untoward symptoms had marked any of these cases.

Gregory's nervousness, his most evasive replies, his sudden changes of front, were decidedly mysterious.

And there was that red *thing* on the hood of the car.

CURTIS, IT DEVELOPED, was quartered in a private cabin some little way from the main building. The path through the pines led past a low rambling structure which Gregory explained was his experimental laboratory. He did not dwell on the subject further, seeming most reluctant to do so, and that served to arouse Frank's suspicions still more.

"Biological?" he asked, striving to speak pleasantly.

"Partly so," Gregory implied by his air that it was none of his visitor's business.

But Frank had seen a skulking figure at the rear of the building. It was the gaunt and colorless individual of the soiled dungarees.

"Who's that?" he demanded.

"Rufus Ballinger. Sort of helps me in the laboratory. Expert botanist." Gregory hurried along the path, obviously wishing to avoid the neighborhood of the laboratory.

Frank cudgeled his memory. Ballinger's name was familiar but most elusive. Somehow, somewhere, he had heard of this man. And in an unsavory connection, he felt sure. It would come to him later. He looked back, saw the thick-spectacled one bending over a most curious milky-stemmed plant that grew waveringly from a pot he was removing from an open hotbed.

"Here's where Curtis is," said Gregory, indicating a small green and white house with broad sleeping-porches and awninged windows.

It was a most attractive place, ideally located, and obviously of most modern design. Entering with his host, Frank saw that it was arranged to take care of two patients and had a well-appointed room for the nurse between the two bedrooms. Only one bed was now occupied, and this by Lemuel Curtis, who lay reclining on his side with his paper-white hands outside the covers.

"Glad to see you, Doc," he greeted Frank in a weak voice. "Thought you'd never get here."

In one swift glance Frank noted that the mastoid bandages were tight and clean and that they were tied in the approved manner. But his heart sank when he observed the wanness of his former patient's countenance and the bloodlessness of his lips. It was unbelievable that the man could have failed so much in the few days he had been here.

"Got to you as soon as I could, old man," Frank said cheerily. "And how goes it? Feeling better?" He had known the young bro-ker for a number of years, and counted him as an intimate friend.

"Pretty good for an old guy." Curtis essayed a smile but was obviously trying to signal with his eyes. And his hand crept out over the covers unostentatiously.

"Would you like to see his chart?" Gregory asked Frank amiably.

"If you don't mind."

As the older physician turned to reach for the daily record, the nervous fingers of Lem Curtis twitched into view and crammed a folded paper into Frank's fist. He covered it at once, then pocketed it. Curtis grinned knowingly.

GREGORY WAS EXTENDING the chart, but Frank gave it scant heed. It was only a tabulation of temperatures, respiration rates, feedings, and the usual run-of-mine hospital information.

"How about his blood tests, blood counts?" Frank inquired.

Reluctantly, Gregory brought them. Amazed, Frank saw unmistakable evidence of the dread pernicious anaemia. The daily increase in deficiency of red corpuscles was indeed alarming. He looked again at the chart and noted that the use of calves' liver was properly recorded. Everything *seemed* to be in order.

"You haven't considered blood transfusions?" he asked.

"Not as yet. As you know from your own experience, the latest practice does not encourage their use too much." Gregory smiled in his unctuous, insincere manner.

"Right. Well, I've seen enough for the present, Doctor. Shall we return to your office?" Frank was anxious to get where he could read the note Curtis had been so anxious to get to him.

"Yes, suppose we do." The older physician was actually beaming. This had turned out to be easier than he had anticipated. "And, Doctor, you'll not be able to get away from the Pines tonight; suppose I assign a room to you and have your bags brought in. Perhaps you'd like to remain a few days here yourself?"

"I had hoped to; in fact I planned to—if you agreed, of course. I like it here."

Gregory did not know quite how to take this, but he let it pass. With his guest so affable, he could hardly do otherwise.

"See you later, Lem." Frank waved airily and followed his host from the cabin.

LATER IN THE SECLUSION of his room, he puzzled over the shakily penciled note.

"*Something mighty queer here,*" it read. "*Nurse on duty at day but not at night. Gregory visits late and gives me medicine that's not reported on the chart. Dope, I think, because I get so drowsy I just have to pass out. Wake every morning weak as the devil— and mentally depressed. That whisper is still in the air. Do something, Doc, or I'm a goner. I KNOW it.*"

This called for thought, for watching and waiting. The note did not clarify things at all. Frank determined, though, that he'd see this through, regardless of professional ethics or of consequences. He considered several possibilities. None seemed logical. This man Ballinger might be involved; possibly not. Gregory, on the face of it all, seemed to be the one to suspect. If Ballinger were in on it, in what connection could it be? Again the surgeon racked his brain for memory of that odd name. The connection still eluded him.

If Gregory were administering drugs to Curtis, why? What could it have to do with the apparent anaemic condition? Of course, there was the possibility that Curtis was so greatly concerned over his own condition that he was inclined to exaggerate ordinary happenings in his own mind. But something was very much wrong here. He would have to find out what it was.

Late that afternoon he strolled down toward the laboratory and, from a distance, saw Gregory and Ballinger stooping over one of the many hotbeds outside. They were so absorbed they did not notice his coming.

Taking advantage of their preoccupation, he circled the building cautiously and secreted himself behind a clump of bushes within sight and earshot. Immediately the plant those two were examining took his entire attention. It was like no growth Frank had ever seen, having a mass of rubbery, vine-like branches that seemed always to be in motion. Weirdly so, as if actuated by some external force. Yet there was no sign of a breeze that might have blown them about.

At the tips, the rubbery members were milky-white in hue and nearly transparent, but near the heavy main stem they shaded off into a deep pink hue. As the doctor watched, the rosiness near the stem of the unnatural plant began to rise and fall, much as if it were a liquid boiling in a test tube. A sickly-sweet odor assailed his nostrils and his instant impression was that it came from the growth. Ballinger was lifting the pot that held the vegetable incongruity and was removing it from the hotbed.

"Careful, Rufe," Gregory cautioned.

His face was turned toward the hiding-place and Frank saw with a start that the older physician's eyes were fixed—staring—as if he were in a trance.

"Lemme be!" snarled the uncouth Ballinger. "I know what I'm doin'. This here's the last time *this* one comes outa here, too."

It was quite incomprehensible. Frank drew himself into the smallest space possible as the other two made for the laboratory, Ballinger carrying the potted monstrosity. The door closed behind them. Frank moved stealthily to one of the windows, hoping to peer inside. But he found it curtained so heavily that nothing could be seen. Disappointed, he returned to the porch of the main building.

Dusk came quickly and with it came the return of Martin Gregory, who dropped heavily into a deck chair beside Frank. His eyes looked better now but there was still a deliberation in his movements that bespoke some sense-deadening influence. The man must be a narcotic addict. A strange place, Gregory Pines. Robeson's nerves chilled.

"Find your room satisfactory?" Gregory drawled.

"First rate. Couldn't be better. All the same I can't seem to get Curtis out of my mind. What is your honest opinion of the case, Doctor?"

The older man's eyes narrowed. No sign of drowsiness or of a lethargic disinterest was in them now. "It's just as I told you; you saw for yourself, didn't you? And you can examine Curtis again in any way and as often as you like. Perhaps you can help me in the case."

This last was said with a knowing smirk.

Frank shifted his attack. "Fond of your botanical research, aren't you, Doctor?"

The change in the man was startling. He purpled; cleared his throat noisily. "You been spying on me?" he demanded.

Frank raised his left eyebrow quizzically. "Would that worry you?" he countered.

"Now you look here!" Gregory sprang from his seat and his pudgy fingers clasped and unclasped in the sheer fury that was within him. "I've been more than courteous, allowing you the run of my place and I've seen fit to put you up for awhile and let you see this patient of yours as often as you please. But I warn you; keep your meddling nose out of my affairs or you'll find yourself in a peck of trouble."

With this outburst he stalked off, slamming the screen door alter him.

AFTER SUPPER, Dr. Robeson wandered through the grounds aimlessly, still without seeing Gregory or Ballinger. Finally he decided to return to his own room and await developments, or at least to plan a course of action. He had not realized how physically tired the day had made him and dozed off in an easy-chair while merely contemplating the events which had led up to the situation.

Awakening with a start, he looked at his watch and saw that it was well past the midnight hour. Something told him he should not retire at once; he paced the floor for the better part of a half-hour, then decided to get out in the open. Perhaps it was only a hunch, but he felt that he might learn something of value by another round of the premises.

All was quiet. There was no moon, but enough of the light of the stars was there to enable him to make his way down the path which led past the laboratory to the cottage where Curtis was housed. He was disappointed—no lights in the cabin. About to return to his room, he was stopped in his tracks by the unmistakable sound from within that marks a deeply drugged man—a heavy shuddering snore. Lem Curtis! Frank stepped to the door of the cabin, found it open and walked in. It was a surprise to find that his patient—and friend—was in a stupor, from which nothing could arouse him at the moment. The nurse was off duty, of course, and on the spur of the moment Frank ransacked her cabinet, obtained the necessary materials and with the aid of a hand flash withdrew a generous sample of Curtis' blood. He observed a fresh puncture almost at the point where he himself needled.

The man did not stir or even groan at the sharp stab; his face was a ghastly mask in the light of the flash. But Frank was all professional now; his personal feelings were put aside. He snapped off the flash and tiptoed from the building, sprinting down the path toward the laboratory. The grounds, seemingly, were deserted, the main building dark excepting for the dim lights of the corridors.

FRANK WAS NO SECOND-STORY WORKER, nor had he the slightest knowledge of or sympathy with the back-porch-casement-opening burglar. But he learned somehow the way to get into Ballinger's laboratory.

With the blood sample carefully protected in its tube, he cautiously felt his way to the bench of the microscopes and with only a single palm-shielded flash from the electric hand lamp found the switch of the illuminator of one of the excellent instruments. This gave him plenty of light without any betraying glare. Quickly he found a slide, stain and cover glass, and prepared his specimen.

He searched the brilliant field of vision carefully. The smear was a perfect one. The deficiency of red corpuscles was so evident as to require no count. But no microcytes, those minute elementary granules associated with anaemia, were present. Curtis was *not* an anaemic. *His blood was being drained artificially from his weakening body.* That other puncture meant that Gregory had robbed him of his life fluid, not infused it.

It came to Frank instantly, this horrible thing, and thoughts of Rufe's squirmy and rustling plant rushed in to show the solution.

Rufus Ballinger was killing men to satisfy his insane lust for experimentation with plant life, there could be no doubt of that. He was endeavoring to produce flora that was half fauna—probably *all* fauna in his crazy mind. Worse than this . . .

A whispering sound close at hand startled Frank into something like normalcy. He turned his head in the direction from which the eerie noise had come and saw slimy pink tentacles reaching over the window-sill from outside. One of the plants had gone berserk! The thing was alive and it was gigantic! Flowers, blood-red in hue, with faces like crimson gargoyles, budded and bloomed in a second of time, looked at him with sinister gloating . . . advanced with the speed of a pack of stalking wolves.

Breath-takingly, a pungent odor assailed his nostrils. The lights of the laboratory flashed on blindingly. Abruptly he knew no more.

WHEN CONSCIOUSNESS RETURNED, slowly and painfully, Frank found himself flat on his back in dewy grass. Dawn was just breaking, as evidenced by the paleness of the eastern horizon. There were sounds of men talking in low monotone and he strained his barely aroused senses to recall what this was all about and his ears to learn the meaning of the muttered intensities of speech. Suddenly, as if he had snapped out from under an anaesthetic, he remembered.

He sat up, stiffly—they had not tied him. He *had* been drugged; the odor of nitrous oxide was strong in his nostrils. What they had used to supplement that first whiff he did not know, nor how they had managed to accomplish it. In the semi-darkness he saw Gregory and Ballinger working over one of the hotbeds of the strange plant growth.

"If I was you," Rule was saying, "I'd put him outa the way. Dead men don't talk, Martin, and he'd be easier'n the others."

"Come, come," Gregory responded slowly and with apparent difficulty in his speech. "There are more important things right at this time. Watch what you are doing."

Ballinger squealed shrilly—like a rat, Frank thought. "The damn thing nearly tore my hand offa me," he whined. "Why'd we take that extra pint from Curtis?"

Still in somewhat of a daze, Frank reflected that there are about thirteen pints of blood in the average human body. That even a professional blood donor can hardly give up more than about a quart every two weeks and still remain robust. But this!—these devils must have been taking a pint a day from the young broker—an extra pint tonight! No wonder the external symptoms of anaemia were manifest in Curtis! No wonder those other lives had been cut short.

Frank, his head clearing by now, rolled over on his side and saw that forms were taking shape more distinctly in the brightening dawn. He saw that the two men were working over one of the wriggly plants, that it was more gigantic than any he had before seen and infinitely more active. Its tendrils whipped about like the arms of an octopus, and Gregory was quite terrified at the swift movements of the horrid appendages, ducking and cowering like a frightened schoolboy.

"Get yourself together, Doc," snarled Ballinger, and he struck the older man's cheek with the flat of his hand.

An incomprehensible thing happened then. The plant, like a faithful hound protecting its master, struck out at the uncouth botanist.

The unfortunate man screeched and fought horribly. He was helpless in the clutches of the thing he had created.

Frank forced himself from his horrified helplessness.

"Gregory!" he yelled leaping forward. "Watch out! The damned thing will get you when it's finished with Ballinger."

The botanist suddenly ceased struggling. The plant, dripping red now, was writhing its members about Martin Gregory's face and neck. Gregory screamed like a trapped and horribly injured animal.

Tingling with artificial paralysis as his hands were, Frank felt in his pockets. Of course he always carried his hypodermic kit with him. It was there.

Gregory now was only half conscious. Frank loaded his hype with phenol—full to the neck. He crawled toward the dying man. The wriggling plant had him almost completely wrapped up in its tentacles.

He plunged the needle into the heavy root-stem of the *thing*. Its charge shot home. A wildly thrashing tentacle knocked him down. It coiled about his neck, and stinging pain shot through him. He fought desperately to escape.

Gregory screamed again, obviously helpless again the octopus-like thing which was engulfing him. Despair gripped Robeson. The poison wasn't working. He choked as the tentacles tightened convulsively.

Then those blood-dripping flowers shrivelled their faces. The arms relaxed. With a gasp of relief, Frank tore away the dripping things with suckers that stuck graspingly and drew away his life-blood.

Ballinger was dead—his body a waxy husk.

Lemuel Curtis now would be no more molested. Gregory, Frank realized, had been innocent. And Gregory would live.

Gregory, hypnotized by the mad botanist—who would never again kill human beings—had been only a tool.

Curtis's life was safe now; he would recover with proper treatment. Building him up with the proper vitamins would take care of that.

Frank climbed erect and tottered to the small cabin to assure the young broker of his ultimate safety. And then, reviving his own faculties, he hobbled back to the scene of the plant's extinction.

By now Gregory's mind was almost normal. Frank helped him to his room . . . they helped each other.

"It was a bad dream," was all Gregory said. Frank nodded. Better let it end that way.

Ingalls and Galloway were gone beyond recall. Curtis was safe. Ballinger was dead—and in the morning they'd kill the young plants. Yes—it *had* been a bad dream.

THE GARDEN OF HELL (1943)
LEROY YERXA

THE BOOTH WAS BY FAR the most attractive along the line. A Mexican girl stood behind the high-banked roses, her deep brown eyes raised to him questioningly. Jeff Flynn wasn't aware of her at once, so absorbed was he in the lush, blood-red flowers.

Then, raising his eyes, he saw for the first time the shapely oval face, full lips, and the long flowing brown hair that framed her features so beautifully.

"I beg your pardon." Flynn's hat came off in a quick gesture of admiration. "I didn't see you. Your roses are superb."

A flush of color spread over her face and the long lashes dropped shyly.

"They are not mine," her voice was low, and husky. "This booth belongs to Trujall."

As though answering to the name, another head appeared over the top of the display. Involuntarily Jeff Flynn stepped back a pace. He had opened his lips to compliment the owner of the booth, but no words came. The eyes into which he stared were black as swamp pools. Trujall was an old man. His head was hatless and a thick, black stubble grew from it. The skin of his cheeks stretched tightly over high cheek bones. He was smiling, but the smile was a grimace that showed rotten, toothless gums.

"You like my pretty ones?" The words were sharp and high-pitched.

Flynn controlled himself quickly and a smile lighted his face.

"They're the finest I've ever seen," he confessed.

A claw-like, hand swept up and plucked one of the largest blossoms.

"A gift to a rose lover," Trujall's smile was set and vacant. "It is not often an American stops here."

Flynn took the flower, noticing the long, dirt-blackened nails on the hand that offered it.

"Thanks," be said. "I'd like to see your gardens. Are they near here?"

Trujall's smile vanished. He stared straight at Flynn.

"No one visits Tipico," he growled. "It is a far journey."

Taken aback by the unfriendly tone in Trujall's voice, Flynn fumbled for words.

"I'll be around in a few hours to buy some of your roses," he said.

Was it his imagination, or did a fleeting look of fear suddenly darken the girl's face?

"We will be gone within an hour," Trujall answered. "My flowers fade quickly here."

Trujall's ox cart was drawn up close to the adobe wall behind the booth. It was covered with a coarse cloth, but under the cloth, a half-dozen bulging objects were visible. Flynn's eyes caught a movement there, and as he stared, two long octopus-like tendrils dropped over the side of the rough boards and wrapped tightly around the wheel. They were perhaps two feet long and covered with brown scale.

Flynn stared. What sort of plant was that? The bulge under the cloth moved. Trujall wheeled around, noting the direction of Flynn's gaze. He was across the booth swiftly, grasped the tendrils with both his skinny hands and yanked them from the wheel. They withdrew suddenly and the movement stopped.

Trujall turned, his face hateful.

"You will go at once," his words were a command.

Flynn caught the wide-eyed expression of horror on the girl's face, hesitated, slightly angered by Trujall's attitude, then turned on his heel and crossed the street.

That Mexican girl had been badly frightened. Jeff Flynn, strangely disturbed at the knowledge, made an effort to thrust it from his mind. After all, it was none of his business. But what was it that was in the ox cart that Trujall was so anxious to conceal? Some forbidden plant he was smuggling?

HERBERT ROSS WAS NO FOOL. Fat and passing the age where romance held sway over logic, he could appreciate a woman of Gwenn's ability.

The plane was hovering over Oaxaca when Gwenn turned to talk to him for the first time during the trip down. Gwenn Hamlin, only a few hours divorced from Ross, was pretty in a heady sort of way. Her green eyes, tall slim body and luxurious red hair made men half insane. Herb Ross knew. Gwenn had given him no peace during the two years they lived together. Brainless and brittle was his description of her; the willing plaything of any man who had money.

"Herby," Gwenn said. "Why don't you go home?"

Ross smiled.

"Chicago has a meat packing plant for me to go home to," he answered. "Why should I forsake you for a line of frozen beef?"

She sniffed, but a badly repressed smile flitted over her face. She was secretly flattered that he still pursued her.

"You'll get the cold shoulder down here," Gwenn said warningly. "Besides, Herby, it isn't right."

"What isn't?" he asked shortly.

"Why—when a girl's divorced, she doesn't just go about with her ex-husband. What will Jeff think?"

Ross snorted.

"Jeff Flynn is a good boy," he said. "But Jeff's young and spoiled by money he hasn't any use for. Gwenn, you only like Jeff's money. You'll be tired of each other in a week."

Gwenn's face sobered. She intended to marry Jeff Flynn, and Ross would never keep her from it.

"Look," she said. "I've been square with you . . ."

He interrupted her with a short laugh.

"You've never been square for a minute," he said quickly. "That's the part you don't understand, Gwenn. I'd have been willing to give you your head if you'd have held to the bridle just enough to impress my friends and business associates."

Gwenn was angry. She turned her head away and hunched her shoulders down into the seat. They were coming down for the landing. Ross fastened his safety strap.

"You want me to act as a front for you," Gwenn said. "I was playing second fiddle to your business."

"In a manner of speaking," he answered, "that's not what I want. I love you, Gwenn, but you won't return my affection. I took the best bargain I could get."

The plane came down smoothly and rolled across the field.

"You've lost me, Ross," Gwenn said. "Jeff will be at the airport. After that, we'll get married and you can pack your bag for the next plane home."

Ross was silent. Waves of blood swept up around his thick neck and colored his cheeks. The plane stopped before the small hangar, and he stood up.

"Flynn is a good kid, but he's got some crazy ideas," he said. "You're not going to marry him, Gwenn. Be sure of that."

She was standing before him, her eyes blazing into his. She stamped her foot impatiently.

"And what can you do to prevent it?"

Ross bent his heavy face close to her.

"*I'll kill you if I have to,*" he said in a hoarse whisper. "But I won't have to. You're going back to Chicago with me."

Speechless with rage, but frightened by this new Herb Ross, Gwenn followed him from the plane. A half-dozen passengers had gathered outside and a dilapidated station wagon stood by the road. The words *Oaxaco Hotel* were printed across its side.

She saw Jeff Flynn, tall and dust covered, a pipe in his mouth. She went toward him quickly, relieved that he was here to meet her.

Gwenn was less sure of herself than she had been when they last met. Herb might be right after all. Jeff was young and looking for adventure.

Her ex-husband filled her with foreboding over what his next move would be. She had never seen him pursue anything in this manner. He was frightening with his huge body and bullying voice, following her thousands of miles, never letting go the bull-dog grip he had on her past.

She went across the field quickly, and into Flynn's arms. His kiss was on her cheek, rather cool she thought. Her ex-husband came up quickly, his hand held toward Flynn.

"Hello, Jeff," Ross' voice was friendly enough. "No doubt you wonder why I winged all the way down here under the circumstances. Well, I couldn't leave Gwenn in a wild country without friends. Acted as her personal bodyguard."

Flynn took the pudgy hand with mixed emotions.

"It *does* make an odd situation," he looked at Gwenn questioningly. "With your approval?"

Gwenn's face clouded.

"I tried to leave him in Reno," she said. "But I can't choose my flying companions. He's tried to make trouble all the way down."

Flynn clamped the pipe tightly between his teeth and picked up Gwenn's bags. Ross followed them across the dusty, cactus-grown field to the station wagon. He sat with the driver.

They were silent on the way to the hotel, and Flynn's hand drew away as Gwenn's fingers closed over it. He pretended to adjust the pipe, but she noticed that he carefully avoided her contact.

Gwenn was a lonely, shallow woman. The adventure of this new project was gone. There were two men for her, and she felt suddenly as though both of them had seen through her shield of glamour and were tearing her real self apart under steady scrutiny. She wished fervently that she had never seen Jeff Flynn, nor Reno. She wished for Chicago and the big mansion that Ross had kept for her. Gwenn felt tired and old and the mascara started to run on her lashes. The town was hot and airless and she had a dull, painful ache in her head.

Flynn arranged with the sleepy Mexican at the desk for a room for Gwenn opposite his own. Grinning, complacent Herbert Ross took the next room. The three of them climbed the worn stairs together and at his own door, Ross hesitated.

"Good luck, Jeff," he said, "you'll need it."

Before Flynn could reply, he was inside and the door closed with a slam. Flynn tried to smile reassuringly at the girl but it was no good. Away from soft lights and low music, she was a tired woman.

"You'd better rest," he said. "I'll be waiting on the sun porch when you're ready, to go out."

ALONE, FLYNN TOOK OFF his clothes and stood under the shower. The cold water felt good against his dusty skin.

He thought about Gwenn. From the first it had never been right. Gwenn had seen him first at the Chez Paree. They had met on the dance floor and she was alluring and lovely in that setting. They had seen each other for a month, always at night and always in quiet, restful places where lovers talk.

She had waited to tell him of Ross. Waited purposefully, he realized now. A quick divorce had been arranged and they were to meet in Mexico City. Flynn knew now that he had lost any love he might have had for Gwenn.

Flynn left the shower, dried himself quickly and dressed in gray flannels. He went along the hall to the second floor, porch and sat down in a cane chair to wait for Gwenn. The sun was warm and the heady sweetness of roses drifted from the flower booths down the street. His head relaxed against the back of the chair and he slept.

How long he had been there, his face baking in the sun, Flynn did not know. When he awakened the sun was slanting low across the red tile roofs and a slight breeze came from the west. He rubbed the sleepiness from his eyes and stretched.

Odd that Gwenn hadn't called him. She had plenty of time to bathe, apply new makeup, and look for him. Considering that she was eager to impress him favorably, she would have never willingly remained away from him so long.

A feeling of alarm entered his mind. Herb Ross wasn't a man to give Gwenn up after following her from the States to prevent her from remarrying. Flynn entered the hall with some misgivings and walked toward Gwenn's door. He knocked. It was quiet. He pushed inward. The door opened.

Herbert Ross sat on the single chair, his head lowered on the palms of his hands. He looked up, and his eyes were dull and cold.

"She was dead when I came in," he said.

Flynn went to the bed.

Gwenn's body was stretched out across the sheet, her legs hanging over the side of the bed. Her neck was twisted and thrown back at an odd angle. Her lips were swollen and blue and the eyes stared up at him, glazed and sightless. The skin of her neck was bruised. Her dress was torn.

FLYNN WHEELED ABOUT.

"You fool," he spoke in a low, tense voice. "You damned fool. You didn't have to do this."

Ross arose slowly, steadying himself with one hand on the back of the chair.

His eyes were red and his shoulders slumped forward in despair.

"I didn't kill her, Jeff." His lips quivered. *"Honest to God, Jeff, I loved her.* I came to plead with her again. She was lying here—like—this . . ."

Flynn wanted to believe him. The fat man seemed sincere enough, but the evidence was damning. No wild stretch of imagination would put another person in Oaxaco who hated Gwenn.

"You choked her," Flynn said. "No one would ever believe that you didn't."

Ross sat down again, looking away from the body. He tried to gain control of himself.

"I knew you'd say that," he looked Flynn straight in the eye. "That's why I've been sitting here, waiting for Heaven knows what. I couldn't come and tell you."

"When did you find her?" Flynn asked.

Ross was eager to talk.

"It was right after we came up," he said. "I decided to have one last talk with Gwenn. I found the door open and came in. I can't expect you to believe me, Jeff, but it's the truth."

Flynn walked to the window and looked down the street toward the flower show. The carts were gone. The street was dark and deserted.

"Jeff," Ross was close to him, his eyes low. "I want you to see something before you call the police. I— I can't think straight yet."

Flynn turned and Ross walked to the opposite side of the bed. He shuddered, reached out and touched the neckline of the girl's dress.

"Above her heart," he whispered.

Flynn watched as Ross drew the dress away. *There was a circular hole in the white flesh over the girl's heart. It was the size of a silver dollar, clean and deep. No blood soiled the flesh around it.*

Ross drew the dress up again quickly. "What did it, Flynn?" he asked in a hushed voice.

Jeff Flynn shook his head. No bullet or instrument that he could imagine would have left the deep bloodless wound he had seen on Gwenn's body.

"I'm damned if I know," he answered slowly.

Flynn put a firm hand on the older man's shoulder.

"I'll do everything I can," he said. "I don't believe now that you killed her. If it helps any, I didn't intend to marry her when I saw how much you cared for her. I was a fool I guess. We'll tell the police that we found her together."

Ross turned and grasped his hand. The grip was warm and grateful.

"Flynn, you're tops. You'll never know how much . . ."

He stopped talking and bent down over something on the floor. He started to pick it up, a shiver passed through his body and he dropped it again.

Flynn picked up the small object and held it between his fingers. It was about three inches long, fleshy and covered with brown scales. He had seen a thing like that before.

The thing in his hand was the cleanly chopped end of a feeler, *like the one he had seen creeping from the wagon of the rose gardener, Trujall.*

"WE'RE GOING TO GET OUT OF HERE," he said sharply. "This is a clue I can follow. We'll call the police and leave before they get here."

"But they'll hunt us down and convict both of us," Ross protested. "I can't let you take the rap."

Flynn's eyes were icy.

"They'll lock us up and we'll never have a chance. If we escape now, perhaps we can find the murderer."

"But where—how?" Flynn looked doubtful.

"I'm not sure," he confessed. "But we're going to visit the valley of Tipico."

"Never heard of it," Ross answered.

"You'll hear a lot from now on," Flynn said grimly. "It's a garden of roses, and I think—a garden of hell."

COUNT AVON BICARDA owned the valley of Tipico; owned the roses that grew in rank profusion within its warm borders; owned the souls of the people who straggled from the village each morning to tend the thorny, green plants on which his roses grew.

Since the Spaniards had come and gone, the Bicarda family had lived within the protected valley of Tipico and their power had not been questioned.

True, in the village there was one small group who kept to themselves. They neither toiled in the gardens nor slaved on the roads. But they were few and they did not trouble the Count.

He stood beside his horse on the hill above Tipico, staring first across the vast sweep of blood red roses beneath him and then anxiously toward the road that came from Oaxaca.

His dress was the dress of a Spanish nobleman. The flabby, weak face, the dreary eyes confessed weakness of character. A casual onlooker would have thought the Count on a movie set, attired as he was in the silken trousers, long silk stockings and tightly-buttoned white cloak of past centuries.

Closer study might betray the wrinkled stocking and the broken garter that hung at his knee, the torn cuff of his shirt that someone had forgotten to mend. Science would brand Avon Bicarda as mentally unbalanced.

His eyes brightened suddenly and the hand on the bridle tightened with excitement. An ox cart rolled toward him from over the hill. On the board seat, a young girl and an old man sat side by side. Trujall, the gardener, was returning from Oaxaca.

The Count mounted his horse clumsily and galloped toward them. At the side of the wagon, he stopped and dismounted. Trujall tapped the oxen with his staff and they halted. The girl watched the Count with surprise and distrust.

Ignoring Trujall, Count Avon Bicarda rounded the cart and bowed low before the girl.

"It is a pleasure to welcome Leona, the daughter of Textan, home once more," the Count said. His lips were set in a leer. "Will you allow me to take you to the village?"

Leona Textan's face paled with disgust.

"My father knows not of my journey to Oaxaca," she protested. "I must hurry straight home to him."

A sneer made the Count's face more simple to read.

"You may as well know that you will not return to the town," he hesitated. "Now or ever."

The girl turned to Trujall, her eyes pleading.

"You begged me to brighten your booth," she accused. "It is your duty to see that I am taken home safely."

Trujall's head came around slowly. His eyes were amused. Planting the heavy butt of his staff in her stomach, he pushed with all his strength. She toppled into Count Bicarda's arms, and a scream of terror escaped her lips: Trujall poked the oxen and the cart rolled away.

Holding her tightly with one arm, the Count called after Trujall and the wagon halted.

"Your task," the Count shouted. "It was again successful?"

For the first time real satisfaction showed in Trujall's eyes. He turned, lifted the cover from the wagon and the Count hurried toward him. Leona Textan dropped to her knees in the dust, tears spilling down her cheeks. The Count glanced hurriedly under the cover and smiled.

"Bigger and stronger," he licked his lips. "You do well, Trujall."

Trujall smiled.

"Thank, you, master," he answered humbly. He turned to the oxen again, to conceal a sneer that was etched on his face.

"Master?" he whispered sneeringly under his breath. "*Fool!*"

He moved forward along the road into the valley.

Leona was on her feet, running toward the timber that bordered the upper valley. Count Bicarda mounted his horse and galloped after her.

Once she fell, scratched her knee and the blood ran from the wound. Looking back quickly she saw that he was almost upon her. She arose and limped forward, too frightened to call out. She reached the trees and ran in among them.

The man jumped from his horse and pursued her. She could hear his heavy footsteps on the soft earth and knew he was close. His arm reached her shoulder and jerked her roughly to a halt.

"Please—my father . . ." she gasped.

"Your father can't do anything," he snarled and tried to press her lips to his. She kicked and clawed him, fighting like an animal.

"You are going to my palace," he said. "It is useless to fight."

Suddenly Count Bicarda felt a heavy hand on his shoulder. He was whirled around, and a fist smashed solidly against his jaw. He went down in a heap, gouging one shoulder into the earth. It stained his white coat.

JEFF FLYNN TURNED to the girl, who had slumped to the ground, wide-eyed. He helped her to her feet.

"Are you all right?" he asked.

She nodded.

"Where did you come from?" she asked in bewilderment. "Seeing you here is so . . . so unexpected. No one comes so far off the beaten path . . ."

Flynn smiled at her.

"I came to get some of those roses. Remember, I said I'd be back to buy some?"

He turned to the fallen Count, who was sitting up, rubbing his injured jaw and rather foolishly trying to brush the dirt from his coat.

"Who is he?'

A look of terror crossed the girl's face.

"You shouldn't have hit him. He's Count Bicarda. He rules all of Tipico. He will make plenty of trouble for you."

Flynn shrugged.

"Not much more than we're in now, eh, Ross?"

Herbert Ross came forward, nodded glumly.

"This the fellow we're looking for?"

"No. We want a fellow named Trujall."

Flynn turned to the girl.

"Where is Trujall? . . . and by the way, what is your name?"

"Leona Textan," she answered. "But what do you want with Trujall?"

"We'd like to ask him a few questions," said Flynn grimly. "Where is he?"

There was terror in the girl's voice.

"You must go away! You must not go to him. It will not be wise . . ."

"It will not be wise not to!" exclaimed Flynn. "Will you take us to him?"

Leona stared at hi intent eyes a moment, then nodded.

"Yes," she whispered. "I will take you to him."

THE VALLEY OF TIPICO had a strange effect on Jeff Flynn. He had been vaguely worried since he first saw the fat Count pursuing the girl in the forest. Everything in Tipico went wrong. They were hardly out of the forest, Ross riding his horse beside that of the glowering Count and Leona Textan sitting before Flynn on his horse, when the odor of the roses started to penetrate Flynn's brain.

Tipico was one vast rose garden, stretching red as blood along the ten-mile floor of the valley. He felt the first rich fumes of the blossoms drift up to them as they went down the dusty road. The perfume filled his head and made him drowsy.

"I'd hate like the devil to *live* in this place," Ross said suddenly. "Those flowers are like opium. The smell is so sweet it deadens my brain."

Flynn could see a change in the girt also. She relaxed against him in the saddle, her eyes widened and her lips parted, almost like rose petals themselves. Her breathing was soft and she looked at him through half-closed lids.

"It is always like this," she said. "The valley is so pleasant that we who live here could not stay long in any other place. It is like a spell that casts itself upon us, making us happy where we are."

The horses jogged on slowly. The sun was bright above and they entered the boundaries of the town. Tipico was small—barely a dozen houses, a store and a few warehouses.

Count Bicarda began to bristle, and he grew truculent. Obviously, now that he was in his own bailiwick, he was losing his fear of the Americans. He glared at Flynn hatefully.

Leona saw the glare and she turned pale. She turned to Flynn and whispered in his ear.

"Please," she begged. "Run away now! While there is time. Take me with you!"

Flynn blinked.

"Take you with me. . . Good Lord, girl, aren't you being just a little . . ." Flynn had intended to say "dramatic" but his lips closed on the word. The fear in her eyes, the tenseness of her body beneath his encircling arm, spelled the sincerity of her convictions.

"No," he said grimly. "No two-bit local emperor is going to scare me out. I've come for a purpose. I want to see Trujall!"

"You will see him!" snarled Bicarda. "And you will see something else . . . *Halto!*"

They came to a halt before a building that Flynn took to be a general store. In the doorway stood a little man, not over five-foot-three in height, with a fierce black mustache that gave him an oddly friendly appearance. Dark, serious eyes hinted at their own ability to twinkle with humor. Right now they were sober and puzzled, and a frown wrinkled the skin at their corners.

"General Harzo!" snapped Bicarda. "Arrest these people!"

HARZO STARED AT BICARDA. He seemed somehow contemptuous, but at the same time there was an unwilling respect in his eyes. Something that was not fear, but yet was compulsory. Obviously, Flynn thought, Bicarda did have power in this valley—enough even to make this pseudo-general respect his commands.

"What is the charge, Count?" Harzo asked respectfully. But he made no move to comply with the arrest request.

The Count began to bluster.

"That gringo—he struck me. He attempted to interfere . . ."

Flynn interrupted;

"Absolutely, General Harzo," he said. "I did interfere. In fact, I pasted the Count in the jaw—where he had it coming. He was molesting this young lady here, against her will, and I did what any gentleman would do—what you would do in the same circumstances. And if I had time, I'd stay to prefer charges and ask you to lock him up."

Harzo turned to the Count.

"What about that?" he asked.

The Count's eyes narrowed.

"I repeat," he said, "this man attacked me. I was merely kissing the girl I have selected as my wife. We are to be married. In fact, we were on our way here to have you perform the ceremony."

Flynn swung down off the horse, lifted the girl down. He looked at her, startled.

"Is that true?" be asked incredulously.

Stark terror was in her eyes. She looked into his a moment, then looked away, tore from his grasp, and ran to stand beside the Count. She uttered no word.

"I'll be damned!" came Herbert Ross' exclamation.

Flynn paled with anger. He wheeled to face General Harzo. He reached forward and clutched the little General's shoulders.

"Listen," he growled in a low voice. "I did the girl a favor, understand? As far as the Count and his two-bit power are concerned, he can go jump in the lake."

General Harzo blinked, but his lips curled into an amused smile. His eyes held a peculiar look of approval.

"Good words, *amigo*," he said. "Now if you will let me go, I will give you some advice."

Flynn let go of him.

"The Count grows roses here," Harzo said. "The people do as he says simply because they have done so for a thousand years.

Perhaps that is why this girl wishes to wed the Count. We shall ask her and see."

The General turned to the girl.

"Do you wish to marry this man?" She stared helplessly a moment at Flynn and Ross, then looked at Bicarda.

His eyes were fixed on her with a glare. "Yes," she said to Harzo. "Yes, yes!"

"You are not being forced to do this thing?"

"No," she said, face pale. "I am not being forced."

Harzo turned to Flynn and bowed.

"You see, amigo, it is all right."

"All right hell," growled Flynn, staring at the girl, who dropped her eyes before his accusing gaze. "But I guess there's nothing I can do about it."

"Do your, duty, General Harzo," Count Bicarda spat out. "Or it will go badly with you."

Harzo's eyes flamed, but he said nothing to Bicarda. Instead he turned to Flynn.

"Therefore," he went on, as though ignoring Bicarda's outburst, "it is obvious that you have attacked Count Bicarda in a criminal manner, and I shall have to arrest you."

FLYNN LEAPED FORWARD, fists doubled. "Why, you . . . !"

Harzo clapped his hands and a soldier leaped out from behind a corner of the building.

"Arrest them!" snapped Harzo. "Take them over to my office. I will take care of their cases immediately after the wedding—"

He turned to Bicarda.

"—You wanted to have the ceremony immediately?" He waited for a confirmation.

"Yes," said Bicarda. "At once."

Leona Textan nodded dumbly.

Flynn walked across to Leona and grasped her arm.

"I know you're not doing this because you want to," he said. "I know you're afraid of something. Maybe it's the same thing I came here to uncover. Maybe it's Trujall . . ."

Count Bicarda shoved forward, tried to disengage Flynn's hand from Leona's arm. Flynn shoved him roughly back, so that he tripped over a bush and sat down. He ignored the Count's sputtering.

"It is Trujall, isn't it?" he pursued. "Tell me the truth."

The girl looked at him tragically.

"Go away," she whispered. "Go away, far from here. You will only come to harm in this valley. I am doing what I want to do. You have no right to interfere."

Flynn released her arm in bafflement, noting as he did so that Harzo had made no move, or order his soldier to make one, in assistance to the Count.

"Okay," he said. "But I'll find Trujall, and wring the truth out of him. Also, the truth about what happened back at Oaxaca!"

The soldier stepped forward now and motioned with his rifle. Flynn and Ross walked ahead of him up the stairs and into the general store. At the rear of it, Flynn saw that they were in some sort of office. There was a desk, several chairs, and another door. Flynn noticed with amazement that this inner office was cool, air-conditioned.

They were marched into a room with a barred window. The guard sat down outside the open door and held his rifle across his knees. He didn't close the door.

Ross looked at Flynn soberly.

"Well, we're in the clink. But at that, it's no worse than where we'd be back in Oaxaco."

"No," said Flynn darkly. "But there's something damned fishy in this valley; more than what happened back there. I intend to find it out."

"I hope you do," said Ross despondently. "Because it looks like a murder charge for me, if you don't!"

FLYNN WALKED SWIFTLY BACK and forth across the floor, white-hot anger burning inside him. Ross sat quietly by the barred window, looking down the sun-swept street. Ross understood Flynn's feelings better than Flynn thought, remembering how *he* had felt when another man took Gwenn away. He didn't speak of it to Flynn. There was nothing they could do.

Ross watched Count Avon Bicarda's carriage come up the street. He saw Leona Textan sitting at the Count's side, her face drawn and pale. The Count was leaning back in the carriage, his eyes closed, face smug. The Count, Ross thought bitterly, was taking the whole thing quite calmly.

The carriage swept by the house and went down the road toward the far end of the valley. General Harzo walked toward their prison, his boots kicking up dust as he walked. Several minutes later another carriage went by. In the seats, several soldiers sat with rifles carelessly held. Their carriage disappeared down the road also. A guard for the Count and his new bride?

The General came in. He carried a stiff, folded, document in his hand. Crossing the room he knelt at a large wall safe and put the document inside. Once he had twisted the knob and locked the safe he rose and faced Flynn.

"You can come out now," he said with a smile. "And if you gentlemen will honor me with your presence, we will go out and dine. Perhaps then you can confide to me the trouble and the mission that brings you here."

"What's that?" asked Flynn, astounded.

"You can come out. You are free. You are not, and have never been, under arrest. I am sorry that I had to inconvenience you, but you will understand that it was the simplest way to avoid trouble all around. Count Avon Bicarda is a power in the valley—although not as great as his mad mind conceives himself to be. So humoring him was the best policy. He will never think of you again."

"But that girl," said Flynn angrily. "She did not want to marry him. She was terrorized."

Harzo shrugged.

"She signified her desires very directly," he said. "Come, we will dine. No doubt you are hungry."

He led the way toward a restaurant and they ordered.

It was one o'clock then. At three, the carriage of soldiers returned from their ride down the valley. They brought with them the news that the carriage of Count Avon Bicarda had been attacked by strange bandits halfway to the palace.

The Count had been shot through the heart and had died at once. The girl was unharmed and being escorted to her new home. The carriage of soldiers had arrived in time to fight the bandits, but too late to save the Count.

GENERAL HARZO, his lips stern and face expressionless, ordered the news to be posted at once. Count Avon Bicarda was dead and the valley belonged to his new wife, Leona Textan.

"Señor Flynn," Harzo said suddenly, placing his half-empty wine glass on the table before him, "I have a question to ask you."

Flynn looked up with moody eyes.

"I'm afraid, General," Flynn said, "you and I have little to discuss. You can perhaps see now the heritage you gave that girl. She's widowed before she reached her home."

"I'm sorry, American, that you think harshly of me. I think it is best that you know the truth. Perhaps you can give me the help I so badly need."

Flynn was watching the mustached man carefully. Ross' head never came up from his food.

"You were angry that I insisted the girl marry," the General went on. "You wonder why . . . ?"

"Insane," Flynn broke in. "I'd like to drag you before the authorities anywhere outside the valley and watch you sober up."

General Harzo rose to his feet.

"It was necessary that, to fulfill my plan, Leona Textan marry Count Bicarda. I had no intentions of letting them reach their home."

Flynn's glass dropped to the table with a crash. Ross stopped eating, mouth open, fork poised.

"You see," Harzo added, "my full name is General Harzo Textan. Leona is my daughter."

FOR SOME TIME the three men faced each other, but none of them spoke. Flynn arose, rounded the table and offered his hand to the General.

"Accept my apology," he begged. "I don't know what you've got in mind, but I'm sure you won't allow them to harm your own daughter. If we had known, we'd have kept our mouths shut."

Harzo Textan smiled and took Flynn's hand.

"I know," he said quietly, "I guess I can trust you. Perhaps it will be best if I tell the story of Tipico."

He pushed his chair from the table, crossed to the fireplace and stood before it. A frown passed over his lace.

"I have not always lived in Tipico," he started. "Many years ago, before Leona was born, I lived in Mexico City. I was a *politico* at the time, und held some high offices. My wife died at Leona's birth and I asked for retirement. They wanted to do something for me, in return for my services to the government."

He paused, smiled wearily and went on.

"Some one knew of Tipico, and thinking it a quiet, sunny place, suggested that I come here. Oddly enough I was given the governing power of the valley and the Mexican government will back up my word here."

"Have you ever had to call upon them?" Ross asked curiously.

Harzo nodded and smiled.

"But once," he answered. "Since the soldier came to the valley and the people realized I was the governor, they have done as I say. There was one exception."

"Count Avon Bicarda?"

"Yes!" Anger blazed in the General's eyes. "Bicarda has lived here since birth. Before him was his father and so back into the years. The family is degenerate and low. They know but one industry. Every year, the petals of the roses are taken to Oaxaca and made into perfume."

"I've noticed an odd thing," Ross said. "The air conditioning in your office, in this restaurant, wherever you go."

Harzo nodded and smiled slightly.

"Yes, you are right," he admitted. "That is how I remain free of the spell of the flowers. The people here live in a semi-awakened state. The power of the flowers is so great that they have no will to fight. They stay here and work until they die *or are murdered*."

Flynn's jaw stiffened. He was thinking of Gwenn. Gwenn with that strange round hole in her flesh.

"Murder?"

The General's fists were clenched.

"There are many things one does not mention," he said. "But now I can tell you the whole story. The Count needed men and women here to work in his gardens. He also needed them for another purpose. For the second he demanded one qualification."

"And that?"

"Death," the General answered in a low voice. "They were found dead in the fields. I am sure it was murder."

"But great God, man," Flynn protested. "Surely you could have stopped it?"

"That is where you are wrong. Every flower-drugged man in the valley would have risen against me, if they had cared. I could not act."

"I'd like to ask you a question, General," Ross said. "You married Leona and the Count for a purpose?"

"I had planned that for years," he admitted. "It was the one way of getting control of Count Bicarda. With Leona married to him, I could go to his palace and find out for myself what was happening there."

"But surely there were other ways," Flynn said. "With your soldiers you could have forced your way in and searched the place."

General Harzo Textan shook his head. "There was but one way to break the power of the Bicarda over this valley."

Ross looked hostile.

"So you did it by marrying your daughter into the family and then killing her husband. The valley of Tipico belongs now to Leona Textan—and to you!"

The General's eyes flashed.

"You are a smart man, Ross," he said. "But I am not responsible for the bandits who killed the Count."

"But it was you who sent soldiers after him as the Count left town," Ross said. "Not more than a quarter of a mile separated the two carriages. There would hardly be time for an outside attack."

Harzo nodded.

"That is all very logical," he admitted, "but not the truth."

"I'm not so sure of that," Flynn interrupted. "There are some things I don't like. General, what do you know about Trujall?"

"I don't know . . ." began Harzo worriedly.

He was cut short by a loud commotion in the hall. The door to the room swung open and a soldier staggered in. His uniform was torn and covered with mud. He tried to salute the General and fell forward on his face.

Flynn dropped to one knee and turned the man over. The fellow's eyeballs were turned up queerly and he was gasping for breath.

"General . . . your daughter . . ." Flynn's ear was close to the quivering lips, "Trujall . . ."

The voice faded to a whisper. The dying man clutched his heart and a shiver passed over him. He tried to speak further, but his lips gurgled wordlessly and closed.

Flynn stood up quickly.

"You have horses?" he asked of the General.

Harzo nodded.

"I'll get them." He rushed out.

When the General had left the room, Flynn drew the stiff white hand of the soldier gently away from the bloodied shirt. A whistle escaped his lips.

"Look at that, Ross!"

There was a deep, circular hole in the flesh over the heart. "The same thing that killed Gwenn! We're on the right track!"

The General came in and two men were with him. He spoke quickly in Spanish and the soldiers picked up the dead man and carried him away.

"Let's go," Harzo said grimly, "and may the Saints protect my daughter until we reach her."

FLYNN AND ROSS rode close to each other on the big horses Harzo Textan had supplied.

Harzo rode ahead of them, his eyes focused on the building three miles away, that was the Bicarda palace.

Flynn felt a strange sleepiness coming over him. The valley air seemed warm and muggy.

"It's a fight to keep awake here," he said.

The General spoke to them sharply.

"Breathe as lightly as possible. It is the power of the roses," he cautioned. In my own town I have clean, cool air and I am not affected. Here, men and women go unprotected. The roses numb the brain like a drug."

Flynn watched the palace ahead of them grow and take shape beyond terraced slopes. It was as lovely as the valley. Roses spread up across terraces and about the lawns. Trellises against the walls were alive with red flowers.

"When we get close enough," Flynn said, "I'll drop off behind. You and the General ride straight in and go to the front door. I'll take a look around before anyone suspects I'm here."

They reached the bend in the road where it turned toward the palace. Flynn reined his horse out of sight behind the bushes. He watched as the two men rode up to the palace, tied their mounts and went to the door. As the door opened the General walked in, followed by Ross. The door closed.

For some time Flynn waited. A gathering storm was hastening the dusk.

He studied the house. In his mind was the image of those plant tendrils under the cover of Trujall's ox cart. Flynn wanted to see that ox cart and its contents again. Perhaps a search of the out buildings . . .

He crossed the lawn quickly and went behind the palace. There was a small vegetable garden.

He saw the carriage house looming, perhaps fifty yards beyond the garden. The small plot in which he stood was planted with bulblike plants that protruded eight or ten inches above ground. He started to walk among them quickly, caught his boot on the roots and fell.

A tiny, whip-like object snapped out and struck his face. Another wrapped quickly about his boot.

Flynn struggled to his feet only to find that he was trapped. The tentacles had suddenly come alive. More of them were stretching toward him. The tendrils were much smaller and yet he recognized the form. They were small plants of the same type he had seen in Trujall's wagon!

Flynn's feet were solidly held in place now, perhaps a dozen of the tendrils wrapped tightly about his boots. He whipped out his knife, slashed them away. It was a foolish move. Two plants were close to his hands. They flashed toward him and secured his wrists tightly. He jerked with all his strength. Thin, watery stuff oozed from the cut vines. His hands were bloody. The knife fell from his grasp.

One bulb-plant under his body moved. He felt a soft, petal-like substance brush across his shirt and the plant or creature, whichever it was, pushed a round snout against him.

Horror stricken, Flynn strained away from the sharp snout and tried to break away. It was useless.

This was the way Gwenn Ross had died!

THE SCALY, EAGER SNOUT was sucking at his flesh now. His shirt was torn and he felt the thing cutting into him bringing blood to the surface.

Flynn shouted hoarsely.

"Ross, help. I'm behind the house in the garden."

Almost at once he heard a door open and saw three faces over the porch rail above him. The light from the room flashed out across the garden and he could see other plants waving and leaning toward him. The pain over his heart was terrible.

"This is it, Ross!" he shouted. "Trujall's plants are killers. Help me!"

Flynn saw Ross wheel about and send a crashing blow into Trujall's face. A gun exploded; a shot sang through the air. Ross cleared the rail with a leap and hit the ground on his feet. He carried a huge knife; a machete snatched from where it hung on the wall, obviously for just the purpose for which he was now going to use it.

Trujall's curse came from the porch. There was the sound of a scuffle. Flynn could no longer see the porch. His eyes were filled with pain and his body contorted, fighting the awful tendrils.

Ross swore loudly and came wading in. The huge knife swung wildly on all sides. Sometimes he staggered and seemed about to fall. Then, howling oaths at the top of his voice, he tore away a blade covered with wriggling tendrils and came on.

At Flynn's side he reached down and sent the knife shooting into the plant under Flynn's body. The suction stopped and the thing dropped away. He cut the bonds from Flynn's body and dragged him to the edge of the garden. Flynn fell forward on his face and lay still. He was breathing hard.

"Entertaining," it was Trujall's triumphant, but angered voice. "But you have ruined my new crop of plants. For that you will all pay."

Ross helped Flynn to his feet. The General had been overcome in his scuffle on the porch with Trujall. He was covered now by the same pistol that menaced Flynn and Ross.

"Thanks, Ross," Flynn recovered his breath. "I didn't know what I was walking into."

They mounted the porch and faced Trujall. His face held a smile of complete triumph.

"Where is the girl," Flynn faced the dwarf, his fists clenched. "You've done something to her."

Ross took his arm.

"Never mind, Flynn," he urged. "Leona is safe. We've seen her already. We'd better take it easy."

Trujall held his gun ready.

"That is wise," he said. "We have already had enough excitement. To wander around here longer might result in a disaster that could not be avoided so easily. Enter and be entertained."

THEY ENTERED A HIGH, WELL-LIGHTED ROOM. It was pleasantly furnished and warm. Trujall motioned to a couch at the far end of the place. Leona Textan was there, lying with partly closed eyes. The room was rich with the scent of roses and they were piled about the girl.

A strange mixture of relief and anger spread over Flynn as he stood there, looking at her. She was clad in the same rough dress, but the flowers spread a perfume about her that made the whole room shimmer under her spell.

"You will be seated?" Trujall asked, pocketing his gun. "There will be coffee."

Flynn wanted to go toward the girl, but something robbed him of energy. It didn't seem important.

"She is all right?" he asked the General.

Harzo Textan nodded listlessly.

"The roses," he explained. "They make her tired and restful. Otherwise she is safe."

Flynn felt tired. He wanted sleep very badly. A serving woman brought a tray of coffee and he sipped his while the others drank. Leona closed her eyes and slept. Her father went to her once, and felt of her forehead. He seemed satisfied.

"She has had a hard day," he announced vacantly. "It will be better for us to stay here tonight and go to the village with the morning."

Trujall went to the door.

"There are only myself and the serving maid here," he said. "I am sorry about the incident in the garden. They are but a hobby of mine and I was angry when I saw the plants destroyed. If you stay out of my gardens you will be safe."

He went out and they heard him leave the porch.

The maid came and led them to their rooms. Flynn was worn out. He sank to the bed and was sound asleep before he had time to remove his clothes.

FLYNN AWAKENED SUDDENLY, his body covered with perspiration. It was dark. His head ached dully. Why was he here in this bedroom? He could not remember leaving the lounge where Trujall had faced them with the pistol. Leona Textan had been stretched out before them, asleep on the divan.

He had succumbed to the sweet odor of the roses, and Trujall's insistence that no harm would come to them. Flynn remembered accepting a cup of coffee from the house maid and watching Ross and General Textan do the same.

That was it. The coffee had been drugged. That, and the roses!

Flynn sat up quickly, saw that he was fully clothed. He rushed to the door.

He stepped into the hall and listened. No sound came from the rooms below. It seemed sinister. Trujall was the power behind this garden of hell. He used the people of the valley like pawns, never soiling his own hands with murder. He left that to . . .

Flynn thought of Leona. The girl had been in the main lounge below the staircase. The thought of her shocked his brain more fully awake.

Halfway down stairs, Flynn stopped short. A high-pitched scream of terror came from the rose garden behind the house. He rushed across the room and out on the high porch. Leona Textan was visible several hundred yards away. She was running between long rows of rose bushes.

The moon made her shoulders glisten. Once she looked back— screamed again and rushed onward. Flynn's boot struck something. He reached down and retrieved the heavy knife that Ross had used earlier in the evening.

Flynn cleared the rail with one leap. He ran swiftly across the lawn and into the rose garden after Leona.

"Stop, or I'll shoot."

Flynn saw the stubby figure of Trujall on the porch with pistol aimed.

"Go to hell!" he shouted and kept on running. Leona had disappeared now. A shot rang out and the bullet whistled over his shoulder.

The second shot hit the bricks of the carriage house close to his head and sang away into the bushes.

"Leona," he shouted. "Leona. Where are you?"

The silence was maddening. Forgetting Trujall, he ran over the soft dirt and down the lanes of rose bushes.

He ran onward, glancing back once to see a light visible on the second floor. Perhaps Ross or the General had finally awakened. He shouted something hoarse and wordless over his shoulder, hoping one of them would hear the sound.

There was a small opening ahead. It was perhaps ten feet square and bordered by the rank, luxurious growths of roses. At the far side he saw Leona, cowering down. Her body was twisted as though she were trying to run—to go farther, but couldn't move. Her lips were opened in a round O of horror and one arm was thrown before her face as she sought protection from her pursuer.

Flynn saw the thing that had caused her panic and stopped short. The other octopus-like plants had been bad enough. Now he knew he was looking straight at the thing that had killed Gwenn and the soldier.

It had the same general characteristics as the others, but it was almost as tall as a man. The thing, plant or animal, walked on nine short feeler-like legs. It moved swiftly, its thick, scaly body vibrating smoothly as it moved. A half-dozen long, root-like feelers protruded from the body. They reached out and wavered in the air, the tips reaching three feet from the body. Its head was a net of muscular fiber with a sharp, cup-like opening at its top.

The cup was the identical size of the wound he had seen on Gwenn's body.

From the edge of this cup a blossom grew. It was a type of orchid, huge and spotted, but unclean. Out of its center came two feelers that evidently gave it a sense of touch and smell that allowed it to pursue its victims.

The thing was crossing the clearing slowly, warily, seeking the girl. It knew she was there. The footsteps had halted and the prey was close.

Flynn went forward slowly, the knife raised over his head. Close to the creature, he brought the knife down in a wide arc. It struck from behind, just below the cup-like neck. The spotted blossom flopped to the ground and the neck fell with it.

The creature whirled around and feelers swept out and around Flynn's waist. Red blood started to pour from the cleanly severed neck. Flynn dropped his knife and tried to release the tentacles that held him. The girl came toward them. Flynn felt the tentacles go around his throat and remembered how easily Gwenn had been strangled.

Leona waited until the feelers were tightly wrapped about Flynn. He was on the ground now.

She clutched the knife firmly and pushed it deep into the creature's body. The movement stopped.

The feelers grew limp one by one and fell away from him. Shaking from the strain, Flynn stood up slowly and kicked the thing away from him.

SHE RAN TO HIM QUICKLY, throwing her arms about his neck. For a moment Flynn forgot Trujall and the men at the house. He was conscious only of the frail, lovely girl in his arms.

"You understand now why I married Avon Bicarda?" she whispered.

Flynn nodded.

"Your father told me everything," he said.

She snuggled closer.

Men were coming from the house. He took his arms from her and turned to see Ross, Trujall walking before him, as they came through the roses. Trujall saw the bloody monster that lay at Flynn's feet, and sobbing, knelt on the ground before it. Ross looked down with cold hatred in his eyes. He carried a pistol. Flynn recognized it as Trujall's.

"I heard you shouting," Ross said quietly. "Found Trujall in the garden trying to release more of these things. He's got a whole cage of them behind the carriage house."

"They didn't escape?" Flynn asked.

Ross shook his head.

"Still behind bars," he said. "We'll starve them to death. Trujall had to fool with the door and I took the liberty of kicking him in the stomach and taking his gun away from him."

The ugly face of the dwarf turned up to Flynn. Blood stained the man's hands where he had fondled the dead creature and tears were in his eyes.

"You killed him," he accused. "You killed my pet."

Ross' eyes were flinty.

"And I'll kill you!" he snarled.

Flynn shook his head.

"No, Ross. When the General awakens," he said. "I think he'll take a certain pleasure in sentencing Trujall and putting him before the firing squad."

"Trujall, why in hell did you pick on my wife?" asked Ross.

Trujall had arisen slowly, his long arms hanging at his side. He shrugged his shoulders.

"I had to have a white woman," he said slowly. "She was the only one in Oaxaco. Many Mexican women and men have given their blood to my *king-plants*. I could give life to the tuber bodies of the plants by shooting certain injections into them. They did not react to natural emotions without the blood of humans in their body."

Flynn was filled with a deep disgust. "But you," he asked coldly. "What were you gaining by this?"

Trujall shrugged his shoulders.

"I have had everything I wished from the house of Bicarda," he admitted. "The *king-plants* were my hobby. They drank blood and became things alive and powerful. I raised them to make up in a way, for my own lack of power. You see my body is very ugly. Not at all tough and strong like my pets."

Ross' face was a mask of loathing.

"You murdered these people and gave their blood to these—these creatures of hell, for no reason other than to satisfy your own lust for power?"

Trujall did not answer. Instead he was on his knees again, carefully gathering up the remains of the thing on the ground.

Ross turned to Flynn and his eyes were pinpoints.

"You'd better take the girl away from here, Jeff," he said.

Jeff took Leona by the arm and led her up toward the house. They were hidden from the two men in the roses.

"What is he going . . ."

Her lips remained parted, but her voice was broken by the sharp crack of the pistol. Two more shots sounded behind them. Jeff stopped, standing very quietly. He thought he heard a groan of pain, then quick footsteps in the dirt.

Ross caught up with them, and walked toward the house without a word. They reached the garden and Flynn looked away across the peaceful rose gardens and then back at the strong, handsome house. He took Leona close to him in the darkness.

CACTUS (1950)
MILDRED JOHNSON

THE PACKAGE CAME by first-class mail. It was from Edith's old friend in Los Angeles, Abby Burden. She opened it with interest, picked out some cotton wadding, a bulky letter, more cotton wadding. That was apparently all, but since nobody, not even Abby, would package a letter so tenderly, she reinspected the cotton and found a small prickly object. The explanation was undoubtedly in the letter.

It was written, as usual, on thin paper; typewritten with hand interlineations and annotations crawling about the pages and into the margins, and Edith had to turn it upside down and endways and trail sentences for sheets before capturing the sense. It dealt with the Burdens' trip to Mexico, but not until the end did it divulge the mystery of the enclosure.

"And now about the cutting," Abby wrote. "I may as well tell you Robert is against my sending it to you. He thinks I'm very silly. Let me tell you about it, though:

"I picked it up in an out-of-the-way, God-forsaken spot about a hundred miles from Chihuahua, where we had a flat tire. It was desert country, ninety in the shade—although there was no shade—and there was poor Robert faced with the prospect of changing a tire. I offered to help but he said the best way for me to help him would be to keep quiet for a while. You know how cranky a man can get under those conditions. The car was like an oven so I took a little walk around to look at the vegetation, such as it was, but there seemed to be nothing for hundreds of miles but sage and scrub and sand, and heat rising and shimmering all about. And then, a short distance away, I seemed to see a kind of fog, an overhanging mist. I thought it was an optical illusion—because whoever heard of a fog in the desert?—but, since it wasn't far away, I walked over to it. And as I approached it I smelled the sweetest, sourest, muskiest odor I've ever known. Suddenly the ground dipped and I was looking at a strange and lovely thing. Do you remember the meteor crater in Arizona? What I saw there was the same thing, much smaller, of course. It was a scoop in the earth, like a great dimple, and it was filled with cactus growths, marvelous, unearthly, beautiful—eight, nine, ten feet tall—gray-green giants stretching their twisted arms to the sky. There were hundreds of them, some of them already blooming with dark red flowers. It was the latter that gave off the strange, sweet smell.

"Edith—actually I felt as if I were on another planet, and what with the heavy perfume and the heat, my head swam. But finally I pulled myself together and rushed back to Robert to beg him to come and see what I had found, and ask him to cut me a slip of one of those weird plants. But his reaction was most peculiar. You know how sensible Robert usually is, but for some private reason he took a dislike to the whole area and became very difficult about getting a cutting for me. He said he wouldn't want a thing like that. He said they looked like goats and smelled like them too. He was positively silly. He said there was something about the little valley and the phalanxes of tortured shapes that gave him the creeps. But finally he gave in and cut me a tiny piece from the nearest plant. He scratched himself doing so and that didn't make him any happier. The spikes on the stem are rather tricky, you'll notice.

"As soon as I got it home I planted it. Edith, it's the finest specimen I've ever seen and grows like—I was going to say like a weed, but it's faster than that. In a week I had to transplant it to a larger plant pot.

"Robert is still angry about it, though, and that's why he thinks I'm crazy to send you a cutting of it. But knowing your fondness for cacti, I had to share my discovery with you."

EDITH FOLDED UP THE LETTER and inspected the little cutting, holding it in her palm. It was no more than an inch in length, brown and shriveled, and so lifeless she doubted that it would grow at all. However, she would give it a chance. She found a small pot, pressed it in, watered it and set it on the shelf with her other cactus plants. "If you're going to be a giant cactus," she said, "you've a long way to go, little friend."

On examination the next morning, she was pleased to see that apparently its grip on life was secure. Watering it on the following Monday with the rest of her cactus collection she decided the infant was going to be a prodigy, for not only had it changed its wizened brown covering for one of healthy green but had straight-ened up and grown fully two inches. Its shape was somewhat comi-cal: with the fat, spinous stem and the two little horns sprouting from the top, it resembled a rampant tomato caterpillar. Edith wrote to Abby that afternoon thanking her for the little plant.

Six weeks afterward, by the end of May, it was no longer little. In fact it had outstripped all the other cacti on the shelf. Now fifteen inches tall, it had been transplanted to a large urn and, in Edith's mind, was being groomed for a star appearance at the horticultural show in the autumn. Her friends admired it and, at club meetings, inquired about its health as they would about a child's.

When Mrs. Ferguson, her next-door neighbor, viewed it, however, she asked the question: "When's it supposed to stop growing?"

"Well," laughed Edith, "my friend who sent it to me said they were eight, nine and ten feet tall—the ones she saw growing in Mexico, but I don't imagine it will grow so much. I haven't a con-tainer large enough for it, for one thing."

"And your porch roof isn't high enough." Leaning over and ten-tatively feeling the two parallel spikes at the head of the plant, she added, "Not that it couldn't bore a hole right through if it wanted to with these things. They're like daggers."

Her remark prompted Edith to ask Abby how the parent was getting along, and she heard, with slight dismay, that it too was hyperexpansive, already two feet high and showing no signs of stopping. When it outgrew the house, wrote Abby, she had plans for it in the yard, but Edith thought grimly: when it outgrows my house it outgrows me. Goodbye, cactus, in that case.

It blossomed early in June with flowers of a peculiar liverish color. Though she never would have admitted it publicly, Edith thought them unattractive, almost repellent. They were almost like sores, she thought. And their odor was pungent enough to cause comment, the baker's delivery man asking if gas was escaping, the meter reader wanting to know if she had something burning in the oven. But her handy man, Mr. Krakaur, who came on Mondays to put out trash cans, mow the lawn, etc., and who was the local philosopher on the side, stated frankly that it "stank."

"Stinks like a goat," he said.

"Mr. Krakaur, how can you say that?" Laughing, she recalled what Robert Burden had said about it.

"And it looks like one too," Mr. Krakaur went on, shifting his cud reflectively. "Got horns and everything. Looks like a sick goat with boils."

But in two weeks the blooms were gone. Most of the smell went with them, although it lingered unaccountably in various portions of the house far away from the porch, in closets, in her bedroom, and seemed to be contained in air pockets for often, usually at night, she would smell it strong and musky, but in the next second lose it. It was as if the cactus itself had passed her open door. She smiled at her fancy, but was surprised to hear from Abby that Robert Burden had the same idea, although he was carrying it to ridiculous extremes, averring, for instance, that he had caught a glimpse of the cactus floating along in its own emanations like a jellyfish in an ocean current. Abby wrote that if he thought that frightening her would make her dispose of the cactus he was mistaken. He was being very stupid and unreasonable, she said. He was even threatening to warn Edith about the danger—"So if you hear a lot of nonsense from him you'll know what it's about."

SHE WAS NOT GOING TO ALLOW herself to be influenced by such palpable friction in the Burden household, Edith thought, but just the same, after reading Abby's letter, she went to the porch and took a good look at her cactus. It *was* a grotesque thing, she admitted, a frame on which mental aberrations could easily be hung. Cruciform in shape, its upraised "arms" were terminated in spiked nodules, like taloned fingers; the forward-sweeping horns were truly formidable; and the withered flowers at the "head" were arranged to suggest an evil face, a demonic, leering, loathsome face.

In sudden revulsion she decided she must destroy it but then, remembering her promise to exhibit it at the flower show and the admiration and interest of her friends, canceled the impulse by laughing herself out of it. "You're not going to pay any attention to Robert Burden's crazy notions, are you?" she asked herself, reminding herself in addition that she had always thought him neurotic. He sounded positively psychotic now.

But that night she dreamed about the cactus. It seemed that she was in bed and, awakened by a slipping, slithering sound from the hall, got up to investigate. In a shaft of moonlight there sat a tiny animal, like a chipmunk, all agleam with silver light, dainty and pretty, and she was about to approach it when suddenly Ted appeared. He looked young and slim, the way he had been when they were married, but his face was grave. Laying a hand on her shoulder, he shook his head as if to restrain her, but she paid no attention and walked towards the little animal clucking softly. But, as she reached it and was crouching to it, it began to swell and grow and in a second had become the cactus, writhing with vile delight, its malevolent face close to hers, its long arms pinioning hers to her sides in sickening embrace. She screamed for Ted but he had gone. He had left her.

Choking, heart beating wildly, she awoke and lay shaking in terror. Oriented at last, she looked towards the door, and it was as if a hand clutched her heart for the area in the hall was bathed, it seemed, in a deep, oily fog, like a swamp miasma, behind which something gray and green was stirring. She sat up, stared hard, cautiously reached for the bedlamp and quickly turned it on. There was nothing.

There was nothing but moonshine and sinister groupings of shadows and her own heavy breathing.

IN THE SENSIBLE LIGHT of day she marveled and was ashamed of the mantle of fear she was weaving for herself out of odds and ends of suggestions, fancied resemblances and nightmares—she, Edith Porter, middle-aged, matter-of-fact, a professed scoffer at all superstition. Was she going to allow an odor, a shape and a bad dream to push her into unreason? And as for Robert Burden's vaporings, for all she knew he might be joking.

She would take hold of herself firmly and, in the meantime, try to rid the house of the meandering gamey stench.

It was nine o'clock on the following Sunday evening. Having spent the day riding in the country with the Fergusons, Edith was finishing reading the newspaper and was beginning to yawn with delicious weariness and plan early retirement when the telephone rang.

It was a girl's voice, blurred with crying, sharpened by hysteria, and Edith could not recognize it.

"Mrs. Porter? This is Nancy, Nancy Winnick, the Burdens' daughter."

"Oh, yes, Nancy—how are you? Is anything the matter?" Edith's mind skipped about frantically for an explanation.

The girl was apparently trying to control herself. At last she said. "The most horrible thing happened this morning. Dad's dead!"

"Oh, no! How—how did it happen?" She felt herself turning cold with shock.

"I don't know the whole story because Mother is half out of her mind and she's given it to us in bits and pieces. She's resting now under a sedative, but all afternoon she's kept begging me to call you and let you know. It's about that cactus she gave you. She wants you to destroy it, because she says—" Here Nancy burst into sobs and was a few seconds recovering herself. "She says it killed him. She knows it killed him deliberately, and it's all her fault. She's afraid something will happen to you too and she'll have two deaths on her conscience."

"But how? How did it kill him?"

"This morning Mother finally agreed that he could get rid of it. You know what controversy there's been about it. Mother said she wrote you about it, how Dad hated it so and Mother was set on keeping it. Well, this morning they had it out it seems and she told him to go ahead and destroy it if he felt so strongly about it. He didn't wait a minute. He took it out to the rubbish can—it grew to an enormous size, you know—and threw it on top of the rubbish, pot and all and then—" Nancy started whimpering again. "I don't know what made him do it, except that he wanted to get rid of it quickly and couldn't wait for the trash collection, but he set it afire and stood there watching it burn. Mother said she shouted to him from the window, but he seemed fascinated by the sight of the flames traveling up it, and then all of a sudden it broke in the middle and the top half flew at him, all ablaze, and landed on him— and it clung to him—he couldn't tear it off—it was all over his face and head—"

"Oh—how horrible—how terrible—" Edith broke down then and wept with Nancy, who at length completed the story:

"When my husband and I arrived we found Mother in a faint, and when she came to she just screamed and screamed; and then my husband went out into the yard, but he wouldn't let us see Dad. He himself was sick because his face and head were all—they took him away to be cremated. We thought that was best."

Lenitive words, condolences—what good were they now? And Edith could not say them; she was too shocked.

After hanging up she sat frozen, staring ahead; then she rose quickly, strode to the porch, lifted down the cactus from the shelf, and, grasping the horns as one would the ears of a rabbit, tore it up by the roots. From the gaping hole there rose the fetid odor so concentrated and powerful that she choked and coughed, but her anger gave her courage and, without looking at the plant in her hand, holding it far oft, she ran down cellar and threw it into the trash barrel. She returned for the pot and carried it down too, set it on top of the barrel, took a hammer and smashed it.

She was still panting when she sat at her desk in the living room to write to Abby all the sympathy she had been unable to express on the telephone and her hand shook so much she had to rest before beginning.

A hand touched her shoulder, gentle but firm—a warning hand; it rested there; she felt the pressure of the fingers. Slowly she unveiled her eyes. All about her was a mist pouring in ever thickening clouds from the area behind her and obscuring the light and a foul stink wafted to her nostrils, but she could not move: in that growing fetor, that dankness, that accrescence of vileness, she sat still. The hand pressed hard, and, coming to her senses, she half-turned her head. On the wall, just behind her head, was the shadow of horns.

She lurched to her feet, tore open the casement and flung herself into the darkness, landing on her hands and knees in the soft earth of a flower bed, scrambling to her feet and hurling herself forward across the field separating her house from the Fergusons'. She stumbled, fell, clambered up, ran on and at last reached the back door and pounded on it. When it was opened to her she fell in and pressed against the wall.

Mrs. Ferguson was staring at her, plump, red-faced, round-eyed. "What's wrong?" Edith could not answer.

"Harry!" Mrs. Ferguson called. "Come here!"

Ferguson appeared and together they led Edith to a chair. "Somebody trying to break into your house?" he asked.

"I don't know," she gasped. "I don't know. I've just had a terrible fright."

She sipped the glass of water they gave her, her teeth chattering against the rim.

"Call the police, Harry!" urged Mrs. Ferguson as Edith Porter sat frightened.

Edith raised a protesting hand. The police to rout something from another universe, another stratum of existence; the law to command the. supernatural? "Don't call the police," she said, setting the glass on the table and sighing.

"But if there's a prowler around—"

"There's no prowler. I'm sure I imagined it." She looked at these solid, sane people and wondered if it were true. Perhaps she had dreamed it all. Nevertheless she could not return to the house. It was difficult to confess her fear of staying alone, but she had to do it. They said they understood, offered their guest room, but were puzzled. Ferguson went over and locked up and brought her keys back as directed.

When Mr. Krakaur put in an appearance on the street the next morning she joined him and walked with him.

"What you doing out so early, Mrs. Porter?" he asked.

"Last night I had a kind of brainstorm. I had a notion something—someone was breaking in, and so I ran over to the Fergusons and there I stayed. You know how we women get nervous at times."

"At times?" cackled Mr. Krakaur who fancied himself something of a misogynist. "I'd say all the time."

She was in no mood for badinage. Trying to be casual, she said, "I wonder if you'd be good enough to put out the trash barrel right away. I want to straighten up the cellar."

Standing fearfully in the kitchen, not daring to go down the cellar stairs but filled with curiosity, she heard him open the outer doors and come back for the barrel. She was not too surprised, though, when he called from the foot of the stairs: "Mrs. Porter, what happened to your cactus?"

"I broke it," she said from the door.

"Did it fall off the shelf?"

"Yes." If one waited others would always provide the answers.

Without realizing it she had moved to the head of the stairs and was peering over the rail just as he was picking up from the floor one of the pieces of the plant pot. Her heart leaped. It could not be coincidence this time, nor a dream. That every piece of the pot had remained in the barrel and none had fallen out she was positive. The sickness of terror rolled over her.

"It don't look too bad," he was saying. "All you got to do is put it in another pot. I think it'll grow just as good."

"No," she said.

"O. K. You're the boss."

SHE MUST GO AWAY and rest, cleanse her brain of this horror which kept her trembling, made her afraid to go to bed, had her staring hard at shadows, sniffing the air, starting and glancing over her shoulder. She was sure now that the hand on her shoulder had been Ted's and that only her enormous danger had enabled him to get through to her. But it was over; the peril was gone; and perhaps a summer in Maine, at the little hotel in Winter Harbor where she and Ted had spent their honeymoon, would eradicate its immediate effects.

When she took one of her keys over to Mrs. Ferguson the latter expressed approval of her decision. "To tell you the truth Harry and I have been worried about you. It's so easy to go into a nervous breakdown, you know." She gave some instances of friends who had slipped into them. She would step in once a week and water the plants and see that everything was all right, she promised. "That was too bad about your big cactus," she said then. "Krakaur told me it fell off the shelf. And after you set such store by it too. But that's the way it is: it's always the things we like the most that get smashed."

It was September when Edith returned. Riding in the taxi from the station, listening to the church clock bong eleven in the clear air, she felt calm, able to pick up her life where she had abandoned it on that Sunday evening in June. It seemed far away now. The peaceful summer, the new friends, the fresh stimuli, they had helped her forget. And she was not afraid. Never again would she be completely sure of herself and of the order of existence, for something strange and unearthly had touched her she knew, but she was not afraid. There was good to surmount evil, a tender hand to warn her of its approach.

The driver set her trunk in the hall, took his money, thanked her for the tip and left, closing the door behind him. And now she was alone; but everything was in its place, familiar and dear and homey: the grandmother's clock tick-tocking in the corner (Mrs. Ferguson hadn't forgotten to wind it, then), the Meissen figurines, a man and woman, in their perpetual saraband on the table, the Regency mirror reflecting a portion of the living room and beyond it the porch with its greenery of plants. She released the breath she had been holding, smiled, walked to the mirror and took off her hat. Then she felt it, the hand on her shoulder.

"This is ridiculous!" she said aloud. "Now I'm sure I dreamed the whole thing!" The pressure was renewed and she wheeled about and shouted, "It's gone, don't you know that?" In hysterical triumph she ran to the porch and turned on the light. "See?" she cried, standing in the middle and sweeping her arm around. "It's gone, I tell you. It's gone!"

But, on the wall, she saw the outline of its horns and, simultaneously, smelled its sickly odor. Her cry was guttural. With hands stretched out protectively, mouth squared in fear, she stepped backwards, crashed into a hard object, turned, and in the last second of consciousness saw the cactus teetering and falling. . . .

"But I feel responsible. I feel that it's my fault." Mrs. Ferguson had said it over, and over. She would never be done saying it nor forget the sight which had met her eyes when, seeing the light, she had gone over to welcome Edith home. Again she explained. "I knew she was fond of that cactus and when I found it growing with the rubber plant I was so pleased. I didn't tell her. I wanted to surprise her. And so I planted it in a pot of its own and it grew even faster than the other one. I should have let her know, though— shouldn't I?"

"It was an accident," Harry Ferguson said patiently. "You're not to blame. Anybody would have done the same in the same circumstances. It was an accident, that's all."

"But it would never have happened if I hadn't done it. Oh, God, when I walked in and saw her lying there with those spikes in her throat—"

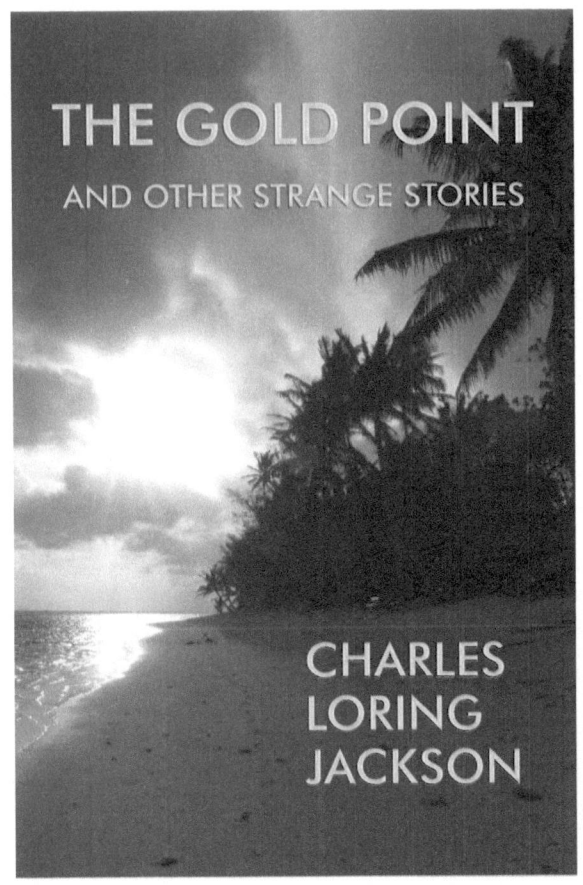

The Gold Point and Other Strange Stories
ISBN 1-61646-085-7

COACHWHIP PUBLICATIONS

ALSO AVAILABLE

Flora Curiosa: Cryptobotany, Mysterious Fungi,
Sentient Trees and Deadly Plants in
Classic Science Fiction and Fantasy
ISBN 1-61646-219-1

COACHWHIP PUBLICATIONS

ALSO AVAILABLE

BOTANICA DELIRA

MORE STORIES OF STRANGE,
UNDISCOVERED, AND MURDEROUS
VEGETATION

Botanica Delira: More Stories of Strange,
Undiscovered, and Murderous Vegetation
ISBN 1-61646-025-3

Bestiarium Cryptozoologicum

Mystery Animals and Unknown Species in Classic Science Fiction and Fantasy

Bestiarium Cryptozoologicum:
Mystery Animals and Unknown Species
in Classic Science Fiction and Fantasy
ISBN 1-61646-009-1

COACHWHIP PUBLICATIONS

ALSO AVAILABLE

INVERTEBRATA ENIGMATICA

GIANT SPIDERS, DANGEROUS INSECTS, AND OTHER STRANGE INVERTEBRATES
IN CLASSIC SCIENCE FICTION AND FANTASY

Invertebrata Enigmatica: Giant Spiders, Dangerous
Insects, and Other Strange Invertebrates in
Classic Science Fiction and Fantasy
ISBN 1-930585-65-9

WULF

TALES OF WOLVES
AND WEREWOLVES

EDITED BY
CHAD ARMENT

Wulf: Tales of Wolves and Werewolves
ISBN 1-61646-056-3